Terri NIXON

A Cornish Promise

PIATKUS

PIATKUS

First published in Great Britain in 2020 by Piatkus

3 5 7 9 10 8 6 4 2

A CIP catalogue record for this book
is available from the British Library.

ISBN 978-0-349-42399-9

Typeset in Caslon by M Rules
Printed and bound in Great Britain by Clays Ltd, Elcograf S.p.A.

Papers used by Piatkus are from well-managed forests
and other responsible sources.

Piatkus
An imprint of
Little, Brown Book Group
Carmelite House
50 Victoria Embankment
London EC4Y 0DZ

An Hachette UK Company
www.hachette.co.uk

www.littlebrown.co.uk

Terri Nixon was born in Plymouth, England, in 1965. At the age of nine she moved with her family to a small village on the fringe of Bodmin Moor, where she discovered a love of writing that has stayed with her ever since.

Since publishing in paperback (through independent small press BeWrite) in 2002, Terri has appeared in both print and online fiction collections, and published *Maid of Oaklands Manor* with Piatkus in 2013.

For Mum and Dad, who have been the perfect cheerleaders from day one, and who became my 'support bubble' when I needed one most.

DRAMATIS PERSONAE

Helen Fox: Widow of reformed playboy, Harry; between them the toast of the wealthy Bristol set in the years following the Great War. Their marriage had been picture-perfect, and it was only after Harry's death that Helen discovered he had been hiding the extent of his debts. She was unable to remain in their home in Bristol, and took their three children to stay at the Fox family's hotel in Cornwall, with the intention of selling her inherited share. The temporary arrangement became permanent when she realised Harry had already sold the hotel, and that his mother now merely managed it for the owner. She took over its running and is now part-owner.

Adam Coleridge: Harry's best friend, and the person who had persuaded him to invest in the shipping company that had ultimately destroyed him. Helen cut him off from all contact with the Fox family, and especially the children, whom he adored. When Fox Bay Hotel came under threat from developers, Adam's remorse led him to employ illegal tactics, and embezzle money from his investment firm, in order to buy the hotel and gift half of it back to Helen. He now lives at the hotel and has regained his lost 'family'.

Leah Marshall: A regular guest at the hotel, from Wales, who is in the habit of adopting different personas to suit either the situation or her mood. Leah befriended Helen when she and the children first moved to Cornwall, and, like Adam, she became an honorary member of the Fox family. Her history was revealed to be more complicated than she'd admitted to; with her husband in prison she had lived as a married woman with his brother Daniel, who had been killed in the war. She had attempted to help save the hotel from developers by running a confidence trick with Adam Coleridge as the 'mark', not realising he was trying to do the same thing. Adam had fallen in love with her assumed character, and although Leah now knows her feelings for him are stronger than his for her, they remain in a relationship.

Roberta Fox: Helen's eldest daughter; a keen motorcyclist who had planned to accept a place on a racing team run by her new friend, Xander, himself a champion racer. Bertie was involved in a freak accident when returning from the racetrack, and her mother had been forced to make the decision to save her life by allowing doctors to amputate her leg. With Bertie's dreams destroyed, her relationship with Helen has also been severely damaged, and remains difficult.

Benjamin Fox: Helen's only son, the eldest of the Fox children. On his arrival at Fox Bay, at the age of fifteen, Ben developed an instant interest in the running of the hotel, and in particular the wines. He was taken under the wing of family friend and bar manager, Guy Bannacott, and when he was old enough, he became the night manager, and trained as a sommelier.

Fiona Fox: The youngest Fox daughter, now sixteen years old. She had always been obsessed with the outdoor life, and though only six when they'd moved to Cornwall she immediately fell in love with the beach and the sea. Fiona began visiting the local lifeboat station at a very young age, and is now one of the shore crew – women who assist with the launching and recovery of the Trethkellis lifeboat, the *Lady Dafna*.

Fleur Fox: Harry's widowed mother. She and her husband had built Fox Bay Hotel together, and when Harry had sold it he had made her continued residence, and role as manager, part of the deal. When Helen and the children moved in, she gave Helen a job to ensure the family had a home. Fleur is extremely stylish, with an aristocratic manner, and is a leading voice in the local WI. Her closest friend and ally is Guy Bannacott, who had stayed by her side throughout the difficult years after Harry had sold the hotel.

Guy Bannacott: Guy is the restaurant and bar manager at Fox Bay. The family know him to be gay, but he is usually extremely discreet about it; there had been a scandal some years ago which had been hushed up and is only referred to obliquely, involving a bawdy song, and Fleur's best gown and heels. Guy is not a cross-dresser, and the incident is his one black mark at the hotel. His slightly haughty attitude masks a deep affection for the Fox family, Fiona in particular.

The Nancarrows: Farmers at Higher Valley Farm, which backs onto Fox Bay Hotel. **Beth** is the widowed mother of twins, **Jowan** and **Jory**. Their father **Toby** had died as the result of a shocking accident, caused by the boys, and as the farm started to slide towards bankruptcy Toby's brother **Alfie** moved up from Porthstennack, to try and keep it running. Beth has long been in love with Alfie but cannot tell him due to their shared loyalty to the memory of Toby. Jowan's romantic relationship with Bertie Fox has suffered since her accident. Jory is the wilder of the twins, and is prone to throwing his money away on drink and gambling.

The Nicholls Siblings: **Xander** and his sister **Lynette** are Bertie Fox's best friends, and live in Brighton. Lynette is an outwardly flighty girl, used to following her glamorous brother around to race meetings, which he teases are her way of finding a husband, but are really her way of taking care of her brother. She'd met Bertie at the race meet where Xander had promised her a place on his team, and has remained a staunch friend throughout Bertie's traumatic recovery from her accident.

Key hotel staff:

Martin Berry, head receptionist – days
Ian Skinner, head receptionist – nights
Jeremy Bickle, head barman
Nicholas Gough, head chef
Miss Tremar, cleaning supervisor
Piran Burch, handyman
Arthur Foley, groundsman

CHAPTER ONE

Trethkellis Lifeboat Station, Cornwall
December 1929

Fiona Fox wiped her condensed breath from the window of the lookout station and leaned on her crossed arms, straining for sight of the *Lady Dafna*. Beside her, the lamp flashed out its Morse-coded message to the 40-foot lifeboat fighting the tide in pursuit of the floundering cargo ship: *vessel rounded headland south*. A moment later the lifeboat's own lamp signalled back, and Fiona's practised eyes decoded it: the *Dafna* would change direction and follow the path of the stricken ship, to pick up any survivors.

Since October the coast had been battered by wind and rain that surpassed even their usual ferocity, and today was no different; the sky seemed to skim the surface of the sea like a lowering grey blanket, and the rolling, heaving water dragged it down until the two became one. December rain lashed at the window of the lookout and dripped through the leaking roof, but Fiona remained in her place while the coastguard tracked the lifeboat's progress with the telescope. As usual he'd forgotten she was even there, which suited Fiona perfectly.

She'd arrived today, just after the call had come down from the lookout station, and had immediately joined Geoffrey Glasson, the coxswain, in rousing the sea-going crew, running from house to house, knocking on doors and yelling through letter boxes before returning to the station with eight men at their heels, along with the women; wives, sisters and daughters who formed the willing shore crew. She had watched with envy as Glasson pulled his oilskin over his head.

'Can't I come out this time?'

Glasson's head popped out of the oilskin and he wrestled his beefy arms through the sleeve holes. 'Not in a month of Sundays, maid. Anyone joins us today it'll be Barry.' He'd nodded at the retired helmsman, who still spent most of his days here, then held out his arms, and Fiona had sighed, unsurprised, and slipped a cork life jacket over them. She'd left him to secure it, then hurried down to the slipway to assist with the launch itself. It never failed to thrill her, watching the *Lady Dafna*'s bow plunge from the slipway into the water, and when the tide was high, as it was today, the spray drenched everyone within shouting distance. Icy water had soaked her from head to toe as the petrol engine coughed into life, and she'd watched, her heart in her mouth as always, until the lifeboat had stopped rocking and begun powering through the waves.

At just sixteen, and the youngest of the women who supported the boat, she was often given the grunt-work to do; cleaning and sweeping puddles of water from the station, fetching water to boil for hot drinks, and picking up and re-hanging oilskins that were often dropped where they were shed. She didn't usually mind it in the least, and for a few minutes today she'd contentedly helped Barry Hicks re-coil the heavy, wet ropes before growing impatient to see what was happening at the sharp end. She'd taken a quick look at the others, to check she'd not be missed, and run up here to the lookout to watch Pasco Penberthy communicating with the *Lady Dafna*. She could have watched for hours as the Morse code flickered between them. It was like magic.

The latest information sent, Pasco seized the telescope mounted in the wall at the front of the lookout station, and swung it towards the jutting headland. 'They'm away,' he muttered.

'Good luck to them.'

Pasco jumped and turned to her. 'What are you still doin' here, miss? They'll want you down there sharpish, and ready. And fetch Tam Rowe, just in case. Go on!' He made a little shooing gesture, and Fiona grinned.

'Alright, I'm going. But can I come back after?'

'You'll be bored. Better off running back home to your posh 'otel.'

Fiona gave him a look he clearly recognised, because he winked, and deliberately turned his back on her to forestall further conversation. She stepped back outside and pulled her sou'wester lower as she turned into the bitter wind and hurried across to Doctor Rowe's house. By the time she was at the door he already had his bag in hand and was dismissing the two patients who were waiting to see him.

'Saw the signal,' he said grimly. 'Had a feeling I'd be called today.'

He strode away towards the station, leaving her to hurry after him. Rain drenched the rough path down to the beach, and as she splashed through puddles Fiona blinked away the drops that ran into her eyes, and blew them off the tip of her nose, but instead of taking up her place in the shelter of the station, she went straight past and onto the beach, ignoring the exasperated shouts of the women who watched her pass. Since they were all volunteers, the only person Fiona answered to was Mr Glasson, and he was out with the boat, so let them shout. The *Lady Dafna* had not yet come back into view, and there was no telling how long it would be before she did, but Fiona meant to be here, on hand and ready to help drag her ashore.

She waited, shivering, beside the slipway. After what might have been twenty minutes, but felt like an hour or more, the dark, bobbing shape came into view around the headland again. Up in the lookout Pasco would have seen them already; Fiona watched the light flashing from the lifeboat: *Ship safe. 3 casualties.*

Fiona instinctively moved closer, as if that would speed up the progress of the boat, and the freezing water lapped over her boots, drenching her to the knee once again. The lifeboat came closer, and her engines cut just beyond the beach, letting the tide push her up onto the shingle. Fiona darted forward, along with the others who had come down from the hut, and then re-wetting her boots was the least of her worries, as she waded in to seize the ropes and begin dragging the *Dafna* up the beach.

All was bustle and shouting for a while; two unknown men, and one all-too familiar, were handed on to the shore crew. Donald Houghton, younger brother of Bertie's mechanic friend Stan, was white-faced and clutching at his thigh, where a gash half a foot long had been hastily wrapped but still gushed blood. He was divested of his cork life jacket, and gently laid onto a stretcher and borne away up the beach, Tam Rowe hurrying along at his side.

The two men from the cargo ship were walking wounded, swaying on their feet but grateful to be ashore, until one of them clutched at Glasson's arm, a look of alarmed realisation on his face.

'The small boat! Still out there!'

'What?' Glasson leaned closer, shouting over the rest of the noise. 'What boat?'

'The old man ... he took it. Some others too.'

'Damn!' Glasson looked around at his exhausted crew. 'Turn her back, lads!'

But the crew had already begun backing the *Dafna* the way she had come, and Fiona and the others lent their waning strength to the task.

As soon as the boat was afloat again Glasson turned to Fiona, spitting out seawater. 'Girl! Fetch Barry, we're one down!'

Fiona turned to run up the beach, but her gaze fell on Don's discarded life jacket and, before she realised she was going to do it, she had stooped down and snatched it up. She struggled with it at first, on her way back down to the sea, but thanks to its larger size she was able to draw it on without help.

'Hoi! No you don't!' Glasson tried to catch her arm as she splashed past him, but she was too quick for him.

'I can help!' she flung over her shoulder. 'Quicker than fetching Barry!'

'Your mother will skin me—'

'Then don't tell her!'

Glasson boosted her into the boat, glaring at her with an exasperation they both knew he had no time for, and a moment later the engine rattled into life once more and the *Lady Dafna* headed back out to sea. Davey Tregunna set to work signalling Pasco on shore, and Fiona pictured the coastguard skimming the rough seas with his telescope for any sign of a smaller boat in trouble, and getting ready to signal back.

Part of her felt guilty for the rush of fierce excitement poor Don's plight had afforded her, but a larger part revelled in the sensation of the smacking of waves against the prow, and the salt spray that dashed across her face. The wind pulled at her old, thin coat beneath the cork vest, and she wished she'd had time to seize an oilskin as well, but if she'd stretched her luck too far she would have been left at the beach with the others, and this once-in-a-lifetime chance would have been and gone.

The boat's speed made her dizzy; she'd last been out on it before it had been converted to petrol, when it had still been a pull-and-sail boat, and even though that hadn't been on a rescue it had seemed to take forever to reach the open water beyond the headland. Now they were approaching the rocky outcrop within minutes, and the boat rose on the waves, slamming down into each trough hard enough to knock the breath from Fiona's body. Her wet hands had been ripped from the rail with the first plunge, and were so frozen it had taken three attempts to lock her fingers around it again, but once she did, she hung on grimly for her life.

It was a miracle anyone spotted the drifting rowing boat through the ferocious swell, despite signals from the coast, which suddenly seemed a hundred miles away. But, just as Fiona thought they'd have to turn back, the helmsman shouted, and Glasson signalled to cut back on the engine. The roar settled to a loud rattle, and the boat slowed almost to a halt while everyone peered through the driving rain and blowing spray.

'There!' the helmsman yelled again, pointing away to the starboard side, and the *Dafna* began turning in that direction. Fiona, her teeth chattering so hard her jaw hurt, prised her icy fingers off the rail and made her uncertain way along the water-washed deck to where Glasson stood. She slipped as she reached him, and grabbed at his arm, immediately furious with herself for doing so, but he righted her without comment, and pointed.

Just ahead, and only visible as the *Dafna* slipped into a trough, a small rowing boat floated upside down, battered sideways and backwards at the whim of the tide, but with no sign of anyone in the water beside it.

'Underneath!' Glasson shouted back to the crew. 'But I only saw two, they're holding on to the seats, I think.'

'How will we get close enough?' Fiona yelled, blinking salt water out of her eyes. It was impossible; the *Dafna* was rising and plunging like a terrified horse, and the tiny rowing boat drifted farther away the longer they waited. But she soon saw that getting close enough was not on the minds of the lifeboat crew at all. The men were a blur of practised motion; barely a word passing between them as ropes were pulled from the end box at the bow, tied around Danny Quick and Andrew Kessel, and secured by the others.

Fiona swallowed hard, suddenly humbled. These men that she, and everyone else, would pass on the street with hardly a second look; who returned home without fanfare and calmly went about their usual business . . . These men were preparing to throw themselves into a violent, icy sea, with only a hastily tied rope to anchor them to relative safety. Knowing vaguely what they did when they were out here was one thing, but seeing it for herself gave Fiona a strong surge of emotion that was a little like love.

The two men eyed the swiftly disappearing rowing boat, nodded to one another, and a moment later they were both gone. Fiona cried out and instinctively lunged forward, but a large hand grasped her upper arm.

'Don't be stupid!' Glasson growled. 'Just keep watch.'

Fiona nodded, and turned to watch for signals from the coast-guard's lookout. It hardly seemed possible that under an hour ago she'd been back there herself, staring out to sea and yearning to be out here instead. The motion of the lifeboat was becoming more familiar under her feet, and she finally felt safe enough to stand without support as she stared through the rain towards the shoreline, but there were no flashing lights there now.

'Not the day you'd choose to be out here,' Damien Stone, the mechanic, observed with admirable calm.

'It's horrible,' Fiona agreed, tucking her hands into her armpits.

'I was thinkin' more of the date. Friday the thirteenth,' he added, when she looked at him blankly.

'Oh!' Fiona had never been particularly superstitious, but she knew it would have been the first thing her mother would have said, and she tried not to think about it now in case Mum was suddenly proved right.

A commotion behind her made her turn back, and she watched with growing fear as Bill Penneck and Damien joined forces to wrestle with one of the ropes. Without being asked, Fiona picked up the slack behind Damien and began pulling, aware she was doing very little to help. She heard a gruff laugh behind her, and Glasson eased her aside and took her place.

'Just be ready,' he told her, not unkindly. 'First aid kit's under there.' He nodded to the end box, and Fiona scrambled forward and dragged out the large metal case, but before she could open it she heard distant shouts, cutting through the wind and the heavy slapping of the waves against the *Lady Dafna*. She rose from her kneeling position in time to see Bill and Damien reaching down to pull a limp form from Danny's grasp.

'One more,' Danny gasped, before he slipped away again and struck out in the direction of the rowing boat.

While Bill and Damien returned their attention to the two ropes, Glasson bellowed for Fiona to bring the first aid box. The unconscious survivor was a man of indeterminate age, but certainly no younger than sixty; slight of build, with a ragged-looking beard, and dressed in a uniform of sorts. He would be lucky to have survived much longer in those icy temperatures; thank heaven for the petrol motor. Glasson made a brief examination, then ordered Fiona away to fetch a blanket while he stripped the man's wet clothing. She hurried back to the end box, acutely conscious of every passing second, but when she returned, she was met with a minute shake of the head, and Glasson's gaze dropped.

'Too late,' he said, so quietly Fiona wasn't sure she'd heard properly over the sound of the wind. 'Old fella probably had a heart attack.'

Fiona looked down, strangely unshy at the sight of the pathetic nakedness of the old man. Until ten minutes ago he'd been clinging to the upturned rowing boat with living, capable hands. Now all that strength and desperate hope was wasted, and he lay here nameless and empty. She felt a sudden rage, as strong and unpredictable as that earlier surge of pride, and a look at Glasson's face told her that those feelings would never fade.

'There's still hope for the other,' he said with surprising gentleness as he pulled a heavy tarpaulin across the body. 'Be ready with that blanket.'

When Andrew and Danny appeared again, they were supporting an even smaller figure between them.

'Little boy!' Andrew shouted, and Bill and Damien pulled on their ropes with great care until they were able to relieve the exhausted men of their burden. The child was bleeding from a head wound; the water washed away the streak of blood, but it reappeared each time with frightening speed. Bill and Damien lifted him onto the deck, and then turned back to help their flagging crewmates pull themselves over the gunwale.

The child looked to be about twelve years old, with white-blond hair turning crimson as the blood soaked into it. It wasn't until the wet clothing was summarily stripped away that they realised the slight figure was that of a girl. Glasson wrapped her in a dry blanket while Fiona rummaged for a bandage, and the girl's clothing, along with a rather odd-looking necklace, was put into a box with a number scrawled in charcoal.

There was little they could do for the casualty now, beyond making their way back towards the shore as quickly as possible. Fiona lay with her arms around the child, to offer as much warmth as her own chilled body had to spare, and tried not to look at the still, shrouded figure of the dead man. He might have been this girl's grandfather, and what she couldn't comprehend was that they were *there*! He'd been alive when they pulled him out, so how could he be dead now? And if she felt this guilt so deeply, how must the others be feeling?

She raised her eyes to the two men who'd put their lives at risk, and once again felt that wash of shame that she had never truly understood what they did out here. Twenty-year-old Danny Quick, who'd habitually teased her back at the station until she'd crossly told him to 'drop dead', at which he'd roared with laughter and told her to be wary of what she wished for. Andrew Kessel sat beside him; Andrew, whose large family owned bakeries all over Cornwall and who boasted that one day he would oversee every one of them. He sat silent, huddled into a blanket, his head down, fatigue rendering him silent for once. Tomorrow he would be making people's eyes roll again with his prideful declarations, but today he was a hero, and not one of those people would ever really know it.

The *Lady Dafna* crunched onto the sand and shingle of the beach, and Fiona found she had stiffened into the position in which she'd lain. It had not been more than a few minutes, but her clothes seemed to be frozen against her skin, and her muscles locked. Glasson lifted the girl up, and only then did Fiona find herself able to move, and she rolled to a kneeling position to watch as the girl was taken ashore. Danny helped her to her feet, without any of his usual flippant remarks, and Fiona mumbled her thanks, wishing she could tell him she understood now.

A miserable cry echoed across the bay as the girl woke, and Fiona's limbs came to life. She slithered across the wet deck and jumped onto the beach, and when the girl at last opened her eyes, her terrified gaze fell first on Fiona. The eyes, wide and blue, remained fixed on Fiona's face, and didn't waver until someone – Tam Rowe, Fiona saw – unwrapped the bandage from her head. Then she tried to twist, to see who was touching her, but it must have cost her to move because she cried out again, and her eyes slipped shut.

'Don't worry,' Fiona said, and took the girl's hand. 'You're safe now. My name's Fiona, what's yours?'

The girl gave a single nod to indicate she'd heard and understood, but did not volunteer her own name. Instead a tiny sigh escaped her, and her hand went limp in Fiona's.

15

'It's alright,' Doctor Rowe said, lifting one of the girl's eyelids. 'I'd say it's not as bad as it seems, but you can't be too careful with a knocked head. We'll take her to hospital; she'll likely need a few stitches. Make haste if you're coming.'

'I ought to stay and help,' Fiona began, looking around at the shore crew who were already working on restoring the *Lady Dafna* to her usual sea-going state.

'I should tan your hide for sneaking on board like that,' Glasson said grimly, making her jump. 'Don't you dare do it again.'

'It was hardly sneaking,' she pointed out.

'Still, you can't just—'

'Please, don't tell my mother,' Fiona broke in. 'She'd stop me coming here altogether.'

Glasson looked at her narrowly for a moment, then shrugged. 'Up to you, maid.' His expression softened. 'You did alright, in the end.' He looked over to where Doctor Rowe was settling the unconscious child in the back of Andrew's bakery van. 'Get on then, or you'll miss your ride.'

The girl remained unconscious for the journey. Fiona couldn't help fretting as she saw the growing red stain on the freshly applied bandage, and as she waited in the little side room at the hospital, she feared the worst. But the nurse who'd tended the girl assured her that there was no serious damage, and that the cut itself was shallow and wouldn't need stitches after all.

'Always seems worse, where the skin lies so close to the bone,' she said. 'You can go in and see her now if you like. How's your sister, by the way?' she added, as she led Fiona towards the girl's bed. 'She was a lovely patient, I'm sure lots of the nurses here would be glad to know how she's getting on.'

'A lovely patient?' Fiona gave her an incredulous look, then saw the nurse was quite serious. 'She's doing well,' she said. Clearly Bertie had been a lot easier to care for here than she'd so far been at home. Not that Fiona didn't have sympathy for her in spades, of course, losing a leg was unimaginably awful, and she loved her sister dearly, but sometimes Bertie just made everything far more difficult than it needed to be.

They arrived at the girl's bed, and Fiona's first thought was that she looked like a doll lying there; so small, with the sheets still pulled tight as if she hadn't moved at all. Her hair, now dry, stuck up white and fluffy above the bandage.

'Hello, dear,' the nurse said, drawing Fiona forwards. 'This is Miss Fox, who came in with you after the accident.'

The girl ignored her. 'What happened to the ship? Did it ... did it sink?'

The nurse looked questioningly at Fiona, who shook her head. 'No, it made it around the headland at least.'

The girl twisted her head on the pillow. Her face was almost as white as her hair, but her eyes looked more alert, and the bandage no longer seeped blood. She observed Fiona for a moment, without expression, but as soon as the nurse had melted away her face brightened in a startlingly sunny smile.

'Hello, Miss Fox. And thank you for coming with me.'

'You're welcome.' Fiona hesitated, unsure what to say now. Although such a short time had passed, the experience on the lifeboat seemed as if it had happened to someone else, and that she'd just been watching from the outside. 'You can call me Fiona. What's your name?'

The girl's face clouded again. 'I don't know. The nurse tells me I'll remember soon enough, so I'm not too worried.'

17

'You don't sound as if you're from here,' Fiona ventured, pulling up a chair. 'I can't tell what your accent is.'

The girl shrugged, then winced. 'Remind me not to do that again,' she said, and her grin reappeared. Fiona realised then that she was older than she'd first seemed, perhaps even the same age as Fiona herself; the face was heart-shaped, and the eyes childlike, but there was something in the way she spoke, and in the direct blue gaze, that belied her appearance.

'They said they're keeping me overnight,' the girl told her. 'But I'm perfectly well.'

'I should think they'll probably keep you until your memory's come back,' Fiona said. 'They have your clothes safe in a box.'

Abruptly the girl's hand went to her throat, and her eyes widened further, but now they looked distraught. 'My necklace! Where's—'

'It's safe,' Fiona assured her quickly. 'With your clothes. You were still wearing it when they took you from the sea.'

The girl subsided, but, witnessing her distress, the nurse returned. 'I think the poor love needs to sleep now, Miss Fox. Come and see her again tomorrow.'

'I will,' Fiona promised. 'If you'd like me to?' she added, and the girl looked at her for an unsettlingly long moment before she nodded.

'Yes, please. I don't know anyone else.'

'As far as you know, you don't,' the nurse pointed out. 'You're bound to be missed off that ship, and someone'll come looking, don't fret.'

Fiona realised the girl had yet to be told the rest of it. 'How many of you were on the rowing boat?'

'I don't remember.'

'What's the last thing you *do* remember?'

'Miss Fox, now's not the time.' The nurse gently urged her to her feet, and Fiona held out her hand to the girl.

'I have to work tomorrow morning, but I'll come after lunch. I hope I'll find you fully recovered then.'

She stopped off at the lifeboat station on her way home, to pass on news of the girl, then walked slowly back to Fox Bay, growing more and more subdued as she relived the moment when she'd looked on the limp and lifeless form of the old man. She wondered how many others had struck out for safety in that tiny boat, how well the girl had known them, and if she knew yet that she'd been the only survivor.

CHAPTER TWO

Fox Bay Hotel

Helen closed the office door, feeling like the keeper of the world's best secret; Christmas was about to be turned on its head in the best possible way. In the meantime everything looked normal out in the lobby; guests were milling about waiting for friends, and Guy Bannacott was thumbing through the heavy guest book, while Martin Berry was wiping wet handprints off the counter top and scowling out at the weather.

Helen's smile faded as she followed his gaze. 'Is Fiona back yet?' She hated the thought of her youngest daughter out there at the lifeboat station at any time, but in winter her fears doubled, and this had already been a more than usually vicious one . . . She pushed the significance of today's date to the back of her mind, it wasn't helping.

'She came back a short while ago, Mrs Fox,' he told her. 'Her clothes were wet, so she went upstairs to change.' Martin gave the wood a final wipe and dropped the cloth back beneath the counter.

'Thank you. I'll go and find her in a minute.' Helen turned to Guy, unable to contain the news any longer. 'You'll never guess!'

Guy raised an elegant eyebrow. 'You'd better tell me then.'

'We're having *very* special guests this Christmas. A couple of Hollywood film stars.'

'We've had Hollywood before,' he reminded her, and he was right of course, but they'd never had anyone quite like this.

'Go on then,' he said, with exaggerated indulgence. 'Who is it?'

'I'll give you a clue.' Helen tried to think of one. 'Oh, I know.' She put both hands to her face and opened her eyes as wide as they would go, her mouth an 'O' of apparent dismay. '*Mercy*, Aunt Mercy!' Her American accent wasn't anywhere near as good as Leah's, in fact it was awful, but Guy looked suitably impressed, and Martin's mouth dropped open, though not, Helen was sure, due to the accuracy of the impression.

'Not Daisy Conrad?'

'*And* Freddie Wishart,' Helen said, looking directly at Guy, whose eyes widened slightly though he gave nothing else away. But Helen had seen the shelf in his room where he kept every issue of *Motion Picture* magazine that featured the fresh-faced young star. He sent away for them especially, and when they arrived he would devour every page with all the hunger of the movie fanatic he was. Once read, he left those in good enough condition in the guest sitting rooms, but the Freddie Wishart ones he kept.

'Really?' he murmured. 'How exciting.' His tone was dry, but Helen noticed his hand was trembling a little as he turned the page of the ledger. 'We must make sure the first-floor rooms are beyond reproach, then. When do they arrive?'

'Next Saturday. The twenty-first, that is, not tomorrow. The producer arrives on Monday.'

Martin shook his head. 'Why on earth would they want to come *here*?' He flushed as Helen raised an eyebrow. 'I only meant to say—'

'Don't worry, I asked myself the same thing.' She smiled to ease his embarrassment. 'At first I thought it might be a way to escape prohibition over the holiday, but they could have gone anywhere, including any of the top London hotels, if they just wanted to get tight. The thing is, the producer of their next film is an old acquaintance of Harry's.' She waved the letter at Guy again. 'The film is going to be set in an hotel just like this, and he's keen to make sure the set is authentic. He's flying Miss Conrad and Mr Wishart over early so they can get a feel for the place.'

'Away from home over the holiday?' Guy looked mystified. 'Americans are rather fond of Christmas, I thought.'

'They'll be even fonder of it by the time this one's over,' Helen said, with determination. 'At least, we're going to do our best to make sure they are.'

After that impossibly difficult first year without Harry, Christmas at Fox Bay had gradually become *the* place to be. To all intents and purposes the hotel was closed, but each year twenty regular guests were invited to make bookings if they wished, and it was rare that such an opportunity was turned down. Society magazines were always trying to secure an invitation, even down to cultivating a relationship with the hotel throughout the rest of the year, but Fleur had the uncanny knack of sniffing them out and alerting Helen to a seemingly innocent booking. Fox Bay guests could be assured of their privacy, particularly over Christmas.

'So, I'm to meet the famed Clifford Brennan, am I?' Guy rubbed his hands. 'He's a genius, I've so much to ask him. His work on *Stagehand Sally* was—'

'Wait a moment. Who?'

Guy gestured at the letter, a little impatiently. 'The producer. He's done all the Wishart–Conrad films.'

Helen had to smile at the way he switched the accepted order of the names around to put Freddie's first. 'No,' she said, 'this is a Mr Rex Kelly, he's not worked with them before. *Dangerous Ladies* is his first since he took over this studio.'

'Oh.' After a flicker of disappointment, Guy rallied. 'I've heard of him, at least. Oh, well. It'll be wonderful to have them all over here.'

Helen handed him the letter. 'It was all down to you, you know. Once you told Harry and Adam how the motion picture industry was taking off, there was no stopping them.'

'I didn't realise they'd all kept in touch after the investment fell through.' Guy skimmed the note. 'They're staying a long-ish while, aren't they? And it says here that they'll be flying a child over after Christmas, too.'

'Well they wouldn't want to take him away from his family over the holiday, he's only ten.'

'Jimmy Haverford,' Guy mused. 'Never heard of him, but good grief, child stars can be obnoxious.'

'Guy!' Helen couldn't help laughing. 'Don't forget your precious Freddie was a child star once.'

'He was a child *actor*,' Guy corrected her, with an aloof look. '*The Boy at the Window* was a piece of art. Freddie's silent work with Stone Valley Pictures was—'

'Well then,' Helen broke in, 'let's not judge poor Master Haverford until we've seen *his* work. I'm sure there'll be something about him in one of those magazines of yours. Anyway,' she went on hurriedly, as a flush touched his features, 'much as

23

I'd like to stand here and chat about Hollywood all day, we both have work to do.' She held out her hand for the letter. 'Have you seen Fleur today?'

'She went out for her afternoon walk early,' Guy said. 'She's been doing that more and more lately.' He pursed his lips, looking unusually hesitant. 'I think perhaps it's all the changes Mr Coleridge is making. It's unsettling for her.'

'It can't be easy,' Helen said, 'stepping back even further than she did when we first came. But it's not as if he's changing the place beyond all recognition, it's still the same but with a few improvements. And I suppose he's perfectly within his rights. He did save the place for us.'

'And you saved him from prison,' Guy pointed out. 'Don't let him ride roughshod over your own plans. Or Fleur's.'

Helen smiled a little at that. Sometimes Guy sounded more like a benevolent uncle, or even a father, than an employee, albeit a valued one. 'Don't worry, I won't.'

She was still mulling over this promise as she added to the list of fresh produce they would need over the next few weeks; Beth Nancarrow would be over from Higher Valley within the hour, and Nicholas Gough, the head chef, *would* keep changing his mind about the menus. It was a wonder they ever got the ingredients in time.

Around her the kitchen seethed with activity; pots and pans crashing, steam hissing through tiny vents in lids, the odd curse as something caught on the edges, or a finger strayed too close to a knife or a burner. Mr Gough stood like an island in the very centre of it all, staring into the distance as if he looked out over a calm sea rather than this ocean of orchestrated chaos.

'I think the cauliflower,' he said at last. 'Yes, the cauliflower.'

'You're sure?' Helen's pen hovered over her list, knowing she should have just written it down and walked away while she had the chance.

'Absolutely. No, wait. I'll ... yes, the cauliflower.'

'Mrs Fox?' A maid appeared at her elbow. 'Mr Nancarrow's here. In the kitchen.'

'Mr?'

'The elder,' the girl qualified, a faintly disappointed look on her face, and Helen couldn't help smiling, the poor girl would evidently have preferred one of the twins. She saw Mr Gough's mouth open to change his mind again, and took her chance. 'Perfect timing, Milly, please tell him I'll be through in a moment. Thank you, Mr Gough.'

She made a note on her paper and checked it through one last time, then went out to the staff kitchen to see Alfie, already furnished with a cup of tea. 'Where's Beth today?'

'It's Friday,' he reminded her. 'She's visiting the same coven as your mother-in-law.'

'Coven? Oh! The WI meeting.' She shook her head by way of a mild reprimand, and sat down with a little groan of relief to be off her feet.

'She told me before she left that they've apparently fixed a date for the memorial,' Alfie said. 'New Year's Day.'

'Ah, Fleur's not mentioned that yet. Mind you, I've been a bit preoccupied, so we haven't had chance to talk for a while.' She nodded at his cup. 'Any more where that came from?'

He twisted in his seat and lifted the teapot from the stand on the dresser behind him. 'Some hostess you are,' he observed as he passed her a cup. 'And to think people talk of you up and down the county, you and your immaculate manners.'

25

'That's not me,' she said, taking a blissful sip. 'I have someone who dresses up and pretends to be me, being nice to people while I lurk in my turret and make dastardly plans to annoy my head chef.'

'Well to be fair, you can be a bit of a tyrant.'

'You just wait,' Helen said, her eyes narrowed dangerously, 'you haven't met that side of me yet, but you just might one day.'

He grinned. 'Let's see the list, then.'

'For goodness' sake don't tell me you haven't enough cauliflower, or Nicholas will resign on the spot.' She passed him the much crossed-out and blotched order sheet, and he scanned it and tucked it into his jacket pocket. 'Should be alright. I'll check with Beth when she gets back and let you know if you need to have words with your chef again.' He linked his fingers around his teacup, which looked tiny in his grasp. 'How are things here? It's been a while since I've come down.'

'Oh, you know. Busy.' Helen felt a little guilty when she compared her 'busy' with that of the Nancarrows. 'How are the boys?'

'Jory's still being a bit of a tearaway.' He shrugged. 'He'll grow out of it, hopefully before he lands himself in trouble. Jowan, well ... Has your stubborn daughter forgiven him for being an idiot yet?'

Beth would never have phrased the question in this way, despite their long-time business partnership, but then Beth hadn't been with her when Bertie had almost died, hadn't held the girl's blood-soaked and writhing form as they'd struggled to get her into the van without hurting her further ... And Beth hadn't stayed with Helen at the hospital, and given her somewhere to weep where no one would see. Alfie was a friend, and he knew them well enough to speak the bald truth.

'I think she realised long ago that she had nothing to forgive him for. But—' she shrugged '—you know Bertie, she finds it easier to feel she has to make her own way, it's so hard for her to accept that someone truly cares for her.'

He nodded slowly. 'She's a complicated young woman, I've come to realise that over the years.' His eyes were kind on hers. 'But you're not just thinking about Jo now, are you?'

'Well, Leah too. And . . .' Helen lowered her face, so as not to let the hurt show. 'And yes, there's me.'

'She knows,' he said quietly. 'Just give it time.'

Helen nodded, and sensing melancholy creeping into the conversation she summoned a brisk tone. 'Speaking of time, I'm running out of it. And I'm sure you have better things to do as well, than sitting here in the warm, drinking tea.'

'Me? I certainly do.' He stood up and lifted his work jacket off the back of the chair. 'I've got a drainage ditch to finish, a dry stone wall to build, and some roof tiles to fasten down. Oh, and there's always the joy of moving the pigs out while we finish fixing up their sty.'

'There, you see?' Helen rose too, and picked up his empty cup to carry it to the sink. 'You have such an easy life. Spare a thought for me, won't you? Planning all these parties and dinners, struggling with endless cushion plumping, and having to make vital decisions about whether to greet guests with a Dom Pérignon, or a Moët.'

Alfie paused, his jacket half-on, and adopted a dismayed look. 'Oh no! I've *just* remembered we have no cauliflower.'

She started to protest, then shook her head and laughed. 'You just would too, wouldn't you?'

'Will you tell Mr Gough, or shall I?'

He ducked out of the door before she could throw her tea towel at him.

That evening, after she'd gratefully handed the reins of management to Ben, she took a well-earned gin and orange over to her favourite alcove in the lounge, and sat down with a sigh of relief. Normally Leah would have joined her, but she and Adam had gone to Bude to see the sound version of a film called *Atlantic*, apparently based on the real-life tragedy of the *Titanic*. Helen shuddered; she couldn't think of a worse night's "entertainment" than watching hundreds of people drowning. She couldn't imagine it was Leah's cup of tea either, but that woman would go to the ends of the Earth to make Adam Coleridge happy.

'Helen? Might I join you?'

She looked up to see Fleur hovering uncertainly by the vacant chair, and nodded, surprised. 'Of course. You needn't ask.'

'You looked a little ... distant.' Fleur sat down and placed her own drink on the gleaming square table. 'I didn't like to intrude on your thoughts.'

'Not at all. I was just thinking about this film Adam and Leah have gone to see. Sounds dreadful.'

'It's Adam I wanted to talk to you about,' Fleur admitted. She twisted her fingers into the rope of pearls at her neck, and didn't say any more for a moment. Helen waited, and finally Fleur found the words she was looking for. 'You know I'm fond of him, but I don't like what he's doing.'

'Ah. Guy did mention he thought you might be finding it unsettling.'

'Guy could always read my moods,' Fleur said, and a fond smile banished some of the shadows on her face. 'Though it's not so much the changes themselves, it's more ... how quickly he's doing it. As if he's had it in the back of his mind for ages.'

'You know Adam. Once he has the bit between his teeth there's no stopping him.'

'But he only owns half of the hotel, Helen. You own the other half, do *you* like what he's doing?'

'Mostly, yes. He has the interests of the guests at heart, they'll enjoy their own private, sectioned-off pool area when the tide's in. Not everyone enjoys jumping in the waves, it's nice to be able to swim.'

'And what of that thing he's building on the beach?'

'It does make sense to have a decking area. You know people are always asking if we really do own that beach, so to have the Fox emblem engraved in the wood means no one need waste their time. And he's doing it tastefully, you must admit.'

'So you agree with all these changes, and the cost of them.'

Helen sighed. 'You know cost isn't really an issue.' Since Adam had sold the farmland to Mr Pagett, his finances had rocked back onto an even keel. She eased aside the niggling reminder that she only had Adam's word for it that Hartcliffe's books had been adjusted, and subtly enough that Simon Hill had no suspicion that Adam had temporarily embezzled such a huge sum of money. He insisted it was being paid back, albeit gradually.

'Besides,' she went on, 'we're going from strength to strength guest-wise. You've heard who's coming to stay, and for how long?'

'Of course.' Fleur picked up her drink again. 'But you must remember that what they're paying for, you have to give them. They're going to expect the freshest food, the most luxurious linens, the top-quality service ... It's not going to be free money.'

'I know that,' Helen said patiently. 'But it's no more than every other guest gets. And they're staying for *six weeks*! Besides, once they go home they're sure to point out what a marvellous time they had. Word will get out, as it has done before. People will want to see for themselves – not all that glitzy set like to stay in London every time, they get enough of the high life at home.'

After a pause, Fleur nodded. 'I hope you're right.'

'It's not really the cost though, is it?' Helen ventured, but Fleur didn't reply, nor did she have to.

Since mending those long-broken fences with Adam, Helen had given in to almost every suggestion he'd made for the hotel. She had wanted to step on some of his ideas, just to try and re-establish some authority, but the truth was they were all good ideas, and all affordable.

Fleur had always liked Adam well enough, as she was keen to point out, but it was obvious she was finding it hard watching everything she'd known from the age of seventeen changing before her eyes. *When Robert first opened this place* . . . was becoming a familiar phrase, and Helen had to remind herself not to dismiss Fleur's fond memories, yet it was impossible to argue with the tale told by the accounting books; the hotel was flourishing, even now, during this time of financial instability.

'Adam's going to visit his family in Leith tomorrow,' she said. 'He'll be away for about a week, I think. But when he gets back I'll . . . *we'll*, keep an eye on him. I'm not going to discount something that works, just because Adam suggested it.' She softened her tone. 'But I promise that neither am I going to let him ride rough-shod, as Guy puts it, over the way you and Robert built this place up.'

'I know, love,' Fleur said, though her smile was a little forced. She sat back in her seat and changed the subject. 'Did I tell you we have a date now, for the war memorial?'

Helen nodded. 'Well, Alfie told me. New Year's Day. It'll be wonderful to have that, at last.'

'It's taken a long while,' Fleur said. 'Most of the families have been contacted, and Daniel's name will be on it, of course. I hope Leah takes some comfort from that. How are she and Bertie getting along now?'

'Much better. Bertie doesn't need Leah nearly as much anymore, and Leah has finally persuaded her, I think, to go and see the consultant about getting a prosthetic made.'

'Good. That will change things.'

'She'll still never ride a motorcycle again,' Helen said quietly. 'And that's what she misses the most. I have no illusions that having a new limb will turn her back into the girl she was.'

Her throat caught on the words, as a picture of a younger Bertie, still Roberta, flashed into her mind, fierce concentration on her face as she got to grips with the basics of riding her first bicycle. She had moved on to the Nancarrow boys' motorcycle all too soon, and Helen had felt sick for a long time seeing it, but the first time Roberta had successfully kick-started the old machine was the first time Helen had seen true happiness on her daughter's face since Harry had died.

'She'll be able to go back to work at the telephone exchange,' Fleur said. 'And that will take her back out into the world again with Sally and her other friends. Who knows what could happen then? A nice new beau, even.'

'I'm sorry she and Jowan have become so distant from one another.' Helen stood up and stretched her aching back. 'He steadied her, and she adored him. Still does.'

'She'll soon learn she was foolish to push him away.' Fleur rose too. 'Well, I'm going to have a chat with Guy about the Christmas Eve dinner. Do you have any messages?'

Helen shook her head. 'I've got to make preparations for Mr Kelly, he's coming on Monday.'

'Why *are* they coming, anyway?'

Helen told her what she'd told Guy, adding, 'The film is supposed to be some kind of crime caper. Daisy plays an English character, and Mr Kelly thinks it will be good for them to spend some time in England, and in the same kind of setting as the film. Besides, Daisy needs to learn an authentic English accent, so Leah will be put to work there, I think.'

'That's quite some dedication to the craft,' Fleur mused.

'Maybe that's not the real reason they're coming,' Helen said with an exaggeratedly mysterious air. 'Maybe Mr Wishart secretly plans to propose marriage to Miss Conrad, and doesn't want the eyes of the world on him while he does it.'

'For heaven's sake don't share that theory with Guy!' The last of Fleur's tension dissipated in a chuckle. 'Well then, we're going to have to pay close attention to that young pair, and be first to offer our services for a wedding reception.' She gave Helen a sly smile. 'And you can tell Mr Coleridge that was *my* idea.'

CHAPTER THREE

Fiona wondered, all the way into the village, why she had lied; she'd done nothing wrong, after all. She'd been working, and thinking about yesterday's rescue with a rush of remembered excitement, when Miss Tremar had come to call her to the telephone.

Martin had looked at her quizzically as he'd passed her the receiver. 'It's the police, Miss Fox. For you.'

The police? She'd listened in growing surprise, then handed the phone back with a few mumbled words about some lost property from yesterday. 'Nothing important, but I'd better go now. Please tell my mother for me.'

Once in the village she turned up the path to the police house, her heart hammering, glancing around to see if anyone was taking any notice. She didn't see anyone looking at her; those who were out and about were hurrying to complete their own errands before the rain started again. Fiona sloshed through several sizeable puddles that had gathered in the uneven slate paving, flicking water off the toes of her boots.

In all the time she'd lived at Fox Bay she'd never had any reason to actually go into the police house, and had no idea what to expect; in her mind it had always shown itself as an implausibly huge place behind the unremarkable façade, split into barred cells filled with snarling captives.

Instead she found herself in a short hallway, with a telephone on a table, and with only one other door. She pushed it open, and stared around a square, plain room featuring a small counter top, a single cupboard, and a large desk where the constable sat writing up notes.

He looked up, smiled briefly, and put down his pen. 'Thank you for coming, Miss Fox. I'd have had to take her over to the station in Bude otherwise, and it's just me today. She'd have been in there 'til suppertime.'

In where? Fiona couldn't see any other door in the room, apart from the one she'd come in through. No cells, no vicious-looking villains. 'What has she done?' She took the seat Constable Quick indicated, but sat forward on the edge of it, her hands clasped tightly. 'I thought she was staying in hospital for a few days.'

'I don't know about that. All I know is she was found nickin' stuff in Mrs Burch's, and Mrs Burch marched her over here herself.'

'And she asked for me, specifically?'

'More like we told her if she didn't have someone to speak up for her, she'd be taken over to Bude like I said. She gave us your name.'

'So where is she now?'

'In the shed,' Constable Quick said mildly. He caught Fiona's appalled expression, and grinned. 'Don't fret, miss. It's not as bad as it sounds. It's just what we call the place where we hold people until we can take them over to the station.'

'Oh!' Fiona relaxed a little. 'So it's not actually a shed, then?'

'Certainly is.' Constable Quick opened the drawer in his desk and took out a set of keys. 'I gather my boy was the one dragged

34

her out,' he said, unmistakeable pride in his voice as they crossed the yard. 'Was you there, then? On the beach when they came in?'

Fiona silently thanked Danny for keeping quiet about her reckless dash for a place on the lifeboat. 'I was there, yes,' she said truthfully. 'That's why the girl knows my name.'

'Even if she don't know hers, eh?' Quick fitted the key into the lock of a small but sturdy-looking outhouse, and Fiona heard a scrabbling from the other side of the door, as if the girl inside had scrambled to her feet. 'It's quite cosy in there,' Quick assured her, noticing her frown. 'Not so cruel as it seems from out here.'

The door creaked open, and Fiona saw that there was indeed a pleasant enough room beyond; electric light, a bunk, an armchair, and a pile of books and magazines. But no windows, and no clock – it would be hard for anyone to know how much time had passed.

The girl was now dressed in a frock that had probably looked nice on its original owner, but hung off her slender frame like an overly floral sack. It drooped almost to the floor, but didn't quite cover the tatty-looking boots Fiona remembered from yesterday. The white-blonde hair sticking up in clumps added to the appearance of a Victorian street urchin; no wonder Mrs Burch had kept an eye on her. But nothing could disguise the beauty of the large, bruised-blue eyes, the finely pointed chin, or the calm poise with which the girl held herself.

Her worried face broke into a smile as she saw Fiona. 'I'm so glad you came!'

'What happened?' Fiona accepted the enthusiastic embrace awkwardly. 'Why were you trying to steal—'

'Time for that later,' Constable Quick said. 'Come with me, miss, I've got your belongings back in the office, and you need to sign a form.'

He led the way back to the house, and the girl turned her face up to the overcast sky as she and Fiona followed, blinking in pleasure at the dull, half-light of the hidden sun.

'You've only been in there an hour,' Fiona pointed out, amused. 'You're behaving as if you've been locked up for days!'

'Oh, but it felt like it,' the girl said. 'I didn't know you'd come, you see, and all I could think about was, what if they put me in prison?'

'Why did you leave hospital then?'

They'd reached the house now, and the girl slipped her arm through Fiona's. 'I'll tell you everything. But you *must* tell the constable that you'll have me to stay at your house, otherwise he won't let me go.' She tightened her hold. 'Promise me you will?'

Fiona struggled for something to say, but in the end she could only shrug. 'Alright.'

Back in the office, Constable Quick assured the girl they were doing all they could to contact her family. 'The main trouble is, the captain of that ship you escaped from has no knowledge of you,' he said, eyeing her disapprovingly, 'so that's no help. Stowaway, were you?'

The girl held her hands up, helpless. 'I don't feel as if I could do something like that, but I suppose I must have been.'

'And there were no survivors from that little boat to vouch for you, either.'

At this, the girl paled and she blinked rapidly. 'None?'

'How many of you were there?'

'I, I don't remember.' She pressed her fingers to the plaster at her hairline.

'What *do* you remember?'

The girl chewed at her lip. 'I think I can remember climbing in. Unless I dreamed that, and I did have some fierce dreams last night. Someone was helping me, an old man, that was real enough.' She leaned forward. 'Didn't *he* survive, at least?'

'They brought him onto the lifeboat,' Fiona said gently, 'but I'm sorry to say he died soon after. There was no one else left when the rescuers swam out to you.'

"Twas my boy saved you, you know,' Quick said, that pride creeping into his voice again. 'Him and Andrew Kessel between 'em. If it weren't for that fact I doubt I should be so lenient.' He turned to Fiona. 'Now, the young lady here remembered your name from the hospital, and I've told her that, if you was prepared to come in here today and take her home, and keep her out of bother 'til she remembers where she came from, she'd be allowed to go free. Will you sign to that effect? You don't have to,' he added. 'Not at all. Your choice.'

Fiona glanced at the girl and saw such pleading in her face that she silenced the questions in her mind, and scribbled her name on the form.

'Thank you,' Quick said, scooping up the page and signing his own name. He passed it to the girl, who pulled a face and put a cross next to where Quick had written: *unknown survivor (female), RMS* Drake, *Plymouth.*

'Do you know what happened to make the ship dangerous?'

Fiona shook her head. 'No. Danny said he couldn't work out why it would have floundered so badly, even in a storm like that. Mr Glasson said it was probably something about the steering gear being put out.'

'But it made shore safely?' the girl persisted.

Quick nodded. 'Docked off Porthstennack, last I heard. Glasson said the engineers were working on it, but he don't know how long it'll take.' The constable slipped the form into a file and closed it. 'Right, on you go, I've got work to be doing.'

The two girls pushed their chairs back and thanked him. 'It looks like rain,' Fiona added. 'Would you mind if I telephoned for Guy to come for us?'

'From here?' Quick gave her a meaningful look. 'I don't think you want that, do you? If I were you I'd call from here, then get across to Mrs Burch's, say your sorries, and get picked up from there.' He pointed through the open office door, to the telephone on the hall table.

'Who's Guy,' the girl asked, 'your brother?'

'No, he's—'

'Oh! While I think on.' Constable Quick opened the cupboard and removed the box Fiona had last seen on the lifeboat. 'Here, your things. Mind you call in at the shop and apologise now.'

'Alright,' the girl sighed, but she seized the box eagerly. 'Thank you.' She looked as if she were dying to open it and rummage through her belongings, but was probably aware it would appear rude. As if she didn't trust those who were helping her.

'Guy will collect us in ten minutes,' Fiona said when she'd replaced the receiver, and together they hurried across the square to Mrs Burch's post office and grocery shop. Fiona made the girl promise not to mention her by name, and then waited outside.

'What do I call you?' she asked, when the girl emerged, red-faced and quiet. 'I can't just call you, *survivor, female*, can I?'

'You could call me ... Amy.'

'Why Amy?'

The girl looked nonplussed. 'Why not? You wanted a name, didn't you? It's the first thing that popped into my head. Why didn't you want me to give her *your* name in the shop, anyway?'

'We can't let my mother find out you were caught stealing.' Fiona stared up the road for sight of Guy's motor. 'She won't even have you to stay for tea if she does, and Mrs Burch is married to our handyman, so the first whiff of it getting to him would put the cat among the pigeons. We can just tell her you were let out of hospital.' This time the lie felt more like a fun, shared secret, and she had the feeling she was going to enjoy it; she was beginning to see why Leah had so much fun play-acting.

'Do you think you're an habitual thief?' she went on, curious. 'I mean, why not just telephone me from the hospital and ask me to come? Why leave at all? Where were you going to go?'

'There's no need for all these questions at once,' Amy grumbled. 'Let's get back to your house and talk there. Have you any clothes I could borrow? Oh!' She stopped dead, and eyed Fiona's favourite, tatty coat. 'Will you have enough room for me?'

Fiona suppressed a smile. 'We have plenty of room. Look, Guy's here.'

The Alfa Romeo drew to a smooth halt outside Mrs Burch's, and Guy climbed out; Amy's face was a picture when she saw his debonair manners and sharp, up-to-the-minute suit, and she turned to Fiona. 'How big *is* your house?'

'Good afternoon, miss.' Guy held the door open for them to scramble into the back, then returned to the driving seat without asking questions. Seeing Amy burning with them, however, Fiona supplied the introductions.

'Guy, this is Amy, who they rescued on the *Dafna* yesterday. I said she could stay with us a while. Amy, this is Mr Bannacott. A very good friend of the family, and an absolute brick for driving out to pick us up. Thank you, Guy.'

Guy nodded and started the engine, saying nothing as they drove back down the winding lane. After only a few minutes, which would have been at least twenty if they'd been walking, he slowed and turned off the main road. They swept up the long driveway towards the front of the hotel, and Fiona smiled as Amy's awed gaze went to the large new sign that Uncle Adam had had made, that stood on the closely cropped grass halfway up the drive.

WELCOME TO FOX BAY HOTEL

'*Fox* Bay. As in . . . ?'

'As in Fiona Fox, yes.'

'Gosh.' Amy stared at the building as they stopped outside the front door. 'It's massive!'

Fiona's rare sense of pride swelled. 'It is, isn't it?'

'But not very pretty.'

Guy's eyes met Fiona's in the rear-view mirror and slid away, expressionless, but Fiona had to admit Amy was right; the exterior *was* impressive, but not particularly attractive apart from the soaring arches of the cloisters that ran the length of the building. 'No, I suppose not.' She peered through the freshly falling drizzle at the former monastery. 'Not from the outside at least. But wait until you see inside.'

'I can't believe anyone actually lives in a hotel.'

'We moved from Bristol when I was six,' Fiona said. 'It's quite famous, you know,' she added, a little defensively.

'I suppose that depends on how rich you are,' Amy said, and Fiona thought she detected a faint note of bitterness.

'Well, for all you know you might live somewhere just as grand,' she pointed out.

'That's true.' Amy brightened a little. 'I might even have come to stay here in the past, perhaps the inside will remind me.' She looked at the smaller, but just as elegant, painted glass door to the side of the huge revolving doors. 'Why do you have two doors right next to each other?'

'My mum and Uncle Adam had that new one put in when my sister had an accident earlier this year. She uses a wheelchair now, so the steps and the revolving door are both a problem for her.' She pointed to the smooth, Cornish slate-paved slope. 'That means Bertie can come and go by herself.'

'Bertie's a girl?' Amy grinned. 'Perhaps I should pick something more interesting than Amy too.'

Fiona led the way into the hotel, gratified now at Amy's awed reaction to the familiar surroundings. Deep, comfortable sofas were carefully placed for light and view, and strewn with gilt-edged cushions; drapes made from white and gold silk framed the tall, angular mirrors; the walnut-topped reception desk dominated one wall, its brass fittings polished to a high shine and the light and dark mottled wood gleaming with a satin finish.

The entire lobby had the look of quiet elegance, and smelled of winter spices, perfume, and rich tobacco, and smartly turned out guests were either signing out, or seated in little groups as they waited for transport to the railway station.

'In another hour or so the Plymouth train will arrive in Trethkellis,' Fiona explained, 'and then we'll have our last regular guests of the year before the Christmas fun starts.'

Amy's face fell, and Fiona silently berated herself. Amy must be distraught at not being able to contact her family, and with Christmas fast approaching it must be doubly hard. 'We'll work on bringing your memory back,' she said gently. 'Let's go and find you a room.'

'Will it be near you?' Amy hung back, looking worried.

'Well, we – that is, the family and live-in staff – have rooms on the third floor. They're just normal, not nearly as nice as the guest rooms.'

'I don't mind. Can we share?'

'But you won't have to pay—'

'Can we?'

'Of course, if you really want to. I'll have another bed brought into my room. Are you worried about those dreams you were talking about?'

'A bit.'

Fiona nodded and squeezed Amy's arm. 'Come on, then. We'll find Mum and tell her what's happening.'

'Is she nice, your mother?' Amy still looked reluctant. 'Will she be cross?'

'Not in the least. She's busy, we have some really important and exciting guests coming next week, but she'll want to meet you.'

She led the way behind the counter and knocked at the office door. Her mother called out for her to come in, and Fiona smiled back at Amy and dropped her voice to a whisper. 'Don't worry.'

Her mother did look somewhat distracted. 'Is this important? Because I've a dozen things to do before lunch. And, by the way, where did you ... oh!' Her expression softened when she saw Amy, hovering slightly behind Fiona. 'Hello, who's this?'

'This is the girl they rescued off the cargo ship yesterday.' Fiona briefly explained everything, except the shoplifting part and Constable Quick's involvement, implying instead that she'd fetched Amy from the hospital. 'So,' she finished hopefully, 'I thought I'd ask a couple of the bell boys to bring the bed from Miss Tremar's old room, now that she's living in the village.'

42

'Good idea,' Mum said, 'but see you don't trouble them until after the new guests are settled. After lunch will be soon enough.'

'Thank you so much, Mrs Fox,' Amy put in shyly. 'I hope I won't bother you for long.'

'Well you must stay just as long as you need to, but I hope you'll find it all comes back to you soon, so you can go home to your family in time for Christmas.'

'Oh, so do I!'

'You can help me with my work,' Fiona said, as they left the office. 'I'll give you half my pay, and we'll have twice as much time for me to show you around.'

Upstairs in Fiona's room, Amy at last opened her box, and her expression melted into relief as she reached in and took out the unusual necklace Fiona had noticed before.

'Is that . . . is it a *spoon*?' Fiona asked, as Amy fastened it around her neck. It certainly looked like the tarnished bowl of a serving spoon that had probably once been a bright silver.

Amy nodded, and when she didn't elaborate, Fiona shrugged and opened her wardrobe. 'That dress is hanging off you. Here.' She withdrew one of the dresses she rarely wore, and held it up to Amy's chin. 'That'll do, we'll find some more later. Meantime get out of that thing you're wearing, and I'll take everything to be washed.'

She left Amy alone to change while she took the clothing to the laundry, but halfway down the stairs a thought struck her, and she stopped, remembering how, from the start, Amy had fretted over the safety of that pendant. How did she remember it was so important to her, if she had no idea who she was? A little chill tickled at the base of her spine; this game didn't seem quite so much fun after all, when she was one of the people being lied to.

CHAPTER FOUR

Higher Valley Farm

Beth Nancarrow replaced the brass shovel on the fireplace companion set, and picked up the ash bucket. She hurried out to the compost heap, where the twins had finished work and were going their separate ways: Jory off to the Saltman, the pub in the village, and Jowan to wash for tea. Whereas he might once have bolted his food and rushed off to an arranged meeting with Bertie Fox, nowadays he took his time, pushing food around his plate, and disappeared to his room immediately he'd finished.

Beth shook her head; the poor lad hadn't known what to do with himself since Miss Fox had cut him adrift. Not that she blamed the girl exactly, it must be hard for her, when Jowan was so active, and it was only natural she'd be a bit withdrawn, but she didn't have to push him away completely.

The van roared into life, and Beth blinked against the sweep of headlights, and then Jory was gone. She went back indoors, wishing her son would stay home for once. The Saltman wasn't particularly rowdy, but it was Jory's habit to meet up with so-called friends who were only too happy to throw their money into some game or other. Sometimes they even went all the way into Bude to do it. All very well for those who could afford it, but at Jory's age he should be thinking about his future. He'd been courting that Sally Penneck, from the telephone exchange, for a while now, and she'd been heard in the village talking of marriage. But Jory was in no position to provide a home for her, nor did it seem likely he ever would be.

Jowan's feet, heavy on the stairs, told her he'd gone up to change his clothes, and soon another evening would be passed and gone, and nothing achieved. Alfie's voice drifted across the yard through the darkness, and Beth automatically checked her appearance in the darkened window glass and tried to see herself through his eyes: same old face, the one he'd known since they'd all been tackers, starting school together in Trethkellis; same old hair, twisted up off her face in one of her tatty scarves; same old eyes, bright and blue in the sunshine, dull and black in the reflection of the kitchen window.

What *did* Alfie see when he looked at her? Toby's widow? The twins' mother? Or a woman in her own right, and with her own wishes and desires? Because if he ever saw that, he'd see himself, reflected in those tired eyes. He'd see his own sweet smile, a contrast with the broad, strong frame; his own dark hair, greying at the temples but still full and thick—

'Staring at the weather won't bring on the spring!'

He'd appeared in the kitchen doorway without her even noticing, and shucked off his coat, hanging it on the back of the door while Reynard went to his water bowl and began lapping loudly.

'Tea's not done,' she said, turning back to prod at the carrots boiling in the pan. 'How's the wall coming?'

45

'It's coming,' he allowed, making for the sink. 'I lost my hip flask, though. Suppose it's been trodden into the mud somewhere up there by now. Ah well.'

'Oh no!' Beth heard the dejection behind Alfie's matter-of-fact tone; he and Toby had exchanged matching flasks on their eighteenth birthday, each with a picture engraved on them by their father; Toby's was an eagle, Alfie's a dog. They'd each spent all their savings on them. 'I'd give you Toby's, but I've not seen it for a good while now. I'll see if I can unearth it.'

'No matter.'

But again, she sensed the disappointment. 'Boys pulling their weight are they?' she asked, to change the subject.

'Jory couldn't wait to get away. Jowan's upstairs I suppose?'

She nodded, then realised that with his face over the sink he couldn't see her. 'He went up the moment he got in. Can you talk to him? He'll listen to you.'

Alfie snorted, blowing water through his fingers, then grabbed the threadbare towel hanging by the sink. 'Bloody won't, you know. Have you tried?'

Beth felt the usual tightening in her belly as his head emerged from the rough towelling and his eyes found hers. 'I've had a word,' she muttered, 'but I'll try again after tea if you make yourself scarce.'

'Right you are, I'll take Reynard out.' Alfie replaced the towel, and began laying the table. It was the picture of domestic peace, and a tiny glimpse into the past, except that Toby would have come up behind her and slipped his arms around her waist, nuzzled her neck, and asked in his typically blunt fashion if there was time for some loving before tea was cooked.

Sometimes she could even convince herself that that was the

reason she was so unhappy, that missing Toby was manifesting itself as loving his brother. But Alfie wasn't Toby, he had his own wisdom, his own humour, his own bewildering logic and frustrating habits. He also had a way of making her feel special, and that wasn't like Toby's either. It wasn't like anyone's. That wife of his from his Porthstennack days wanted her bumps felt, running off like that while he was away fighting. How he hadn't been snapped up again by some lonely war widow by now … Heaven knew there were enough of them. It crossed her mind briefly that perhaps he had been, on the quiet, but she dismissed that immediately; Trethkellis was not the kind of place to keep anything quiet for long.

After tea, when Alfie had pulled his wet coat on again and left, Beth touched her son's arm. 'Come in the sitting room, and sit down a bit.'

He blinked. 'What for?'

'I want to talk to you.'

Jowan groaned. 'Not about Bertie *again*.'

'Don't let her push you away, Jo,' Beth pleaded. 'She don't know her mind. Not really.'

'She knows it well enough to tell me to get lost!'

'You don't believe she means that, no more than I believe it.' Beth abandoned the attempt to persuade him into the comfort of the sitting room, and slid back into her chair at the kitchen table. 'She's—'

'Going through a difficult time. I know.'

'I was going to say proud,' Beth said softly. 'And confused. And lost. She needs you, Jo, even though she can't bring herself to admit it.'

'I can take not being told I'm needed,' he said, his voice grim. 'I can even take her yearning after that Xander Nicholls bloke, but what I'm not prepared to sit down and accept is her bloody *rudeness*! It's been one long string of insults and belittling since she came out of hospital, and I'm—'

'Another proud one,' Beth sighed. 'And why is it, d'you think, that she's so rude? About you, your bike, your life here at the farm?'

'Because she's a spoiled brat. Because she's suddenly best friends with Nicholls's fancy sister, and now she's too good for the likes of me.'

'Because all those things are what she wants, but can't have, you silly boy!' Beth rose and began putting plates into the sink.

'But she *can* have me!' Jowan protested. 'I never once made her think she was less than she was.'

Beth turned to him again. 'It's not enough to *not* tell her she's lacking, Jo.'

'What does that mean?'

'Think on this.' She pondered a moment. 'You buy me a nice coat from the second-hand place down Fisher's Row. It's a lovely colour, it's warm, and got a collar like them movie stars have, that turn up to their ears. But it's got a big hole in the sleeve.'

'And?'

'And you hand it to me, all proud as you like, and I'm grateful and polite, I don't mention the hole, and how long it'll take me to mend it. But I don't say how warm it'll keep me, either, or how I'll secretly feel like Clara Bow or Daisy Conrad when I wear it into town.'

Her son briefly raised his eyes to her. 'I've been an idiot, haven't I?'

'Yes.' Beth sat beside him and took his hand, forcing him to look at her again. 'But I understand it, love. As far as you're concerned nothing's changed, so you shouldn't have to put anything into words. I know you've never been good at saying it. Not even to me.' She gave him a little smile. 'But *you're* not the one who's had your belief in what you two had shaken. Bertie now …' Beth kissed Jowan's work-roughened knuckles, as if he were still a schoolboy instead of a man of twenty-eight. 'She's had everything she's ever known ripped away from her, and she needs to get it all back. Bit by bit.'

'Should I go and see her?'

'Not now.' Beth nodded at the clock. 'You'll only have to rush off again. Go tomorrow morning, when you've got the whole day.'

'But the wall—'

'Oh, your Uncle Alfie can manage a bit of dry stone walling, with Jory's help. He'll understand. Besides, I'm not saying you have to *take* all day, but at least the time'll be there if you need it.'

'Thanks, Mum.' Jowan stared at the table and took a deep breath. 'You might have just saved Bertie and me and our whole future.'

'Get away with you. You'd have worked it out.' Beth tugged gently at his hair, and went back to the sink. She waited until Jowan had left the room, then picked up the towel Alfie had used and pressed it to her cheek. Saved their future, had she? If only she could do the same for her own.

* * *

Fox Bay Hotel

Fiona had no idea what time it was, but the horrid feeling she'd had on the stairs earlier wouldn't go away and it was keeping her awake. Not so Amy; Fiona could hear the gentle snores coming from the other bed, and listened hard in case the girl muttered anything in her sleep. The more Fiona thought about it, the more convinced she was that she was being duped. Unable to wait any longer, she raised herself on one elbow and clicked on the lamp on her bedside table.

'Hie! Amy!' she hissed. 'Wake up!' There was no response, so Fiona reached behind her and pulled out her pillow. 'I said wake *up*!' She flung it the five or six feet across the gap between their beds, and gave a grunt of satisfaction as Amy sat up, gasping.

'What . . . ?' She threw the pillow back. 'What on earth are you doing?'

Fiona pushed her curls out of her eyes. 'I need to talk to you.'

'What about? What time is it?'

'I have no idea. Tell me about the spoon.'

'Why?'

'I want to know why it's so important to you.' *And how you know it is.* But she didn't say that, not yet.

'I . . . think it must have been a gift,' Amy said, somewhat lamely.

'A gift from whom? Your parents?'

Amy's hand went to the pendant. 'Maybe. It looks unusual enough to be special, after all.'

'But you knew it was missing,' Fiona insisted. 'Why are you lying to me, after all I've done to help you?'

'I'm not!'

'Tell me the truth, or I go to Constable Quick first thing.'

There was a long silence, then Amy shuffled forwards on her bed until she was perched on the very edge with her legs crossed, like a child. She held Fiona's eyes with her own. They

50

were opened wide, hypnotic. 'If I tell you the truth, you have to promise to keep it a secret.'

'I knew it! I'm not promising until I've heard it.'

'Then I won't tell you.' Amy sat back again, her face set and stubborn.

'At least tell me this,' Fiona persisted, 'do you know who you are really?'

The girl remained silent for an agonisingly long time, then nodded slowly. 'That's all you get, unless you swear to help me.'

'Help you?' Fiona considered; promising to help wasn't quite the same thing as keeping a secret, helping might even necessitate giving that secret away. 'Yes, alright. I'll help you if I can. I promise,' she added, as Amy prompted her with raised eyebrows. 'A Cornish maid's promise is a bond forever.'

'You said you came from Bristol.'

'Alright, I'm not Cornish. But my father was, and that's as good.'

Amy looked at her for a long, thoughtful moment. 'My name is Amy Markham. I live in Devon with my adoptive parents.'

'*Devon?* Then what were you doing on a ship off this coast?'

'I'm looking for my real mother.'

Fiona sat up straight, suddenly fascinated. 'Where is she?'

Amy gave her a withering look. 'If I knew that I'd—'

'Alright, alright!' Fiona held up a hand. 'You know what I mean. But that ship was going *somewhere*, so you must have had some idea where to start.' She settled back against her pillow again, wide awake and ready to stay up all night. 'Start from the beginning.'

Amy pondered a moment, then sighed. 'Okay. I was born in 1913, up in—'

'So was I! I knew you were older than you looked at first!'

'Do you want to hear this or not?'

Fiona subsided. 'Sorry, go on.'

'I was born in London. I have no clear memory of being there though, nor of my mother. No one ever *said* she'd died, exactly, but I'd just assumed, from the way people talked. Then one day Kitty and I were having a row—'

'Who's Kitty? Your adoptive mother?'

'Yes. Anyway, she let it slip that my mother's alive. It appears my father had arrived out of the blue when I was about four, and took me away from her while she was working.'

'Oh!' Fiona bit back a further declaration of outrage, and gestured for Amy to continue.

'All I had with me, that was truly mine, was this spoon.' Amy squinted down at it. 'From what my father told me it was my comforter from long before then, the way some children have a blanket. I don't remember where I got it. Anyway, my father wasn't really able to care for me; he'd lost part of his arm in the war, and couldn't even work alone at his own trade.'

'Which is?'

'He's a butcher. He admitted he tried to pass me off onto his family, but they didn't want me either.'

'If he couldn't cope any better than your mother, why did he steal you to begin with?'

Amy shrugged. 'Perhaps he thought he was better than her, no matter what. But I won't hear anything said against him, before you start,' she added quickly. 'He's told me more about my mother than Kitty ever would, anyway. She and Archie have their own baby now, and they love him much more than they do me.'

'Oh, I'm sure not!'

'It's true. It's natural I suppose, but we started arguing a lot.

This last fight, she yelled that she didn't blame my mother in the slightest for not trying harder to find me, that she was better off without me.'

Fiona stared, appalled. 'That's awful!'

'That was just before my last visit to Frank.'

'Your father?'

Amy nodded. 'I was trying to find out more, but Kitty absolutely refused. She wouldn't tell me how or why I ended up with her and Archie, either.'

'And what did Frank tell you about your real mother?'

'That she used to work as a kitchen maid at a big manor house, near where he has his shop in Cheshire. All he knows is that she's got a new man now, and they've gone to some little place in Ireland. But . . .' Amy shot Fiona a triumphant smile '. . . I found the name of the village, looking through his old letters while he was at work, and I found out her name, too. She's called Ruth.'

'Ruth Markham. Hmm. Shouldn't be too hard to—'

'They weren't *married*, you idiot! She wouldn't have been working at Oaklands if she were married!'

Fiona flushed. It wasn't nice to be called names by someone who hardly knew you, particularly one you were trying to help. 'Ruth what, then?'

'I don't know. Kitty wouldn't tell me either, even after I told her what I'd already found out. So we had another argument, a *really* big one . . .' She trailed off, and touched her necklace again, and her eyes took on a faraway look. 'Kitty can be very cruel when she doesn't get her own way. Anyway,' she said more briskly, 'I packed a few things after she went to bed, and headed down to Plymouth, to the dockside. I found a cargo ship that was sailing from Plymouth to Cork, and hid on board.'

'Was it that easy?' Fiona stared, astonished.

'Not really *easy*,' Amy conceded, 'that's cut a long story a bit short. It took a day or two to find a ship, and I ended up sleeping in an alley on the Barbican to save my money. And you know what the weather's been like.'

'It must have been terrifying,' Fiona breathed, fascinated and horrified at the same time.

'We had to go to Roscoff first, so it took much longer than I'd thought it would. I'd have been alright if it had just been the one night like I thought it'd be, but by then I was starving. I thought the galley was empty, and sneaked in for food, but I got caught by the cook.'

Fiona could feel her eyes widening, it was like something from an adventure book.

'I thought I was in massive trouble,' Amy said, 'but he . . .' In the low light, Fiona saw the animation fade from the delicate features. Amy cleared her throat after a moment, and went on, 'he ended up helping me, gave me a bag of proper food, and a blanket. He told me jokes to make me laugh, and I stopped being so frightened. Then, when things went wrong he came to find me, and helped me into the lifeboat.'

Her voice trembled, and, realising who that cook had been, Fiona scrambled from her own bed and sat beside Amy to take her hand. 'I'm so sorry he died,' she murmured. 'You must be heartbroken.'

'Did *all* of them in that boat drown?' Amy turned pleading eyes on her. 'Was that true?'

Fiona nodded. 'How many were there?' she asked gently.

'Six. Myself and Mr Downing – that's the cook – and four others, but I didn't notice if they were crew or passengers.' She gave a short, dry laugh. 'Should have stayed on board the *Drake* with everyone else. Thank goodness they were all safe, at least.'

'You thought you were doing the sensible thing,' Fiona said, trying to imagine how Amy must have felt, to trust a stranger with her life.

'Will the lifeboat men tell the police about me? When they ask about the others?'

'I don't know. Maybe.' Fiona saw Amy's fingers clutch at her nightgown. 'There's no sense worrying though, there's nothing we'd be able to do. Will you telephone Kitty in the morning, and tell her you're alright?'

'No!' Amy pulled her hand away. 'She'll stop me from finding my mother. Besides, there's no telephone at the farm.'

'Really? Telegram then. You don't have to tell her where you are,' Fiona pointed out, 'just say you're alright.'

'No. You promised me!'

'I said I'd help you, not that I'd keep your secret, remember?'

Amy gave her a betrayed look. 'She's been lying to me for years, about my own *mother*. Would you want me to be dragged back to that dirty old farm and worked until I drop? Not to mention lose any chance I might have to learn the truth, and why my father took me away?'

They fell silent, and for a few minutes Fiona listened to the clock hollowly ticking away the night. She thought about how distraught her own mother had been when Bertie had gone missing for just one night, and imagined an unknown woman in tears, her head pillowed on her arms as she sat at her table. Then again, as Amy had said, she'd lied for years and could be cruel too. The sympathetic image changed, to become a stern-faced woman, tall, cold-eyed, and angry, looming over a sobbing Amy, her indistinct features twisted in a scowl.

'I promise I won't tell anyone,' she said at length. 'And I'll try and get you on another boat to Ireland. But this time as a passenger. We can afford to pay for a ticket if we save our earnings, and what we can't save I'll ask Mum to lend me. You can call it a Christmas present.'

Amy drew a gasp. 'Oh, *thank* you—'

'On one condition,' Fiona cautioned. 'You send a telegram to your adoptive parents first thing in the morning.'

'Do I have to?' Amy's pleasure subsided a little. 'They're sure to—'

'Yes, you do,' Fiona said firmly, 'but to stop them looking for you, you can tell them you're spending Christmas with friends.'

'They know all my friends.'

'New ones then! As long as they know you're safe.'

'Oh, alright then!' Amy gave a little squeak and threw her arms around Fiona's neck. 'I'm sorry I called you an idiot! Are you sure your mother won't mind me staying?'

'Quite sure, provided she thinks we're helping you, not hiding you.' Fiona disentangled herself and went back to her own bed. 'You shouldn't send your telegram from here, and the post office will be shut, but if you knock at the side door Mrs Burch will send it for you.'

'Mrs Burch?' Amy's face fell again. 'I'm not sure, after what happened.'

'You apologised, didn't you? Don't worry, she'll understand.'

'But she'll know *I* know who I am,' Amy fretted. 'She's bound to tell that constable. Or her husband, and you said he works here.'

Fiona frowned. 'A letter then. It won't get there nearly as quickly, but at least it's something.'

'Only if I can post it somewhere else. Trethkellis is so small, it'll be easy to find me from the postmark.'

'Alright, we'll think of something. Bude, maybe. I have some Christmas shopping to do.'

They fell silent again, but Fiona was still not ready for sleep. 'Tell me about *you*, then,' she said, as Amy climbed back beneath her own covers with a little shiver. 'Not about your parents, or why you left home, but other stuff.'

Amy pondered a moment, her fingers pulling the odd pendant up and down its chain. 'I love to dance, when I'm allowed to. Which isn't very often,' she added sadly. 'I have to work from dawn until late at night every single day.'

'You're a dancer?' Fiona reflected that she shouldn't have been surprised really, given Amy's willowy frame and strong, assured movements.

'I can't claim to be a dancer, but I took lessons with Belinda Pearce in the village hall at Yelverton. She taught us all the new dances.'

'So you *were* able to get out and about a bit, then?'

'I used to sneak out. If Kitty caught me she'd threaten me with her husband's leather belt. It was worth it, though.'

'We have a dancer who stays with us sometimes,' Fiona said, feeling uncomfortable and looking to bring the light conversation back. 'She's called Lucy Kempton.'

'She stays here?' Amy breathed. 'Oh, I love watching her, she's so . . . *free!*'

'Is she?'

'Did you ever see Isadora Duncan dance?'

'That poor woman, I can't believe it was two years ago now.' A shiver ran down Fiona's spine at the memory. Lucy had been staying with them at the time, and when they'd heard how Miss Duncan's scarf had become entangled in the back wheel of her

57

friend's car, they'd all been rendered speechless with shock. Lucy had been inconsolable.

'She had a rotten life,' Amy agreed sadly. 'But her movements were like water. Lucy's like that.'

'Well *she* won't be here at Christmas, but Daisy Conrad's a surprisingly wonderful dancer.'

'Who?'

'Daisy Conrad. Remember I told you we had some important guests coming? Well, it's her and Freddie Wishart!' If Fiona had been hoping to impress her new friend she was left disappointed.

Amy shrugged. 'I've never seen them, but she can't be as good as Lucy and Isadora.'

'From what you've said it's a different style entirely. But at least you'll have someone to talk to about dance.'

Amy looked at her as if she were mad. 'I can't *tell* anyone!'

'No, of course.' Fiona bit her lip, feeling foolish again. 'Well, I'm glad you told me. Now go to sleep, and tomorrow I'll introduce you to the rest of the family.'

As she snuggled beneath the warm blankets she heard Amy give a heavy sigh of contentment, and shook her head. She still didn't know if she entirely trusted the girl, but things would certainly be interesting while she was here.

CHAPTER FIVE

Sunday 15th December

Leah watched carefully as Helen poured their tea, and reflected on the change that had come over her friend in the past few months. Or more properly, she amended, Helen's reversion to her old self. The pall of worry had lifted, leaving Helen's youthful face open, fresh, and with a ready smile. Her contentment was infectious, and people visibly reacted to it; it was no wonder Harry Fox had been drawn to her, and had remained so faithfully at her side.

Or that Adam was, still.

Leah blinked and took the cup Helen handed her. 'All caught up with your Christmas cards then?'

'I sent the overseas ones in good time,' Helen said, 'but annoyingly enough I'm all behind on the ones in this country. Still—' she rolled her eyes '—Harry's uncle Geoffrey in New Zealand will get his, which is the important thing.'

Leah grinned. 'Of course.' She looked around a little wistfully. 'I'll miss you all.'

'And we'll miss you. But it's only fair your aunt gets you for Christmas this year, it's been a while.'

Leah sniffed. 'She's only asked me this year because the Carters are the only neighbours she has left. If Red Brenda and her sister still lived on the other side I'd not get a seat at the table!'

'Well the time will pass quickly enough.'

'Thank goodness, and she'll be pleased, so I shouldn't be uncharitable. Anyway, when does this Hollywood producer arrive? Adam will be furious he didn't know about it before he left.'

'He won't miss anything.' Helen settled back in her seat. 'Mr Kelly is due tomorrow, but Miss Conrad and Mr Wishart won't be here until the following Saturday, he'll be back by then. Will you telephone and tell him?'

'Certainly not! He'll use it as an excuse to come back sooner, and he needs to spend more time with his family.'

'They were never very nice to him growing up, so I wouldn't blame him.' Helen looked up as Bertie came in. 'How are you feeling today, love? You've been very quiet for the past week or so.'

'I'm alright.' Bertie positioned her wheelchair so she sat alongside her mother, rather than facing her, and Helen sent Leah a helpless shrug. They both knew Bertie was struggling, especially now that Christmas was beginning to creep into the edges of every activity. For the first time, she would be unable to do much more than watch it all from a distance. She couldn't help string the lights outside on the gazebo this year, or climb the ladder to pin the holly around the lobby, and, most importantly, she wouldn't be able to go out with Ben and fetch in the huge, wide tree that was transplanted every year by the barn, and help drape it with garlands and toys.

This year it would be Fiona's turn to go with Ben, and although she knew Bertie might ordinarily have given over those tasks quite happily, Leah recognised that it was a blow to have had the choice taken from her.

'The doctors in Bude are still keen to talk to you about a prosthesis,' she ventured into the silence. 'Perhaps you could telephone to make an appointment for next week? Before the Christmas festivities start.'

'Maybe.'

Leah suspected that meant, *no*. She caught Helen's eye, saw her about to urge Bertie on, and shook her head slightly; as Bertie's nurse she had learned to gauge the young woman's changeable anxiety level, and could sense what would cause her to lash out. She hated to see the way Helen flinched whenever a Bertie-barb, as she privately called it, struck home, and she didn't want that to happen now.

'Well do let me know when you decide,' she said, her hopes dwindling further. 'It's only to talk, after all.'

'Bertie, guess who's here to see you?' Fiona had appeared in the doorway, and went on excitedly, before her sister could hazard a guess, 'It's Jowan! Looking very dapper too, I might add.'

'What does *he* want?' Bertie muttered. But she smoothed her hair into place, curling the sleek bob under with her fingers. 'Tell him I'm busy.'

'You are not!' Fiona rolled her eyes. 'Come on, he's waiting!'

Leah wished she understood Bertie's reluctance to meet Jowan face to face; in hospital she'd turned to him like a drowning woman, but since his first visit she'd mostly kept him at arm's length. The few times they had met had been taut affairs, resulting in Jowan stalking off, holding his temper in check with a visible effort, and Bertie glaring after him with a mixture of frustration and despair. Despite all that, Leah was sure it wasn't all over between the young lovers, and as Bertie gave an exaggerated sigh of annoyance and wheeled herself from the room she crossed her fingers, and silently willed the two of them to reach the same conclusion.

Her message delivered, Fiona turned to her mother. 'Amy and I are going to Trethkellis when I've finished my shift this morning.'

'What on earth for?' Helen looked out at the drizzle. 'I wanted you to fetch down the tree ornaments later, and sort through them.'

'We'll do it this evening,' Fiona promised. 'We ... we just thought it might help Amy's memory if we went back to the lifeboat station.'

Leah hid a smile. The girl just couldn't keep away. 'No change yet, then?'

'No, but we're hopeful.' She vanished as quickly as she had arrived, and when she and Helen were alone again, Leah picked up her tea and settled back against a cushion.

'So, Mr Kelly arrives tomorrow, and his glamorous little worker bees arrive next Saturday. Will everything be ready for them?'

Helen regarded her with shrewd eyes. 'You sound very disapproving.'

'Not at all. Why do you say that?'

'For a start, *worker bees* isn't a very nice way to describe two of the biggest screen stars in the world.'

Leah shrugged. 'No, you're right. That's Adam's phrase.'

'And you're just madly jealous of them.' Helen grinned.

'Well, who wouldn't be? Daisy is adorable, and have you seen that beautiful boy in *Pirate Jim*? And the two of them in *One Morning in Paris* ... hilarious!'

Helen smiled. 'I haven't seen them all, but I do feel as if I have, and a dozen times, thanks to Guy. Anyway, changing the subject, when do you go back to Wales?'

'Aunt Mary's expecting me next Monday evening.' Leah heard the reluctance in her own voice. So much happened at the hotel over Christmas, and she felt far more at home here than she did at the house that now belonged to her aunt.

Since August, and everything that had happened with Adam and with the hotel, Leah had resigned her secretarial position in Wales, citing her new job here, and had written long, guilt-ridden letters home, though she suspected her aunt was quite happy to remain in the little house alone. She'd also tentatively asked about her estranged husband, Glynn, and whether he'd stayed in the village since his early release from prison. Aunt Mary had said, with some relief, that he'd moved away, gone to Liverpool, or Manchester, or some such place, which came as no surprise; he'd always yearned after brighter lights than Mountain Ash could provide.

'I'll be back by the 30th,' Leah said, 'so at least I'll be here for New Year's Eve. A brand new year. A new decade!'

'I hadn't really thought.'

'Thought about what?'

'The last new decade, and the party we had for it.' Helen put down her teacup. 'It was the night I found out Harry had ... had lost everything. I can't bring myself to believe it's actually been ten years.'

'Ten years in which you've re-built everything, and given your children the best of lives. You've got every reason to celebrate.'

'You'll miss Adam,' Helen said, clearly keen to distract herself. 'Your first Christmas too, it seems a shame.'

63

'It is.'

'Why don't you take him back to Wales with you?'

Leah laughed, though the thought gave her a wistful pang. 'Can you imagine me trying to prise him away from here? Not to mention from the cubs. Not after all these years of ...' She stopped, but Helen arched a brow.

'Being kept away from them, by me?'

'Well, yes.' Leah shook her head. 'No point avoiding the issue, is there?'

'I suppose not. We understand each other now though. Anyway, he might surprise you. Did you mention it to him?'

'Of course. You'd have thought I'd asked him to perform the Dance of the Seven Veils in Truro Cathedral.' Leah laughed away the little lump of envy. 'No, he was quite clear he wouldn't shirk his duties here in favour of a holiday in Wales.'

She had to stop talking then, because in her heart she knew the choice hadn't been Wales or Cornwall, and it hadn't been leisure or work. The choice had been Leah or Helen, and Leah had lost.

* * *

Bertie's heart tightened as she rolled into the lobby and found Jowan perched uncomfortably on the very edge of one of the velvet-covered chairs. He leapt up, and she could see how he'd made a huge effort to look smart but still felt out of place, by the way he kept tugging his waistcoat straight, and smoothing his hair back. It looked as if he'd used a whole tub of Uncle Adam's Brylcreem, and it still wouldn't lie flat. He had that in common with his own uncle, except that Bertie couldn't imagine Alfie Nancarrow ever using such a thing.

She only realised she was smiling at that thought when Jowan smiled back, and she wished he hadn't; she could never resist it, it lit his whole face, and his mouth always seemed made for her own lips when it lifted like that. He strode across the floor to meet her, and braced both hands on the arms of her chair as he leaned down, that wide, generous mouth less than a foot from hers.

'I love you,' he said. 'I know I've not said it enough. Not made it clear enough. But there it is. I hate that I can't help you, but you are *more* to me now than you ever were.'

Bertie stared up at him, for a moment unable to speak, then she grinned. 'Have you been rehearsing that all the way over here?'

'Of course I bloody have!' Jowan looked helplessly at her for a moment, then leaned forward and kissed her, with an enthusiasm that could not be argued with. When he pulled back, his hands were still planted on the arms of her chair and his voice was still cross. 'I've been rehearsing that too, in my head.'

She laid one hand gently over his, and with the other she reached up, and slid it around the back of his neck. 'That lacked finesse,' she murmured. 'I think you need to practise it a bit more.' She pulled his mouth back down to hers, and he sank to one knee beside the chair, moving closer. Ignoring the fact that there were guests beginning to emerge from the breakfast room, Bertie tangled her fingers into Jowan's carefully smoothed hair and deliberately messed it up. She could feel the laughter bubbling between them, but the kiss did not end until she reluctantly released him and took a deep, relieved breath.

'Thank you for not giving up on me,' she said quietly. 'I know I've been absolutely horrible to you, and I'm sorry. More sorry than I can say.'

The humour in his eyes faded with the sweep of his lashes as he blinked slowly. 'Does this mean you're not going to push me away anymore?'

'I was pretty stupid to do that,' she admitted. 'But I couldn't be sure you still ... you know.'

'I was the stupid one, for not spelling it out to you. I thought you knew by now.'

'And who pointed out that I couldn't have known? Should I guess?'

'No need.' Jowan smiled. 'She said something about a coat with a hole in the sleeve ...' He trailed away, shrugging. 'It doesn't matter.'

'Has your uncle realised yet, about her?'

Jowan looked up at her, startled. 'Realised what?'

'That she has feelings for him. Deep ones,' she clarified, though she knew it was unnecessary; Jowan had a way of pretending ignorance over something he didn't want to discuss.

He stood up and moved around to the back of her chair. 'Where shall we go?'

'The cloisters. Well?'

'He's her brother-in-law,' he said carefully, pushing her towards the side door. 'Are you sure you want to go outside? It's pretty nasty out there.'

'Don't change the subject. And yes, I do. I need fresh air like you need a haircut.'

He gave a low laugh, and Bertie's heart gladdened at the sound. 'I'll get one before Midnight Mass,' he promised, as he pushed open the door.

He rolled her along the smooth walkway, and she let her head fall back, enjoying the icy brush of wind that lifted her hair.

He shivered, used to being out in all weathers, but also to working up a sweat to counter the chill. 'You're mad.'

'*Does* Alfie know yet?' she persisted.

'No, he doesn't.' He parked the chair, and sank to his heels against a stone pillar so he could look up at her. Out here he looked more settled, more at ease, and as his hair blew in the wind it reverted to its usual bouncy, Nancarrow mess. 'And I'm glad, because if he did, he'd have to break her heart. It wouldn't be his fault, but I'd find it hard to keep loving him like a dad if he did that.'

His certainty was disconcerting, and Bertie frowned. 'How do you know he'd break her heart?'

Jowan shrugged. 'I just do. Anyway, let's talk about you. I've missed you.' He said this last in a voice so soft she could hardly hear it over the wind blowing down the stone throat of the cloisters.

'I've missed you too,' she said, and reached for his hand. 'How are you, Jo?'

'Me? I'm the same as ever. Bit worried about Jory, he seems to be spending his wage as soon as he earns it, and with nothing to show. How about you, though? Have you spoken to the doctors yet about . . .' He nodded at her leg.

'Leah wants me to go in and see them this coming week.'

'And will you?'

'I wasn't going to,' she confessed. 'I didn't see the point.'

'And now?' He squeezed her fingers to make her look at him. 'Are you thinking about it?'

'In a way.'

'You seem distracted.'

Bertie didn't want to spoil the new-found peace between them, but she had to be honest. 'I had a letter last week, from Lynette Nicholls.'

His lips tightened predictably enough at the name. 'How is she?' he asked, all politeness, but she knew it wasn't Lynette he struggled with.

'Still hunting for a husband.'

Jowan's smile was forced as he eased back, sitting down on the wet floor. He didn't speak, but his eyes were on her, and they compelled her to continue, to get to the nub of things.

'Xander is training to become a pilot.'

'I see.'

She took a deep breath. 'And I've decided I want to do the same.'

Incomprehension faded quickly into incredulousness. 'A pilot. You.' His tone was dismissive, almost amused, and sick disappointment swept over her.

'Yes, me.' She tried not to let her dismay show. 'Why is that so odd?'

'Because you're a woman.' He stood up, as if looking up at her suddenly put him at a disadvantage.

'So was Harriet Quimby.'

'Who?'

'First *woman* to fly across the English Channel,' Bertie said tightly. 'There are lots of women with pilot's certificates. Why shouldn't I be one?'

His gaze flickered towards her right leg, although it was little more than a reflexive glance. 'It's ... dangerous,' he managed.

'No more dangerous than racing a motorcycle. Or even just meeting a dog while riding one, apparently.' She'd hoped a flash of dark humour might help, but the tension in his frame did not lessen.

'Was?'

She frowned. 'Was what?'

'You said this Quimby person *was* a woman. How did she die?'

'Just a figure of speech,' Bertie lied. That Harriet Quimby had died in a plane crash, barely two months after her flight, was not something that would help her cause. 'Jowan, listen, this is something I really want to do. I *can* do it, I know I can.'

'It's not your ability I'm questioning. *I* know you can do it, too.' Jowan crouched at her side again and his blue eyes searched hers, as if hoping she were playing some kind of joke. His voice was no longer dismissive, now there was real worry in it. 'Bertie, this is ... I can't take it in. It's only been a few months since you wanted to race motorcycles, and look what happened. We nearly lost you! And now *this*?'

'It's not something I've suddenly decided today, I've been thinking about it every minute for the past week.'

'Since you found out your flashy racer is doing it.'

'It's got nothing to do with Xander,' Bertie said hotly. 'It's just that it made me think.'

'Nothing to do with Xander, eh?' Jowan folded his arms, presumably so Bertie wouldn't see that his hands had curled into fists. But he didn't look angry, he just looked as if he were battling every urge he possessed not to speak up against this choice. Perversely, this reaction, and his determination not to try to put her off, touched her more deeply than if he'd embraced it wholeheartedly.

'What happened to his big dream about running a racing team?' he asked at last. 'He was all for it, and was about to rope you in too.'

'He wasn't *roping me in*.' She tried not to sound annoyed again. 'It was what I wanted, you know that. Anyway, that was before the stock market crashed. He lost all his likely investors, and a huge amount of his own money, so he had to look elsewhere for his excitement. At least this way he'll be paid.'

'Paid? For pilot training?'

'He will be if he joins the military.' Bertie saw the shock on his face, and rushed on, 'That's not what I want, though. I want to fly civilian planes, and once I get a prosthetic leg fitted there's no reason I shouldn't be able to do that as well as anyone.' She laid a hand on his rigid forearm. 'Jo, this will give me back what I've lost.'

'But if you're going to get a new leg anyway, you could go back to riding.'

She shook her head. 'It's not the same, you know that. Using the kick-starter, slamming your foot into the ground when you go into a slide . . . You need *feeling* in your feet for that kind of thing, and I don't think any false limb will be able to give me that.'

Another silence fell between them, and Bertie half wished she'd told him about the idea without bringing up Xander Nicholls, but she didn't want to start off with a secret like this between them. 'I'm going to look into it,' she said at length. 'Will you be with me?'

He tore his gaze from the long stone corridor and searched her eyes. 'Let's just get your leg fixed,' he said at last, 'then we can talk.'

'You think I'll have gone off the idea by then?'

He gave a short huff of laughter. 'Come on, Bertie. I've known you long enough to know that's not going to happen.' He shook his head. 'No. I'm hoping that by then *I'll* have come to terms with it.'

'So am I.' Bertie tucked her hands beneath her arms. 'Let's go inside, I'm freezing.' She gave a theatrical sigh. 'Fancy bringing someone out here, on a day like this? What kind of a boyfriend are you, anyway?'

'One who's got to go scuttling back to the farm, get changed, and go back out in the cold to finish the dry stone walling.'

'Do enjoy that.' Bertie grinned up at him as he pushed her back into the warmth of the lobby. 'I'm going to put my foot up and read.'

She felt the chair twitch as he reacted to her words. It had cost her a lot to make the joke, but it was worth it, to twist just in time to see the flicker of pride and love on his face as he shook his head in mock disbelief. But, to his credit, he did not attempt to make a joke of his own – she wasn't quite ready for anyone else to do that.

'Go away now,' she said. 'Build a wall. Come back soon.'

He leaned over her shoulder and pressed his lips to hers. 'I'll be over again for Midnight Mass, so you'd better start thinking about what wonderful present you're going to get me this year.'

'How about a motorcycle?'

'What?'

'The Flying Squirrel. I want you to have it.' Bertie's eyes stung as she said it, but it had been something she'd thought about a great deal, even when they'd been at odds. 'I've been beastly to you, and besides, I'll never ride it again.'

He parked her beside one of the sofas and sat on its edge. 'Didn't Stan want it back?' He looked bemused, but a flicker of excitement lit his eyes and she knew she'd made the right decision.

'Neither of us could even talk about it for ages,' she said, 'and by the time he asked about it, I'd already managed to keep up most of the payments.' Adam had tried to pay it all immediately, but she'd been so furious at the idea that he'd backed off, and instead insisted on employing her in the hotel office, paying her the wage she was missing from the telephone exchange. To this she had put up no argument, after all it had helped them both. 'It's almost mine to give,' she added. 'By the second week in January it will be.'

'But you could *sell* it back to him, surely?'

'I want *you* to have it,' she repeated. 'Will you? And soon? I can't bear to think of it out there in the barn, it's only going to depreciate the longer it's left there. It deserves to be ridden, and I want it to be by someone I care about.'

Jowan didn't speak for a moment, but he must have read the sincerity in her face, because he swallowed hard, and nodded. 'I can't give you anything like as wonderful,' he murmured.

Bertie looked pointedly down at her left hand. 'Can't you? That's a pity.'

He followed her gaze, and the smile was all in his eyes. 'I'm sure I'll think of something.'

'I'm sure you will.'

CHAPTER SIX

Monday 16th December

'So we'll have the treasure hunt on the Tuesday. Give everyone an appetite for the big Christmas Eve dinner, and keep them out of the hotel while we decorate.' Helen noted it down, then followed Leah's squinting gaze through the window, to the swaying trees and the rain bouncing off the gleaming red bonnet of Ben's new Bugatti. 'It's been a filthy end to the year so far.'

'You might need to supply boats just to get across the grounds.'

'Hmm.' Helen tapped her teeth with her pen. 'Maybe we should set an alternative hunt inside the hotel this year, just in case.' She made another note; her pad was starting to look like a child's scribbling book. 'I'll see to it once the bookings are finalised and we know which rooms will be free.'

Leah smiled. 'I imagine the cubs are excited about the Hollywood guests.'

'Bertie and Fiona are. Ben is trying hard to convince us that he isn't holding the biggest torch in the world for Daisy Conrad, by insisting she's a spoiled brat with a head full of champagne bubbles.'

73

'Poor Ben! Let's hope he's right, then, or Lily Trevanion is going to find herself out in the cold. Fiona and her new friend can come up with some indoor clues, that'll keep them out of mischief. I'll let them know. What do you make of her, anyway?'

'Amy?' Helen considered. 'She seems very polite, I suppose. I was thinking of putting some posters about the village, to see if anyone knows her.'

Leah pulled a sheet of paper towards her. 'We can put a notice up in the shop too, with our telephone number. The girls can take them this afternoon.'

'Absolutely, I'm sure the poor love would like to be home for Christmas. There's nothing quite like it.'

She fell silent, suddenly aware that being "home" for Christmas wasn't necessarily the same great joy for Leah that she herself always believed it to be. 'Sorry, I know you'd rather be here.'

'Duty calls,' Leah quipped, her voice light, but some of the cheeriness dropping from her features. 'Now, what's next?'

'The farm delivery due next week.' Helen flipped open her diary. 'Monday afternoon. I must check they'll be able to supply extra cream.'

'Speaking of the Nancarrows,' Leah said, 'has Alfie proposed to Beth yet?'

Helen shrugged. 'I don't know, it's not as if he'd have told me if he had.'

'Oh, I think he would,' Leah protested. 'You two are friends, after all.'

'I envy Beth,' Helen said with a little sigh. 'She's going to have such a happy life now, and she's certainly earned it.'

'So have you. You've both been widowed for ten years.'

'It's different for me, I've not set my heart on anyone new. Beth's waited for Alfie for so long.'

'And he's a decent one,' Leah added. 'She could have done a *lot* worse.'

'Well it's about time he woke up to what's in front of him,' Helen said firmly. 'Right then, treasure hunt at ten, dinner at seven to leave time to get ready for Midnight Mass.' A knock at the door stilled Helen's pen. 'Come in.'

'Mrs Fox.' Martin Berry, head receptionist, popped a flushed, excited face around the door. 'You asked me to let you know when Mr Kelly arrived.'

'Thank you. Attend to his bags, and seat him in the lounge, if you wouldn't mind.' When he had gone again Helen shook her head, smiling. 'Martin's met people far more important than Rex Kelly.'

'Ah, but now Mr Kelly is producing Conrad and Wishart,' Leah said. 'That's an entirely new level, even for Fox Bay.'

'Good point, in which case I'd better not keep him waiting.' Helen stood up. 'Coming?'

'Me? Why on earth would I?'

'Because you're my best friend, and you're helping me to arrange the big Hollywood holiday.'

Without waiting to see if Leah was following, Helen marched out from behind the reception desk just in time to see Martin holding back the engraved glass doors, and showing a tall, spare-framed gentleman into the lounge. She tried to remember everything Harry had said about the man, upon his and Adam's return from America, but all she could recall was a general approval; they'd hit it off rather well by all accounts.

After Harry's death she had received a letter of condolence

from Mr Kelly and his wife Julie-Ann, and an assertion that Harry had been one of the classiest and finest people they had met. At the time it had simply been one more in a seemingly endless outpouring of sorrow, and had meant little, so when the letter arrived to say Mr Kelly was coming to Fox Bay she had been hard-pressed, at first, to remember who he was.

She felt absurdly nervous now, meeting the man for the first time, and wished Fleur hadn't gone off to Bude for the day; if Mr Kelly had thought Harry was classy, he would lap up Harry's mother and her impeccable manners. She signalled to Jeremy Bickle, the head barman, to attend to him, and then waited until the American had been served his drink before going over to introduce herself. He twisted in his seat as she approached, a narrow-shouldered man, with white hair and a kind face, who rose to his feet with a ready smile.

She smiled back. 'Mr Kelly. How lovely to meet you at last.'

'Mrs Fox. Please, call me Rex.' He shook her hand with both of his, and she noted with a little wince that he hadn't eased up on his grip in deference to her smaller bones. 'I can't tell you how sorry I was to learn of your husband's passing.'

'Your letter was very comforting,' she said. 'Harry spoke well of you. This is my friend Leah Marshall, who's helping me get everything organised for your stay.'

They shook hands and murmured polite greetings, then Helen gestured for Rex to sit again, and took the seat opposite. For a few minutes they talked about his journey down from Southampton, but soon the conversation slid, inevitably enough, onto the reason for his trip.

'It's going to be *the* big new production for Good Boy,' he said, leaning forward, as eagerly as if he were selling it. 'This is one time I'm glad to be studio head as well as a producer, I green-lit it the moment it landed on my desk. *Dangerous Ladies*, written by a brand-new guy on the block, name of Andy Discaro. Remember that name, he's going to be big!' He winked. 'He's a friend of Freddie Wishart's, and his screenplay is just perfect for the public mood right now. Quirky, fun, a little exciting . . . George Faber's playing the second male lead, and I'm getting one of our best directors on it. Anyway,' he finished, as if embarrassed by his own enthusiasm, 'I wanted to get here ahead of the kids, to get a feel for it before they arrive and everything goes crazy.'

Helen couldn't help smiling at the description of the two film stars as "the kids". But he was right, seeing the hotel as it really was would be impossible once word got out who was staying there. None of the guests had yet been informed.

'Well I'll be glad to show you around myself,' she said. 'Just let me know as soon as you're settled and ready, and I can answer any questions as we go.'

'I'm happy to note anything down for you, to read over later,' Leah offered. 'I can take shorthand.'

'Thank you, ladies.' Rex raised his glass. 'Will you join me?'

'Thank you, but no,' Helen said. 'I have to keep a clear head while I'm working. Is there anything else I can help with, before I leave you to get settled?'

'I think I'm all good, thank you. But don't rush off. How are your children? Three, isn't it? Harry couldn't stop talking about them when he was over.'

'That's nice to hear,' Helen said with a smile. 'Ben, the eldest, is actually the night-shift manager here, so if you have any questions during the night he'll be happy to help you. Fiona is very keen on the local lifeboat service, and helps out there whenever she can, and my middle daughter, Roberta, had a dreadful accident earlier this year. I'm only telling you because when you meet her later on you'll notice she often uses a wheelchair to get around.'

'Oh, what a terrible shame,' Rex said, his brown eyes creased in sympathy. 'You know, Harry talked about her more than any of them.'

'They were devoted,' Helen said quietly. The pain might have faded but it never went away entirely. 'Do you have children?'

'Two boys,' Rex said. 'That's why Julie-Ann stayed home for Christmas. They're grown-ups now, but that doesn't make any difference at this time of year, does it?' He laughed. 'Jimmy, Haverford that is, didn't want to come for the whole of the holidays, but he'll be here just after what you guys call … Boxing Day, I think?' He raised a questioning eyebrow, and when she nodded, he went on, 'I'm glad to see you settled here, anyway. From everything Harry told me it's a special place.'

Helen rose to her feet. 'I hope you'll think so. I'll leave you to it then, and you can just speak to Martin on reception when you're ready for me to show you around.'

Rex stood up and held out his hand again. 'You ever hear from that other guy? The one who used to work with Harry?'

'Adam Coleridge?'

'That's the one. I heard he dropped off the map after Harry died.'

'He did, for a while. But actually he's—'

'Slimy little creep deserved everything he got,' Rex said. Helen started, and from the corner of her eye she saw Leah stiffen as she smoothed her skirt. Rex shrugged apologetically. 'I know he was a friend of your family, Mrs Fox, but he had no class. No conscience.'

'What do you mean, no conscience?' Leah asked. Helen

detected a note of sharpness in her voice, and sent her a warning look which she ignored. 'What did he do?'

Rex turned his steady gaze on her, and seemed about to answer, then shook his head. 'Doesn't matter. It's all in the past.'

'No, please,' Leah persisted. 'What do you mean?'

'Leah,' Helen murmured, but Leah was staring at Rex, who raised his hands, effectively ending the conversation.

'I'll speak to your guy on the desk,' he said to Helen. 'I look forward to looking around later.'

'About Adam—'

'No, I'm sorry. I shouldn't have been so blunt, it's unlike me. Put it down to travel exhaustion, and forget it. Please.'

Helen was about to push further, but she needed to find out what it was all about in order to even think about smoothing things over, and there was clearly only one way to do that.

She led the way out to the lobby and summoned a bell boy. 'Please show Mr Kelly to his room on the first floor, and see that his luggage is there.' When they'd gone, she turned to Leah. 'When's Adam due back from Scotland?'

'Next Saturday.'

'You'd better find out what he's been up to, the very minute he gets back. I'm going to have to try and mend some fences now, without even knowing what broke them.'

'It will have been long before we met,' Leah protested. 'He won't feel obliged to tell me anything.'

'I know it's not your fault, and I'm sorry to put this on your shoulders, but I'm not risking Rex turning tail and going off to London after all.' She smiled to soften what sounded, to her own ears, like a boss talking to an employee. 'We need to find out what went on, or he could cost us an absolute fortune. Not to mention destroy our reputation. If it's something that can be smoothed over, please do it. If not we're going to have to think of a way to persuade him to stay away.'

'I'll talk to him the minute he gets back,' Leah said, sounding less than certain. 'I'd better go and do that notice, and get the girls to draw some posters.'

Helen watched her go back to the office. She had a suspicion her friend was still treading on eggshells around Adam, which was not the sign of a healthy relationship. She had no idea what was wrong between them, but they'd better sort it out before the rest of the Americans arrived.

* * *

Higher Valley Farm

Another day was drawing to a close, it was almost dark already, and Beth glanced out into the yard to see if the boys and their uncle were coming so she could dish up the evening meal. There was no sign of the twins, but she supposed Alfie would fetch them in directly. He was leaning on the gate talking to Michael Sherborne, who'd come to help finish the dry stone wall separating the remaining farm land from the new golf course ... What had, until last summer, been Nancarrow land.

But there was no sense bemoaning what they'd lost, and, as Alfie kept reminding her, selling that land to Hartcliffe Developments had meant they could keep the larger part of the farm going. And a golf course was better than a housing development, so Pagett's subsequent purchase of it wasn't such a bad thing either.

For a moment she allowed herself the secret pleasure of being able to observe Alfie without him knowing, and as the last of the day's light faded she stored away in her mind the image of the easy way he straightened up to laugh at something Michael had said, and then braced his forearms on the gate again, his booted foot on the lower bar as if he was ready to stay there and talk all night.

He would, too, Beth acknowledged with a mixture of exasperation and affection; the concept of indoors held little appeal for him, even when it offered food, warmth, and comfort. How like his late brother he was, in that respect. But Alfie seemed quiet and reserved, until you got to know him, where Toby had been garrulous with anyone and everyone, and while Toby had been as gentle a soul as you'd wish to meet, there was an edge to Alfie that most people never saw.

He had once told her about an altercation that had taken place on Priddy Farm when he'd worked there before the war, with Keir Garvey, a man who'd later become one of his best friends. Since Garvey was even more strongly built than Alfie himself, it could have turned very nasty. Yes, Alfie was kind and popular, he was hard-working, and he was generous with his time ... but he was no saint. Still Beth felt her stomach liquefy when he turned his smile on her, or if they happened to pass by one another in the narrow hallway.

It had begun to rain now, and through the kitchen window she watched him simply pull his hat down further, and turn up his collar, in preparation for continuing their conversation. But Michael had had enough, and made his goodbyes, patting the top bar of the gate in farewell.

Alfie turned, and Beth stepped back away from the window though she knew it was unnecessary; he would never assume it was him she'd been watching anyway, he was as oblivious to female attention as he was to the elements. She peered out again, and clicked her tongue as she saw him head towards the outhouse to check the generator. A flickering light across in the barn told her that must be where the twins were, so she'd have to fetch them in herself after all.

She pulled a face and plucked her oilskin off the hook, and hurried across the yard. But as she reached the open barn door she stopped and listened, her face breaking into a smile as she heard Jory give a whoop of approval.

'When? You sly bugger, you kept that quiet!'

'We only talked about it yesterday,' Jowan said, laughing. 'We haven't talked about a date yet. And keep it hushed! It's only between Bertie and me for the minute, and even that's not official yet.'

'So when *will* it be so-called "official" then?' Jory wanted to know.

'Not until I've got her a ring. And God only knows when that'll be, on what I earn.'

Beth winced; he was only telling the truth, but it was a painful one.

'Well why don't you sell that bike she's given you?' Jory persisted.

'She hasn't, not yet. Besides, she'd hate me to do that.'

'I'm sure she'd rather have a diamond or two!' Beth could hear the grin in Jory's voice. 'Or do you prefer the bike to the girl?'

'Don't talk stupid!'

'Well, if you take the bike off her hands and sell it, you can afford to buy her the best. Those Foxes'll be used to that, don't forget. And if you *do* sell it, you can spare me a bob or two. I'd pay it back,' Jory added quickly. 'It's just I owe a couple of mates for covering me the other week when I was shy.'

Beth stiffened. Jory's voice was light, but it was a familiar request, and Alfie had already covered the lad more than once.

'I'm not selling it!' Jowan insisted. 'She wants me to ride it. You'll have to win the money back, you'll enjoy that.' He gave a short laugh. 'Or you could earn it, like the rest of us.'

'Says the man who can't afford to buy his girl a ring,' Jory scoffed lightly. 'Alright, I'll shut up about that now. I'm happy for you both. For truth. Now hurry up and finish that, and let's get in before the rain gets any worse.'

'Me? You're the slow one ...'

Beth backed away from the barn; it would sit uncomfortably with them both, for different reasons, if they knew she'd listened in, and it sounded as though they had no need of being rushed by her. She heard them banter back and forth as she crossed the yard back to the house, and her misgivings eased. They were often at odds over stupid things, but they were brothers, and twins ... they always found their love for one another again.

Over dinner, Beth found her eyes drawn more and more often to Jowan, trying to see him through the eyes of a wealthy young lady, as if she hadn't been part of that young lady's growing up for the past ten years. Bertie had been a regular visitor at the farm all that time, first befriending the twins, then learning from them, and finally accepting that one of them loved her with all his heart. Now that she was on the verge of agreeing to wed him, and to be brought into the Nancarrow family, would she still view them with such affection? Or would she resent the simplicity of a life that would no longer be a mere diversion?

The Nancarrow family had always been respected, and when young Toby had chosen her as his bride she'd been eyed with envy and delighted to accept. But then, *she* hadn't been the elder daughter of some rich family who owned a hotel that rightly belonged somewhere like London.

She noticed a tension in Jowan as he ate, and wondered if his thoughts were taking him down a similar path. Alfie caught her eye, and indicated his nephew with a barely perceptible jerk of his head. She gave him the hint of a shrug and returned her attention to her meal. Jory was talking about borrowing the van again, and Alfie was muttering something about payment for fuel, but Beth allowed their familiar discussion to fade into the background as an idea came to her.

She thought about it as she and Alfie cleared the table, and as soon as the twins had gone – Jowan to his room, Jory into the village – she went to the bureau in the sitting room and took out a shoebox.

Alfie put a scuttle of coal beside the fire, and sat down with a little grunt of relief and stretched his long legs out, easing his stockinged feet towards the crackling fire. 'I'm glad that bloody wall's finished.'

'Does that mean Michael's finished here for a while too, then?'

He nodded. 'He's got work over to the tannery for a bit though. He'll be alright.'

'Plus the lifeboat.'

'Well that doesn't pay, but it'll keep him occupied. Speaking of which, they were called out last Friday. The thirteenth, would you believe? Talk about unlucky.'

'Hmm?' Beth was hardly listening as she poked around in the box.

'What Mick was telling me, just before he left. Did you hear about the girl?'

'What girl?' She looked up, interested at last, and Alfie grinned. 'You can't tell anyone, 'specially not Jo, but Bertie's little sister went out on the *Dafna* the other day, and they brought a girl ashore.'

'Went *out* on it?' Beth looked at him, incredulous. 'Does her mother know?'

'That's why you can't tell,' Alfie cautioned. 'Helen would blow up.'

'And who's the girl they brought back?'

'No one knows,' Alfie said in an exaggeratedly mysterious voice. 'Slip of a thing apparently, with white hair. They thought she was a boy at first. No memory. Got caught shoplifting at Mrs Burch's though,' he added with a laugh. 'Garth Quick said he'd let her off if she stays with the Foxes, and keeps out of trouble until her memory comes back.'

Beth found what she was looking for, and put the shoebox on the floor. 'Michael was on that rescue himself then?'

Alfie nodded. 'And Garth's boy Danny helped bring the girl in.' He crossed his ankles with a little sigh of contentment. 'Those lads do a hell of a job,' he said. 'I'm glad ours haven't got involved though, I'd never sleep for worry.'

Ours . . . Beth felt a warm glow at the casual word. 'Me and all,' she said softly.

'What've you got there, anyway?' Alfie nodded at the little box in Beth's hand.

She sat forward, suddenly nervous; this involved him too. 'It's the ring that belonged to yours and Toby's mother,' she said. 'Toby wanted it kept for if we had a daughter.'

'Ah, yes,' Alfie said. 'Don't look so worried, I'm not going to demand a share of it just because you had boys instead. I've none of my own, after all.'

'It's the boys I'm thinking of,' Beth said. 'Or rather, one of them. Jowan's going to ask the Fox girl to marry him.'

Alfie smiled. 'Good. I hoped he would.'

'Well we're not to know it yet, not 'til he tells us, all official. Thing is—'

'He can't afford a ring worthy of her,' Alfie guessed, closing his eyes. 'Good idea to give him Ma's, he's earned it.'

'But what about Jory?' Beth persisted. 'Won't he resent us giving this to Jo?'

'Probably.' He yawned. 'But we'll do our best for him too, when he eventually finds someone he wants to wed. I can't see it being very soon.'

'Sally Penneck would disagree.'

He grunted. 'Sally Penneck's going to be waiting a long time if she thinks Jory's going to propose.'

Beth opened the little box and looked down at the slim gold ring, with its three sapphires in a row, and two tiny diamonds separating them. It had been Sylvie Nancarrow's greatest treasure, and its delicate design would sit so well on Bertie Fox's slender finger and not look even slightly out of place or cheap. Her mind made up, she shut the box and tucked it into her apron pocket.

Alfie settled back again and crossed his arms over his chest. Beth watched him for a few minutes, until his breathing had steadied and slowed, and his tense frame relaxed into sleep, then she closed her own eyes and let the same peace steal over her.

CHAPTER SEVEN

Bude Hospital

'The process is a heat treatment of the aluminium, which strengthens it.' Mr Russell spoke to both Bertie and her mother, but it was on Bertie that his eyes rested most frequently. After all, it was she who would make the decision. 'Developed by Desoutter's own brother, in fact.'

'Desoutter?'

'Marcel Desoutter was given a wooden leg after he crashed his plane. It was too heavy to allow him to fly, so his brother adapted a new model, using a lighter, aluminium alloy. After that, the sky was his limit.' The consultant cleared his throat. 'So to speak.'

Bertie couldn't suppress a smile, and her heart beat a little faster as his words sank in. 'So ... he was able to, to fly again, once it was fitted?'

'Indeed. He and his brother were in the business of creating and developing prosthetic limbs. Invaluable since the war, of course.'

'And how long would it take to have one fitted?'

'Well, we don't have to consider a knee joint for you, so that would speed things up. We'll take measurements today, and once we've ascertained that your stump has healed completely, and that you will be able to bear weight on it, we'll have one made within a few weeks. It'll take some time to learn to walk on it, mind.'

'We'll all be there to help you,' Helen urged, her voice hopeful.

'You won't know yourself, Miss Fox,' Mr Russell added, with an encouraging smile. 'We've had patients with all kinds of upper and lower limbs made for them, yours will be one of the most straightforward, but I promise you it will change your life entirely.'

Bertie looked at her mother, who gave her a tentative smile.

'I know you've been resisting this, but I also know it's not because you don't want it.' Her voice softened. 'Bertie, wanting a normal life doesn't make you weak. Quite the opposite.'

With those words Bertie unexpectedly felt something shift in her mind. For the first time she wondered if the reason she'd been fighting this was because it had seemed as if she was reaching back, into a life that was gone forever. She'd believed she had to learn to live with her new self, or else appear broken and desperate, but perhaps her mother was right; the real courage lay in seizing what had been left, and shaping it into something new.

She *did* want it. And she was ready.

On their way out of the hospital Bertie moved slowly on her crutches. She knew she had to tell her mother what she was planning, and that she must do it today, but the peace they had regained since the accident had been too hard won. This might fracture it all over again.

'I gather you and Jowan are making another go of it,' Helen said into the silence.

'I think he's going to ask me to marry him,' Bertie said. 'And just before you hear it from someone else, I'm giving him the Squirrel.'

'Very sensible,' Helen said. She held the door open and Bertie swung through. 'But what's really bothering you?'

Bertie stopped, surprised. 'What makes you think anything is?'

'I know you,' Helen said simply. She drew Bertie aside, out of the way of the hurried comings and goings in the doorway. 'Something's been troubling you for weeks. I thought it was Jowan, but now you're back together I realise it's something else.'

There was nothing for it but to tell her. Bertie took a deep breath. 'I'm thinking of learning to fly an aeroplane.'

There was a stunned silence. Helen looked away, towards where Guy sat waiting for them in his car. She folded her arms, cupping her elbows, and Bertie saw her shoulders rise and fall in a very slow, controlled way. When she turned back her eyes were bright, but the smile on her face was genuine.

'Well, now I know why you lit up when Mr Russell mentioned that Desoutter bloke.' Her voice caught as she added, 'I'll help you in whatever way I can.'

'Mum, I—'

'Truly. I'm not just saying it to avoid another row.' She took Bertie's hand. 'I don't know how you'll do it, or when. I don't know what'll happen when you do. But—' her smile now held the hint of a grin as she pointed to the sky '—if I have to fire the cannon myself, I'll get you up there.'

Bertie laughed, partly in relief, and partly in response to the image of her smartly turned out mother dressed as a circus ring-master. 'I think you might have to join a queue.'

'Behind whom?' Helen helped her into the leather straps of her crutches again, and the two of them set off towards the car.

'Leah, for one. And definitely Stan Houghton, for two. I think he was sadder about his precious Flying Squirrel than he was about me.' She handed her crutches to Guy, who slid them into the back of the car, and swung herself into the back seat. 'Are you really alright about this?'

'Not in the least,' Helen said, tucking a blanket around Bertie's knees, and now Bertie could see the fear that tightened her mother's mouth. 'But I've come to realise that all three of you are completely beyond my control, and all I can do now is be glad you've all chosen to live your lethal lives here with me.'

She climbed into the back seat beside Bertie, instead of into the front with Guy as she normally did, and her closeness was a surprising source of comfort; Bertie had never felt more like a frightened child, looking into an unknowable future. In this crowded and bustling world, and regardless of the love that surrounded her, absolutely no one she knew could fully understand what cruel and glorious tricks her mind was playing on her now.

The car moved slowly away from the hospital, and as they left the grey stone building behind them Bertie began to relax and allow herself to imagine what it would feel like when her new leg was attached. It was a little overwhelming, so she concentrated on the little things; what would it be like to slide a shoe on and not feel it? To tie shoelaces and not know how tight they were? To walk across deep carpet or stony road, and yet only feel the different textures of the ground beneath one foot? Would she look normal in a pair of trousers, or would people still stare at her with looks of guarded sympathy?

The car slowed, and Bertie idly looked out of the window, her heart suddenly speeding up for no apparent reason. She felt sick, and just for a moment longer she couldn't work out why, then she realised Guy had turned off at the short cut that led to the back of the hotel – the same short cut she herself had taken on the way home from the race in Bude back in August. Her fingers instinctively curled and she closed her eyes, determined to say nothing, but to her relief her mother spoke up and broke the tense silence.

'Take us back through the village if you wouldn't mind, Guy?'

Guy braked gently so they rolled to a stop. 'This way's quicker, I thought you'd want—'

'I'd like something from the shop,' Helen said. 'Does Mrs Burch still sell those lovely little gift sets of hand-made chocolates?'

'Not usually once the summer season's over. But perhaps over the Christmas period she might put some out.'

'Good. I'd like to get Leah something nice for her train journey.'

Guy reversed back onto the main road, and Bertie's heart slowed again. She unclenched her hands, and let out a breath she didn't know she'd been holding, and kept her gaze locked on the passing hedgerows as they wound through the lanes towards Trethkellis.

Guy parked across from Mrs Burch's shop, and strode across the square, raising a hand here and there to greet people he knew, and then vanished into the darkness of the shop doorway.

The quiet ticking of the cooling engine was the only thing to break the silence until Bertie cleared her throat. 'Thank you.'

'For what?'

'You didn't need to come back this way, did you?'

'I told you,' Helen said mildly, 'I wanted to get something for Leah.'

'She doesn't leave until next Monday.'

Helen seemed about to argue further, but in the end she

shrugged. 'I saw your face, even if you didn't say anything.' She smiled faintly. 'Your father would be unbelievably proud of you, you know.'

Bertie's eyes stung and she turned away again, staring out across the square, but her mother's hand folded around hers, and she returned the pressure and the last of the rancour between them melted away. With her gaze still on the shop doorway she blinked rapidly to clear her eyes, and saw Guy emerge once more, a gaily wrapped package in one hand, and a plain object in the other.

He tucked the gift under one arm, and stopped beside the bin near the shop doorway to unwrap his own chocolate bar, but as Bertie watched, he frowned and stared harder at the bin, even going so far as to prod at something in there. He glanced quickly at the car, then back into the bin again, and when he re-joined them he handed an oblivious Helen the gift chocolates, but said nothing about what he'd seen. Bertie met his eyes in the rear-view mirror, but they shifted away again immediately, and she knew it would be pointless to ask now.

It wasn't until the following morning that she was able to find Guy alone. What little sleep she'd had the previous night had been filled with dreams of plummeting aeroplanes, and crowds of laughing people, led by Jowan, pointing at a leg made of gift-wrapped chocolate that was melting away beneath her knee.

As a result, she was short-tempered and anxious as she rolled slowly through the lobby towards the fresh outside air, hoping to blow the lasting images away with the stiff west wind that was blowing off the sea. Guy came out of the office with today's notes, his lips moving as he flicked through them, storing the information away in the neat filing cabinet in his mind, no doubt; with just two days before their guests of honours' arrival there was still a lot to do.

'Guy!'

He turned, and an automatic, welcoming smile started to cross his face, but even as Bertie watched the smile abruptly became polite and distant.

'Good morning,' he said, recovering himself. 'Is there something I can help with? Only I'm just about to—'

'Just a word, if you have a moment?' Bertie gestured towards the sitting room. 'I won't keep you.'

She preceded him into the room, and waited until he'd closed the door behind him, wryly amused to see how he took his time, delaying the inevitable. Her own impatience won out, and before he'd fully turned to face her she blurted, 'What was in that bin?'

'Bin?' His face was carefully bland, but Bertie had known him long enough to see beyond that.

'Outside Mrs Burch's,' she said patiently. '*Something* stopped you in your tracks, and since then you've been behaving like … like Mata Hari!'

The comparison brought a glimmer of animation back to Guy's face, and as his eyes widened Bertie remembered the story she'd heard about his one foray into cross-dressing, which had involved her grandmother's favourite gown and a good deal of local scandal. She froze.

'Well,' he said at last, into the awkward silence, 'if you're going to compare me to a spy you might at least have chosen Samuel Wingfield. At least he was wearing a smart uniform when they found him.'

Bertie bit her lip hard, but when she saw the glint in Guy's grey eyes, the laughter wouldn't be held in. He joined in and it eased the tension, but when the chuckles had died down Guy shook his head regretfully.

'I'm sorry, I can't tell you what I saw. It's really not my place.'

'Of course it's your place! The first thing you did was look at the car to see if anyone was watching.'

'I couldn't see into the car from that distance.'

Bertie knew deflection when she heard it, she was a master of it herself. 'That makes no difference,' she pointed out. 'Your instinct was to check and see if Mum and I had seen *you*. Why? Come on, Guy, it was clearly something to do with us or the hotel, so you'd better just tell me and get it over with.' Her frustration gave her voice an imperious edge she recognised as her grandmother's, and she could see the same recognition on Guy's face as his resolve faltered.

'It's not to do with the hotel,' he said at length. 'At least, not directly. Look, let me see if I can get to the bottom of it first.'

If Bertie could detect deflection in others, she could also accept a stubbornness that matched her own. She held Guy's gaze for a moment longer, then sighed. 'Come to me the minute you have anything to tell me. Alright?'

'I will,' he promised. 'And now, if you'll excuse me I really must be getting on.'

'Of course.'

Bertie watched him go, irritated almost beyond belief; there was no chance he'd ever come to her voluntarily . . . Sometimes, for her own peace of mind, she wished she didn't know him so well.

* * *

Work was almost all done for the day, and Fiona and Amy were bundling the used bed sheets into the laundry cart when they heard a brief knock at the door.

'Cleaning,' Fiona sang out automatically. 'Please come back in an hour.'

'It's me.'

'Guy?' Fiona lowered the lid of the cart and went to open the door. 'It's not like you to come up here. What can I do for you?'

'Your mother told me which rooms you were doing,' Guy said, sidling in with a quick look into the hallway behind him.

'Well you've found us, but we're not doing the tablecloths and bar towels. You need the other Fiona.'

'I'm not looking for Miss Tremar,' Guy said. 'I wondered if I might have a word, in private?' He flicked a glance towards Amy, who spread her hands in a shrug and took hold of the laundry cart.

'I'll take these down.' She wheeled the cart from the room, but when she turned to close the door behind her Fiona saw a troubled look cross her face, and knew it was mirrored on her own.

'What's the secret?' she asked Guy, busying herself with straightening the covers on the newly made bed.

'I saw something yesterday that gave me cause for concern.'

'Oh?'

'How well do you know Miss Amy?'

Fiona stilled, but her mind raced. 'A little better than the rest of you, I spend more time with her. But nothing about who she is, of course.'

'Of course,' he echoed, and Fiona looked at him sharply.

'What did you see?'

'It was more where I saw it that was remarkable.'

'Which was?' Fiona was hard-pressed to contain her exasperation.

'The bin outside Mrs Burch's shop. I saw some posters, and a notice.'

Fiona felt the blood drain from her face. 'Posters?'

'The notice was written by Mrs Marshall, with the hotel details on it, and the posters are the ones drawn by you and Miss Amy, to ask if anyone had any information about her. *Those* posters.'

'Wh-why would they be in the bin? Has someone pulled them down?'

'They didn't look crumpled,' Guy said quietly. 'In fact they were all still together, half-unrolled.'

Fiona's heart sank further. He was looking at her as if he hoped he were breaking some kind of bad news, and that she hadn't known a thing about it. It would be the easiest thing in the world to set his mind at ease, but that would put all the blame on Amy, which wasn't fair.

'You might as well tell me,' Guy said. 'I'll find out sooner or later.'

Fiona gave in. 'You must understand, Amy's had a very difficult life.' She sat down heavily on the bed. 'She's just looking for her mother.'

Haltingly she explained everything Amy had told her, and finished with how she'd promised to try and help her get to Ireland after Christmas. 'So there was really no need for the posters, see?'

'Yet you still made them.'

'We have to pretend she's keen to find out who she really is.'

'Sly,' Guy opined. 'Don't you remember how distraught your own mother was when Bertie went missing?'

'Of course I do. But Amy wrote to her adoptive parents, I don't think she's posted it yet but she will soon. We were waiting until we could get into Bude but we've been too busy.'

'Did she tell *them* she's travelling to Ireland?'

'No. Just that she's safe. There's no reason she would want to worry anyone, even if they've treated her badly.'

'And have they?'

'Yes. Horribly.'

'Why is she continuing to lie to everyone here?'

'Because the more people who know, the more likely something will slip out. Amy knows Kitty and her husband are dead set against her finding her mother, so as soon as they get a sniff of where she's hiding they'll come down and take her back. You will keep our secret, won't you? Please?'

'You've put me in an impossible position,' Guy said. 'My loyalty is to Mrs Fox.'

The fact that he'd reverted to her mother's formal name made Fiona quail inside, but she couldn't think of anything further to say so she waited. And hoped.

'When's the next crossing to Ireland you can get her on?' Guy asked.

'Mr Glasson says it's not until the new year. The fourth, he thinks.'

'And how do you propose going about it?'

'Amy's memory will ... return, just before that, and I'll tell Mum I'm going back to Plymouth with her. I'll put her up in safe rooms on the Barbican, and then come home on the next train.'

'And you'll pay for all this, and for the passage? How?'

'I've got some savings, and I'll have a couple of weeks to earn more, if I don't buy expensive Christmas gifts. Then I'll ask Mum for the shortfall, which shouldn't be too much.'

Guy shook his head. 'It doesn't matter how much it is, or how little, but it's not fair to ask your mother for money to perpetrate such a lie. Imagine how she would feel if something happened during the passage, and she discovered she'd helped you? How do you suppose that would make her feel?'

So bluntly put, Fiona saw how the deception was widening without intention, and she had the sense that she was disappearing into a mire of her own making. That stupid promise! After a moment's silence Guy seemed to make up his mind, albeit with deep reluctance.

'Alright, I'll hold my peace. I might even be in a position to help out with a bit of money, enough for steerage anyway. Come and see me when it's time.'

'Oh, Guy . . .' Fiona breathed. 'Why would you do that?'

'I told you, I don't want your mother involved. Besides—' he lowered his eyes briefly '—I've had experience of searching for a parent, and I wouldn't wish it on another soul.'

'I had no idea you'd had to do something like this too.'

'Why would you?' He looked genuinely surprised. 'I'm just an employee, after all.'

'Oh, you are not! Thank you!' She moved to hug him, and for a moment she thought he'd hold her off, but unlike her brother and sister she'd been a young child when they'd moved here; hugs had become natural for them very early on despite his outwardly formal demeanour.

After a moment he held her at arm's length. 'If word reaches your mother that I knew about this, I'll lose my job and my home just like that.' He snapped his fingers, and Fiona winced.

'She won't.'

'I'll deny everything,' he warned.

'I won't say a word.'

'See that you don't.' Guy frowned a little as he looked at her. 'I hope this girl's not making a fool of you, Fiona. There's something about her . . .' He shrugged. 'I don't know. She's too good at lying, in my opinion. She and Mrs Marshall would make a good pair.'

'She's just desperate.'

He nodded, then turned to go. 'Don't tell her I know anything about this, you're not obliged to tell her what I wanted to see you about, and if she's got any manners at all she won't ask. But if she does, you can just say I wanted to discuss a private family matter.'

'So lying isn't always bad?' Fiona had intended it to sound teasing, but Guy's face darkened.

'No. Not always. Sometimes it's for the very best of reasons.'

CHAPTER EIGHT

Saturday 21st December

Leah found Adam on the beach, standing on the rocks and supervising the finishing touches to the decking before the pool area could be declared completed. She'd seen his luggage in the lobby and known this was the first place he'd come, even after returning from Scotland on the Edinburgh sleeper only that morning. His blond hair was lifted and tugged by the stiff wind, defying Brylcreem and comb, but he still managed to look suave and set apart from it all, as he called instructions.

'I recognise that foreman,' Leah said, coming up behind him. 'You've poached him from Pagett's golf resort build, haven't you?'

'Not at all.' He turned and smiled, a bright, welcoming smile, and she wished she didn't have to spoil things. 'I simply borrowed him during the hiatus in the construction.'

Leah gave him a wry look. 'By "hiatus", you mean his weekend off?'

'He's good at his job.' Adam jumped off the rock to land beside her. 'And he needs the money while building is suspended.' He shrugged. 'Everyone wins. Now.' He tugged at the belt that held her coat closed, and slipped his hands around her waist. 'This is the first time I've seen you in a week. You haven't come all the way down here in this horrible wind to ask me where I procured my workforce, have you?' He silenced her reply with his lips, and for a moment she gave in to the pleasure of his touch, kissing him back with what she hoped would be enough enthusiasm to take the edge off what she had to ask him.

He kept his arm around her when they broke apart. 'I hear we've got distinguished guests arriving today.'

'They're due around mid-morning. The little boy actor's been unwell, and he isn't coming now, until later, but their producer arrived last week.'

'Ah yes, I gather Clifford Brennan's not producing them any more?'

'No, it's someone called Rex Kelly.' She watched his face carefully, but his expression didn't alter. She found that unnerving rather than comforting. 'Helen and I had a chat with him the day he arrived.'

'Hope he's settled in alright.' Adam affected to notice an errant worker, and gave a shout. 'We have three days to finish this, Bowden! Mistakes cost time, and time is money!'

Leah didn't even turn to see who Bowden was, or what he was supposedly doing wrong. 'He said something that's made Helen very nervous,' she persisted.

This, finally, brought Adam's attention back, and Leah bit back a surge of frustration but Adam didn't appear to notice. 'Really? What did he say?'

Leah re-fastened her belt, then brushed a blowing curl back from her face and tucked it into her hat, deliberately taking her time over it all. Adam was looking at her, seemingly calm, but she noticed a nerve jumping in his jaw.

'He said he thought you deserved to lose everything,' she said. 'He doesn't know you've built it all up again, and he certainly doesn't know you own half of this place.' She folded her arms. 'Are you going to explain why he hates you so much?'

For a moment Adam faltered, then gestured for her to accompany him away from his workforce. 'I suppose I owe you the truth, at least. I don't come out of it very well, though.' He guided her to the foot of the cliff, to some rocks in the shelter of an overhang, and courteously wiped the wet sand away. But Leah had the feeling that, as with her own actions, it was more in the way of delaying his story than in sparing her a wet behind.

She fought rising impatience while he removed a few pieces of bladderwrack seaweed and settled beside her, and tried to still the nervous fluttering in the pit of her stomach; he reminded her all too much of Glynn when he was bracing himself to tell her of some scheme that had gone wrong, or cost them dear. Or worse.

'What were you doing in July 1911?' he asked, surprising her.

Leah thought for a moment. 'Glynn and I had been married a year by then, and I remember we went up to Carnarvon Castle around the middle of the month, hoping for a look at Prince Edward's ceremony. Apart from that we were probably up to no good somewhere.' She hoped her honesty would prompt him into a like-minded response. 'Why?'

'Harry and I were all aboard for the motion picture lifestyle,' Adam said with a wry smile, 'it was just taking off in Los Angeles. An old friend of Guy's married well out there, and Guy told us there was a brand new movie studio being set up in Hollywood. Which did actually launch in October, as it turned out. Anyway, back then we had money to burn, so we took a trip over there, and got talking to a bloke called James Conrad.'

'Daisy's father?'

He nodded. 'Back then Conrad ran a small-ish production company outside Hollywood, called Stone Valley Pictures. It had just produced Freddie Wishart's first film, *The Boy at the Window*.'

'Freddie must have been awfully young.'

'He was eight, and adorable. An instant child star. Daisy was six, and James was determined to get her into pictures too, but he didn't want it to be seen as giving her a leg up, so he'd called in this other company, Horizon, and promised investors if they gave Daisy a minor role.'

'Sneaky.'

'Just business. And you know she's talented anyway. They advertised in magazines, inviting people to sink money in return for promised shares in the company when it went public. Anyway, Horizon was run by Rex Kelly, who was all for the deal, and we all got along famously, invited to parties, dinners, and so forth. We were introduced all over.'

Adam started to fidget now, and Leah knew he was coming to the crux of the story. 'At the time,' he said, 'I was seeing this absolute pill of a girl, with ambitions in the silver screen. In fact when I'd told her where Harry and I were going she'd begged and begged for me to put in a word for her.' He shrugged. 'I was a bit rotten to her when we broke up, so it seemed the least I could do.'

'So you got her a job with Conrad?'

'No. Stone Valley had nothing for her, but I thought this Rex chap might be worth a shot. He was a bit of a frustrated producer himself, at the time, though he ran the whole shooting match. His top man was Clifford Brennan.' He fell silent again, and once more Leah resisted the urge to prompt him. After a moment he continued. 'I couldn't ask him directly, of course, not after Conrad had done exactly the same thing for Daisy, so the next best thing was to persuade someone a little further down the chain, that Corinne was the next big thing. So I struck up a sort of ... relationship, if you like, with Rex's wife, Julie-Ann.'

Leah stared at him. 'You mean you seduced her?'

'It wasn't all one way!' Adam protested, somehow still managing to sound like the injured party. 'She thought I was a bit of a novelty, I suppose. English charm and all that, they lap it up out there. Look at Charlie Chaplin.'

Leah stood up, appalled. 'I don't want to hear any more.'

'Don't go feeling sorry for her, darling, she was in no way backward in coming forward.' Adam reached for her hand to pull her back down, but she jerked it away. He sighed. 'I misjudged her entirely. As soon as I broached the subject, and very subtly I thought, she realised I'd only been after a job for Corinne, and she blew up. Told Rex I'd ... tried it on with her.'

'But not that it had gone any further?'

'Of course not, she'd be mad to say that. This way her reputation remained as pure as the proverbial driven. He took me to one side, and told me that if I ever came anywhere near Julie-Ann again he'd ... I think his actual words were, *pound the crap* out of me.'

Leah tried to equate the kind-faced, refined gentleman she'd met a few days ago, with a furious studio head, threatening violence. Then she looked at Adam, and the bewildered puppy expression on a face handsome enough itself to grace the screen; Rex Kelly must have privately known only too well that his wife had been a willing participant. Which had doubtless made matters even worse for Adam.

'Did Harry ever find out about this?'

'No, he was blissfully oblivious. But then you know Harry.'

'Not really. I only know the Harry that Helen's told me about.'

'Well, he'll be one and the same.' The old remembered loss painted Adam's eyes a darker blue. 'He never really saw the bad in anyone, simply because he was such a good egg himself. An innocent in a way, despite being worldly.'

'What about the investment?'

'We put money into Horizon and settled down to enjoy the ride, but after a few pictures they were swallowed up by Good Boy Productions anyway, and we lost it all.'

'So they never went public at all?'

He shook his head. 'Rex weathered the takeover of Horizon, and now he runs Good Boy. Seems he's made good on his ambitions to be a top producer, too.'

'Well he's quite likely to transplant the whole Christmas thing somewhere else if he learns you're here, so perhaps it's better if you're not.' Leah wondered, for a moment, if she were mad to continue with her hopes of a future with him, but despite everything there was still something infuriatingly compelling about him; he had the same roguish appeal as Glynn, but without the sense of real danger attached. In short, he belonged in one of those movies Rex Kelly and his ilk made. 'Come with me to Wales,' she said, crossing her fingers behind her back.

'With your husband lurking behind every corner?' Adam gave a short laugh. 'I don't think that would make for much peace on Earth and goodwill to men, would it?'

'He's gone. Liverpool or Manchester, Aunt Mary says. There's not much opportunity for his brand of money-making in the Valleys. Come on,' she urged, 'just until after Christmas, so Helen won't have to worry about Mr Kelly finding another hotel.'

Adam stood up. 'Absolutely not. If this bloke's staying for six weeks, then we're going to have to straighten things out so we can bury the hatchet.' He paused, a cloud passing over his face, but it wasn't in response to the disappointment on her own. 'He hasn't brought his wife with him, has he?'

'No. She's at home with their children.'

'Right, then. I'm staying. I'll talk him around, don't worry.' He dropped a kiss on her cheek. 'Go back indoors, darling, you'll freeze. I won't be long, I just need a word with the foreman so I can tell Helen how much longer we'll be. What time are the worker bees arriving?'

'I'm not sure, they might already be here. And don't call them worker bees.'

Adam grinned. 'Alright. Anyway, I'm sure they're wonderful, and will perk things up here nicely.'

Leah felt a small twinge of satisfaction; on this subject she knew more about the hotel than he did. 'Christmas at Fox Bay hasn't needed perking up for years.'

'So I gather. I've yet to see it for myself, though.' He gave her a sad little smile. 'I'm sure you'll miss it horribly, just as we'll all miss you, of course.'

Of course. The satisfaction melted into a pang of envy for all that would be happening here over the next few days, and for the fact that Adam and Helen would be at the heart of it, together, while she sat in Aunt Mary's parlour and made polite small talk to visitors she barely knew and would likely never see again.

She watched Adam leap nimbly up the concrete steps onto the almost completed decking, and immediately go into a huddle with the foreman, their heads bent against the wind. Then, with the awful, hollow sense that she had already lost him, she turned and made her way back up the cliff.

* * *

The atmosphere at Fox Bay had subtly tightened as the morning progressed, and Bertie had come out into the lobby after breakfast, where she could sit and read her magazine while she watched the guests arriving for Christmas. It had been hopeless trying to draw Guy out once more, about what he'd spotted in the bin outside Mrs Burch's shop; the time would come where she would get it out of him, but in the meantime there were much more interesting things on both their minds. Today was the day Hollywood royalty came to Cornwall.

Bertie had been captivated by Daisy Conrad since the actress's first adult role, in *One Morning in Paris*. She and Guy had often talked about her screen presence, and her ability to tell an entire story with her face; the title cards were almost irrelevant. When her first talking picture, *Silver Shoes*, was screened in Bude last year, Guy had driven her and Fiona to watch it, and they had all emerged enraptured.

'Now I know why Ben is so envious he couldn't come,' Fiona said, as they made their way back to the car. 'I wondered why, since Lily's dragged him to it twice already, but I can see now. I'm ready to watch it all over again myself.'

'Ben is besotted with Daisy,' Bertie said. 'I was too, and after that film, I think she's even more wonderful.'

Guy was equally enthusiastic. 'Who would have thought she could dance so well!'

'I thought you'd be disappointed this film didn't have Freddie Wishart in it,' Bertie said, with a wink at Fiona.

'I must admit I prefer it when they're together,' he allowed, '*One Morning in Paris* is wonderfully funny. But I had no idea Daisy could carry a film so well alone.'

Fiona had grinned at Bertie behind Guy's back, and kept her voice earnest. 'But Freddie would have played Philip's part much better than George Faber. Don't you think so, Guy?'

'Faber was adequate.'

And that was all they were permitted of their teasing.

The last of the Christmas guests finished checking-in, and vanished to their rooms to change out of travelling clothes. Mum and Granny were upstairs putting personal finishing touches to the guests of honours' rooms, much to Miss Tremar's irritation; Ben usually went straight to bed after his night shift, but today he had found it necessary to check every name in the guest book and make various notes beside them, while simultaneously trying to smooth his hair flat; and Guy was drifting around flicking a duster over every piece of already-shining brass he could find. Only Fiona had abandoned all pretence, and was waiting outside on the drive with her less than enamoured new friend.

A commotion in the doorway dragged every eye to it, but it was neither Daisy nor Freddie.

'Bertie! You look wonderful!' Lynette Nicholls gestured to the disappointed bell boy to take her bags over to the desk, and crossed the lobby to the seating area. 'I saw Fi outside and she said they were waiting for a special guest to arrive. I hadn't even told her we were coming!' She laughed at her own joke and leaned down to hug Bertie.

Bertie accepted the embrace with a smile. 'We?' she repeated, hoping she'd been wrong, for Jowan's sake. 'Is Xander here too?'

'Parking the car,' Lynette said, and took the seat opposite. 'Who's the *actual* special guest, then?'

'Guests.' Bertie stressed the plural. 'Daisy Conrad and Freddie Wishart.' She laughed at the look of awe on Lynette's face. 'I bet you're doubly glad you were so nice to me at the racetrack now!'

'I sure *am*, Aunt Mercy!'

'That accent is terrible.' Bertie grinned, rolling her eyes.

Lynette shook her head. 'I can't believe it. How exciting!'

'They're due any minute, so if Xander isn't careful he's going to ruin their big entrance.'

'Very likely!' Lynette laughed. 'It'll all go right over his head, of course.' She waved at Ben, who waved distractedly back, and lowered her voice to a conspiratorial whisper. 'He's rather a dish, your brother, isn't he?'

Bertie shrugged. 'If you like that sort of thing.'

'What, tall, dark-haired and handsome, and with a jaw that could cut diamond?' Lynette winked. 'I could manage.'

'Better not let his girlfriend hear you talking about him like that. Why didn't you tell me you were coming down?'

'Helen knew we were coming, of course. We were so pleased to get the invitation, particularly as we're not generally guests. We wouldn't have intruded, but I was so sorry to hear you and that lovely farmer were no more that I wanted to cheer you up with a surprise.'

'But Jowan and I are back together,' Bertie said, feeling a bit of a fraud now.

'Well that's no reason to look miserable.' Lynette leaned forward and patted Bertie's hand. 'It's *good* news, silly!'

'But it means you've come all this way under false pretences.'

'Not at all! I'm still thrilled to see you again. Besides, I'll get to meet the gorgeous Freddie, and Xander was planning on coming down soon anyway. He's taking up his training immediately after New Year, so it just means he's come down a week earlier.'

Before Bertie could answer, Lynette pointed to the stairs. 'Who's that? Looks rather important.'

'Rex Kelly, the producer. Owner of the film studio, actually. Lynette, where's—'

'Does that mean they're here?' Lynette stood up.

'Probably.' Bertie saw Rex check his pocket watch as he reached the lobby floor, and both she and Lynette turned expectantly towards the door.

'Caernoweth Air Base,' Lynette said, distracted and clearly not realising the impact her words would have. 'Xander's training, I mean.'

Cornwall? Bertie could only imagine what Jowan's reaction would be when he found out. 'I thought he'd be training at Brighton.'

'He's bored with Brighton, and since his racing tour last summer he fell oddly in love with this place.'

'Oddly!' Bertie tried to take offence and couldn't. 'But Caernoweth? I thought that place more or less lived and died with the war.'

'It was defunct for a while,' Lynette agreed, 'but the Royal Air Force have ... Oh!' Her voice dropped reverently. 'There she is!'

A group of five or six people were gathering outside, having climbed from two motor cars. Two of the party were fussing over the fall of a coat belonging to a third, and Bertie recognised the face beneath the green, beribboned bucket hat as it peered around.

'She's so beautiful,' she breathed.

'She looks a bit spoiled though,' Lynette said, straining to see better. 'There's Xander, the silly ass, marching up to them as if they're old friends! He hasn't a clue, you know.'

'Doesn't he go to the pictures?'

'Never. Where's Fabulous Freddie? Oh, no! Xander's talking to him.' She shook her head. 'I shall never live this down.'

The lift bell sounded, and Bertie's mother emerged. 'They're here! I saw them from the window upstairs.'

'Mum, honestly!' But Bertie couldn't help grinning at her mother's uncharacteristically childlike excitement. 'What would you say to Fiona if she behaved like that?'

Helen chuckled. 'I know, I'm dreadful. Hush now, I have to be a grown-up.' She looked around. 'I thought Leah would be here.'

'Me too, where is she?'

'Maybe she's still talking to Adam. She'll be sorry to have missed this.'

The group began filing through the doors one at a time, and Rex greeted them as they came in. Daisy and Freddie were the last to enter, and while their companions went to the reception desk, the two young stars stood aside, paying scant attention to whatever their producer was telling them as their gazes wandered over the lobby.

Freddie Wishart couldn't have appeared more different from his on-screen persona, who was so often seen dishevelled and bemused. His hair was neatly greased and parted, and his pale blue eyes were half-lidded, in contrast to the wide-eyed innocence of the characters he played. The pencil-thin moustache appeared drawn-on, and he constantly ran a finger along it as he stared around him, as if taking mental notes already.

Bertie studied Daisy. The short, but famously voluptuous form was swathed in a deep green wool coat fastened with a single button; only a few inches of her legs showed, ending in sensible brown leather Oxfords. She might have been anyone, until one looked at her face: the expressive eyes, the small nose and the wide, laughing mouth, all framed by a thick fur collar and the dark green hat ... that face had filled the screen, had brought laughter in waves, and unreserved admiration – even from the critics who were usually so quick to question a star's popularity.

Freddie's tall, blond appearance was such a perfect foil for Daisy that, from their very first film together, they had become the epitome of youthful romance. *One Morning in Paris* had taken Hollywood by storm, and their next two films the same; funny, witty, and deeply romantic, Conrad–Wishart films were a magical escape from the despair caused by the Great Crash, as they were calling it. And here they were, in Fox Bay Hotel ... Bertie could scarcely believe it. She glanced over at Ben, who, to give him credit, was behaving like a good manager, helping Martin book in the new arrivals, but his gaze kept slipping towards Daisy, and his expression fell somewhere between admiration and a rather desperate kind of disapproval.

Guy had very smoothly joined Rex just before the party had come in, and now stood with them, nodding sagely, and making notes as Rex passed on his service requests.

'Look at him,' Bertie murmured to Lynette. 'Every inch the cool, calm manager he isn't.'

Lynette's laughter rang across the lobby, and drew the curious eyes of both Daisy and Freddie, and she hushed at once, blushing. 'Sorry,' she said. 'He is *sort* of a manager though, isn't he?'

'Dining room and bar,' Bertie allowed, 'but Mum and Ben are the actual hotel managers. He sometimes forgets that, but we love him so we forgive him.'

'Here's Fiona and her friend,' Lynette said. 'Gosh, but that girl's pretty. Look at that white hair! Who is she?'

'We don't know.' Bertie gave her a quick explanation of all she knew of Amy's rescue. 'She seems nice enough, and it'll be good for Fi to have someone of her own age here over the holidays. Look sharp, Mum's bringing Daisy over.'

'This is my elder daughter,' Helen was saying, 'Bertie.'

'Bertie? That's a great name.' Daisy held out her hand. If she'd noticed the wheelchair behind Bertie's seat she didn't mention it. 'Roberta, I guess?'

Bertie nodded and shook her hand. 'This is Lynette Nicholls.'

'Delighted, I'm sure. Oh, did you say Nicholls?' Daisy turned to look back at the doorway, where Xander was talking to Freddie. 'Is that your husband?'

'My brother.' Lynette grasped the gloved hand in both of hers and shook it fervently. 'It's wonderful to meet you, Miss Conrad.'

Close up, Daisy looked tired, but her smile was wide and seemed genuine enough. 'You too. Both of you. It's so beautiful here, we can't wait to go take a look around outside later.'

'If you can prise Freddie away from Mr Bannacott,' Lynette said.

Guy looked up at the sound of his name, and brought Freddie over for his own introductions. By now some of the other guests had come back downstairs, changed and ready to walk out in the fresh air, and there were a satisfactory number of double-takes that the Hollywood pair affected not to notice. Or perhaps they were so used to it that they genuinely didn't.

'Good to meet you.' Freddie shook hands with them, then turned to Guy, all business. 'We'd better go get changed, then we have to talk to Rex. Will the bar be open in around, say, a half-hour?'

'Of course, Mr Wishart.'

'Freddie,' the young man insisted.

'Freddie.' Guy inclined his head politely, but Bertie was sure she could detect a light flush of pleasure.

As they left, Guy leading them up the stairs, Xander slid in and took the seat temporarily vacated by his exasperated sister. He grinned at Bertie. 'Swanky home you have, chum.'

'Not to mention the guests,' Lynette said, pulling up another chair. 'What were you and Freddie talking about?'

'Do you know—' Xander sat forward, his face earnest '—I had absolutely *no* idea they were famous types, until that Rex fellow mentioned Hollywood.'

'And now do you know who they are?'

'Well of course I do, I don't live under a rock! I mean, I've *heard* of them, who hasn't?'

'Lynette tells me you're doing the next part of your training at Caernoweth Air Base?' Bertie said, secretly hoping her friend had got it wrong.

'Yes. It all kicks off on Jan the sixth, though I'm travelling down on the second. I have to go down there sometime before I start too, to sign my life away.' He prodded Bertie's knee. 'You should come too, Bertram, ask a few questions if you're serious about what you wrote to me. I've heard it's a nice little seaside town, too, is that right?'

'I've never been there,' Bertie said. 'Seems silly really, when it's so close.'

'Well there you are, then. It's settled. I'll drive us down tomorrow, shall I? There's a lovely pub there, apparently. Something to do with Tintin, if you can believe that. Or perhaps I've misheard.'

'I can't come tomorrow. Perhaps Monday, if you're not busy? Tuesday's the treasure hunt, so I can't get away then.'

'Monday it shall be.' His wide smile softened as he looked at her. 'I'm glad to see you doing so much better. I'm sure you were only being held back by—'

'She's back with Joel,' Lynette broke in.

'Jowan,' Bertie corrected. 'And I was *not* being held back by him.'

'I was going to say fear, darling,' Xander said gently. 'It must have been so frightening, getting used to the way things have had to change.'

Bertie subsided, and her eyes prickled. 'It was. And I'm sorry for jumping to conclusions.'

He regarded her for a moment, then nodded. 'That's alright. You can make it up to me somehow.' He winked. 'Right, I'm going to check in and unpack. Coming, sis?'

Lynette stood up and straightened her coat. 'I'll come and find you later, Bertie, and we can talk properly.'

As they walked away Bertie heard Lynette ask, in a voice not quite low enough, 'Were you really going to say *fear*?'

'Of course not, you idiot! Thanks for saving me the embarrassment.'

Bertie knew she should have been disappointed in him, even annoyed, but she only smiled. They were irrepressible, irresistible, and, against all likelihood, her very best friends. If only Jowan understood.

* * *

Leah was packing when Helen went looking for her, and doing a very poor job of it. It wasn't until she turned around that Helen saw the reason why; her eyes were red and watery, and her frustration with every single movement resulted in her abandoning the idea of folding altogether. Plus fours were jammed into the front of the case with the legs hanging over the edge, and the gown she'd had washed and pressed especially, to wear on Christmas Day, was balled up and shoved into the corner.

'Whatever's the matter?' Helen lifted the pink beaded dress out and shook it. 'This is your favourite! I'll send it down to be pressed again, and packed in tissue paper.'

'Don't bother.' Leah sighed and sat down heavily on the bed. 'The only people who'll see it are Aunt Mary and her friends, and they won't care about a few creases.'

Helen took the chair by the dressing table and studied her friend. 'What's he done?'

'Adam?'

'Who else? Did you find out what the problem is between him and Rex?'

'Yes.' Leah's accent slipped into impeccable American. 'Pin your ears back, Mrs Fox, it's a doozy.'

Helen listened, with growing dismay, as Leah told her everything Adam had said. She half-stood, then sat again, then jumped up and went to the window, as if she expected to see the two men meeting on the driveway and exchanging blows. She had to keep them apart until she'd found a way to prepare the producer for the role Adam now played in the running of the hotel.

'Thank goodness Rex didn't bring Julie-Ann with him,' she muttered. 'Oh, God, Adam was always a fool, but this . . . *this*!'

'He said he'd talk to Rex,' Leah said. 'But to be honest, after seeing the way Rex spoke about him I don't hold out much hope for a reconciliation.'

'Exactly.' Helen gave the crumpled dress another shake. 'I'll put this in for a pressing, and then see if I can find Rex before Adam comes back.' She nodded at the shambles on the bed. 'You'd better get that sorted out, or you'll regret it when you get to Wales.'

She left Leah pulling out the contents of her suitcase, and hurried downstairs to the laundry. But seeing Rex Kelly talking to one of his party near the door, she dropped the dress behind the counter instead, and changed direction. She only hoped her anxiety didn't show.

Rex looked up as she approached, and a smile cut across his lean face. 'Mrs Fox!' He turned to his companion. 'We'll continue this later, when Freddie and Daisy are ready.' He held out his hand courteously and clasped Helen's when she took it. 'Can I just say again how beautiful this place is? It's perfect to get a feel for what we'll be creating back home. Did you know they're building a golf resort just up the road? Of course you did!' He beamed, and Helen's hopes lifted; if he liked the place this much perhaps there was less of a chance he'd be driven out once he found out who co-owned it.

All the way down the stairs she'd been seizing half-baked ideas and casting them away, and now she realised the only sensible way was to tell him the truth. Or at least most of it.

'I'm so glad you like it,' she murmured, as she drew him away from the door and towards the lounge. 'You might be surprised to find out we almost lost it earlier this year.'

'*Lost* it?' He craned his neck as he looked around at the shimmering perfection of the lobby. 'How so?'

'Harry had got into ... difficulties, just before he died, and the hotel was bought by someone else. We kept it running throughout the twenties, but the owner had to sell back in the summer, and it was almost converted to holiday flats.'

'Holy hell!' Rex shuddered. 'Pardon me, Mrs Fox ... Helen. But that would have been a travesty. *Holiday flats?*'

'Indeed. Anyway, there was someone who'd made some shrewd investments nearby, including the land where they're building that golf resort you mentioned. He owed Harry a great deal, financially and morally, and he sold his assets to buy this hotel, which he then gifted to my family. Half of it, at least. He still owns the other half.'

Rex smiled. 'Good to see a man pay off his debts.'

'Oh, he's a changed man,' Helen said, crossing her fingers at her side. 'He was something of a rogue in his youth, but he's spent the past several years making up for it.'

Rex stopped. He had not become the head of a multi-million-dollar company by accident, he clearly had a quick mind and it snapped into action now. 'You're talking about Adam Coleridge,' he said flatly.

'I am.' Helen kept her voice calm and reasonable as she took her final gamble. 'I do understand you've had some bad dealings with him in the past. I have no wish to ask what they were, but, having thought it over I feel it's only fair to let you know he's living here, and to give you the opportunity of changing your plans. I can recommend a good hotel in Bude that will still have rooms.' She could feel her fingers aching as she crossed them even harder. *Please don't, please don't ...*

'Enough rooms for me, the kids, our team, *and* Jimmy Haverford?'

Helen nodded. 'Like us, they run at reduced capacity over Christmas, and would be absolutely honoured to receive you at short notice.'

'I see. Perhaps it would be for the best. Which hotel is it?'

It was an effort for Helen to keep the disappointment from her voice, but it was her own fault for pushing her bluff too far. 'It's called the Summerleaze. Actually the assistant manager is Ben's girlfriend, so we know her quite well. Would you like me to call now and have your luggage sent over?'

Rex raised an eyebrow. 'You'd do it too, wouldn't you?'

'Of course.'

Rex eyed her shrewdly for a moment, then he smiled. 'You're a class act, Mrs Fox. No, I'm not going to up sticks and move out to Bude. And thank you for your honesty.' He looked around the lobby, then back at her, and nodded. 'Time's a healer, I guess, so I'm prepared to accept the hand of friendship from Adam Coleridge, if he offers it.'

'Oh, he will,' Helen said, and saw from Rex's grin that he'd heard the schoolteacher determination in her voice.

She and Rex parted company by the lounge door, and Helen went to fetch her coat for the walk down to the beach. Adam had a lot of making up to do, and he needed to start now.

CHAPTER NINE

Monday 23rd December

Fiona had originally baulked at the idea of a day out in Caernoweth with Bertie and the Nicholls siblings; it was embarrassingly obvious she and Amy had only been invited to spare Lynette's boredom while the other two were at the air base. It was her only day off, and she'd much rather have gone to the lifeboat station, but when Amy realised that the fishing cove of Porthstennack lay at the foot of the town she had begged her to accept.

'Didn't you say that's where the RMS *Drake* ended up?'

'Constable Quick said it anchored off the coast there while it was fixed,' Fiona corrected her. 'It'll be long gone by now.'

'What if it's not? What if it took a long time to fix? Come on, we have to at least find out!'

'And how will you get to it, even if it is? It won't be sitting prettily in a dock waiting for you, it'll be anchored maybe a mile out to sea!'

'I just want to find out. Maybe some of the people saw ... some of the passengers, or something,' Amy finished lamely. 'Come on, it'll be good to get out of here for a while anyway, won't it? And,' she added, 'I still have that letter to post to Kitty, since we haven't managed to get into Bude yet. Caernoweth is far enough from here that she won't know where to find me.'

'That's true. Though from what you've told me I doubt she'd be worried anyway.'

'She wouldn't be worried, she'd be . . .' Amy shook her head, her face pensive again. 'Anyway let's go, shall we? Come on.'

Fiona had to admit a day trip might be fun, especially now that Leah had left for Wales and Mum was once more immersed in the Christmas preparations. It wasn't even as if they saw anything of Daisy and Freddie either; the two stars were being chaperoned by their producer as if they were five-year-olds; Aunt Leah hadn't even seen them before she'd left, much to her disappointment. Ben had evidently decided Daisy was as empty-headed as he'd assumed her to be, though on what basis it was impossible to imagine. Still, he was as dismissive whenever her name was mentioned as if she'd been anyone he passed in the street, and no longer made any attempt to cross her path.

Amy couldn't possibly have cared less about the Hollywood visitors, she hadn't recognised them when they'd arrived, and had told Fiona that the only time she'd ever been to a picture house was to watch her idol Isadora Duncan. She couldn't see the point in lavishing praise and adoration on someone who simply pretended to be someone else for a living, and had grumpily asserted that if she could be paid a tenth as much for her own acting skills, it would pay, not only for passage to Ireland, but for a whole new life. Her growing annoyance with it all was becoming wearing.

It was also good to be getting out from under the sharp eyes of Guy Bannacott. The last three days had been awkward, but she'd kept her word; Amy still did not know the restaurant manager had seen anything, and had questioned Fiona every time she had shied away from speaking to him. Now here was a chance to get away for a whole day and maybe even forget the need for such exhausting subterfuge.

Xander's Bentley was a tight squeeze for the five of them, but, with much giggling and shoving, Fiona, Amy and Lynette managed to climb into the back, leaving the front passenger seat free for Bertie. The roof was up, against the chilly December wind, but the day stayed miraculously dry, and soon enough they were barrelling along the winding Cornish lanes towards Caernoweth.

Fiona could hear that Bertie and Xander were engaged in a lively conversation in the front of the car, but whatever they were saying was drowned out by the engine, the wind rattling the windows, and the excited chatter between Lynette and Amy. The discussion was doubtless something to do with the air base and Bertie's idea of becoming a pilot. Fiona's feelings about that were so mixed she had given up trying to unravel them; on one hand the possibility had brought Bertie right back into herself, and her argument that, while riding would be impossible, flying was well within reach made perfect sense. On the other, what if she were turned her down for the training? What would that do to her fragile recovery? And if she were successful, would that be better? The entire family would be permanently terrified—

'Tell me all about where we're going,' Lynette demanded, nudging Fiona, and pulling her out of her reverie. 'Does it have shops?'

'Not the kind you mean, I shouldn't have thought. Probably somewhere to buy food and things, but it's still mainly a working town from what I've heard. Nothing there for the tourist.'

Lynette sighed. 'There's the hotel on the cliff, though, I've heard a lot about that. Surely there must be *some* nice places for the guests?'

'They come for the sea air and the scenery, just like at Fox Bay. If they want more, they probably go to Bodmin, or Truro.'

'Oh, well.' Lynette leaned forward and peered past Amy at the fields they were passing. 'A little walk and a nice hot lunch will do. How far is it, do you suppose?'

'I have no idea, but we must be close by now. That mine chimney could be Wheal Furzy, though that's defunct now.'

'And there's the air base,' Amy said, pointing. 'We must be almost there.'

'We are,' Xander said. 'I'll drop you off on the edge of the town.'

The car drew to a stop at the top of a long hill, where what had once been an impressive-looking hotel had been turned into holiday flats. Remembering how close Fox Bay had come to the same fate, Fiona wondered if Mr Pagett had had a hand in this, too. It seemed likely.

Xander came around to open the door. 'Right, you lot can push off now. Bertram and I'll meet you back here at around one o'clock, and we'll drive down to that old fort hotel place on the cliff for lunch.'

The three back seat passengers scrambled out, and Bertie waved to them as Xander turned the car around to face back the way they'd come. She looked nervous, Fiona reflected, but excited too, which was good because even if nothing else came of her visit to the air base today, at least she'd had that excitement for a while.

'Right,' Lynette said, when the car had vanished around the bend. 'Where to first?'

'I want to see the beach,' Amy put in at once. 'Fiona said it's the same place where the ship I was on ended up.'

'I'm not walking all that way in these shoes, just on the off-chance of seeing a ship!' Lynette protested. 'We can ask someone though, if you like, and if it's there you have my blessing to go down by yourselves, and I'll meet you for lunch.'

Fiona nodded, and drew her scarf tighter. 'Let's just walk down through the town and see what we find.'

The three of them started down the hill. Fiona had been right; there was little in the way of shops, apart from a butcher, and grocer, and one or two others, though she smiled to see a Kessel's bakery halfway down the hill. She remembered Andrew's constant boasting at the lifeboat station, and since this was doubtless one of his oft-mentioned family she decided to call in and buy a pastry on their way back up, just so she could tell him she'd done so.

They wandered past the civic offices, where a rather wind-tattered poster was pinned, advertising weekly gatherings, run by an organisation called the Widows' Guild, on Saturday mornings. These meetings offered a discount for those who lived and worked at the air base.

'Strange to think Xander will be socialising somewhere like this from now on, instead of his club,' Lynette mused. 'And Bertie too, no doubt.'

'If they allow her in,' Fiona added, still not sure how she felt about it. She looked up, shivering slightly at the thought of her sister all the way up there, swallowed up by clouds, and nothing between her and the ground but a flimsy metal floor. Across the road she saw a neatly painted sign over the front window of what looked like another ordinary house converted to a shop: *Penhaligon's Attic*.

'Books!' Amy followed her gaze. 'Let's go in. Looks like they sell all kinds of other knick-knacks too.'

Lynette pulled a face. 'Second hand?'

'Don't be such a snob!' Fiona grinned. 'I bet you haven't got a Christmas gift for Jowan yet.'

'Hardly, since I didn't think we'd be seeing him.'

'Well then, why not have a look?'

Lynette shrugged. 'Alright. It's not as if there's much else to be doing.'

The three of them crossed the road and peered through the window.

'It looks lovely and cosy in there,' Fiona said. She turned to Amy, who had stepped away. 'Aren't you coming in?'

'No.'

'What's wrong?'

'Nothing!' Amy pulled her hat lower as the wind cut around the side of the building. 'I just don't want to go wasting a nice day looking around a dusty old shop.'

'It was your idea! And it's not at all dusty,' Fiona protested, her hand already on the door handle. 'It's quite bright and clean.'

'Still. You'd only have to carry anything you bought, and it might get damaged.'

Fiona was struck by a thought. 'Is it because you don't have any money to spend? Because I can give you—'

'I said no! You go in, I'll just wait here.'

Fiona looked at her a moment longer, then shrugged, and she and Lynette stepped inside.

It was clearly just the front room of a house, with a door at either end of the room, and several bookcases of varying sizes. Most were stuffed with books but there were some shelves devoted to ornaments and hand-sewn items, and one or two with watch chains and other pieces of second-hand jewellery, and it was to these that Lynette went.

Fiona smiled at the dark-haired woman who stood behind the narrow counter. 'This all looks lovely,' she said. 'Are you Mrs Penhaligon?'

'No, I'm just standing in for my friend for an hour or so. The shop belongs to her family. My name's Emily Parker.'

'Fiona Fox. Very pleased to meet you.' Fiona introduced Lynette, and Miss Parker looked interested when she heard where they'd come from.

'Fox Bay? You're one of the hotel Foxes?'

Fiona nodded. 'You know it then?'

'Oh, yes. Mrs Kempton and her husband stay there sometimes, so I hear.'

'She does, if you mean Lucy Kempton, the dancer?'

'That's her. Her family home is just up the hill, at Pencarrack House.'

'Of course! I'd forgotten that.' Amy would be thrilled. 'She and her husband are lovely. We just want to have a little look around if that's alright? It's such a beautiful little shop. So much to see.'

'Explore away! I'm sure Freya would be delighted to know you find her placements appealing. Personally, I always go straight for the books, I've always been something of a bookworm.' Miss Parker glanced at the window. 'Didn't I see there were three of you?'

'Yes, our friend has decided to stay outside while we have a look around.' Fiona opened the door again and called out to Amy, who was leaning against the wall further down. 'Amy! Are you sure you—'

'Shut *up*!' Amy's face contorted as she managed to cut across Fiona's shout with only a harsh whisper. 'No, I don't want to come in. Leave me alone!'

Startled, and embarrassed, Fiona closed the door again, harder than she'd intended, and the jangle of the bell brought Lynette around to the front of the shop again.

'What's bitten her?'

'How rude,' Fiona muttered. 'I'm terribly sorry, Miss Parker.'

'Oh, don't fret on my account,' Miss Parker said. But her face was thoughtful as she looked at the empty road beyond the window.

Lynette settled on a watch and chain for Jowan, and Fiona chose a copy of Agatha Christie's *The Mysterious Affair at Styles*. The title seemed appropriate, as she was still puzzled by Amy's sudden change of heart; there certainly seemed nothing even faintly sinister about either Emily Parker or the shop.

'I want to go back to Fox Bay,' Amy said, levering herself off the wall as Fiona and Lynette re-joined her.

'Don't be silly,' Lynette said. 'We've only just got here. Xander and Bertie won't be nearly finished yet.'

'Then I'll just wait for you all at the top of the hill.'

'If you insist.' Fiona made little attempt to hide her resentment, especially after all that fuss Amy had made about coming here, making her miss out on her day with the crew of the *Lady Dafna*. 'You haven't posted your letter yet,' she reminded her coolly. 'There's a letter box outside the baker's shop.'

'Alright,' Amy said, 'I'll post it on the way up.'

'But it's over an hour yet before we meet Bertie and Xander. It's only just gone twelve.'

'Then let's go to the beach.'

'Goodness, and walk all that way back up again?' Lynette eyed her shoes. 'No thank you. It might be fun to see if that's open, though.' She pointed down the hill, to where a sign hung outside a tiny inn, squeaking back and forth in the stiff wind.

'The Tin Streamer's Arms,' Fiona read aloud, and remembered Xander's vague musing on the name. 'Tintin indeed!' She couldn't help smiling despite her annoyance with Amy. 'We can't go into a pub though. You go if you like.'

'You can drink lemonade,' Lynette pleaded. 'Do come on, it's such a pretty little place!'

'It might be nice,' Fiona conceded. 'Amy, you could ask about the ship.'

'You ask. I'll go up to the bakery, post my letter, and ask there. I'll wait for you by the flats.'

Before they could respond, she began walking quickly up the hill. Fiona sighed and followed, running a few steps to catch up.

'Gosh, I never had you down as a spoilsport,' Lynette called after her. 'Oh, alright!'

She too followed, though much more slowly, and when there was enough distance between them, Fiona grabbed Amy's sleeve and pulled her to a stop. 'Why wouldn't you go in that shop?'

'It looked boring.'

'Rot!' Fiona remembered how Amy had pulled her hat down, covering her distinctive white-blonde hair. Nothing to do with the wind then, after all. 'It was something about that woman, wasn't it?'

'What woman?'

'The one in the shop! Look, you don't have to worry, we didn't talk about you, we just said that we'd come down from Fox Bay. Do you know her?'

'How could I? I've never been here before.'

'That's not an answer!'

'And you're not getting one!' Amy's eyes blazed, but only for a moment, then she relented and lowered her voice. 'Not now, alright? I'll tell you later.'

'Promise?'

Amy's gaze slipped past Fiona to where Lynette was labouring up to meet them, and she nodded. 'Cornish-promise. Go and talk to her while I post my letter.'

Fiona waited for Lynette, while behind her Amy hurried up to the posting box outside the bakery, and then the three of them went into the shop. She spoke to the baker for a few minutes, extolling Andrew's bravery, and then Amy asked after the RMS *Drake*.

'Did anyone come ashore?'

'No, miss. Never saw hide nor hair of anyone. Don't think they'd have been able, not the way the seas is now. They sent tugs out to square her up, so she could be fixed, but even they were hard pushed in those tides.'

'And the ship's gone now?'

'Oh yes. Sailed two days after she anchored.'

Amy nodded her thanks, looking despondent, and as they went outside Fiona leaned in close and whispered, 'I thought you'd laid low for the entire time? How did you know who was on board?'

'I was *hoping* someone might have bothered to come ashore and ask after their cook,' Amy said bitterly. 'Not to mention the others in the small boat with me.'

Fiona remembered how devastated Amy had been to learn of the old man's death. 'Don't worry,' she said more gently, 'they'll have been told everything by the coastguard.'

129

They walked on in silence, and it wasn't until they reached the top of the town that Fiona remembered what Emily Parker had told her about Pencarrack House. It would be something to cheer Amy up.

'Guess whose family home is just down that lane?' She pointed towards the outline of a large manor house away to their left.

'Whose?'

'Lucy Kempton.'

Amy's mouth dropped open, then closed again quickly. 'She doesn't live there now though, does she?'

'No, Liverpool I think. But that's where she grew up.'

'Well come on, then!'

Amy grabbed Fiona's coat and began to run, and they heard a faint cry of protest from behind them. 'I can't run in these shoes, you rotten pair!'

'We won't be long!' Fiona yelled back, and heard Amy's laughter dancing in the wind. Amy pulled harder, and there was a loud, tearing sound as the stitching in Fiona's sleeve gave way. They both stopped dead, and the look on Amy's face was one of such comical dismay that Fiona burst into breathless laughter of her own.

'It's my oldest coat, come on!'

She grabbed Amy's hand and began to run, feeling like a carefree child for the first time in what seemed like years.

* * *

Caernoweth Air Base

'What do you think?' Xander's voice cut across the sharper than expected rattle of the propeller, but Bertie waited until the plane had lumbered away across the field before she turned to answer.

'It's like another world!' She shielded her eyes against the low winter sun to watch the plane take off, but it remained on the ground, rocking its way across the grass before turning in a slow circle to face them again.

Xander echoed her disappointed sigh. 'Well, I've got to go over there to sign some papers.' He pointed to a squat building across the yard, behind a huge wire fence. 'That's the Royal Air Force part of the base, but you should be alright to look around this part. Feel free to join me, otherwise I'll find you later, alright?'

Bertie nodded absently and lifted her hand in a wave, following the progress of another biplane further away. From the moment she'd told Jowan, and despite his words, she had known he was silently holding on to the hope that she would change her mind. She even suspected herself that her determination was wavering. What had she been thinking, after all? That the interest in pursuing this new, rather lunatic dream, would somehow ease the loss of her beloved motorcycles, the lifelong passion she would have shared with her father had he lived? How could it? In fact, most of the way down here in the car she'd been privately listing reasons she could give others, as to why flying wasn't for her, and imagining the relief on Jowan's face when she told him.

But from the moment Xander had helped her from the car she had felt a tight coil of excitement deep inside. A wholly unexpected visceral pull towards the noise, the smells, and the sight of the different types of aircraft dotted around the vast field. The buildings that housed the training aircraft were unlike anything she'd ever seen before, either. Hundreds of feet in width and length, soaring, arched roofs with iron trusses, and one of the closest even stood open to reveal three aircraft inside, one of them with its propeller off and an engineer only visible from the shoulders down as he worked on it.

'You'll be Miss Fox, then.'

Bertie turned to see a friendly looking young man in greasy overalls. 'Yes, how did you know?'

'Xander Nicholls is an old pal,' the young man said. 'He told me to look after you. Tommy Ash.' He put out his hand, then looked at the oil on it, and dropped it again apologetically. 'Let me show you around.' He didn't give the crutches a second look, but took a slow pace as he led her towards the hangar at which she'd been staring. 'Those in there are the type of thing Xander will be flying. They're Type 76 Jupiters, developed for training now. We also have a couple of Sopwith 1½ Strutters. They're bombers, left over from the war. Those, over there—' he pointed to a corner of the field, where two larger planes were nose-to-nose '—they're great for training fighter pilots.'

Bertie followed him inside the hangar, and stared up at the plane closest to her. She'd known they'd look very different on the ground, but she hadn't expected this jolt of emotion at seeing one close up. She reached out a hand and gently brushed it over the casing.

'What about civil planes?'

'We mostly use the Simmonds Spartan, I'll take you over to the hangar in a minute. Before I do though, I have to ask … How serious are you then, about learning to fly?' Now he finally acknowledged her folded trouser leg, and when he met her eyes again his expression was both fascinated and curious.

Bertie looked around the hangar, and up at the plane towering above her. 'Deadly,' she said quietly, and let out her breath in a slow release of pent-up tension.

'Good, you'll need to be. Xander tells me you're ... *were*,' he amended, 'a keen motorcycle racer.'

'I was.' It gave her a little pang to say it, to acknowledge its passing in those two blunt little words, and she wanted to rush on and explain herself, but looking at Tommy's face she didn't think she needed to. 'I'm being fitted for an aluminium leg,' she said instead. 'It's lightweight, and once I'm used to it I should be able to do everything he can.' She gestured to where Xander had gone to complete his forms, and Tommy laughed.

'Never mind, I'll stand as a witness for your defence, if it comes to that. Now—' he nodded towards the open door '—let's go and look at those Spartans before you change your mind.'

Cliffside Fort Hotel was bigger than Fox Bay, and like Fox Bay it had been restored beautifully, maintaining the outward appearance of the fortification put in place against the Spanish, but affording the guests a degree of comfort never imagined by the soldiers garrisoned there. The only concession to modern luxury visible from the outside were the lights, placed strategically around the weathered granite walls and softening the hard grey daylight.

Bertie looked around with real appreciation as they went inside. It was a haven of subdued lighting and warmed stone, and in deference to the season a goose feather tree stood in the corner of the lobby, decorated with wooden baubles and paper bells, and with a twist of fairy lights through its branches instead of candles. It wasn't in Fox Bay's league for modern luxury, but the owners clearly had their own way of making Christmas a special event, and there were plenty of people around to enjoy it.

The waiter seated them by a large picture window that

overlooked the otherwise hidden inlet at the foot of the cliff, and left them to peruse the gaily printed menu with holly painted around the headings. Amy's eyes kept flicking from table to table, and Bertie guessed she was looking for any clue that might help her remember anything. It must be awful for her, not knowing herself.

As for her own news, she sensed the questions hovering on the lips of the other three, but only when they had selected their meals and handed back the menus, did Lynette finally bring up the subject of the air base.

'Well, Xander? All braced, ready for the sixth?'

'Ready as they'll ever be,' he quipped. 'They've been warned.'

'Good thing too,' Lynette said. 'They'll need to keep an eye on you that's for sure. What about you, Bertie? Did you have the chance to speak to anyone?'

'I did.' She met Xander's grin and finally returned it. 'It's too soon yet, of course, but there's a strong possibility they'll take me on in a few months, to begin training.'

'She'll need the peg leg first, of course,' Xander put in, and Fiona audibly caught her breath, but Bertie just dipped her fingers into her glass and flicked water at him.

'I spoke to the doctors last week if you must know.'

'And it won't be a peg leg, you perfect oik!' Lynette added a few drops of her own. 'It's a skilfully engineered, precision-crafted prosthetic.'

Bertie's mouth dropped open. 'Which medical book have you swallowed?'

'Excuse me, I listen!' Lynette protested.

'There's a first time for everything.' Xander returned fire with his water, making Lynette splutter in mock outrage.

Fiona and Amy exchanged a look and giggled; whatever had

been niggling away between the two younger girls on the drive over seemed to have been put aside for the time being, and the Christmas spirit was settling over them all again.

The time passed quickly as they ate, with all five of them talking over one another, comparing and exchanging bites of food, and generally enjoying the festive air of a party. The food itself was outstanding, and it was the most relaxed and easy mealtime Bertie could remember in quite some time, perhaps as far back as her birthday, before their own hotel had fallen into its darkest time in ten years. Towards the end, however, she noticed Amy's gaze still travelling around the room, as if she expected to see someone she knew.

'Does this feel familiar to you, Amy?'

Amy looked startled. 'Familiar? How?'

'Well, I noticed you'd gone a bit quiet, and were having a good look around. I thought perhaps this town's somewhere you know. Maybe even your home?'

'It isn't.' Amy's attention returned to her food. 'I was just looking, that's all.'

'That's a pity.'

'We went and had a look at Pencarrack,' Fiona said. 'Did you know that's where Lucy Kempton grew up?'

Bertie nodded. 'Mum told me. What's it like?'

'Huge. There was a fire, you know, so quite a lot of it was rebuilt in about '11 or '12. Oh, and you know that architect who's working on the golf resort?'

'James someone-or-other?'

'That's him. We talked to his wife. Did you know he was blind for almost a year, after he was beaten up and thrown into the valley at the back of Pencarrack?'

'A blind architect?' Bertie winced. 'How awful for him, he must have felt his life was over.'

'What golf resort is this?' Amy asked, reaching for a piece of bread. 'I didn't hear his wife mention that.'

'The one near home,' Bertie told her. 'They sold off part of the farm where Jowan lives, and James Fry is working up there for Norman Pagett.'

'They've stopped for the time being though,' Fiona added. 'They've only done the basement foundations, but they need to drain some of the worst of the flooded ground above it.'

'I found this up at Pencarrack too, buried in the mud.' Fiona rummaged in her pocket and drew out a dark, unevenly shaped coin. 'It's a copper Cornish penny, the miners used to use them.' She rubbed at the dirt with her thumb to show the date better. 'See, it's got 1811 stamped on it.'

'It's filthy!' Lynette exclaimed. 'Put it away at the table.'

'What did you pick it up for, anyway?' Bertie wanted to know. 'It's not as if it's worth anything now.'

'You know what Mum says,' Fiona said. 'See a penny, pick it up—'

'All day long you'll have good luck,' Bertie finished with her, smiling. 'I've never known you to be superstitious in your life! But Lynette's right, it needs a good clean. Better put it away.' She looked at Fiona's coat. 'And speaking of Mum, you'd better get that sleeve stitched up before she uses it as an excuse to finally throw that old coat away.'

'She wouldn't dare!' Fiona smoothed the sleeve as if it were a cat. 'And if she does, I'll only fetch it back.'

'Again.'

'Again!'

'This food's delicious,' Lynette enthused. She turned to summon a waiter. 'Please pass on my compliments to the chef.'

The waiter bobbed his head. 'Of course.'

'Never mind that, just tell him to come out,' Xander said. 'I'd like to thank him myself.'

The waiter disappeared, and Lynette took a swig of wine and turned to Bertie. 'So, tell us more about what you'll be doing when you earn your wings.'

'What a fanciful phrase.' Bertie grinned. 'I suppose I shall be doing what Xander is doing, at first. Just the same, nothing more and nothing less.'

'But will you be able to? You know, even with . . .' She nodded at Bertie's leg.

'The leg I'm being fitted for was actually designed for a pilot,' Bertie pointed out, 'so yes. Even with.'

'Well I'll drink to that!' Lynette raised her glass again just as the kitchen door opened and a young man in grubby whites came into the dining room. He looked to be about Ben's age, not as obviously good-looking, but with a certain rough charm for all that. Lynette certainly seemed quite taken. The waiter led him over to Bertie's table and he bowed briefly.

'I'm pleased you've enjoyed the food,' he said. His voice was more refined than his appearance, and Lynette was still staring at him with fascination. The chef cleared his throat, as he noticed it too, and nodded again. 'Well. Uh, thank you for taking the time to tell me.'

'It was delicious,' Xander said, shooting his sister an amused look. 'I'm sure you'll be going far, once you leave this poky little backwater, and I'll look out for you. What's your name?'

'Thank you, sir. My name's Henry Batten, but I'm generally known as Harry.'

Bertie had taken a sip of her own wine, and swallowed hurriedly when she heard this, hoping to stop Xander from saying anything else. The coughing fit that ensued did the same job, but only for a moment.

'Well,' she heard him go on, through the noise of Fiona banging on her back, 'this is a nice enough little place, very quaint and all that, but I'm sure you're too good for the kind of clientele you get here. Present company excluded of course!' He grinned around at the others. 'Seriously, Harry, you ought to apply for a position at Fox Bay, much more suitable for someone of your talent, the kitchen has a Michelin star already.'

Bertie, her eyes streaming, shook her head frantically at him, but the chef was smiling.

'Very kind of you to say so. Enjoy the rest of your meal.' He nodded around at the others, and caught Bertie's mortified expression. 'I'll ask the waiter to bring you a glass of water, miss.' He backed away, still with a little smile on his face, and Bertie groaned.

'What was all that about?' Xander demanded.

'A *backwater*?' Bertie shook her head. 'His family owns this hotel, you idiot!'

Xander looked at her steadily for a moment, and she could almost see his mind going back over everything he'd said. Then he let out a loud bark of laughter. 'Well, never mind who his mother is, give him a job at your bloody hotel! Speaking of which.' He gestured for his coat. 'Let's go and see what *your* chef's preparing for dinner tonight.'

'Do you ever think of anything except food?' Lynette scolded, rolling her eyes.

Xander pretended to consider. 'On occasion. Used to be easily distracted by motorcycles, and pretty girl racers.' He winked at Bertie. 'Now it's aeroplanes. But yes, you're right, it's mostly food.'

'Well you'd better make sure you're not distracted by any pretty girl fliers,' Lynette said, 'the stakes are a bit higher up there.'

The familiar, good-natured bickering continued as they paid the bill and made their way outside, and Bertie stopped on the hotel steps and rested on her crutches for a minute, letting it wash over her while she stood looking up at the iron-grey sky. A lone Sopwith 1½ Strutter from the training field cut through the air, and she watched it, squinting, as it circled the town. One day she too would be looking down at people coming and going from this hotel, just as they were today; would anyone glance upwards and wonder how it felt to be up there?

She watched the biplane chug away again, and let out a long, slow breath. The interview had been informal at this early stage, but probing, and she'd felt as if every aspect of her life and ambition had been laid bare and picked apart. Questioned. Tested. It had left her wrung out and wavering, close to wanting to throw it all aside and go back to the comfort and safety of her life at Fox Bay.

That had been the easy part. Now all she had to do was tell Jowan that, not only was she definitely going to train here, but that Xander Nicholls was too.

* * *

Mountain Ash, South Wales

The railway station was crowded, late on this Monday evening. Tomorrow was Christmas Eve, so in addition to the usual commuters there were people fighting their way out with small children and packages. Leah made her way out to the street without any real attempt to rush. If she caught the bus, all to the good. If not, it wasn't such a long walk that it would be impossible. Uncomfortable, wet, and certainly dark, but manageable.

The bus was just turning the corner at the end of the street, and Leah shrugged and took a better grip on her case, and followed its journey. It was such a far cry from Guy Bannacott rolling up in his Alfa Romeo, and whisking her off to Fox Bay, that she couldn't help smiling despite the disappointment. At least she'd be returning to it before too long, and to an exciting job too; Rex had come to find her just before she'd left, and told her Helen had been singing her praises as someone good with accents. He'd been hoping she might consider helping Daisy Conrad learn to speak with an authentic English accent, and had even promised her name would appear on the credits of the film. Her own name, immortalised on the reel of a Hollywood picture! It was a miraculous thought. She still didn't know if Daisy was aware of Rex's request, but he was the boss, after all.

She entertained herself with thoughts of the hotel as she manoeuvred through the crowd. There was the treasure hunt tomorrow, of course. The prizes were never anything grand, but everyone got involved, and while the guests were outside all day, weather permitting, the family mucked in together to decorate the hotel. It was a wonderful chance to rekindle the intimacies denied them for much of the year, and Fleur was always in a good mood, Guy revelled in every moment, and played to the gallery beautifully, and this year, as well as the excitement of Hollywood coming to stay, there was a real sense of joyful relief after a difficult and worrying year. Everything had become settled and peaceful since Adam had saved the hotel . . . Well, Helen and Adam between them at any rate.

And that was the problem, wasn't it? Helen and Adam. Everything about the two of them made perfect sense; friends since childhood, knowing each other inside-out, and heart and soul . . . Even if Helen didn't return his love, it was hers for the taking, so what did that make Leah? A temporary diversion? A toy to be played with until it was his turn for the real prize? Certainly second best, if not third or fourth . . . or who knew how many?

Leah set her face in the direction of the house in which she'd grown up, her mind now fully on what she had lost. But Adam Coleridge had never really been hers at all. If only she could have remained Susannah Paterson; that woman had held a fascination for him at least . . . She let out a brief, humourless laugh, startling a passer-by; he'd even come straight out and said he'd preferred "Susannah's" Scots accent to her own Welsh one, and she'd told herself it had come from a place of anger. She had even believed that, for a while, but now she knew the truth and it made her feel stupid and angry.

Side stepping as a car drove too close to the edge of the pavement, she acknowledged that self-deception as just one more sign that she'd been seeing everything through a happy, love-induced haze. But now she was away from that life she could see it all for what it was; she was a substitute for Helen, who'd taken up all the empty places in Adam's heart without even knowing it. Certainly without trying. By the time she returned to the hotel after Christmas she'd be thinking more clearly, she'd be stronger, and she'd be able to tell him that Leah Marshall was nobody's second choice. She was setting him free to pursue the woman he truly loved; it would be her gift to him. To them both.

The thought of watching a new kind of relationship developing between Adam and Helen gave her a sharp pain beneath her ribs, and she caught her breath with the strength of it. They'd try to hide it, because they were both good people and they'd know what it would do to her, but it was as inevitable as the December rain falling from the sky, and just as unstoppable.

The crawling car had slowed further, and to her annoyance it rolled to a stop just where she was in the habit of crossing to take the road that led out to her little hamlet a mile or so away. She tutted under her breath and stepped back to cross behind it, but the driver's door opened and a familiar voice cut through her irritation.

'Sorry I'm late.'

She turned, her heart thudding so hard she could hear it echo through the scarf wrapped around her ears. Her voice was hardly more than a whisper. 'Gregory?'

'We're in Wales now, it's Glynn here, remember?' Then he went on, as casually as if they were the best of friends, 'I meant to meet you off the train, but I couldn't find anywhere to park. Hop in and I'll take you home.'

Leah didn't move. 'How did you know I'd be here?'

'Your aunt, of course.' He stepped around to open the passenger side door. 'Step lively, darling, we're holding up traffic.'

Aunt Mary? Surely she wouldn't have told him, not voluntarily ... A cold feeling swept over her, and he must have read the thought that was suddenly making her feel sick, because he smiled. 'Your aunt is fine, Lee, we've talked.' He took her case and slid it onto the back seat. 'Look, it's a long story, and best told in the comfort of a warm car. Come on. You're quite safe, this is me, remember?'

It was true, no matter what the reason for his being imprisoned, he had never raised either hand or voice to her, never caused her a moment's grief until that final job, and she knew that he loved her still. Perhaps not with the depth of emotion with which his brother had loved her, but well enough, in his own way.

'Come on,' he said again, more softly.

Leah's legs moved her, without thought or protest, and she slid onto the seat and closed her eyes as the passenger door slammed shut. So this had been the Fates' plan all along, then. Daniel, Helen, the cubs, and Adam ... they had all been an exciting, devastating, and finally perfect, little interlude, but now it was over. Her husband was taking her back to their marital home, and soon it would be as if neither of them had been away. Glynn's hand left the steering wheel to press hers where it lay on her lap, and although her face rewarded him with a mechanical smile she felt only a kind of flat acceptance, as, after nearly fifteen years and two new lives, destiny dragged her back onto the path she thought she'd left behind.

CHAPTER TEN

Higher Valley Farm
Christmas Eve morning

Beth closed the ring box and put it into her pocket. Jowan's stammering announcement last night had brought a broad smile to her and Alfie's faces, and even Jory had pumped his brother's hand and lain off the scoffing, for once. The sound of the three male Nancarrows clattering across the yard in working boots brought an unexpected lump to her throat; how long now, before that familiar sound was just a memory?

All the Nancarrows would attend the midnight service at St Adhwynn's, but it would be Jowan's second Christmas Eve sitting with the Foxes, since he and Bertie had become close. Beth enjoyed seeing him lift himself out of his busy working life, even if it were just for one night of the year, but once she gave him this box, that one night would become his life. He'd be part of another family, and would gradually begin cutting ties with his own.

She'd reconciled herself long ago to the fact that her boys would not be with her forever; even if they continued working on the farm they would both want their own homes, with their own families. It was a miracle they'd both stayed at Higher Valley until their late twenties, but in some ways that was going to make it harder when they eventually left. A sharp loss, indeed. She turned back to the table to straighten porridge spoons beside four places that would soon become three. And then two. And then what?

But, she scolded herself, there was no use dwelling on the sadness of that; they'd all been up with the lark, including her, and had already put in two hours of hard work, now they were all ready for a good hot breakfast. She picked up the post and put it next to Alfie's plate. One letter had a Caernoweth postmark, which made her smile; the annual round-up of news from Keir Garvey, no doubt, which always put Alfie in a good mood. He'd settled back in at Trethkellis well enough, but he openly admitted that he missed Priddy Farm, and the friends he'd made since he'd married his childhood sweetheart and moved down there.

The twins kicked their boots off by the door while Alfie seized the coal scuttle and went back out to fill it. Beth waited until Jowan had poured his tea, then wordlessly handed him the box. Jowan stared at it blankly for a moment, then opened it. His face, when he lifted it, was worth every moment Beth had spent chewing over her decision, and his eyes seemed to pick up the sparkle of the brightly polished stones.

'What's that?' Jory asked, leaning across to look.

'It's your grandmother's ring,' Beth told him. 'When you meet your future bride we'll try and do something like the same for you, I promise.'

Jory grinned. 'You don't have to worry about me being jealous,' he said. 'If Jo wants to throw his life away he's more than welcome to a few shiny stones to do it with. I've got more sense.'

'Who'd have you anyway?' Jowan returned smartly. He ignored his brother's snort, and rose to put his arms around Beth. 'Thanks, Mum. She'll love it.'

'Who'll love what?' Alfie set the filled coal scuttle by the door. 'Oh, you've give it him then?'

'It's Midnight Mass tonight,' Beth reminded him. 'He needs time to practise how he's going to ask her.'

Alfie eased off his boots and came over to sit with his nephews. He picked up the post, and sure enough his mouth lifted when he saw his old friend's handwriting on the letter from Caernoweth. Beth put the bowl of porridge on the table and went back to frying bacon, letting the murmur of voices wash over her, and trying to store it in her mind along with the other memories she could sense slipping away.

When she came back to the table Alfie and the boys had almost finished their porridge. Jowan kept eyeing the ring box beside his plate with a look of mild panic, and Beth sent Alfie a smile, expecting either a returning one, or an eye roll and an amused glance ceiling-ward. She got neither, he only looked back at his plate, and ate steadfastly through the remainder of his breakfast without any of his usual signs of enjoyment.

Beth said nothing, but when she looked at the pile of opened post and saw a letter on the top, typed on headed paper: Ministry of Agriculture and Fisheries, her heart sank. What now? Were they finally to be subject to a compulsory purchase order by the council? It had happened to at least two other farms that she knew of, and was a permanent source of background worry. One of many.

Jowan and Jory bolted their food and went back out, Jowan eager to finish his work in plenty of time to prepare for a momentous evening and dress for church, Jory just as keen to smarten himself up, but Beth doubted he'd come with them, his glad rags would probably be paraded around Bude instead. Christmas Eve would be a quieter time now than it had ever been in the past, and although Beth had for years sweated and grumbled her way through all she had to do, she felt a sharp pang at the loss of excitement, noise, and arguing that had always reigned in the house at this time of year.

'Will you help with the veg later?' she asked Alfie, who was still finishing his eggs. 'I want to get it all ready before church.'

He nodded. 'Can do.'

'Are you alright?'

'Right as rain.'

'You look ... off. Is the ministry making things difficult?'

He looked surprised, then followed her gaze to the letter. 'Oh, that. No, it's nothing.' He gathered up the post and tucked it into his pocket. 'Right, I'll be back in time to take you to town later if you still want to go.'

'Yes, please. I just need a few bits to make tomorrow special.' For one sad moment she wondered if any of it really mattered anyway, then she pushed the thought away. If anything it mattered more than ever, after all it was likely to be their last Christmas all together.

'Right then.' He laid down his knife and fork and pushed his plate away. 'Thanks, it was good.'

But the words sounded mechanical, and Beth felt another tremor of discomfort. She watched him tugging his boots back on, and waited for him to speak, because, no matter what he said, she didn't like the look of that letter. But he merely sent her a brief smile and went back out into the cold winter morning.

*

The letter was still foremost in Beth's mind as she selected the bird for tomorrow's table. The barn echoed with loud, frantic clucking and the beating of wings, as she picked up a chicken and turned it upside down. After one quick, practised motion the chicken hung limp from her fingers.

'That's a good one.'

Beth turned to see Alfie in the doorway. 'It'll do,' she allowed. 'Big enough for us four, at any rate.'

'Want any help with it before we go?'

'Oh, are we going now? I wasn't expecting you back 'til a fair bit later. I've not even put the water on to boil yet.'

'Do it when we get back.' He had an odd look on his face, and as he came further into the barn she identified it as nervousness, a touch of determination, and a strange, low-key excitement. Her heart gave an inexplicable little leap.

When she came back down, changed ready for a trip into town, Alfie was reading one of the letters he'd had that morning, but it was the one he'd got from Mr Garvey, not the ministry.

He looked up as she came back into the kitchen, and his eyes were bright. He blinked rapidly. 'You look smart.'

'What's in the letter, Alfie?' she said softly.

He lowered his face again. 'Ellen's died.'

'Mr Garvey's wife?'

Alfie nodded. 'She'd been ill a long while, but they thought she was getting better. She went a few days back.'

'You knew her too, didn't you?'

'I did. She worked up at Wheal Furzy before it closed, then at the Tinner's Arms.' He gave a sad little laugh. 'She was a fierce one, too. Perfect for keeping Keir in his place. Keir's that lost, now. He's . . .' He trailed away and looked down at his feet. 'It makes you think, and to be truthful I've done nothing else since breakfast, but . . . life's short isn't it?'

'It is.' They all knew it; Toby's ghost still sat in the chair by the window ten years on.

He took a deep breath. 'You shouldn't . . . *We* shouldn't . . . I mean, we should all take happiness where we can find it. Shouldn't we?'

He sounded almost pleading, and Beth felt the sting of tears. 'Yes.'

Finally he looked up and his eyes found hers. 'I've been lonely a long while, Beth. A *long* while. Since long before Sarah went her own way.'

'You'd have found another, if not for the war. And then coming here to help us after we lost Toby.' Beth hoped the trembling she felt in the hollow of her belly wasn't reflected on her face.

'Maybe.'

'Plenty of women around here would have been glad to,' she rushed on, hating the sudden silence. 'And with men in such short supply—'

'Thank you,' he said wryly, but his smile told her he wasn't as insulted as he pretended. 'Are we going into Bude, then?'

She stared at him blankly for a moment, then came to life. 'Of course. Just let me get my coat and purse.'

He said no more about the letter during their trip, nor about the realisation that life – and happiness – were passing him by. But now and again, when she sneaked a sidelong glance at him as he drove, she saw the ghost of a smile curving his lips, and the little warm spot inside her spread a little further.

* * *

The buzz of conversation and laughter flourished among the guests waiting in the lounge for the start of the Christmas Eve treasure hunt. Although the bar would not be open until the evening, Ben had been pouring champagne quite liberally and the devil-may-care spirit of Christmas had now well and truly descended.

Fiona and Amy had both been permitted a small glass each, but Amy had set hers aside. 'I don't want to get squiffy and blurt something out,' she murmured, in answer to Fiona's surprised look. 'Can you just imagine?'

Fiona could. It wouldn't take long for the questions to start. 'Well pass it to me, then, when no one's looking.'

'Are you sure?'

'I'm quite used to it, don't worry. I wonder who we'll be paired with?'

'Who's drawing the names?'

'Granny usually does it. Or she might ask Daisy or Freddie to do it this year.' She looked around, but although Daisy was there, there was no sign of Freddie. 'I wish we could stay out longer than lunchtime.'

'Can't we?'

'Well, you're a sort of guest, so I suppose you can do what you like.' Fiona pulled a face. 'But I've got to come in and work with the others. Family tradition. At least I've got my lucky miner's penny.' She pulled it out of her pocket, now cleaned. 'Maybe it'll help us to win nice and quickly so I don't miss out on too much.'

'Ladies and gentlemen!' The ringing sound of a cocktail stirrer on a glass hushed the voices in the room as Helen smiled around at them all. 'I'm *so* sorry to keep you all waiting,' she went on, but Fiona caught the look that flew between her and Adam and guessed it had been a deliberate ploy, in order to allow the guests to drink extra and mingle more. She didn't know whose idea it had been, but it had certainly worked.

'Thank you for choosing your partners for the treasure hunt,' Helen went on. 'As you know, I do like to mix up the groupings a little bit, so you're going to be teams of four, and I'm now going to ask Mrs Fleur Fox to draw pairs from this rather swish-looking Homburg. It was kindly loaned by Mr Rex Kelly, who, as you probably know by now, is all the way from Hollywood!'

A ripple of applause ran around the room, and Rex pretended to doff his hat and only then to realise he wasn't wearing it. He rolled his eyes and pointed to it in Helen's hand, making an exaggerated *gosh, I'm silly* face. The piece of silent theatre turned the polite applause into relaxed laughter, and a louder show of appreciation.

'Thank you, Mr Kelly.' Helen passed the Homburg to Fleur, who drew out a piece of paper and read aloud, 'Xander and Lynette Nicholls.' She drew another. 'Mr and Mrs Walker, two of our most loyal guests, all the way from Manchester.'

The two pairs waved to each other across the room, and drew together in their new team, and more names were pulled from the hat.

'Daisy, dear, you don't appear to have a partner written down,' Fleur said. All eyes swivelled to Daisy Conrad, who stood beside Rex looking sweet and shy, her trademark red hair completely covered by a ravishing blue silk scarf that trailed a fringe down across one shoulder.

'Freddie's not feeling well this morning,' she explained. 'So I thought I'd just tag along if that's alright.'

Immediately there rose a clamour, as various guests sought

to invite her onto their teams, but Helen held up a hand and strained to see to the back of the room. 'Father Trevelyan? You're not partnered either, are you?'

The vicar of St Adhwynn's turned puce. 'I wasn't planning to take part, Mrs Fox, I'm only here to help.'

'Oh, nonsense!' Helen beckoned him forward. 'It's very good of you, but I think your superior brain might be put to better use on the clues we've laid out there for you all, don't you? Ben and Bertie have been particularly fiendish this year, and poor Daisy doesn't know the area at all. Who are they paired with, Fleur?'

Fleur dipped her hand into the hat. 'Fiona and Amy!'

Fiona heard Amy give a little groan, and was inclined, for once, to agree; Daisy and Freddie had proved extremely dull guests, after all the excitement their arrival had created. Daisy certainly didn't seem to have much about her, she was all practised smiles and impeccable manners, and excuses to hide away from everyone. Just like Freddie today.

Daisy and the vicar joined them, Daisy flashing her famous smile. 'Thank you so much, Father Trevelyan. I'll try not to let you down.'

'You must call me George,' he stammered, no doubt aware of the envious eyes boring into his back.

'So what do we do now?' Amy wanted to know. 'Do we just go out and look for clues?'

'We're each given an envelope with our own starting point,' Fiona said. 'Each place has a different first clue, taking the group through a different route to the final prize. It's basically a race.' She looked around and caught Ben's eyes on them, frowning. Her first instinct was defensive; what had she done wrong now? Then she realised it was Daisy he was looking at, and that the frown was more speculative than annoyed; he was obviously less impervious to the woman's charms than he'd pretended to be.

Her head buzzed with the champagne, and she was about to go over and tease him when their mother called for attention again.

'The prize is a magnum of this lovely champagne we're all enjoying, and tonight's dinner will be cooked for you personally by our chef Nicholas Gough, who many of you will know earned a Michelin star for the hotel restaurant just two months ago, when the latest Guide came out.'

'What's a Michelin star?' Amy whispered, under the applause that broke out.

Fiona shrugged. 'Means he can cook.'

She heard Daisy give an unladylike snort of laughter into her glass, and wondered if she hadn't judged the girl too harshly.

They were ushered forward to collect an envelope from the neat pile on the bar. Fiona grinned at George. 'Ah, perfect, we start at St 'Dwinn's.'

'Where's that?' Daisy asked.

'The church. It's not far, come on, we've only got until lunchtime, then you and Father Trevelyan are on your own.'

'Oh! Why is that?'

Fiona told her about her chores, and Father Trevelyan clucked disapprovingly.

'I *told* your mother I'd help!'

'But you wouldn't want to go changing bed linen now, would you? Come on! I want that champagne so I can give it to Bertie and Jowan when he finally proposes to her.' She was also quite keen to get out into the fresh air and clear her head, and saw Amy frowning at her.

'Don't worry,' she murmured, as they crossed the threshold and

153

stepped out into the now thankfully dry day. 'I might have drunk it a bit fast, but I'm not going to say anything.'

'About what?' Daisy asked, appearing at her shoulder.

'About ... about how Ben has a fancy for you,' Fiona said, clutching at the first thing that came to mind, and was surprised to see Daisy flush; she must be used to being worshipped by now. All the same, Ben wouldn't thank her for saying anything, and would certainly think twice about letting her near any champagne in the future, should he find out.

'I suggest you scratch any memory of me saying that,' she advised brightly. 'Anyway, let's get to it, shall we?'

They spent some time searching for the clue at the church, keeping watch for any of the other couples heading towards them, though Daisy spent more time looking around her in awe, and exclaiming over the age of the wooden pews.

'It's all so beautiful!' She ran her fingers over the wood, which was dark and gnarled, but gleaming and smelling of Mansion, ready for the Midnight Mass that night. 'Oh, I'd love to be married right here!'

'My parents were,' Fiona ventured, a little swell of sadness damping the fizzing sensation of the champagne. '*Everyone* came, so they said, and had to wait out in the churchyard because there wasn't room in here.'

'It's tiny,' Daisy agreed, 'but if I could find the man who'd be happy to marry somewhere like this I know he'd be the right man for me.'

George looked surprised. 'But you'll be used to such grandeur.'

'I hate it.'

Before Fiona could question Daisy's blunt response, Amy produced the clue from the font, with a cry of triumph, and read aloud. 'Now that you've found this Heavenly clue, stay here 'til you find out if love awaits you.'

'Love,' Fiona mused. 'The altar?'

Amy started in that direction.

'No, there won't be any more in the church,' George said, frowning. '*If love awaits you*. Where do you meet people you could possibly fall in love with?'

Amy shrugged. 'At a dance?'

'Hmm. But there won't be anything as far afield as the village hall, and the last dance I went to was here, in a marquee. Your sister's twenty-first, Fiona. What a night that was!' The vicar blushed as he mentioned it, and Fiona remembered how Sally Penneck, and Bertie's other telephone exchange friends had taken him under their wing and shown him the newest dance crazes, spinning him until he'd nearly collapsed.

'In a bedroom?' she blurted. 'You know,' she went on, embarrassed at the way her thoughts had followed one another, and how it must have sounded to the vicar, 'dreaming of romance?'

Amy nodded thoughtfully. 'But there are so many rooms in the hotel, whose could—'

'Wait,' Daisy interrupted, perking up. 'You have tennis courts, don't you?'

Fiona nodded. 'Two of them.'

'Right then. Tennis score for zero is love, right? Do you have someplace where people can sit while they're waiting for their turn on court?'

George grinned and pumped her hand, as if she were a parishioner who'd just donated her life savings to the church. 'You're a little genius, my dear!' He turned to Fiona.

'The gazebo!' they said together.

'Shall we take the clue with us?' Amy asked, with a wicked little grin, but Daisy snatched it out of her hand, laughing.

'Better not, though I like your style!'

Amy might have thawed a bit then, Fiona thought, she certainly looked less dismissive. They set off across the churchyard at a trot while Daisy replaced the clue ready for the next team. She followed them quickly, but as she was latching the gate she gave a little shout, and Fiona turned to see she had her thumb in her mouth; Daisy pulled a face at the bead of blood that appeared when she removed it.

'Damn!'

'What did you do?' Fiona said, peering more closely.

'I just caught it on the latch and pinched it a bit. It's nothing, I'll put my glove back on, that'll soak it up.'

'We can't have you bleeding all over your fine glove,' George said, and Amy's face predictably darkened again.

'I'm fine,' Daisy insisted. 'It'll stop bleeding in a minute.'

'Anyway we need you here to help us solve the next clue. I'm sure one of these young ladies would be happy to run back to the hotel and find a plaster.'

'A what? Oh, like a Band-Aid?'

'I'll go,' Fiona said, catching sight of Amy's mutinous expression. Besides, she could just imagine what her mother would say if she found Amy hunting around in the office for the first aid tin. 'Keep sucking your thumb until I get back.' She laughed as Daisy deliberately crossed her eyes and stuck her thumb back in her mouth, and decided the girl had turned out to be quite nice after all. Bad news for Ben.

The hotel was eerily quiet. With most of the work taking place in the kitchen, the lobby was deserted and only the faint sound of glasses being set out at the bar drifted through from the lounge. Ben was in his element at this time of year, and Fiona envied him the joy he found in his hotel work; how could she be expected to find the same level of satisfaction stripping beds and re-filling water jugs? The sooner she was taken on at the lifeboat station, the better.

Guy was supposed to be taking over from Martin Berry, who'd been given the two days off, but he was nowhere to be seen. Mum would be furious if she knew he had left the reception unattended.

Fiona stepped behind the deserted desk, and stopped dead, her hand on the office door handle as an unmistakeable voice came clearly through the door.

'It'd kill my dad!'

The voice was one she'd heard blaring over the cinema screen in Bude, usually speaking with a faintly sardonic lilt, accompanied by the lazy smile that had melted hearts the world over. What was Freddie doing using the telephone in her mother's office, when there was a perfectly good one on the reception desk? Fiona was about to go in and find out, but her hand froze again as Guy's voice responded.

'He loves you, Freddie, that will never change. But don't you think he has a right to know?'

'No! At least ... not yet. Maybe someday. Oh hell, it's such a mess ...'

'Don't worry. Come here.'

Her heart thudding, and her head still spinning a little, Fiona bent and peered through the keyhole, but all she could see was the corner of the desk, and one black-sleeved elbow. The elbow moved, rose, and then Fiona could see a stylishly striped Fair Isle sweater as the black-clad arm went around it.

She backed away, feeling her eyes widen until they burned. Guy had been the subject of gentle teasing, certainly, but no one had ever really thought his feelings for the young man would be returned. Both he and Freddie would be mortified, distraught even, to know they'd been heard, let alone seen; Freddie might even be driven to leave Fox Bay, which would be as disastrous for their reputation as the revelation about his private life would be to his own. *Lying for the very best of reasons, indeed.*

The other nearest first aid tin was in the kitchen, and as Fiona went to fetch Daisy's plaster from there instead, an uncharacteristically dark thought struck her: while she didn't exactly doubt Guy's intention to help Amy, he might just as quickly change his mind, and it never hurt to have another weapon in one's arsenal.

CHAPTER ELEVEN

In November 1923, a short-lived but particularly virulent outbreak of influenza in West Cornwall had given rise to the panic that the Spanish flu had reared its terrifying head again. Many members of the Fox Bay staff had gone down with it, and both Fleur and the then nine-year-old Fiona had been stricken too. To Helen's relief Leah had stayed in Cornwall to nurse them both, and by the middle of December the outbreak had subsided, though several key members of staff were still too weak to return to work.

Bookings at the hotel had been greatly reduced, of course, and Guy had respectfully asked at which point he should write to the guests who still intended to stay, explaining that their reservations would be cancelled, so Helen had promptly called the staff and family together, and made a simple announcement.

'We're staying open for Christmas, and where work needs to be done, we're going to be the ones to do it. Any questions?'

Everyone except Ben, who'd given a little hoot of approval, had been too surprised to respond, and so they had stayed open; those family members who were able had mucked in with anything that needed doing, no matter how menial, and the guests thought it charming and asked if it would be the same next year. After some consideration, the family agreed it should be. It had become tradition that most of the staff were given the night off, and the Foxes donned aprons and uniforms and pitched in to fill the gaps. It never failed to bring a sense of novelty and camaraderie; part of the fabric of a Fox Bay Christmas, for which guests were prepared to pay top price if they were invited to secure a room.

Not everyone was delighted with the arrangement, however; Nicholas Gough could often be seen pacing the grounds with his hands clasped behind his back, his head down, but no one dared approach him to find out whether he was planning menus or walking off a fit of frustration.

Leah's absence was keenly felt this year, and Helen knew her friend would have given anything to be elbow-deep in potato peelings or soapy water, rather than facing days of endless quiet with her aunt. Adam, however, had been sceptical at first, sensing a trick, and resistant. Once he'd finally, reluctantly, become resigned to it, Helen was determined not to allow him any excuse to back out, so when he appeared in the kitchen wearing his suit she sent him off again to change.

'But I've got—'

'No meetings, no consultations, and no need to ruin a perfectly good suit. What you *have* got is a pile of vegetables to prepare, for guests who have paid good money.' Helen smiled, not entirely without sympathy, at the look on his face. 'Besides, it always brings us closer together as a family. I *thought* that was what you wanted?'

'Oh, alright, since you insist.'

Helen half-expected him to vanish and only reappear at dinner time, but he returned after twenty minutes, wearing a striped wool sweater and a pair of green Oxford bags. Helen had rarely seen him looking so casual and comfortable, and she kept sneaking sidelong glances at him as he worked, wondering if he were missing Leah as much as she knew Leah would be missing him. She hoped so, but he had brightened so considerably that she suspected his mind was on anything but the damp cottage in Wales.

'Have you met Rex yet?'

'Years ago. Dreadful man.'

'You know what I mean!' She threw a piece of carrot at him.

'Mrs Fox!' Nicholas Gough shot her a pained look, and she gave him back an apologetic smile and turned back to Adam, her eyes and mouth wide in a look of mock dismay.

Adam grinned. 'No, I haven't seen him, either I've been busy or he's been locked away with the worker . . . with the actors. But don't worry, I'll apologise the moment I do.'

'Make sure you do it before dinner, I don't want any awkwardness between you.'

'I'll find him the minute he comes back in.' Adam pulled a face at Bertie as she rolled by, a bowl of marinade in her lap. 'Your mother doesn't change, does she? Still a frightful nag, just like when she was ten.'

Bertie offered him a strained smile and handed the bowl to Nicholas, who took a small silver spoon from his pocket and dipped it into the paste. The others fell silent as he tasted, and only relaxed as he nodded and wiped the spoon with the cloth at his shoulder. Helen shook her head; the chef did enjoy his theatrical moments. Thankfully his sous-chef was much easier-going, and rolled his eyes when he was sure his boss wasn't looking. It would be a shame to lose him in the new year, but he was deservedly moving on, and up. Helen had entrusted the hiring of his replacement to Adam, much to Fleur's disapproval.

'You know I'm fond of him,' she'd said, which seemed to preface so many of her concerns about Adam Coleridge, 'but what does he know about hiring a chef?'

'As much as either of us,' Helen pointed out. 'Mr Gough has been here an age, and he brought Mr Stevens with him. We've never had to do it either.'

Fleur hadn't found a response to that, but Helen had felt sorry for her blunt words when she saw a look of tired resignation cross her mother-in-law's face. 'I don't mean to let him make all the decisions,' she said gently. 'You and I will conduct the final interview together, once we're down to the last two. Let Adam earn his place by doing the leg work first.'

Fleur had seemed slightly mollified, and had returned to her war memorial project. But even that was nearing completion now, and Helen couldn't help wondering what Fleur would do then to fill her time.

She glanced at Bertie again, who'd taken the marinade back to her station to begin brushing it over the lamb cutlets. The girl had returned from her day trip full of the joys of a suddenly bright future, but today she'd been subdued again, and Helen wanted the chance to talk to her at length, and alone. Since that was going to be impossible today she did the next best thing.

'Adam, would you go and find Ben, and begin putting the tables together in the dining room? Fiona's written the cards, they're in the office. Best linens, but if they look crumpled or creased put them in the laundry and I'll iron them myself after lunch ... Blast!' She'd promised to iron Leah's dress too, which was probably still sitting in a crumpled heap behind the reception

162

desk. She sent a silent apology to her friend, but in all likelihood Leah was right, she wouldn't have occasion to wear it anyway.

When Adam had left, she took up a position next to Bertie's station and began chopping mint for the second batch of marinade. 'Are you alright, darling? Is Jowan still coming to church tonight?'

'I think so.'

'You're not sure?'

'Unless I've put him off.' Bertie sighed. 'I think he wanted to propose in the New Year.'

'And now you think he won't?'

'I haven't told him I've spoken to the recruitment officer at Caernoweth yet.'

'Ah. How do you think he'll react?'

'I don't know,' Bertie sighed. 'He said he'd support any decision I make, but that was before, when we first got back together. Now it's all becoming more likely, it might be a different story. He might change his mind. And even if he doesn't ...' She didn't finish.

Helen used the edge of her knife to scrape the chopped mint towards Bertie. 'Didn't he think it would happen?'

'I don't know. To be honest I'm sure he wouldn't mind at all, if it weren't for who else will probably still be there.'

'I see.' Helen gave her daughter a sidelong look. 'Well, Xander's a glamorous man, and very charming. No one would blame you.'

Bertie looked horrified at the thought. 'I adore Xander, but now I know him properly I couldn't imagine spending an entire day with him, let alone the rest of my life!'

'*You* haven't had second thoughts about flying though?'

'Not a bit.'

'So assuming Jo still wants to marry you, what else is troubling you?'

Bertie looked uncomfortable. 'I hinted that I was expecting a ring. I shouldn't have done that, he doesn't have any money for one.'

'But he won't let *that* put him off, will he?'

'Probably not,' Bertie allowed, 'but I'm worried he might borrow money he can't afford, and then end up selling the Squirrel to pay it back.'

'You've been thinking about this a lot, then.'

'Practically nothing but.'

'My advice is to put it out of your mind,' Helen said, curling her hand over Bertie's short, sleek hair. It had been a long time since she'd felt able to do such a thing without hesitating, and she was gratified when Bertie raised a trusting face to her. 'This is a strange time, Bertie, people say all kinds of things they don't mean, or have given little thought to. I'm sure he knows that. I'm sorry, I don't mean to sound dismissive.'

'No, you're right. There's nothing I can do about it now. I'll talk to him later, and tell him it was just a joke, he doesn't have to buy anything.'

'He'll still want to, but he'll have time to save up, once he knows you're still keen and that this pilot training hasn't changed all that.' But Helen didn't want to pursue that subject any further, not today; she still felt a kind of cold terror at the thought of what Bertie intended to do, and was worried she might slip up and show it. 'What do you think of our guests, then?'

'I haven't seen much of them.' Bertie began brushing the cutlets again. 'You only have to look at Ben to know he's awfully sold on Daisy, though I'm quite sure he doesn't want to be. And anyway, once all the novelty wears off she'll be as keen as anything to run back to her life of luxury.'

'And he's got Lily to think about,' Helen added.

'Poor Ben, a thorn between two flowers.' Bertie grinned. 'I'm sure he won't marry Lily either though, she's too ambitious. She won't want to leave the Summerleaze, and he definitely won't want to leave here.'

Helen wished she could be as sure. 'Right, speaking of Ben, I'm going to pop my head around the dining room door and check he and Adam aren't shirking. I'm sure I heard a piano a few minutes ago, and it wasn't playing anything I'd like your grandmother to hear.'

Christmas Eve lunch for the guests was catered, as it was every year, by a company in Bude. At one o'clock precisely they delivered hot soup, fresh bread, and a hearty plum pudding to the treasure hunters at the gazebo, and brought a few covers to the hotel too, so that the decorating and the dinner preparations continued uninterrupted.

This year the surprisingly reclusive Freddie Wishart was the only abstainer from the outdoor fun, and Guy offered to take his lunch, to be served in his room, as the dining room was closed for the day. Helen handed it to him, trying to detect any sign of nervousness, but there was only habitual cool professionalism as Guy took the covered dish; it seemed the reality of the young man's presence had finally chipped through the layer of fascination his fame had created. She herself was still entranced by "the kids", probably because they had kept so very much to themselves, but hopefully tonight, provided they attended the dinner, of course, they would enjoy the rare chance to relax in company.

Fiona and Amy returned dutifully, but with such evident reluctance that Helen relented and sent them back out again. 'You can make it up tomorrow by being extra helpful during the Christmas lunch. *Extra* helpful,' she repeated firmly, as the girls had looked at each other with glee. She was reminded that Fiona was really quite a solitary girl now she had left school, with only those at the lifeboat station for company, and hoped she and Amy would remain friends once the girl had been safely returned to her family.

The next time she saw her younger daughter, Helen was in the lounge with Ben, putting the finishing touches to the tree decorations. Fiona burst through the glass doors brandishing the small trophy Ben had hidden inside an empty milk churn in the kitchen garden.

'We did it! We're the brainiest!'

'You can't claim the prize!' Helen protested. 'Everyone will think it's a cheat!'

'It was my lucky penny.' Fiona showed her the misshapen piece of copper. 'See a penny, pick it up, and so on.'

'And to think you've always mocked my superstitions!' Helen smiled. 'I don't know that a miner's token works in the same way. Perhaps you're just cleverer than you realised.'

'Actually it was Daisy who solved most of the clues,' Fiona said, shooting a sly glance at her brother. 'She's *really* clever, you know.'

Ben ignored her and gave the brass rail he was polishing one last flick with his cloth. 'All ready in here, I'll go and check the dining room.'

When the door had swung shut behind him Helen turned back to Fiona. 'You shouldn't do that, darling. Daisy will be going back to America soon, what's the use of pushing them together when it'll only break his heart?'

'I'm not trying to push them together, I just want him to stop trying so hard to *not* like her.'

Helen shook her head. The girl didn't realise yet how easily young hearts could be manipulated, but she would learn. She just hoped it wouldn't be the hard way.

'Just leave them alone,' she said. 'Go and give the trophy to either Daisy or Father Trevelyan, before the others get back and start calling it a fixed job.'

'Alright.' Fiona turned to leave, but Helen called her back.

'I can't believe you're still wearing that ratty old coat, and look at that torn sleeve! For heaven's sake, it's time to throw it away, surely?'

'I'll stitch it! I promise.'

'You and I both know your stitching's never really been good enough for something like that,' Helen protested. 'You *always* give it to Guy to do, and you always think I don't know about it!' But she sensed she was losing the battle already. 'Go on then, but see you do it yourself this time, Guy's busy. And wear your good coat to the service tonight!'

Gradually, as other teams discovered the losers' envelope left in the milk churn, they returned with cheerful resignation, muddied and refreshed, and joined the others in the lounge to take a welcome hot toddy from Guy's samovar.

They exclaimed satisfactorily over the exquisite, tasteful decorations that had appeared while they were out. Ben and Adam had hung a luxuriant garland over the fireplace, and Ben had then set to work pinning wreaths of rich green holly to the walls, and setting tiny fairy lights to perfectly catch the glossy leaves, and twinkle along the bar. Adam had then returned to the kitchen, and Ben had enlisted Helen's help to put the finishing touches.

The big Douglas fir tree in the lobby was always the focus of the Christmas decorations at Fox Bay, and both lounge and dining room featured smaller versions, made from feathers but decorated in the same colours. Beneath this one, a model railway ran through a forest of wooden trees on its simple track; Helen had laid cotton wool along the tops of the trees to give it a winter feel, and Rex Kelly drifted over, mulled brandy in hand, to look over it appreciatively.

'It was Harry's when he was a boy,' Helen said. 'Of course it was clockwork back then, but Guy said it would be nice to take it out again every Christmas, so he bought the Hornby engine himself.'

Rex smiled. 'There's something about a model railroad set at Christmas, isn't there?' He paused, and Helen waited, guessing at the real reason for his coming over. She was right.

'I saw Mr Coleridge a few minutes ago.'

'Ah. How did it go?'

'He's a charming man, I remembered that right.' Somehow it didn't have the sound of a compliment. Rex stared into his glass and swirled the drink thoughtfully. 'First thing he did was shake my hand and apologise. No excuses.'

Helen nodded, but was privately surprised; Adam's usual way was to present any reason at all as to why something wasn't his fault. It seemed Leah's straight-talking ways were proving to be a good influence on him.

'So are the two of you going to be able to live under the same roof for a few weeks?'

'Sure. But you can tell him he has you to thank for my being able to forgive him for what he did.'

'Me?'

'If you hadn't put his case so well, I'd have been out of here the second I saw him.' He shrugged. 'But I'm willing to accept that a lot of water has flowed under the bridge, that he regrets what he did, and that he's mended his ways.'

'He's certainly done that.' Helen proffered her hand. 'Thank you, Mr Kelly. You're a true gentleman.'

'As long as he's aware I'm watching him.'

'Of course. I hope you enjoy dinner tonight.' She gave him a brief grin. 'And it might make it more enjoyable to know that Mr Coleridge peeled the potatoes, and hated every minute of it.'

Rex snorted laughter, and his cool, polite expression warmed again. 'It tastes better already.'

* * *

Daisy blushingly received the prize and kissed the beaming, and far less shy now, Father Trevelyan on the cheek, and soon afterwards people began drifting away to change into their Christmas finery for dinner at seven. Bertie went around the dining room with a lap full of heavy, beautifully embroidered napkins, and folded them into the shapes of boats, as had been the tradition for as long as she could remember. As usual she felt the little pinch of envy for the guests, and their superb meal overseen by Nicholas Gough, but she knew their own family meal later would be more enjoyable in other ways.

Dinner was a noisy, uproarious event, as expected. Nicholas was relieved to welcome his returning kitchen staff for the evening, so the family, except Fleur, who sat with the guests as the Fox representative, changed into plain uniforms, donned clean aprons, and served their guests with the usual mix of

169

aplomb and hopelessness. Guy and Ben, naturally enough, were the stars of the show, and swept around the room without spilling a drop or a splash. Fiona, tripping over her new shoes, almost threw an entire dish of peas into the lap of an hysterically laughing Daisy Conrad, and Helen fell into conversation with one of the other guests, and forgot she was supposed to be taking orders for the main course.

Once everyone was eating, Helen, Fiona and Amy dashed upstairs, along with the few remaining chambermaids, and set to work on the rooms, straightening beds, hanging discarded dresses and jackets, and freshening water jugs. Bertie remembered very well what that was like, it hardly seemed a year since she'd been doing it herself, and she found that, despite how much she'd grumbled at the time, she missed it now; not only the ability to dash anywhere, but also the sense of closeness the work brought. There had always been a lot of giggling, rushing, exclaiming over a stray masculine cufflink in a lady's room, and a general feeling of satisfaction when all the rooms were completed in the allotted time. But now Bertie remained downstairs, reliant only on the memories as she set the table in the family kitchen.

Once the guests were enjoying their coffee and brandy, the Foxes and their helpers gathered for their own dinner. During the meal Bertie couldn't help noticing that Adam kept glancing at Helen with a sort of puzzled but smiling appreciation, as if he'd never really seen her before. Of course this was his first Christmas at Fox Bay since Helen had taken the reins, and he'd probably never seen her so flustered, red-faced, and laughing; his memories of her as a hostess would be those of a guest, arriving after the hard work had been done, when Helen was once again cool, composed and ready for smooth conversation. She was certainly in her element tonight, though she didn't return Adam's looks once, and after he caught Bertie's eyes on him he made a point of focusing his attention elsewhere for the rest of the meal.

At around a quarter past eleven, those few guests who had chosen to attend the Midnight Mass at St Adhwynn's assembled by the front door, ready for the short walk to the church.

'Are Daisy and Freddie coming?' Fiona asked their mother, pulling on her gloves.

'No, but I think it's safe to assume the church will be packed tonight anyway, with people hoping to see them.'

Fiona grinned at Bertie. 'At least *you* won't have to worry about getting a seat, you lucky thing.'

Bertie was surprised into a laugh before she aimed a thump at her sister's arm. She couldn't understand why, despite the happy atmosphere, she felt a tightness in her chest, until she remembered the difficult conversation that lay ahead; she had to know how Jowan felt about her future before she could allow herself to embrace it. There was also the thorny subject of Xander to tackle, but that could wait.

Torches bobbed through the grounds as they made their way to St 'Dwinn's. The dry weather had held, giving way to a cold, still night, and breath condensed in the air around them, while one or two of the guests voiced their regret at choosing fashion over warmth, as they re-wrapped pretty silk scarves and tied coat belts tighter. Bertie strained for sight of Jowan in the silhouetted crowds in the churchyard, and felt the smallest twinge of guilt, but mostly relief, when she realised he wasn't there. Christmas would stay happy for a little while longer.

Helen placed Bertie's chair at the end of a pew near the back, where there was a wider aisle, and Fiona and Amy sat beside her.

Helen tried to persuade them closer to the front, but Amy shook her head. The girl looked around her carefully, as the church filled with parishioners from Trethkellis, the way she'd done at the Cliffside Fort hotel yesterday, but something about the way she did it seemed cautious and a little nervous, rather than curious. Bertie was about to ask her to swap places with Fiona, so she could talk to her sister about it, when the organ struck up and the cross began its short journey from bell tower to altar.

Father Trevelyan had hardly begun to speak before the door creaked open again, and the congregation twisted as one in their pews. Jowan came in with his mother and his uncle, but there was no sign of Jory – which came as little surprise. Beth and Alfie remained standing near the back, but Bertie raised a hand to beckon Jowan forward, bracing herself for a difficult night after all.

She rolled back a couple of feet. 'Budge up,' she hissed to Amy, who squeezed up to Fiona to allow Jowan into the pew. She felt the cold air he'd brought in with him, and his fingers, wrapped around hers, were icy too, but his smile was brilliant as he stood to join in with the first carol, his face fixed to the front but her hand still clasped in his.

To her surprise he sat down again before the carol had ended, and started digging around in his waistcoat pocket. Bertie watched in amusement; was he holding in a sneeze, and searching for a handkerchief? Then he gave an exclamation of triumph and pulled out a small box, and Bertie stared, her mouth suddenly dry. Jowan opened the box and there, nestled against a pillow of blue velvet, was the most beautiful sapphire ring. She raised startled eyes to Jowan and, surrounded as they were by a forest of coats and legs, it felt as if they were in their own private little clearing, entirely separate from everyone else.

'Gosh!' Amy whispered as the song ended, indicating that they were perhaps not as separate as Bertie had thought. 'How beautiful!'

Jowan paid no attention, his eyes were still on Bertie, silently urging a response from her. As if there could be any question . . . Bertie nodded. Jowan's mouth lifted in a smile as he took the ring and slid it over Bertie's finger, but it only reached as far as her knuckle and he hissed in frustration.

'Jo, I love it.' Bertie tried to force it further, but it simply wouldn't go. 'It's beautiful, but where on earth—'

'Mum gave it to me, it was my grandmother's.'

Jowan took the ring back, and closed the box just as the congregation received the blessing and sat down with a lot of rustling and shuffling. He leaned in close, and his breath tickled her ear.

'I'm sorry, I rushed this. I'll get it altered and we'll do it properly later, but it was killing me not knowing what you'd say. I had to just let it out.'

She couldn't help but flinch inwardly as she considered her own reasons for making a clean breast of her intentions tonight. But she was too happy to worry for long. 'Couldn't you even wait until the end of the service?' she whispered back, grinning.

'I didn't think I'd make it 'til the end of the *day*,' he confessed. 'Now hush, you're supposed to be setting an example.'

She was tempted to dig him in the ribs for that, but she knew he'd bellow a surprised laugh, so instead she raised their linked hands to her lips, and firmly put all thoughts of aeroplanes to the back of her mind. For now, at least.

When the service ended, she and Jowan sat still while those at the back of the church left. There was no sense in trying to manoeuvre the chair through the narrow doorway while it was clogged with people. As the first of the congregation passed through the tiny porch their voices drifted back in, raised in delight.

'Snow!'

'It's actually snowing!'

'Merry Christmas!'

'Watch your step, there!'

'Come back to the hotel with me,' Bertie said, slipping her hand into Jowan's. 'You can pick up the Squirrel.'

'Look, about that—'

'We've been through this. I *want* you to have it, I can't bear the thought of someone else riding it. But you'll have to push it tonight, it's not been started in months.'

'I'll give you a hand, if it's slippy out,' Alfie said, appearing at Jowan's shoulder.

Bertie smiled up at him, noting, not for the first time, the strength of the family resemblance. Alfie might only be Jowan's uncle, but he and his brother had been peas in a pod. Dressed in his Sunday best tonight he had appeared older than he usually did, but his smile cut through the formality now, and familiarity was restored.

'There you are, Jo,' she said. 'No excuses. Take it. Please.'

'I'll be with you d'rectly,' Alfie said, as they turned Bertie's wheelchair to face the door. 'Just need a word here first.'

'I'll come too,' Beth said. She smiled at Alfie with such deep contentment that Jowan and Bertie exchanged a surprised glance. 'You have your talk to the vicar, Alfie, and just come home when you're ready.'

As they crossed the hotel grounds, towards the barn that housed the Flying Squirrel, Bertie had to ask. 'What's he talking to Father Trevelyan about, Beth?'

'I'm sure I couldn't say,' Beth said, but she replied too quickly, and Bertie suspected the bells at St Adhwynn's might be ringing out again in the not too distant future, after all.

'The snow's not settling,' Jowan said, bringing Bertie to a stop beside the barn. 'You can sit on the bike, Mum, I'll see you home in style!'

Beth laughed. 'Go on, then, why not?'

'I just have a little gift for Bertie first.' Jowan's voice had dropped a little, and Bertie wondered if he were going to propose again, for his mother's benefit. But he felt in an inside pocket this time, and withdrew a short, rectangular box, wrapped in red tissue paper. Snow fell on the paper, wetting it, and by the lights hanging in the trees Bertie could see through it to the silver box below.

Looking up at him in some surprise, she lifted the lid of the box, and when she looked back down she caught her breath. This was even more of a surprise than the engagement ring, and every bit as meaningful. Perhaps even more so.

'Well?' Beth urged. 'What is it?'

Bertie placed the lid on her lap, and with a shaking hand she took the scarf from the box and let it slide through her fingers. It was made in white silk. Windproof. A flyer's scarf. She couldn't look at Jowan, but her heart had swelled until she was sure it would soon stop her breathing. She felt his hand on her shoulder, telling her she needn't say anything.

'Are you ready, Mum?' he asked, and Bertie could hear the emotion in his voice. 'I'll get this bike and then we can leave everyone to it.'

'We have an early start,' Beth explained to Bertie, frowning in a puzzled way at the scarf; clearly she too had been expecting

Jowan to produce the ring. 'Animals have no respect for holidays, after all.'

Jowan swung open the barn door and disappeared into the murky depths, flashing his torch ahead of him as he went. After a few minutes of faintly awkward silence, broken only by the laughter drifting over from the churchyard, he re-emerged, pushing the Flying Squirrel. Bertie found she was able to look at it again without feeling queasy, and was even able to smile as she watched Jowan run his hand across the tank. The Fox family emblem was scratched, but still recognisable, and she wondered what he would do with it.

'I'll just push you back to the hotel,' Beth said to her, 'and then we'll toddle off home. Alfie'll follow when he's ready.' She took hold of the handles of Bertie's chair. 'That's a very pretty scarf...' The question hung in the air, but Bertie wasn't ready to answer it yet. She just looked over at Jowan.

'Very.'

* * *

Helen stood in the small, arched doorway, and watched with tired satisfaction as her guests made their way out of the churchyard. She was glad to have attended the service, but equally so that it was over; it had been a successful day all round, though exhaustion was settling into her bones now. She wished Leah were there, so she could look forward to a nice natter with a nightcap before crawling into bed. She missed her friend's acerbic asides and pithy little observations, and she missed never knowing which accent was going to pop out of Leah's mouth at any given moment.

Still, she would be back in less than a week, ready to begin tutoring Daisy Conrad in her quest to sound authentically English, and to help organise the New Year's Eve party. Tomorrow – or rather, today – would be another busy one, but at least with everyone having the same traditional goose, the kitchen work would be much more straightforward. Several of the staff who had taken Christmas Eve and this morning off would resume work mid-afternoon, and everything would return to normal.

'Happy Christmas to you, Mrs Fox!'

She turned to see Father Trevelyan picking up hymn books from the empty pews, and went back to help him. 'It was a lovely service, thank you.'

He beamed. 'I just wanted to thank *you* again, for allowing me to join in the treasure hunt. I had a wonderful time. And that Daisy Conrad certainly has a sharp mind.'

'So I gather.' Helen smiled. 'Are you joining us tomorrow for our Christmas lunch?'

'I wouldn't miss it for the world.'

'Good. We'll be eating at about two o'clock, and there'll be the usual games afterwards.'

'Wonderful, I look forward to joining you after the Eucharist.'

Helen stacked the hymn books she'd collected on the table at the back of the church, bade Father Trevelyan good night, and pulled on her gloves as she went out into the lightly falling snow. Fiona and Amy were trying to scoop enough to make a snowball, but the ground was wet and it melted where it landed. They were both giggling like children as they turned instead to the top of the low wall, and Helen remembered the wash of gladness she'd felt earlier, when she'd given her permission for the two girls to re-join the treasure hunt. She felt it again now, Fiona was coming to life again in front of her eyes, and it was both a relief and a joy to see it. From tragedy had sprung friendship, and she hoped it would endure, like the one she shared with Leah.

The crowd was thinning, but Helen couldn't see Bertie anywhere; presumably Jowan was pushing her back to the hotel. She waved to Fiona and Amy, and was about to make her own way back alone when a hesitant voice spoke behind her.

'Helen?'

Alfie stepped into the thin fall of light that spilled through from the church. His hat put half his face in shadow, but she could see enough to note the lines of tension around his mouth, and his hands were shoved deep into his coat pockets.

Helen frowned. 'What is it?' She grew more worried as he hesitated. 'Is something the matter?'

'My friend's wife died,' he blurted, and Helen blinked. He looked equally surprised at his own words, as if he'd planned to say something else entirely.

'I'm sorry to hear that,' Helen said after a moment. 'Was it someone from the village?'

'No, back in Caernoweth. It made me think, that's all.'

'It's sure to,' Helen said softly. 'I'm really very sorry, Alfie. A particularly terrible time to lose someone, too, when it seems the rest of the world is rejoicing.'

He nodded. 'Keir waited a long time to tell Ellen how he felt. Too long. It didn't seem like they had nearly enough time together.'

He began to make sense now. 'And now you're going to tell Beth how you feel? Can I just say, it's about time?'

'I'm not ...' He stopped again, then took a deep breath. 'The thing is, ever since August I've not been able to put you out of my mind.'

All Helen's words dried up, and she just stared at him until she found her voice again, smaller than she'd ever heard it. 'But you've never—'

'No, and I wish I still hadn't.' A smile finally broke across his face, banishing the tension. 'I feel a proper idiot if I'm honest,' he confessed, sounding more natural now. 'But at least now I've told you I'll be able to concentrate on other things.' He shrugged. 'Good night, Helen. The peace of the season to you and yours.'

He tipped his hat to her, squinted up at the swirling snow, and strode off.

'Wait!' Helen threw her arms up, exasperated. 'You can't just say that and walk away!'

'Why not?' He glanced around them to make sure no one was paying attention, and returned to stand in front of her. 'I'm not fool enough to think you might have me stuck in *your* thoughts, I just had to get you out of mine.'

'But ...' Helen fell silent, because hadn't she felt a flicker of envy whenever she thought of Beth winning his love at last? Only now did the unwelcome question slide into her mind: was that because Beth had found *someone*, someone honest, upright, and kind, or was it because that someone was Alfie Nancarrow?

He was looking at her with an expression that was part impatience, part hope, as he waited for her to tell him he was wrong. When she remained silent he pressed her arm with his cold, ungloved hand. 'Pay it no mind. Keir losing Ellen like that just hit me strange, that's all. It's Christmas, it's snowing, you're looking so pretty tonight ... Like I said, I just had to get it out.'

Helen looked down at her sleeve, and tried to imagine that familiar hand touching hers, instead of her coat, or even resting on her cheek ... Suddenly it was all too easy, and she stepped away. 'What about Beth?'

'That's the second time you've mentioned her.'

'Because she's in love with you!' Helen shook her head. 'You can't stand there and tell me you didn't know that?'

He looked honestly dismayed. 'But she's my brother's wife.'

'Widow,' Helen said gently. 'For nearly *ten years*! That day I came to find you, to talk about you selling the farm, I was certain she had your heart at last.'

'What made you think that?'

'Well ...' She floundered, trying to remember exactly what had convinced her. 'You were more relaxed than I'd ever seen you.' It sounded foolish to her own ears now. 'It seemed as if the pressure had been lifted so you might finally talk to her about your future.' Then she remembered. 'You even started whistling, remember?'

'Bloody hell,' Alfie muttered. 'Now who's the idiot? I was relaxed because our problems with Higher Valley were over, yes. I was *happy*, because you'd come to talk to me, even joked with me! Look.' He shoved his hands into his coat pockets again. 'Before that, when we talked business, I respected you, and I admit I took a bit of a fancy to you. That was all. After that day by the river I realised I actually *liked* you. It wasn't until after Bertie's accident, when I saw the fiercest Fox of all rise up, that I knew I was doomed.'

'Doomed,' Helen repeated, a sudden light-headedness making her laugh. '*Doomed?*'

'Utterly.' Alfie gave her a rueful grin, and leaned over to drop a light kiss on her chilled cheek. 'Go home, Helen. Get warm.'

She watched him walk away, and removed her glove to touch the tiny warm spot on her skin. The light feeling remained inside her, and when she heard his low chuckle drift back to her across the snowy churchyard she felt the smile start from somewhere in the centre of her. It was still there when she awoke on Christmas morning.

* * *

Later the hotel would be alive with music and games, and the family would be kept busy for the remainder of the day, but for now all was peaceful, and the family sitting room was a cosy haven with the curtains drawn against the rain that battered the windows. The fire was already lit, and now and again a bit of escaping gas exploded with a pop, and with the small tree, the lights, the smell of toast and coffee, and the crackling fire, everything should have been perfect. But as Fiona looked around her this morning she couldn't help feeling that this year she was the only one who was fully appreciating the moment. She'd never seen everyone so distracted. Ben was away with the fairies, as Granny often said, and he kept staring at a spot in the distance before blinking himself back to reality. He must be exhausted.

Her mother smiled her thanks at Fiona's gift of a new mesh handbag and leaned over to kiss her on the cheek. 'It's beautiful, darling, thank you.' But her attention was soon back among the leaping flames, though she didn't seem melancholic. Just thoughtful.

Bertie was in an odd mood, too, though that was more understandable. She was drawing a beautiful white silk scarf – a gift from Jowan – through her fingers over and over again, but her gaze kept going to her right leg, and the pinned pyjama trousers. Jowan and his mother had taken the Flying Squirrel after church last night, and it must have felt awful to see it go, despite knowing she'd never ride it again.

Granny admired the gloves Fiona had bought her. 'They'll be perfect for the memorial dedication next week.' But even she was looking distant, and she kept throwing glances at Adam, joining them for his first family Christmas since those days in Bristol that Fiona herself barely remembered.

'Missing Leah?' Helen asked him, picking up a pile of envelopes from the table. 'It's such a shame you two had to be apart for your first Christmas.'

Adam smiled. 'Do you know, I really am missing her, yes.'

'You sound surprised.' Helen passed various cards around to be opened.

Adam shifted in his seat. 'Well, to be honest, when she left she wasn't altogether pleased with ... with what I had to tell her,' he said. 'So yes, obviously I miss her, but I'm surprised how much. She can light up a room just by walking into it.'

'Well make sure you tell her that when she telephones.'

Adam smiled. 'I will.' He fell silent for a moment, then he looked at the card Granny was reading. 'That's a nice one.'

Fleur nodded, but her voice was oddly cool. 'From Harry's uncle Geoffrey, I don't think you ever met him.' She turned to Fiona. 'Didn't your friend want to join us this morning?' Her dismissal of Adam was bordering on rude, and Fiona met Bertie's surprised look before answering.

'She was a bit embarrassed that she didn't have gifts for everyone.'

'Oh, the poor girl!' Fleur shook her head. 'I hope you told her it didn't matter.'

'Of course I did. She still said no.'

'It must be so difficult for her being away from her own home. She must be wondering what on earth her family are feeling. Not to mention wondering what kind of Christmas she was missing.'

Fiona bit down on the comment that Amy was, in all likelihood, thanking the heavens that she wasn't at that awful farm this morning, but tucked into a warm bed upstairs. 'It must be difficult,' she mumbled instead.

'I wonder what Dais— What Mr Kelly and the others are up to,' Ben mused. Once again Fiona and Bertie exchanged glances, but this time they both smothered smiles.

'Still asleep, I expect,' Granny said. 'But I'm sure they all have very glamorous gifts to exchange when they finally get up. Helen, what *are* you daydreaming about?'

Helen started. 'Nothing!' She gestured to Fiona. 'Come on then, youngest dishes out the gifts, and your brother hasn't had anything yet.'

'Rubbish to Mum,' Bertie chanted, throwing a piece of wrapping paper to Helen. 'Oh!' She held up a dark blue chenille beret, and blew a kiss to Granny before putting it on.

'It looks beautiful, Bertie,' Helen said. 'You do look pretty in a hat.'

'What did Adam get you, Ben?' Fiona craned her neck to see. 'What's that?'

'It's a camera.' Ben turned it over and over, examining it closely.

Adam grinned. 'I thought you might like to use it to take some pictures for our new magazine.'

That got everyone's full attention, at last.

'Magazine?' Helen said, eyes wide. 'That's the first time you've mentioned that!'

'Only a little one,' Adam said hurriedly. 'More of a pamphlet, really. I thought it would be good for advertising. We can discuss it later, though. So,' he went on, wisely, judging by the look on Granny's face, 'what does the rest of the day hold in store?'

'Sleep,' Ben said promptly. 'I've been up for two days.'

'Breakfast, lunch prep, lunch, and then games once the regular staff are all in.' Helen began gathering up the discarded wrapping paper and streamers, and, just like that, family time was over. 'Fiona, see you and Amy are down by eight o'clock.'

'Do you think it's a good idea?' Fiona asked her, picking up the gifts left for Amy. 'The magazine, I mean.'

'I don't know.' Her mother sounded wary as she looked around, but when she saw Granny occupied reading one of her cards, she relaxed a little. 'I suppose it could be good publicity.'

'Not just for us,' Fiona pointed out, 'it would be good for the whole village. Especially Higher Valley, since they provide so much of our food. Just imagine a big, smiley picture of Beth and Alfie, with a wheelbarrow full—'

'Less chatter, more tidying,' Helen cut in, sounding suddenly brusque, but she relented slightly as Fiona fell silent, chastened. 'Sorry, darling. Look, I need to discuss it with Adam and Granny, and just now we really do need to be getting the dining room ready for the guests.' But as she turned away to pick up more paper Fiona saw her smile fade too quickly. What on earth had she said now?

CHAPTER TWELVE

Mountain Ash, South Wales

Christmas afternoon. At Fox Bay the air would be rich with the smells of perfume and cigars, and the festive spices of clove and cinnamon, and there would be music drifting out from the lounge, where Guy would by now have been rather too easily persuaded to don the mantle of Cliff Edwards or Noël Coward. It would be time for games in the lobby now, too; shrieks of laughter as guests skipped out of reach playing *blind man's buff*, or passed an orange, chin-to-chin with the next in a giggling line. Adults, freed from the constraints of their day-to-day lives, behaving like children and enjoying every second of it—

'Do you want to get a breath of fresh air?' Glynn had come over, unnoticed, to where Leah was staring out of the window, and as she turned back into the room the bright, clear picture of Fox Bay shattered, and was replaced by a dull reality: Aunt Mary already at the sink, with Bethan Carter from next door flapping a dishtowel in readiness for the first gleaming plate; the smell of vegetables heavy in the air, mixing uncomfortably with the smoke from the table candle Glynn had just blown out; the gravy boat dripping onto her mother's best tablecloth; brown paper smoothed out and piled neatly by the ottoman, ready to go back in for next year's gifts.

Bethan's husband Dewi sat in the armchair, replete, his eyes closed, and one thumb planted firmly over the bowl of his pipe as he tamped down the first layer of tobacco. Soon the room would be filled with the smell, mingling with the cabbage-water, and with the gradually rising voices from the kitchen. Suddenly Glynn's suggestion seemed like the one thing that would stop Leah from screaming, so she nodded and went to fetch her coat. She pulled it on over the plain dress she had worn today, glad she hadn't bothered with her best frock after all; what place did pink and beaded have here? It was a Fox Bay dress, and it was where it belonged.

Outside was just as grey and gloomy, but at least the brisk wind blew away that crushing, claustrophobic feeling. Glynn said nothing as they walked along the deserted road, and she reflected that he'd not put as much as a step out of place since he'd picked her up at the station on Monday.

Despite promising to explain his presence on the short journey, only the squeak of the wipers had filled the silence between them until he'd stopped at Aunt Mary's house, where they had sat staring out through the rain on the windscreen, neither moving nor looking at one another.

'I was sorry to hear about your mum,' he had said at last.

'Thank you.'

'So,' he went on, after a brief pause, 'the house belongs to your aunt now, does it?'

'Oh, I see.' Leah pushed open her door, but he caught her arm.

'No! I was just … asking. Making conversation.' He sounded awkward now, but Leah didn't want to ease that awkwardness.

'Well it might have escaped your notice, but it's late, it's dark, and I've had a long journey. I've better things to do than sit here and make *conversation*.'

'Right. Of course.' He let her go, but she didn't get out immediately.

'Where are you staying?' She knew, deep down, but she could still hope.

'Here, of course. It's our home, Lee. We're still married, remember?'

'How could I forget?'

'Look, I'm sorry about your boyfriend. He came sniffing 'round, and I didn't know … He's a bit of a mouth on legs, isn't he?'

'He's not my boyfriend,' Leah said, her throat tightening as she heard the words spoken aloud. 'I don't care what you did to him. He said he gave it back just as good though.'

'Did he now?'

Leah heard the grin in his voice, and shook her head tiredly. 'I don't care,' she repeated. 'I just want some peace and quiet.'

That had been the only reference to Adam, to her other life, and to their marriage, that he had made. Everything had been eerily like the old days apart from that; she'd greeted Aunt Mary, gone up to her old room, and seen Glynn's clothes already neatly arranged in the wardrobe. That night they had lain together side by side, not touching, but not arguing either. He had made no attempt to initiate any kind of intimacy, and she had stared into the darkness, her eyes burning, her fingers twisted into the eiderdown, and her heart in Fox Bay.

*

187

Now, as they walked, she found herself wondering how much he knew about her life. He'd never have been so sanguine if he knew she and Daniel had been living as man and wife, in the very town to which he'd sworn never to return.

'It's been a long time since we've talked,' he said now, guiding her around a puddle in the lane. 'I've missed it. Do you still do your Millicent Scripps?'

Leah's surprised laugh turned into a half-sob, and he stopped, concerned. 'What's wrong?'

'Nothing. You just caught me unawares with the question. I was just ... remembering.'

'Honey, she's *worth* remembering!' Glynn's accent peeled back the years that lay between them. They'd played the American couple to great effect, right up until '15, when it had all gone so horribly wrong, and they'd both had enormous fun doing it. When she glanced at him now he was smiling, and she couldn't help returning it.

'That's better.' His voice was surprisingly soft. 'I've missed that, Lee, more than you'll ever know.'

'How much do *you* know?' It was out before she could stop it, and part of her was glad, but a tight band of fear clamped her chest for a moment.

'I know you spend most of your time in Cornwall now, but I don't know where.'

Good. 'What else?'

'I know you tried the inheritance scam down there, of course. That the bloke who came looking for you believed you had some kind of relationship, and it wasn't all one-sided, from what I could gather.'

She nodded. 'We might have been something special, yes. Come on, Glynn, what else?'

He looked up at the sky, then back at her, and the clouds were reflected in eyes that had once held such power over her, compelled her, fascinated her, and now regarded her with deep sadness.

'I know that you and Daniel fell in love after I was put away.' Leah let out her pent-up breath. 'I can't pretend to be sorry.'

'Good.' Glynn cleared his throat as his voice cracked. 'I'm glad you had someone, when I couldn't be there, and I'm ... yes, I'm glad it was him. I loved him, you know that.'

'And he loved you. Otherwise he wouldn't have come up for the trial.'

'And that's truly the first time you ... spent any time together?'

She nodded. 'We joined the war together.'

'You always were a good nurse.' He smiled suddenly, and it was as if it were twenty years ago. 'Do you remember much about that day, in the office at the Alexandra Docks?'

'The day we met?' Leah gave a little laugh. 'Not something I'm likely to forget, is it?'

'My first day on the job, the place had only been open a month or so.'

'My first day in the office,' Leah added. 'You turning up with your hand covered in blood, and the office manager expecting me to patch you up just because I'm a woman.'

'Thank goodness for swinging chains bringing us together. You did a good job, and I'm glad it made you think about taking up nursing.' He looked down at his right hand, at the scar that ran from the base of his thumb to halfway up his wrist. 'I could have lost it.'

The comment awoke the memory of Toby Nancarrow, and then of Bertie Fox, and Leah walked on, faster than before; Glynn had to trot to catch up.

'What's wrong?' He caught her hand and pulled her to a stop. 'Leah, I know you've had a whole lifetime come and go since I was sent down, so tell me about it, I want to know.'

'There's no point. It's over.' Leah took another deep breath, and this time when she let it out she felt the last of her secret hopes go with it. 'You're home, *we're* home. Let's get on with it.'

After a moment of searching her eyes for any sign of wavering, he nodded. 'Are you ready to turn back?'

Intentional or not, it had the feel of a double-edged question, and Leah hesitated, but only for a moment. The sky was spitting at them. Fox Bay was receding, becoming like some perfect place she had read about in a book, and perhaps now it was time to remember things as they'd been before. Before the arrest, before the war, before Daniel.

She turned to face the way they'd come. 'Come on then. Bethan and Dewi will be going back home soon, and Aunt Mary will be feeling lonely.'

For a moment they walked in silence, then Glynn spoke hesitantly. 'I didn't stay here long after I got out, I left not long after your bloke turned up. But I came back because—'

'He's not my bloke,' Leah said. 'And yes, Aunt Mary told me you'd gone, or I wouldn't have come back myself.' She waited, and when he didn't continue she prompted him. 'Go on, you came back because?'

'Well, because I assumed you'd be home for Christmas, and I need to ask you something.'

'So you didn't come home to pick up where our marriage broke off?' Leah couldn't work out whether she was relieved or disappointed, and that disturbed her more than anything.

'Not entirely, although of course I'd want that. If you did too,' he added. 'I won't hold you to anything, I understand you have a new life now.'

Did she? 'What did you want to ask me?'

Glynn looked around them, and his expression was so comically furtive, given their isolation, that Leah smiled, and lowered her voice to a whisper. 'Careful, I'm sure there's someone in that tree, taking notes.'

He automatically followed her pointing finger, then his face broke into a grin. 'I asked for that.' Nevertheless he spoke in a lower voice. 'When I was inside I got talking to a bloke who came up with an idea. But I need you to make it work.'

'This man's still in prison?'

'No, he got out a couple of weeks before me. The thing is, we had no idea just how perfect it would be, until the American stock market crash back in October. I've been in Liverpool setting it all up.'

'Setting what up?'

'Before you dismiss it, remember it could be the answer to all our problems.'

'I can't dismiss anything when I don't know what it is,' Leah pointed out, but she couldn't deny the way her heart was suddenly beating faster.

Glynn's face was alight now, and he looked more like his old, devilish self: handsome, excited, and totally focused on her. He grasped her hands and his eyes held hers, and she knew that, for this moment at least, no one in the world was more important to him. In the face of Adam's indifference it was hard to resist.

'Millicent deserves one last outing, don't you think?'

'Oh, no, not—'

'Imagine it, Lee! Drifting around the swankiest clubs in

Liverpool, attended on by some of the richest men you'll ever meet, and one of them prepared to give up *everything*, to get at what's in here.' He tapped Leah's forehead lightly with one finger, then let it drift down her cheek, stopping at her lower lip. He leaned forward and his own lips took its place, pressing against hers, parting them gently while his hand slipped beneath the hair at the back of her neck. Leah leaned against him, her memories lifting her off this muddy, puddle-strewn lane and into the huge hotel bed in which they'd spent their wedding night, paid for by a much younger Millicent.

It had been the most exciting time of her life, before it had all fallen apart. If not for that one desperate shove, which had killed the arresting policeman, Glynn's prison sentence would have been months instead of years. Of course, he would then have been conscripted and might not have survived the war, but she and Daniel would never have spent enough time together to fall in love, she'd never have felt the terrible ache of his loss, and sought comfort at Fox Bay. Never met Fleur, Helen, or the cubs. Or ... For a second Adam's face hovered behind her closed eyelids, but she felt her husband's arms tighten around her, and pushed the image away. The time for *ifs* was over. She would return to Fox Bay for one last time, make her farewells, and then come home. This was her life now; back in the arms of her first love.

It could be a lot worse.

CHAPTER THIRTEEN

Bude Town Centre
Friday 27th December

The WI meeting had gone on for longer than Beth had expected. With just a few days left until the war memorial was dedicated there had been a lot to talk through, and Fleur Fox had finally released them, with last-minute instructions as she gathered up her papers.

'Don't forget to take your badges to sew onto your coats. See you all on Wednesday, at ten forty-five outside Mrs Burch's shop. The unveiling is at eleven o'clock sharp!'

The ladies of the Trethkellis WI hurried out, eager to make the most of what remained of their half-day in Bude before the coach took them home. Beth wasn't going to be joining them for the homeward trip; she'd arranged to meet Jowan and Bertie instead, who were in town today arranging to have the engagement ring re-sized.

She had about half an hour to spare before she had to be at the jeweller's, so she said her goodbyes to Gladys Finch and Lizzie Burch, and walked slowly down the Strand, relishing the wind off the river after the stuffiness of the meeting rooms. The shops down here were enjoying the few days' normal trading between Christmas and New Year, and Beth made her way towards the cake shop at the far end, thinking to celebrate the four years since Alfie had come to Higher Valley.

On her way she stopped to look in a few windows, though she didn't register any of what she was seeing; her mind was too full of concern for Jory. Over Christmas he'd been withdrawn and distant, not like his usual self at all, and even Jowan's engagement had failed to raise the usual teasing comments. Alfie had come looking for him yesterday, to help Jowan and himself finish building the new pig pen, but he'd taken the van into town and hadn't returned until the early hours of this morning.

Alfie had shown a rare flash of temper, reminding Beth once again of his fiery past, but Beth couldn't blame him; he and Jowan had spent almost all day on a job that should have taken half the time, and Jowan had nearly taken his finger off trying to lift a heavy stone on his own. To his credit, Jory had stumbled from his bed at the usual time this morning, knowing Alfie would be working alone, but the change in him was worrying.

Beth found she had naturally drifted towards the window of one of her favourite charity shops, and she spent a few minutes admiring the crochet-work of a baby suit, and wondering if she could produce something half so pretty for when Bertie gave her her first grandchild. The thought of grandchildren brought a warmth to the chilly day, and as she moved away, smiling, her glance fell on a simple display in the window of the pawn shop next door.

Arranged on a three-tiered stand draped in a tartan cloth, it comprised a pair of leather driving gloves, a smart-looking hat, and a hip flask; a plain pewter one with a worn leather band, and Beth thought of Alfie's much nicer one, lost up by the new dry stone wall somewhere. She hadn't been able to find Toby's to give him, either, which had been both puzzling and frustrating.

She felt in her coat pocket for her purse, and said a silent goodbye to the cake they could have all enjoyed, but the hip flask was a much more fitting gift. Inside the shop she was met by a surprising, and quite depressing, array of goods people had found it necessary to sell. Raising short-term loans, that had evidently become a long-term necessity.

A young woman stood at the counter, in conversation with the pawnbroker, and they seemed to be haggling over a compass. The woman was presenting a good argument for a drop in price, and Beth listened carefully, hoping to adopt the same attitude but fearing she was too timid.

'It's been in your window for a good long while,' the young woman was saying, 'and no one's even asked to see it yet.'

'How do you know that?'

'Because the cloth it was sitting on has faded to the exact shape of the box! It hasn't so much as moved for ages. Look, if you'll put it aside for me until next week, I can pay a little closer to what you're asking. Otherwise I can only offer you five shillings.'

'I see. And you'll definitely be back for it, will you?'

'Of course. It's a gift for someone, but I don't get paid until tomorrow. I'll pay you two shillings of it now.' The woman dug into her purse and withdrew the coins. 'Here.'

The pawnbroker sighed. 'Alright. I'll make a note of your name.'

'Don't sell it to anyone else!'

The broker gave her a sudden smile, which had the air of triumph about it. 'But as you say, miss, no one's so much as asked to see it, so that's not likely, is it?'

The woman laughed and held up a hand to admit he'd bested

her, and Beth realised she was very young indeed. No more than a girl.

'Write my name down, then. Amy Fox. Address, Fox Bay Hotel, Trethkellis.'

Beth started at this blatant lie, then realised the girl must be the mystery survivor from the stricken cargo ship.

The broker finished noting down the details. 'I'll give you until next Friday. The third.'

'I'll be here before then, probably Monday.' The girl peered at the receipt and handed it back. 'Please note on here that this payment is two shillings off whatever price we eventually agree on next week. You know, just in case you . . . *forget*.'

Beth hid a smile in her gloved hand; the girl had gumption, whoever she was.

'Help you, madam?' The broker barely waited until the girl had moved away from the counter before he shifted his eyes to Beth, relief clear on his face.

Beth gestured to the window. 'I'd like to see the hip flask, please.'

'We get a few of these in,' the broker said, leaning into the window space. 'Popular with all manner of gentlemen. 'Course, some of them's engraved, which means a bit of work filing it down, so makes 'em more pricey. This one was alright, though.'

Beth handed over the money, predictably without quibbling, and couldn't help wondering if Toby had in fact pawned his. It would make a horrible sort of sense, given the difficulties they'd had.

With the flask nestling comfortably in her pocket, Beth wandered along to the jeweller's to wait for Jowan and Bertie. Amy was looking in at the window, and she turned when Beth approached, then looked away; clearly she'd been expecting someone else. When Beth didn't pass by, or go into the shop, the girl looked at her again, her eyes narrowing slightly in suspicion.

'Are you following me?'

'Certainly not!' Beth laughed. 'It's alright,' she added with a conspiratorial smile, 'your secret's safe with me.'

Amy drew back. 'Secret?'

'The compass.' Beth gestured towards the pawn shop they'd just left. 'I gather it's a gift.'

'Yes.' Amy relaxed. 'Are you Jowan's mother?'

Beth nodded. 'Is Fiona with you?'

'She's talking to someone she met from the lifeboat crew, I left her to it, and said I'd meet her here. We're getting a lift back with her sister.'

'I take it the compass is for her? It's a good choice, if so. She'll love it.'

'I hope so.' Conversation dried up, as Beth wondered whether to broach the rescue, and Amy's subsequent memory loss, and they were both relieved to see Jowan emerge backwards from the jeweller's shop, pulling Bertie's chair out onto the narrow pavement.

'We're picking it up on New Year's Eve,' Jowan said. He looked down at Bertie, and the two of them exchanged a warm smile.

Fiona joined them after a couple of minutes, and they made their way back to where Jowan had parked the farm van. Beth sat in the front with Jowan, and Bertie squashed between them.

'I've got your uncle Alfie a little gift,' Beth told Jowan as he drove out of the town. 'It's four years next Friday that he came to live with us, did you know that?'

'I suppose I must have known it, but didn't really think. What did you get him?'

'A hip flask. To replace the one he lost up by the wall.'

'Oh, he'll be glad of it,' Jowan said. 'He loved that flask.' He kept flicking sidelong looks at her, and eventually Bertie smacked his leg.

'Stop it, keep your eyes on the road!'

Beth's curiosity was piqued. 'What's the matter, anyway?'

'Bertie reckons you and Uncle Alfie need to get on with things,' Jowan said, and Beth caught the grin on his face as he returned his attention to the road ahead.

'On with things? I'm sure I don't know what you're talking about.' But she knew she hadn't fooled anyone.

Alfie had been subdued when he'd returned from Midnight Mass, but by mid-morning on Christmas Day, after the milking and the mucking out were finished, his mood had returned to its usual quiet contentment. In the warmth of the farmhouse, with the smell of a good lunch in the air and the radio playing carols softly in the background, there had been a sense of peace and real happiness. More than once Beth had looked up from her book to see Alfie's eyes on her, half-closed but thoughtful. She'd looked away again quickly, but he hadn't seemed embarrassed to be caught looking, and it was impossible to dismiss the thrill that ran through her as she considered what that might mean.

They dropped the girls off at the hotel, and when they arrived back at the farm Beth was relieved to see Jory still working with Alfie, patching the barn roof. She hurried indoors, leaving Jowan to help them, and up to her room where she peered at herself through the heavy patina of her dressing table mirror. She pulled off her hat and rubbed at her cheeks to bring some colour back to her chill-whitened skin, then she dragged a hairbrush through her flattened hair, trying to create something a little more fashionable and sleek-looking.

It was no good, he knew her too well to be fooled by any attempt to appear alluring, she was what she was, and it was time to find out if that was enough. She hung her coat on the door and replaced it with her apron, then she took the flask and slipped it into her pocket and went back downstairs to begin supper.

When the men had finished work for the day, Beth laid the wrapped gift next to Alfie's dinner place, and dished up their meal without mentioning it. Alfie splashed his face at the sink, as usual, and joined his nephews at the table, and when he saw the tissue-wrapped package he raised surprised eyes to Beth.

'Happy fourth year at Higher Valley,' she said, trying to smile but feeling it tremble on her lips without properly forming. 'I wanted to mark it in some way, and I found this today when I was in town.'

'You didn't need to,' Alfie murmured, and a flush touched his tanned skin.

Beth watched anxiously as he unrolled the tissue paper, and when the flask fell into his hand he simply looked at it without speaking.

Jowan leaned over to see it properly. 'You're right, Mum, it's a really nice one.'

'What is it?' Jory craned his neck to see, but sat back down again quickly. 'Very nice,' he muttered.

'Do you like it?' Beth stammered. 'I only got it down t' Charlie Templeton's place, it can go back there if—'

'I like it fine,' Alfie broke in. Then he took a deep breath and looked up at her. 'I love it,' he said quietly. 'It was proper thoughtful, thank you.'

Beth watched her sons exchange a glance, and suddenly it hit her too. She silently berated herself; far from the perfect gift, it actually amounted to, *Here, have this to remind you twice over that your brother's dead.*

'Alfie, I'm so sorry,' she began, but he put the flask down and came over to her.

'Hush,' he said, still in that quiet voice. He drew her into his arms and rested his chin on the top of her head so she found herself staring at the open collar of his shirt, until she closed her eyes and rested more naturally against him. When he spoke she could feel the vibration against her cheek. 'It's the nicest thing anyone's done for me in a long time, love. Truly. Thank you.'

'There's nothing in it you know,' she said, striving to lighten the mood again, and he laughed.

'I'm sure we can do something about that. Jo, fetch that bottle Ben Fox gave us for Christmas.'

He released her, and she wished she'd taken the opportunity to wrap her arms around his waist while she'd had the excuse, but he took a step away, holding her at arm's length. 'I didn't get you anything.'

'Well, it's not until next Friday,' she pointed out, smiling. 'There's time yet.'

'Gravy's bubbling,' Jory said mildly, and Beth felt a flash of exasperation and the temptation to snap at him to *take it off the heat, then*. Alfie squeezed her arms once more, then let go and took the bottle of Glenfiddich Jowan had passed him.

Later, when the twins had left them alone, they took up their familiar positions either side of the fireplace. Alfie had poured himself and Beth another measure of the whisky, and filled his hip flask ready to take with him tomorrow, when he travelled to Caernoweth for Mrs Garvey's funeral. The fire crackled between them, creating a companionable peace.

'Was nice of Ben to give us this,' Beth said, looking at the whisky in her glass. 'He's a thoughtful lad.'

'They're a nice family,' Alfie said. 'Brought up well, those kids.' He seemed poised to say more, but fell silent, tilting his glass to catch the firelight.

Beth said nothing, but her heart was still racing. He was even quieter than usual, and kept looking away, into the distance or focusing on some small thing she knew he wasn't seeing. Whether they had a future together or not, it seemed tonight would tell, and she wished he'd just put her out of this agony. It would be better to have her heart broken now, and then at least she could begin to heal.

She thought over all the potential women who might have caught his eye since his wife had left him; several here in the village; some woman named Nancy he'd known in Caernoweth, he'd mentioned her a lot when he first came; and of course Leah Marshall. He got along well with her. Too well, sometimes, despite the fact that she was with Adam Coleridge ... Of all of them, Leah made Beth the most nervous, with her sparky humour and her pretty looks.

But none of them were here, and she was. It was time to speak the truth, while she had a voice.

'I want to talk, Alfie,' she began, and her voice cracked on his name, as if she suddenly had no right to speak it.

'So do I.'

Beth's insides tightened until she could barely breathe. 'Go on, then.'

'You first, you said it first.'

She took a gulp of Scotch, and Alfie, by contrast, put his glass down. He laced his fingers together and Beth focused on them, to calm the trembling in her own. Finally she was ready. 'You've been here four years, and we've worked well together, haven't we?'

'We have. Very well.' But he sounded subdued. 'Listen—'

'No! Not yet. I have to say this. It's like you said, about your friend Keir. Life's short.'

'Beth, let's get wed.'

Beth stopped, certain she'd misheard. 'What?'

Alfie came over and took the drink out of her hand, then drew her to her feet. 'No more dithering. If you'll have me, I'd be glad to be your husband, and a father to your sons. Such as they might need one, now they're grown.'

Beth looked up at him, searching his face for ... something. Anything. But though his eyes met hers, all she could see was her own reflection, and that of the flickering firelight. He was fulfilling her dream, but it felt hollow.

'You don't truly want me, do you?' The words were tugged from her, going against all her instincts to seize this moment of long-awaited joy.

He looked at her helplessly, and now there was more in his expression, there was confusion. 'I do! It's just ... You're my sister-in-law. It feels wrong even though I know it isn't.'

'But do you care for me *at all*?'

'I care a great deal.' Alfie's hands went to her waist, and when he touched his lips to hers she couldn't bring herself to question it any more deeply. 'Marry me, Beth,' he whispered. 'Let's take what we have, and be happy.'

'Of course I will.' She held his face with both hands, so she could study every beloved line and contour. He was a good man, a kind man, and her love for him was as deep a part of her as her own soul. He would come to love her too, in time.

CHAPTER FOURTEEN

Three of the usual staff, from the same family, had gone down with food poisoning over Christmas, and Fiona had stepped in on Monday to cover. Amy joined her without argument, but she was clearly fed up.

'I thought you wanted to go to the lifeboat station today?'

'I did.' Fiona pushed open the door to the laundry with the front of the bedding cart. 'Mum wouldn't ask me to work unless there was no alternative.'

'But it's your day off. And you're *family*, for heaven's sake!'

'We all muck in when we have to, and I didn't want to learn the actual hotel work like the others, so this is what I do instead.' Fiona grinned. 'Don't look at me like that, it suits me better this way. At least I have a shorter working day so I can get outside at some point.'

'I suppose.' Amy sighed. 'I was hoping to get back to Bude, to collect something. How long do you think we'll be stuck in here for?'

'We've almost finished, I think. Leah's back today, too. I can't wait to hear her teaching Daisy to speak with an English accent!'

'Of course Miss Conrad's bound to be wonderful at that, too,' Amy said drily.

'Come on, you have to admit now that she isn't what you thought she'd be.'

'It isn't her as a person that I dislike.' Amy stopped working for a moment, frowning as if she were trying to work it out for herself. 'It's more that ... people like her and Freddie have so much handed to them on big velvet cushions, just because people like the way they look.'

'And the way they act.'

'Anyone can do that! I could get paid for doing it.'

'And then you'd have to listen to people like you being rude and dismissive,' Fiona pointed out. 'True, it can be a question of luck, being born in the right country, and having the right look, but there's a lot of hard work too. Look at what they're asking her to do for this *Dangerous Ladies* film.'

'Have an all-expenses paid holiday in a posh hotel?'

'Didn't you hear what she said in the church, when we were looking for the clue?' Fiona shook her head. 'She hates *the grandeur*, as Father Trevelyan put it. She might not have wanted to spend her Christmas in a foreign country, away from her family,' she went on, hitting her stride nicely in favour of someone she had only just begun to like herself. 'Then there's an awful lot of lines to get perfectly right, knowing where to stand without making it look forced, and now she has to learn to speak English in such a way that—'

'Alright! Anyway, I liked Mrs Marshall when I met her,' Amy said hurriedly, evidently keen to change the subject onto something they agreed on. 'She's got a way about her. She's exciting.'

'Come along, girls, those beds won't make themselves,' Miss

Tremar clucked, before realising it was Fiona she was talking to, and softened the order with a half-nervous smile, as if she'd been joking.

'I hope the others are back tomorrow,' Fiona grumbled, pushing her sweat-damp curls out of her eyes and back under her cap. 'They can take my shift in return, and I can go to the station instead.'

'Are there any nice young men there?' Amy asked. 'What's the man who saved me like?'

'There were two of them.'

'The youngest of them, then?'

'Danny Quick? He's a joker.' Fiona was surprised by the little flicker of jealousy she felt as Amy smiled.

'I like jokers.'

'He's a bit of a show-off about the fact that he's got his own outboard motor. He's too old anyway. At least nineteen.'

'That's only three years.' Amy's smile widened suddenly. 'I have something I want to show you that will make those three years disappear completely.'

Fiona lifted a stack of ironed sheets and dropped them into the cart ready to take upstairs. 'How do you know you'd want them to? You don't even know what Danny looks like.'

'What *does* he look like?'

'Awful,' Fiona said firmly. 'Spots all over his face, and a nose you could launch the *Dafna* off.'

'That's a shame. I bet you could stun anyone.'

'Me?' Fiona blinked. 'I thought you were talking about you.'

'I'm going away, remember?' Amy lifted her own pile. 'No point in me getting to know anyone around here. Now, if I happen to meet a nice Irishman when I'm over there, that's another matter.' She dropped the sheets on top of Fiona's and winced slightly, drawing a sharp breath.

'Are you alright?' Fiona asked, frowning.

'Perfectly. Not used to hard work though, clearly.'

Fiona looked around and lowered her voice. 'But you live on a farm.'

She hadn't lowered it enough though, and one of the laundry maids bobbed up from where she'd been kneeling unnoticed, untangling wet sheets. 'Have you remembered where you're from then, miss?'

'Yes!' Amy feigned a delighted smile, while Fiona groaned inwardly. 'It's wonderful, isn't it? You mustn't say anything though, Fiona hasn't had the chance to tell her mother yet.'

'Tell us everything!'

'Milly!' There was a fine line between informality and unruliness, and both Granny and Mum were wary of allowing the staff to cross it. 'Amy is our guest, don't forget.'

Milly went back to work, and Fiona grimaced at Amy and mouthed, *Sorry*.

'I don't mind, honestly, but you'd better go and tell your mum when we've finished here, I have a feeling word will get out quickly.'

The two of them made their way back to the service lift, and Fiona felt fresh sweat trickling down her temple. The day she could choose to leave this work and spend all her days out in the fresh air couldn't come soon enough, and the idea of a disappearing three years, even if it were only in appearance, suddenly seemed extremely appealing.

'What have you got to show me then?' she asked, trying to sound casual.

'Why do you care?'

Fiona shrugged, but she was still curious, because Danny's nose was actually quite neat, and she'd never noticed so much as a blemish on his outdoor-healthy skin ... She looked up in time to see Amy wink.

When they'd finished their share of the chores, Amy went upstairs to change while Fiona found her mother in the office. 'I thought Leah would be here by now.'

Helen looked at the clock. 'The train's due in about half an hour, Guy's already gone to meet it. Oh, and I need a chat with Arthur Foley before ... Sorry, I'm getting distracted again. So much to do!' She offered Fiona a bright smile. 'Is Amy looking forward to the party tomorrow?'

'That's what I came to tell you, she's got her memory back!'

Helen's genuine pleasure made Fiona feel wretched with guilt. 'But that's wonderful! Tell me!'

'She really is called Amy, so that must be why it was the first name to pop into her head. She's from a farm in Devon, and there's no telephone where she lives, so she's sending a telegram to her mother now, just to tell her she's safe and well.'

Helen came around the desk and hugged her, heedless of her sweaty clothes. 'How did it happen?'

'She just ... remembered, all at once. Maybe seeing Mrs Nancarrow earlier jogged some memory of her own farm.'

'Mrs Nancarrow? I was expecting Alfie this time.'

'Alfie has gone away for a day or two, apparently. I know he prefers your signature on the order sheet, but Mrs Nancarrow was happy for Mr Gough to sign for it. Oh! Did you know Alfie has proposed to her at last? Just think, we're all going to be family once Bertie marries Jo!'

'Wonderful,' Helen repeated, in a faraway voice as she sat down again. 'Well. You must tell me everything when you know it. About Amy of course, not Alfie and, and his ... and Beth. Alright, go and change out of those clammy things. Tell Amy she can telephone her family from here if she wants to.'

'They don't *have* a phone,' Fiona reminded her. Hadn't she been listening?

'On a farm?' Helen shook her head. 'Seems rather foolish. Even the Nancarrows are getting one put in now.'

Fiona could see her mother really was distracted, and was now busying herself with some papers on the desk, and she took it as her cue to leave. 'I'll be down when I've changed then,' she said, and left her mother to it.

She went to her room, untying her apron as she went, and when she pushed open her bedroom door she froze in place. A young woman stood in the centre of the room, dressed in a heavily beaded pink dress that fell only just below her knees. She was about twenty, slender, and she stood dead still, posed with one arm raised, flapper-style, and the other on one jutting hip. Hastily applied make-up made her eyes look huge and her lips startlingly red. Only her hair gave her away after the initial surprise.

'Amy?' Fiona shut the door hurriedly behind her. 'What on earth?'

'I found it.' Amy grinned, switching her pose to a coquettish look, with one finger pressed to her cheek. 'What do you think?'

Fiona looked more closely. '*Where* did you find it? That's Leah's favourite dress. You haven't been into her room, have you?'

'Of course not.' Amy sat down at the dressing table and examined her newly made-up face in the mirror. 'It was lying in a heap behind the counter. I assumed some guest had left it behind. The make-up is Bertie's though, please don't let on!'

'It all makes you look . . .' Fiona gave up.

'About three years older?' Amy suggested with a little smile. 'Try it on, Fi. You'll look gorgeous!'

'It's Leah's,' Fiona repeated, but she couldn't help staring at the way the dress hung off Amy's frame, and showed so much of her slender legs, and wondering if she would look half as good.

'You're built like a matchstick,' Amy said, reading her mind. 'You would suit this dress perfectly. You ought to ask Mrs Marshall if you could borrow it for the party, she's sure to let you. I'll even do your make-up.'

'Absolutely not! You have to take it all off too, Leah's due back within the hour.'

'It needs a good pressing anyway,' Amy mused, examining the skirt. 'How do you do it with all these beads on it?'

'Inside out.' Fiona looked down at herself, at the grubby uniform dress, the clunky shoes, and the sagging stockings. 'Do you really think it'd suit me?'

'Just try it on.' Amy stood up and reached behind her to unzip the dress, and as she did so the material pulled taut against her body. Fiona froze for the second time in as many minutes.

Amy slipped off the dress, and, wearing only her petticoat, turned away to pick up her own clothes. She continued chattering about the party, with her back turned, but it wasn't until she was dressed once more, had wiped the make-up away and reverted to her almost boyish, sixteen-year-old self, that Fiona was able to speak.

'Why didn't you tell me?'

'Tell you what?' Amy looked at her brightly, but Fiona thought she detected a wariness behind the smile.

'When are you due?'

All the strength seemed to run out of Amy's limbs, and she sat down on her bed. 'June, I think.' She sounded defeated. 'I'd almost convinced myself it wasn't true, and even this dress hid it really well. Or so I thought. I've only just started to show, it's come on really suddenly.' She raised pleading eyes to Fiona. 'Don't tell,' she begged. 'You promised—'

'To *help*,' Fiona reminded her, feeling sick. 'Anyway you've lied to me, I shouldn't have to keep that stupid promise now.'

'I haven't lied!' Amy flashed back. 'I . . . saw no reason to burden you with knowing, that's all. I'll be out of your hair soon.'

'Is that why you wouldn't drink the champagne at the treasure hunt?'

Amy played with the coverlet. 'I've heard it's not a good idea.'

'And why you left the hospital so soon? So they wouldn't have time to find out?' The more Fiona thought about it, the more foolish she realised she'd been. 'And that business down in the laundry earlier—'

'It was just a little twinge,' Amy broke in. 'Nothing to do with anything.'

'You shouldn't even have been doing that work.'

'And how was I supposed to get out of it?' Amy countered hotly.

'By *telling me*!' Fiona stared at her, disbelieving. 'I'd have found something else you could do, without letting on!' She slumped onto her own bed. 'I can't believe you've been here for more than two weeks, and not said anything.'

'What will you do?' Amy asked in a quiet voice.

'Listen to you, while you tell me everything,' Fiona said grimly. 'Now. We can start with, who was it?'

'His name's Micky Trebilcock, his dad's a milkman who comes

to the farm sometimes. Micky does casual labouring for us in the summer.'

Fiona did a quick sum in her head. 'And harvest-time in particular, I take it.' A thought occurred to her, and she sat up straight. 'Did, did he force you in any way?'

'No!' Amy looked appalled enough that Fiona believed her. 'It was just ... it was a hot day, we'd pinched some cider from the harvest festival barrel, and ...' She shrugged. 'We just weren't careful, that's all. He's only seventeen himself.'

'Does he know?'

Amy nodded miserably. 'We fought over it.'

'And what about Kitty?'

'She'd be horrified. She'd hate me.' She dropped her voice to little more than a whisper. 'She might make me, make me ... You know.'

Fiona caught her breath. 'I'm sure she wouldn't.'

'You don't know anything about her.' Amy looked desperate now. 'That's why I want to find my real mother. She's been in this situation herself, she'll understand.'

'But what if she doesn't want—' Fiona saw a dangerous glint in Amy's eyes. 'What if she doesn't have what it takes to help you?' she amended.

'Money, you mean?'

'Amongst other things.'

'Well,' Amy looked at the floor. 'I was hoping you might be able to ... send me on with something extra. Your family being so rich, and all.' She brought her gaze back up, a little defiantly.

'It's not that easy,' Fiona said, dismayed at this change in her friend. 'I can't just put my hands on the sort of money you'd need, and if I asked Mum for it she'd have to know why.'

'You could come up with something, couldn't you?'

'A lie, you mean?'

'I wouldn't ask if I weren't desperate!'

'Let me think about it.' Fiona rubbed her face with both hands. 'It's too much to take in just now. Leah will be here soon, there's tomorrow's party, then the dedication of the war memorial, which Granny insists we attend. By the way, Mum thinks you've sent a telegram to your mother, alright?'

Amy nodded. 'Thank you,' she said in a small voice. 'I'll be gone soon and you won't have to worry.'

'I'll do nothing *but* worry, until I get a letter from you saying you've had your baby.' Fiona stood up and stretched her aching back. 'I'll see if I can come up with something, if only to see you don't turn up at your mother's home penniless.'

* * *

Helen eyed the leaves that had blown across the netless tennis courts and clumped in soggy little piles against the net posts, and checked her watch; she just about had time to talk to the grounds-man before Leah arrived. She resolutely put the news about Alfie and Beth from her mind for long enough to talk to Arthur Foley about the leaves, and the peeling paint on the gazebo, but as she left his cottage and made her way back, the sinking sensation hit her again and she had to face it.

If Alfie's matter-of-fact declaration to her on Christmas Eve had been a bolt from the blue, her own reaction to it had both puzzled and dismayed her. All this time she'd been expecting him to take up with Beth as if it were the most natural thing in the world, but she hadn't realised that, along with that expectation, there had been a sort of desperate hope for it – that it had been an unconscious way of dampening a growing affection that didn't belong in her heart, where Harry lived. After all, she and Harry had been two halves of the same whole. The Heavenly Twins, bound in love and mutual desire right to the end. Her natural, easy friendship with Alfie had been something entirely different, and to think of him in the same way she'd felt about her husband was to deny everything she'd always believed, about both relationships. Muddying waters that had been so clear until now.

It was perfectly possible to form a close friendship with an attractive man without wishing for it to go further, she knew that very well. It had been that way with Adam Coleridge for years, and since he'd come back into their lives she'd proved it again; Adam was undeniably appealing; charming, funny, and intelligent. But the thought of becoming physically close to him was absurd. Alfie, on the other hand . . .

Helen shook her head. What was the use in going over Alfie's qualities, when he was now engaged to marry someone else? She had hesitated too long over her reply, and he had done the sensible thing and returned to the woman who, for the past four years, had been as close to a wife as it was possible to get. It *was* too late, and if she were faced with the same situation again, she must again hold him at arm's length. But this time it would not be through indecision.

She was almost at the door when she heard the honk of a car horn. She looked up and saw Guy's motor, but it wouldn't have been Guy who'd tooted the horn, and Helen could just picture his face when Leah had leaned across him to do it.

Leah stepped out of the car before Guy had the chance to hand her out, her blonde curls bouncing where they poked out from beneath her hat. She hugged Helen more tightly than usual, and when she drew back Helen looked at her carefully.

'Is everything alright?'

'Perfectly,' Leah said, and linked her arm through Helen's as they went indoors out of the cold. It reminded Helen a little of the first day they'd met, nine years ago: *I think we're going to be great friends, Mrs Fox.* How right she had been.

They sat in their favourite spot in the lounge, while Helen brought Leah up to date on everything that had happened in the past week. She carefully stepped around the subject of Adam, preferring to wait until Leah mentioned him first.

'Daisy and Freddie have kept largely to themselves,' she said, turning to accept the drinks from Jeremy Bickle's silver tray. 'But that'll change now, of course, when you and Daisy begin your lessons.'

Leah took what looked like a very welcome gulp of gin and tonic, and sighed. 'Would you believe I'd forgotten all about that?'

'You'll be marvellous. She's so looking forward to getting started.'

'As am I, but—'

'Fiona's friend Amy has regained her memory,' Helen went on. Then she steadied herself, intent on sounding just as casual as she went on, 'And Alfie Nancarrow has finally proposed to Beth.'

'At last!' But Leah's laughter faded, and it was her turn to look more closely. 'And how do you feel about that?'

'Feel?' Helen took a slug of her martini.

'Well, you're . . . good friends, you and Alfie.'

'We are. Which means I'm delighted, of course.'

'Look—' Leah put down her drink and leaned forward '—feel

214

free to put me straight, but I've always thought you had a bit of a soft spot for him.'

'As you said, we're good—'

'He's a good-looking man.'

'There are plenty of those around.'

'Are there?' Leah looked around with comical scepticism, and Helen smiled.

'We do have some very suave guests,' she pointed out.

'I'm not talking about suave. Or smooth. Or polite.' Leah picked up her drink again and sat back, eyeing Helen shrewdly. 'Alfie is none of those things, well, he's *occasionally* polite,' she allowed with a little smile of her own. 'But mostly he's good. And yes, he's got the kind of looks that improve with age.'

'And Beth deserves him,' Helen said firmly. 'She's loved him for years.'

'I know what that's like,' Leah said, 'when the two men in your life are brothers. It's complicated, it makes you question everything.'

'The difference is, your husband is a crook, and *he's* the one who's still alive. If Toby hadn't died, Beth wouldn't have been thrown together with Alfie like this.'

There was a pause, then Leah tapped her glass with a painted fingernail. 'Come on, what aren't you telling me?'

'I'm not sure I understand.' Helen avoided Leah's sharp gaze by watching the electric train on its endless loops through the fake forest.

'You're hiding something.'

'Am I?'

'Helen!'

Helen looked steadily at her for a moment, then replaced her drink on the table and explained about Christmas Eve. 'I just

215

stood there,' she confessed. 'I didn't know what to think, or what to say ... so I said nothing. He didn't expect an answer, so it didn't seem to matter.'

'Do you think if you'd said anything it would have made a difference?'

Helen once more hesitated just a little too long, and saw that Leah had noted it. 'No,' she said at last, 'because if I *had* said anything, it would be about how he'd misdirected those thoughts.'

'Because of Beth, or because of Harry?'

'Both! Neither ...' Helen sighed. 'I don't know. I didn't realise, until he'd walked away that there was anything inside me that matched what he'd said.'

'But there is *something*?'

'He was a tower of strength to me over Bertie's accident, and we've shared a solid friendship since then.' She shook her head. 'But when Fiona told me today that he'd proposed to Beth, I thought someone had scooped out my insides and replaced them with ice. I don't know where *that's* come from.'

'Oh God, Hels ...' Leah reached across the space between them and took her hand. 'You have to tell him, before he marries Beth. For both their sakes.'

'Don't be ridiculous!' Helen snatched her hand away, appalled. 'What right do I have, when I don't even know my own feelings?'

'Don't you?'

'No!' Helen realised she'd been raising her voice, and lowered it again. 'Look, I've barely stopped thinking about him since he spoke to me, but that's because it felt good, knowing a man I respected wanted me. I'm no glamour girl and nor have I ever been. But before that I'd barely spared him a second's thought unless he was standing in front of me.'

'Meaning?'

'Meaning that what I'm feeling now is thwarted flattery. Yes, I'm attracted to him, which, incidentally, is the first time I've thought about anyone else in that way not just since Harry died, but since I *met* him. That's nearly thirty years. But Beth loves him, Leah. She *loves* him. I don't.'

'If you're sure.'

'I am. And on that note I think it's time we changed the subject.' Helen vented her frustration in a harsh breath. 'Right. Adam's in Bodmin at the moment, interviewing chefs, but he said he'd be back by five. It's almost that now, so I'm sure you'd like to go up and change out of your travelling clothes.' She stood, expecting Leah to follow suit, but Leah didn't move and she sat down again.

'What is it? Something about Adam?'

'Adam, and other things.' Leah lowered her head, and spoke in a voice so low that Helen strained to hear it. 'I'm leaving him. And here.'

Helen's heart sank. 'Leaving?'

'I've been offered a job, in Liverpool. At a hospital. You don't need me to live in any more, for Bertie, and I've been thinking it's time I made my own life again.'

Helen sat in silence, struggling not to blurt anything that would make her sound selfish. But the thought of Leah no longer living with them – especially after their difficult time back in September – was just as devastating as learning about Alfie and Beth had been.

'I'll come back when I can,' Leah said, 'and I'll stay with you when you'll have me, but ... well, I'll be a nurse again, which is what you've always nagged me to be.' Her smile was uncertain.

'I'm glad for you,' Helen managed. 'I'll miss you though.'

'And I'll miss you. I can't tell you how much.'

'When will you leave?'

'I get the train to Liverpool on the second, Thursday, and I start work on Saturday.'

'Do you have somewhere to live?'

'At the nurses' home. It's all arranged. I'm so sorry to be springing this on you, Hels, but I wanted to tell you face to face.'

'And Adam?'

Leah looked away. 'Adam doesn't care for me the way I want him to. The way I care for him. I don't think I can bear to be around him any more, knowing that.'

'But he does!' Helen urged. 'I'm sure of it. You only have to see the way he looks at you!'

'Bless you, Helen, we both know that's not true.' Leah's eyes glistened, and she blinked hurriedly. 'Anyway, we must make the most of the time I have here, so I'm going to get changed, and meet you back down here so we can talk about the party. Alright?'

'When will you tell him?'

'Oh.' Leah waved a hand. 'I'll pick my moment.' She finished her drink, and left Helen sitting alone in the bar, staring at the Christmas tree and the perpetually running train set, and seeing neither.

CHAPTER FIFTEEN

It was well into the evening before Adam returned. Leah had bathed and changed, and although her bedroom mirror told her she was looking relaxed and rested, she felt as tightly strung inside as she had when she'd arrived. She'd been listening out for the familiar sound of his car, without fully realising she'd been doing so, and looked out of the window in time to see the Lagonda crawling around the side of the hotel to its usual parking space.

When she found him he was in the office with Helen. Of course.

'At last!' He jumped up, his smile wide, unguarded, unforced; she could almost believe he was as happy to see her as she was to see him, but she doubted if he was also feeling the same lurch of panicked uncertainty. He drew her close and pressed his lips to her temple, and she had to force herself to move away.

'How did it go?'

'I was just telling Helen,' Adam said, re-seating himself. 'I've interviewed seven over yesterday and today, in their own kitchens, and it's come down to two. Both currently head chefs, but willing to come here as sous-chef as long as Nicholas Gough remains in charge. They're keen to work under him.'

'And if Nicholas leaves they'll be just as keen to step up?'

'Exactly. He'll meet them on Thursday morning, they'll take turns running the pass for lunch, and, provided they come up to scratch, Helen and Fleur will interview them both in the afternoon.'

'Who are they?' Helen said. 'You didn't get around to that part.'

'Kurt Strommer's one.'

'From the Royal Oak?' Helen looked impressed. 'That kitchen's in line for a Michelin star too. I've eaten there, it's out of this world.'

'The other one's Henry Batten, from the Cliffside Fort.'

'Where's that?'

'Caernoweth.'

'I'm sure that's where the girls went to lunch the other day. They said they enjoyed it so much they had the chef brought to their table.'

'Two good ones then,' Leah said. 'Look, Adam, can you spare half an hour? I'd like to speak to you alone.'

Adam gave her a wicked grin. 'Speak to me, eh?' But he seemed to sense the tension behind Leah's casual attitude, and nodded, looking at Helen. 'We can talk about the other stuff later.'

'Alright.' Helen studiously avoided eye contact with Leah, and busied herself with her handover sheet for Ben.

'What other stuff?' Leah asked, as they made their way through reception.

'Just some artist's work that I'd like to hire, to hang out here.' He gestured at the wall by the stairs. 'Those old prints are getting a bit dated now, and so are the ones in the upstairs sitting room.'

He went towards the lounge, but Leah shook her head. 'No. Upstairs.'

He looked at her, quizzically. 'Is everything alright? Is it your aunt?'

'She's well. We'll go to my room.' She moved past him to climb the stairs. 'Your room's always such a mess.'

'I don't know why you insist on having two separate ones anyway,' he said, not for the first time, as he caught up with her. 'Everyone knows—'

'Everyone knows what happens in a person's private bathroom as well,' Leah threw back over her shoulder, 'but that doesn't mean they want to acknowledge it in public.'

She led the way into her room and took a few deep breaths, working her fingers to ease some of the tension. Adam sat with easy familiarity at the table by the window, and she poured him a glass of whisky and took the chair opposite. She studied him for a moment, without speaking, and could see him growing uncomfortable.

'What's that look for?' He sounded irritable now. 'Come on, Lee, I've had a busy day.'

'I'm just trying to work out if it suits you.'

'If what suits me?'

'All this . . .' she waved a hand '. . . talking about new art for the lobby, interviewing kitchen staff. Generally being a good boy.' A tiny smile crept across her face. 'I don't think it does, to be honest. You need to be in the thick of something. Admit it, even if it's only to yourself and me.'

'The thick of what?'

'Dealing, chasing, exploring . . . Anything rather than hiding away here, signing forms, and adding up what you owe and to whom.'

'I *owe* Helen and the kids.'

'Do you owe it to them to give up your lifestyle?'

'Harry did.'

'Oh, for goodness' sake!' Leah got up again and poured her own drink. 'Just because Harry was ready to give everything up for love, doesn't mean you have to as well.'

The words had just slipped out, but when she turned back to him he'd grown very still, and his gaze was pinned to the tablecloth. Leah wanted to tell him that it was no use, that Helen wasn't within reach for him, that she never would be. But he had to find that out for himself.

'I'm leaving,' she said instead, and told him the same story she'd told Helen. She spoke so convincingly of her nursing job in Liverpool that she almost believed it herself, and part of her even wished it were true. Throughout the telling she could see the thoughts flitting through Adam's mind, as if they were printed on his face: shock, disappointment, guilt ... But the clearest was relief, and as deeply as she felt the pain at losing him, she knew she'd made the right decision; Beth might be willing to accept Alfie while his heart lay elsewhere, but Leah was no Beth Nancarrow.

'Lucky Helen,' she mused, faintly bitterly, when Adam made no reply to her explanation. 'Two men ready to give up everything for her.'

Adam looked up sharply. 'Two?'

'Not pretending any more then, I see.' Leah decided not to bring Alfie into this, it wasn't fair. 'Harry might be gone, but he was devoted to her and so are you.'

He looked trapped, opened his mouth to protest, then shook his head. 'I'm sorry. I care about you, you must know that.'

'But you don't love me.' Leah finished her drink and stood up. 'Well, that's all then. I'll be leaving on Thursday.'

Adam stood too, and tried to put his arms around her but she stood rigid, though it took all her strength not to lean against him one last time for old time's sake, for the fun they'd had, the love they'd made, the new lives they'd both found here.

'I'll see you at dinner,' she said stiffly instead, her arms resolutely at her sides.

Adam looked at her searchingly, and she thought that, for a heartbeat, she could see something real in those eyes, but whatever real feelings he had were not hers to claim.

'See you at dinner,' he echoed, at last. 'Lee, I'm—'

'You can see yourself out.'

When she was alone again, she fumbled a cigarette out of her case and lit it, annoyed to see the tip shaking as she drew on it. She'd known him a matter of months, and emotionally charged months at that. It was ridiculous to think they'd had any kind of hope in a calm, steady environment; Adam was as addicted to excitement as she was. And Glynn, too.

She allowed herself to think about Glynn for a moment, something she'd promised herself she wouldn't do until she was on the train to Liverpool to meet him, but the way Adam had given in, without so much as a protest, had badly shaken her confidence. She'd expected a token argument, at least, something with which she might have comforted herself when she began the journey back to her old life, but there had been nothing.

Glynn, on the other hand, loved her as deeply as he ever had, and he had coaxed her memories to the surface over Christmas, and made her laugh as they'd relived their glory days. He had put no pressure on her to return to full married life, but she knew it wouldn't be long, once they moved to Liverpool. Adam would necessarily become another memory, like Daniel, consigned to the deepest part of the nights when she couldn't sleep.

In the meantime, she had to get ready for her first session with Daisy Conrad. She would only have two days in which to school the actress, and one of those would be taken up in part by the ceremony to dedicate the memorial to the Great War, on New Year's Day. Perhaps it would even be a good idea to take Daisy along, she mused, as she closed her bedroom door behind her; she would hear all kinds of accents, mingling with the villagers and visitors.

Leah went down the first two flights, and couldn't help glancing down the hallway on the first floor, to room eight, where she and Daniel had planned to return every year. Until that telegram had arrived ...

Without realising it, as she'd been thinking about him she'd been walking down the short hallway to the room itself, and arriving at the door she laid a hand on it, closing her eyes and silently saying her last goodbye to the memories that lived behind it.

' ... do a good job.'

The voice was American, and Leah realised with a start of embarrassment that she'd been standing outside Rex Kelly's room like a fame-hungry starlet. She stepped away, but curiosity kept her listening as she heard Daisy's famously smooth tones in reply.

'Mrs Fox says she's real good at voices. I'm sure she'll do her best to help me, but if not then ... well, I'll just listen a lot, and practise. I don't really like to refuse, it seems so rude.'

'I don't see how anyone could be fooled into thinking a put-on accent could be real, anyway,' Rex grumbled. 'I've never heard one that sounded it, for sure, even in the best movies. They expect a certain kind of English. But, if Mrs Fox approves, then I'm willing to give her a chance, I guess.'

'I haven't met her, have you?'

He must have nodded. 'Pretty lady, and nice enough, but I wouldn't get your hopes up. Her own accent's kind of ... well, not like regular English.'

'*That's because I'm Welsh, you rotten little upstart,*' Leah breathed, but she found herself smiling, feeling engaged with life for the first time in days. She liked Rex, and she admired Daisy, but if either of them were to truly trust her she was going to have to pull out all the stops from the outset. She liked nothing more than a challenge, and it would be the best distraction she could have hoped for from the desperate disappointment of Adam Coleridge.

She returned to her room and pawed through the dresses hanging in her wardrobe; many of them had been plucked from charity shops and market stalls, but there was one she had paid good money for, lots of it, and it had stood her in good stead more than once. She registered the absence of her pink beaded dress with a little frown, but her hand closed on the one she was looking for and she drew it out. Perfect.

When she arrived in the lobby a short while later, the first person she saw was Helen, who did a satisfying double-take, and then grinned.

'So nice to see you again, Mrs Scripps.'

'Point me at the stars,' Leah intoned dramatically, and Helen laughed and indicated the lounge.

'Rex knows you though, you won't be able to fool him.'

'I know, honey, I know. But it's not really Rex I have to convince.'

Leah pushed through the double doors, and immediately found the little cluster of Hollywood guests, who stood by the tree, chattering animatedly. She was glad she had toned down Millicent's appearance to something more in keeping with theirs; it had been fun to overplay her part in the past, but she had a feeling that Liverpool was going to be a far more serious affair, and it would be good to test Millicent in these surroundings.

Rex was facing her, and he opened his mouth to greet her, but she winked and gave a brief shake of her head. He turned to his companion again, leaving Leah free to join them unannounced.

'Hello, everyone,' she said, suddenly having less confidence in her own skills, and wondering if she wasn't still too overdressed. But it was Christmas, and her beads and feathers weren't the only ones in the room – nor was she the only one in a dress that revealed almost as much skin as it hid.

'Good evening, Mrs ... ?' Rex raised an eyebrow.

'Scripps. Millicent Scripps.'

Rex introduced himself and the others. 'Are you a guest here, Mrs Scripps? Only I don't think we've met.'

'I'm a good friend of Mrs Fox,' Leah said. 'So nice to meet some fellow Americans here! Miss Conrad, I'm *such* a fan! Tell me, do you like it here? I find it a little *too* quiet at times, after the buzz of the city, don't you?'

'Oh no, not me. I love it here!'

And they were off. The conversation flowed easily, and no one so much as looked at Leah askance. She spoke at length, testing her accent to its limits, and if she'd sought confidence in her ability she found it here. She was also reminded of the pleasure she took in successfully passing herself off as a wholly invented

226

creature, and learned it was particularly sharp when she was with people whose entire lives revolved around that.

She kept up the pretence until after dinner, at which she'd naturally been invited to join them, and where she'd sat between Daisy and Freddie. When Rex started discussing locations back home that might be adapted to replicate Fox Bay, she went out into the lobby to escape the heat and the cigar smoke for a while. It was almost empty out here, with everyone either finishing dinner, or already choosing the best seats in the lounge, but Ben was on duty and she found him chatting to Xander at the desk. She realised with a wash of sadness that she'd have precious little time to talk to the cubs now.

'When do you start your training?' she asked Xander, only just remembering to slip back into her own voice.

'The sixth. Bertie's going to visit when she's had her leg fitted, so she can ask me if it's all we'd hoped for before she officially signs up.'

'Well, she's not one to change her mind once it's made up.'

Ben kept surreptitiously looking over towards the dining room, and Leah smothered a smile. 'She'll be out soon.'

'Who will?'

'Sweetheart, you don't have to pretend with me.' Leah turned to Xander. 'Do you mind if I talk to Ben alone for a minute?'

'Not at all. I need to make sure that horror of a sister of mine isn't making an idiot of herself anyway.'

'One of these days that *horror of a sister* is going to give him the thick ear he deserves.' Leah smiled as they watched him go back into the dining room. 'Good thing we know he doesn't mean it.'

'They're as bad as one another.' Ben looked at her, his own smile fading. 'Mum tells me you're off. For good this time.'

'Well, I wouldn't say *good*,' Leah said, trying to keep her tone light. 'But yes, I have a chance to take up nursing again, and I'd be a fool to pass it up. I'll be back, though.'

'I hope so.' He glanced at the dining room door again as it opened, but turned back to Leah when Mr and Mrs Walker came out.

'How's that beautiful girlfriend of yours?' Leah asked pointedly.

Ben flushed, and began tidying the already neat reception desk. 'I haven't seen her over Christmas, she's too busy.'

'As are you. You can't put all the blame on her.'

'I'm not. I'm just saying.'

'Are you two serious?'

Ben stopped shuffling business cards. 'You were talking about Daisy back there, weren't you? When you said she'd be out.'

'Of course I was.'

'I have no idea why. She's never going to look twice at me when she has Freddie Wishart.'

'Are they an actual item then?' Leah was genuinely surprised. 'I mean, I know that's what the press likes to think, but they didn't seem to be anything of the kind at dinner.'

'We've barely seen Freddie at all, so we wouldn't know. But even if they're not together, she has a wildly exciting life in America. Where she's going to be sailing home to in a few weeks,' he added.

'Do you still think she has a head full of champagne bubbles?' Leah gave him a sly look, and he grinned. Leah reflected that it was no surprise he'd broken hearts all over the village when he'd taken up with Lily Trevanion, he was the image of his handsome father, with the sweet, uncomplicated temperament of his mother. A winning combination in any offspring.

'Alright, I take that back,' he allowed. 'But when you read the papers they all say it. Because of her father owning that other studio, I suppose.'

'She's proved she's more than worthy of her place among the top names. And she's adorable too.'

'Yes.' He sighed. 'It was easier when I believed the papers.'

'So you *are* smitten?'

'Leah!' Ben's laugh was unguarded and loud, and echoed across the lobby just as the girl in question came out. She looked over, and waved, and Leah noticed Ben's hand beside hers, about to rise. She clamped her own over it. 'She's waving at me,' she muttered from the corner of her mouth.

'Thanks,' he whispered back, and Leah patted his hand and brought out Millicent again.

'Hi, sweetheart! Come on over here a second?'

'Leah!' Ben hissed.

'Hush.' Leah smiled as Daisy came over. 'You've met Ben, haven't you?'

'Not really. At least, we haven't been properly introduced.'

'Well considering he's the night manager, I'd say that was very remiss of the management. Daisy Conrad, Benjamin Fox.'

'Pleased to meet you, Benjamin.'

'Ben,' he managed, and Leah pretended not to notice how he dragged his hand up his trouser leg before he offered it. 'I'm sorry I haven't introduced myself before.'

'Oh, it's no one's fault,' Daisy assured him. 'I'm barely around when you're on duty. I've been retiring early to run lines. In fact, Mrs Scripps, it's been wonderful to meet you, but I have to go do that right now I'm afraid.'

'I understand you're going to be learning to speak with an English accent for your new role?'

229

'Yes! I can't wait.' Daisy cleared her throat, and made a passable attempt. 'I'm to play an English *femme fatale*.'

Leah chuckled, and immediately felt bad when she saw Daisy's expression. 'Honey, I'm not laughing at your accent, that's actually pretty good. No, it was just ... *English*, and then the French ... Never mind.'

'Oh! Right, I get it! Anyway, this lady Mrs Fox knows is going to be teaching me to sound more natural.'

'And do you think she can?' Leah studiously avoided looking at Ben.

'Honestly? I don't want to be rude or ungrateful, but I'm not convinced, and neither is Rex. But, you know, I'll give it a shot.'

'I think Rex might have changed his mind about that recently,' Leah said. 'But why don't you think it'll work?'

'Rex says she doesn't even speak normal English herself.'

Leah still didn't dare look at Ben, who she sensed was holding in another of those huge laughs. 'She doesn't? What do you mean?'

'I need someone who has the kind of accent people back home are used to hearing from over here,' Daisy said earnestly. 'But like I said, I'll try.'

'Well if she's no good, or if, say, she suddenly has to go away, I'm sure there's ... *someone* who'd be glad to help out.'

Ben made a strangled sound.

'I'm sure,' Daisy said. 'Anyway, I really must go now. My script awaits!'

'Are you sure you wouldn't prefer to begin your English lessons tonight?' Leah slipped easily into her best, cut-crystal English accent, and smiled as Daisy's mouth fell open in surprise. 'I'm sorry, love,' she said in her own voice. 'I just had to give you the confidence in me that you'll need, if you're going to learn from me.'

'Confidence?' Daisy repeated, her green eyes huge. 'I am in *awe*! Yes, I'd like to start tonight! Holy smokes!'

Her enthusiasm made Leah feel oddly emotional; there was no hint of annoyance at being publicly duped, as she'd feared there might be, just honest appreciation. The girl was a sweetheart, and Leah was suddenly sorry they'd have so little time together. But she also felt certain it would take no time at all for Daisy to pick up what she needed before Leah left. And if not, well … She glanced back at Ben, as they bade him good night. The boy was never overworked at this time of year, after all.

CHAPTER SIXTEEN

Trethkellis Lifeboat Station
New Year's Eve

Fiona dropped the sponge back into the bucket with a contented sigh. How was it that cleaning down the cramped quarters of the station gave her ten times the satisfaction of cleaning the huge, luxurious rooms back at the hotel? There she was a maid, true enough, but she was also very obviously one of the family, and even the formidable Miss Tremar offered a degree of deference. Here she was no more or less than one of the women who maintained the station, cleaned the oilskins, wound the ropes on the capstans, and generally supported the crew of the *Lady Dafna*. But here she felt needed as she didn't at Fox Bay.

Amy had been greeted with pleasure by those women who'd been present at her rescue, then Fiona proudly took her down to the slipway and showed her Danny Quick's little boat. 'Remember I told you he has an outboard motor? This is it!'

Amy didn't look particularly impressed, but she nodded, pulled her coat tighter and looked back towards the station. 'Is he here then?'

'No, but they might all come down for practice later. Anyway, he's shown me how to start it. All you have to do is open the fuel line with that switch, then turn that wheel there on the top, really fast—' she demonstrated in the air '—and off you go! He's going to let me try it one day, he says. Wouldn't it be wonderful if we could go out on it before you leave?'

But Amy had remained disappointingly uninterested, though when they went back inside she had looked at the clock and perked up. 'Remember that surprise I mentioned, the one I'm supposed to pick up this week?'

'I remember.' Fiona hid her disappointment. 'Are you saying you want to go today?'

'You don't have to come. There's a train in half an hour, if I catch that one I can be there and back before you've finished here for the day. Then we can still walk back together.'

'My birthday isn't until February though.'

'It's a combined early birthday gift, and a thank-you. Would you mind if I went?'

'Of course not! But you should be saving your money for … you know what.' Fiona nodded at Amy's waist, its secret concealed behind a heavy coat; a Christmas gift from the family.

'I know. This is only something very little, but when I saw it I thought you'd love it.' She looked around her. 'And seeing the way you are here, I'm doubly sure of it now.'

Geoff Glasson had arrived shortly after Amy had left, and immediately put Fiona to work, as if to remind her that one illicit trip out on the *Dafna* did not make her a crew member. But she didn't mind in the slightest, and when the rest of the crew arrived to take part in another practice run she felt her heart lift as if a group of old friends had arrived – she'd forgotten how much she'd missed being here.

The Dafna was launched and then retrieved, and sat now on the beach as Damien Stone, the mechanic, made a minor adjustment to the fuel mixture while the rest of the crew left him to his work.

'Andrew!' Fiona called out as they made their way up the beach, 'I found one of your family's bakeries, in Caernoweth, and told them all about how brave you are!'

'Proper job!' he yelled back, his voice snatched away by the rising wind.

'Shouldn't have told him that,' Danny shouted, 'he's bad enough already!'

He received a punch in the arm for his trouble, and his laughter rang along the beach.

Donald Houghton was back on the crew after a couple of weeks away to allow his leg to heal, and as everyone grouped in the station they discussed their plans for the celebrations for the end of the decade. Much of the conversation seemed to centre on the party that would be happening in the Saltman, and would feature a popular local comic duo who were renowned for their bawdy ditties. In her heart Fiona longed to be included in it, but it was impossible.

'I suppose you've got a posh party planned,' Danny said to her, as if he'd climbed into her thoughts. 'Got the King coming, have we?'

'Lay off her,' Andrew said. 'You're only jealous 'cos you're not invited.'

'Jealous? Of a bunch of toffs in frills?'

'Oh, I think you'd look *lovely* in frills,' Fiona said with an innocent smile. 'They'd really set off that baby curly hair of yours.'

Andrew guffawed, several others sniggered, and even Danny grinned. 'Alright, maid, you've got me there.'

The chatter was interrupted as the coastguard's siren split the air, and Fiona and the other women melted back against the wall while the crew leapt for their protective clothing. Then they hustled into action, helping the men into oilskins and boots, tugging here, straightening there, making sure the cork life jackets were properly fixed, before running down to the beach to help ready the boat itself. The ropes were heavy, and wet, and the waves tugged at the women's skirts, then plastered them against their freezing legs. Fiona was in her usual trousers, but even those were dragged by the weight of the water, and she slipped more than once, knocked off balance by the surge of the tide as it made its way back in.

Eventually the *Dafna* was far out enough to use its engine, and it roared and spluttered to life, sending the boat rocking wildly before it steadied and began its journey out into deeper waters. Fiona, up to her chest in the rolling swell, coughed out a mouthful of salt water and began wading back with the others. She toyed with the idea of going up to the coastguard's hut as usual, to follow the progress of the lifeboat itself, but after catching a glare from Geoffrey Glasson's wife she followed the women meekly indoors, to re-clean everything they'd scrubbed that morning. Then she sat at the bottom of the slipway, waiting for the boat to return, and glad she'd taken the time to sew up her coat sleeve after all; the wind cut through every strained seam and buttonless hole.

The tide crept up the beach, and her clothes still hung wet and heavy around her shivering frame, but eventually she saw the signal flashing from the hut on the hill, to announce the

Dafna's return. Alongside the other women she seized the ropes once again, her fingers cramping and ice-cold, and her muscles screaming. Once more she was knocked to her knees by a sudden surge, and swallowed a mouthful of brine before she was hauled to her feet again by someone nearby. She gasped for breath, blinking away the salt spray, and put all her strength into pulling the boat up onto the beach. All around her people were shouting: instructions, questions, answers, curses ... Exhaustion was creeping through her bones, but she wished Amy had stayed, so she might have felt the same matchless thrill that went with it.

The damaged fishing boat for which the *Dafna* had been called out was now drifting, crewless, but at least all souls on board had been brought safely ashore. Most of them were men she recognised from the village, and, as always when it was a local vessel that had hit trouble, she felt the vastness of the dispassionate sea like a weight across her own shoulders.

Pasco Penberthy would send a tugboat out to bring the drifting fishing boat in, provided it was still afloat by that time, and in the meantime the survivors and lifeboat crew would need hot drinks and dry clothing. The women would have their chance only when they had served the others, but Fiona was grateful to feel a heavy blanket draped around her shoulders as she refilled the tea urn.

'Don't pay me no mind,' Danny said, low in her ear. 'Andrew's right, I'm jealous.' With that, he vanished to get changed, and Fiona smiled as she watched him go. *A nose you could launch the* Dafna *off?*

Amy returned as Fiona was starting to get warm again, but she had an air of secrecy and urgency about her that seemed out of proportion to having just bought a birthday gift. She drew Fiona aside, only wincing slightly in surprise as her fingers gripped wet clothing.

'I've just seen something!'

'What sort of something?' Fiona released herself from Amy's grasp, and plucked her wet sleeve away from her arm with a grimace. 'And where?'

'In the pawn shop.' Amy took a short breath. 'It was Bertie's ring, I'm sure of it!'

Fiona stared, then gave a confused flick of her head. 'Bertie's ring? Her *engagement* ring?'

'Yes! And Mr Templeton says it was Jowan who pawned it!'

'How do you know it was hers? He hasn't even given it to her yet!'

'Because I saw it in the church, when he first showed her. I was sitting next to her, remember? At Midnight Mass.'

'But they took it to be re-sized, we saw them come out of the shop.'

'And today I saw it in the shop up the road,' Amy insisted. 'It wasn't out for sale yet, it was just lying there on the counter on a bit of cloth. I asked the pawnbroker, he was cleaning it, I think, and he looked at his records and said it was Jowan Nancarrow's. Can't be too many of those around, can there?'

'There's no need to be sarcastic,' Fiona retorted.

'Well, do you think we ought to tell Bertie?'

Fiona thought for a minute. 'No. I'd imagine he's going to be able to get it back, just needed the money for something in the meantime. It's not as if he *sold* it.'

'How long before they do sell it?'

'How should I know?' Fiona snapped. 'I'm not in the business of pawning my belongings!'

'So we should keep quiet about it?'

'Definitely.'

Amy pursed her lips. 'Alright. I won't say anything.'

Fiona eyed her carefully, not entirely convinced. 'Come on, let's go home. I'm freezing, and we need to get ready for the party.'

'Looks like you've been having a party here,' Amy opined, looking at the remainder of the crew who were still milling around. 'Are these the ones who brought me in?'

'Most of them.' Fiona pointed out those she could see, beginning with Andrew Kessel. 'Mick's in the shed with Mr Glasson I expect,' she finished.

Amy looked startled. 'Who?'

'Mr Glasson, the cox.' Then she realised. 'Oh, I see. Mick is Michael Sherborne. Sorry, I didn't mean to remind you of something so difficult.'

'Don't be silly, it's not your fault.' Amy looked over her shoulder as they left the station. 'Which one's Mr Outboard Motor then, the face that launched a thousand lifeboats?'

Fiona grabbed her arm and dragged her away. 'Never you mind.'

* * *

The party didn't officially begin until nine, which was another hour yet, but already the doors were revolving seemingly non-stop, and shrieks and laughter drifted from outside as frocks were whipped over knees, and hats threatened to escape. Bertie and Lynette sat in the lobby where they could watch the comings and goings of guests, and Jeremy Bickle stepped out from behind the busy bar himself to bring their cocktails, along with a bottle of champagne in an ice bucket.

'Where's Xander?' Bertie asked Lynette, smiling her thanks at Jeremy as he laid it all on the low glass table with a flourish.

Lynette picked up the bottle. 'As far as I'm aware he's still chasing some awfully pretty American girl. The one who's meant to be looking after Daisy. Marjorie something, I think.'

'Ah, the lovely Miss Porter.' Bertie grinned. 'And is she enjoying being chased, do you know?'

'I imagine she must be, she's not trying very hard to evade capture.' Lynette splashed champagne into their glasses, on top of the concoction already in there. 'This cocktail is in your honour today,' she announced. 'Aviation Fizz. Cheers!'

'Cheers,' Bertie echoed, with a smile, and took a sip. 'What on earth's in it? Apart from the cherry stuff, I can taste that.'

'Gin, of course. Um, Crème de Violette, bit of lemon juice . . .' She waved a vague hand. 'Usual stuff. And all topped off with a dash of champers.'

'And a dash more?' Bertie held out her glass, and Lynette obliged.

'What time's Jowan getting here?'

'Not sure, it depends how soon Alfie gets back from Caernoweth I suppose. They're all invited.'

'And is Jowan going to . . . you know?'

'To what?' Bertie asked innocently.

'Propose, you idiot!' Lynette took a slug of her drink. 'He's picking up the ring today, isn't he?'

Bertie gave her a slow smile. 'Yes, he is. And yes, he is!'

Lynette gave a short squeal, then looked mortified as Freddie Wishart wandered past. 'That wasn't about you,' she said hurriedly. 'I mean I wasn't . . . I didn't . . . Oh hell!'

Freddie's blond hair was less heavily waxed tonight, and he'd swapped his staid suits for something brighter in light green, and cut fashionably loose. He appeared much younger than he usually did, more like his on-screen appearance.

'I don't expect every woman I meet to fall over me,' he assured her with an ironic tilt to his smile. 'Or even to squeak.'

'Do you think he secretly thinks I fancy him?' Lynette murmured, as he continued on his way. 'Because I truly don't. He's dishy enough, but not my type at all.'

'Who is your type?'

'I don't know, until I see him.' Lynette took another drink, and considered. 'There is someone I certainly wouldn't object to seeing a bit more of, though.'

Bertie suspected it was Ben, and she wasn't quite ready for that, so she changed the subject. 'What do you think of Amy getting her memory back, then? So suddenly, too.'

'Good for her. Her family must have been beside themselves.'

'Hmm.' Bertie couldn't help the little niggle of suspicion; those two girls were always sloping off somewhere, talking in low voices, and looking furtive. Fiona wouldn't say a thing, of course, but Bertie had never quite managed to bring herself to trust the little blonde waif.

'She's a sweet thing,' Lynette said, 'and so adorably pretty. Speaking of which, even little Fiona is looking quite grown-up tonight, don't you think?'

She pointed, and Bertie turned to see her sister coming downstairs, looking disturbingly adult in a dress that was part chiffon, part silk, and altogether too short at the knee. A pang of envy went through her; she herself would never be able to wear such a gown again. Amy was behind her, wearing one of Fiona's dresses; a plain square-cut one that hung off her spare frame and fell to mid-calf. Bertie expected her to be casting equally envious glances at Fiona's party frock, but she seemed distracted.

'So many people here already,' Fiona said. 'Mum's only just gone to change. We've been helping her decorate the small sitting room upstairs, for anyone who doesn't want to have their ears blasted by Billy and the boys.'

'Who are they?' Lynette asked.

'Billy Lang and the Pure Blues. They're a seven-piece from the Bude area, they played at my twenty-first.' How long ago that seemed, now, Bertie thought. Another life entirely.

'What time's Jowan getting here?' Amy was peering at the door as if she expected him to be there now.

'When he's ready,' Bertie said, with more waspishness than she'd intended. 'Why?'

'Maybe she's got a little crush!' Lynette sang, smiling broadly.

Amy scowled. 'Don't be ridiculous.'

'We're just excited to see if he proposes,' Fiona broke in, and tugged at Amy's arm. 'Come on, let's go and see if Billy needs any help setting up.'

'Does Fiona have her eye on anyone?' Lynette asked, as the girls vanished into the lounge.

'I wouldn't have thought so! She's far too young.' But Bertie couldn't help remembering Fiona's first impression of Xander, at the Bude racetrack: *You never told me he was quite so handsome . . .* 'Is absolutely everyone falling in love at the moment?'

'Like who?'

'Well, Jo and me, of course. You and . . . whoever it is you're after, Leah and Adam.' She nearly added Ben and Daisy, but that was all one-sided, and if Lynette really did have her eye on him it would send her mood plummeting. 'Alfie and Beth Nancarrow,' she said instead.

241

'It must be the new decade,' Lynnette surmised, brandishing the champagne bottle again. 'Come on, drink up.'

'New decade. Yes.' Bertie fell silent, and Lynette frowned. 'What is it?'

'I remember the party my parents had for the last one,' Bertie said. 'I was allowed to sit on the stairs and watch everyone arriving, but Ben was the only one of us allowed to actually attend. Everyone looked so beautiful and excited. Like peacocks, strutting around in their bright colours.'

'It must have been wonderful.'

'It was the last party my father ever gave.'

'Oh, darling . . .' Lynette put her hand over Bertie's. 'I'm so sorry.'

'When I was by the river, you know, when I had the accident, I thought I saw him standing by the bridge. He looked so real.'

'He'd be proud of you,' Lynette said gently. 'You've been incredibly strong.'

'I wanted to go to him.'

'And thank goodness you didn't. He wouldn't have wanted you to miss out on all this. And all that's to come.'

'I think—' Bertie broke off, and shook her head with an embarrassed half-smile. 'No. Never mind.'

'Go on.'

Bertie took a deep drink from her glass, and realised she was feeling a little squiffy, or she wouldn't be saying this. 'Do you remember when I said that when I was racing motorbikes I felt close to him?'

'Of course.'

'Well I think part of the reason flying appeals so strongly is that it would make me feel closer still.' Bertie heard the words and they sounded foolish, even to her. 'I said never mind.'

'No, I understand.' Lynette's voice was still quiet. 'It makes perfect sense.'

'Well, whether it does or it doesn't,' Bertie said, drawing herself straighter in her chair, 'I'm doing it.'

'Yes!' Lynette topped them both up and then peered into the bottle. 'More champagne needed, I think.'

'And now I know Jowan approves. Did I show you the shcarf?' She giggled. 'That's harder to say than you'd think!'

'It is after a gallon of champers!'

'I keep it here,' Bertie said, pulling the box out from where it was wedged between her thigh and the side of the chair. 'Makes me remember how lucky I am.'

'How lucky *he* is,' Lynette corrected her. She looked around. 'It's filling up quickly, isn't it?' A crash of cymbals from the lounge made them both jump, and the little run on the drums that followed told them Billy and the Pure Blues were almost ready.

'It's going to get quite loud in here, isn't it?' Bertie said.

'Well, that's why there are two sitting rooms upstairs.' Lynette stood up. 'Shall we?'

'Don't you want to stay down here with the party? Just because I can't dance, doesn't mean you have to—'

'It has absolutely nothing to do with dancing,' Lynette said firmly, taking hold of the handles of Bertie's chair. 'I'm going home in a couple of days, and we shan't see each other for ages. Come on. Bring your glass, and hold this.' She put her own cocktail glass into Bertie's free hand, and pushed her towards the lift.

They ignored the enclosed sitting room on the first floor and came out on the second, where the smaller lounge area lay open to the corridor. Surprisingly, they found themselves alone, and with the sound of the jazz band drifting up the stairs from the ground floor there was just enough background noise to provide entertainment without drowning conversation.

Lynette sank into one of the high-backed chairs near the window. 'Damn. Should have got another bottle before we came up.'

'Someone will be around to take orders in a minute.' Bertie sipped at what was left in her glass, and stared out of the window at the blackness beyond. The coloured lights bobbed madly in the wind, and now and again a tree branch would bend and obscure them, and it seemed they were flickering on and off like coast-guard signals.

'I've never known such beastly weather last so long,' Lynette grumbled, following her gaze. 'That dusting of snow on Christmas Eve didn't last long, did it?'

'Hardly ever does, out here. But it was nice to see when we came out of church.'

'I'll bet.'

'As soon as you feel you want to go back downstairs, you must do it,' Bertie said, still feeling guilty.

'Oh, I will.'

'Do you girls mind if I join you?'

Bertie twisted in her seat, surprised to see Daisy Conrad, looking ravishing as always, but also terribly shy. She was standing at the top of the stairs, evidently ready to continue down the moment she felt unwelcome.

'Gosh, of course not!' Lynette jumped up. 'Come over! Why aren't you downstairs with your party?'

Daisy came closer, the fringes on her green silk and devoré velvet gown swishing around her calves, and her fingers playing with the clasp of her evening bag. She still looked nervous, and Bertie could hardly place her as the same woman who'd bewitched the world from the huge cinema screens. She hadn't seen much of the girl since she'd arrived, but there had always been an aura of the star around her, even when she remained quiet and in the background.

'Are you alright?' she asked.

'I'm fine,' Daisy said on a sigh, and Bertie realised that if she'd thought she herself had been getting tipsy, Daisy Conrad was already well beyond that. Her huge, beautifully painted eyes were struggling to focus on anything, and when she lowered herself into the empty chair next to Bertie her hand slipped and she landed more quickly than she'd intended. A giggle burst from her lips, and it was hard not to smile in response.

'I suppose you're not used to drinking like this,' Lynette said, exchanging an amused glance with Bertie. 'Prohibition and all that.'

'Oh, we have ... places, where we can go,' Daisy said, waving an elegant hand.

'Speakeasies? I've heard of those.'

'Those, and others.' Daisy tapped the side of her nose solemnly. 'There's a Blind Tiger downtown by the ... Oh, but no. I mustn't.'

'Well it's not as if we're going to go there,' Bertie protested. 'Come on, what's a Blind Tiger?'

'Mr Bannacott!' Lynette's chair was facing the open end of the lounge, and Bertie turned to see Guy was indeed there by the stairs, dressed in a smart suit rather than his uniform in honour of the occasion. He'd been peering into the room, and when he saw them he fished his notebook from his top pocket, and flashed his professional smile.

'Can I fetch you ladies something to drink?'

'Perfect timing!' Lynette beamed. 'Three Aviation Fizzes please. And a bottle of champagne you can leave with us.'

'Are you expecting . . . anyone else to join you?' he asked. 'Mr Wishart, perhaps?'

'No, thank goodness,' Daisy said. 'It's just us free birds tonight.'

'Why do you ask?' Bertie felt like teasing him, but her champagne-loosened tongue was likely to push teasing into outright mockery if she wasn't careful, and that would have been crude and unfair so she stopped.

'Just in case you wished to order a drink for anyone else,' Guy said carefully, giving Bertie a particularly hard stare.

'Of course. Very sensible. Still no.' Daisy smiled brilliantly at him, but Bertie could see her eyes were crossing slightly. 'However, if you *do* see Mr Wishart please tell him he's perfectly welcome to . . . stay downstairs where he belongs.'

Lynette snorted, but Daisy kept an admirably straight face as they gave their orders, and Guy left as silently as he'd arrived. Bertie raised an eyebrow. 'Why are you so intent on keeping Freddie away?'

'A Blind Tiger,' Daisy said, clearly equally intent on deflecting the question, 'is a place where you can go . . . Well. There are two kinds.' She held up two fingers, and stared at them for a moment, before remembering what she'd been saying. 'One is a place where you can go look at something exciting, like a . . . well, a tiger! But not usually. Mostly a, a parrot, or something, who tells poems. You know? An attraction. You pay to see it, and you get a drink for free. See? Not selling.'

'And the other kind?' Bertie was still grinning over the idea of a poetry-reciting parrot.

'The other kind is where you put your money in this little

drawer thing in the wall. You tell them what you want to drink, and how you take it, and it arrives. Magic! *Voilà!*' She struck a pose. 'No one gets in trouble because no one can tell who's serving.'

'So if you're quite used to drinking,' Bertie said carefully, 'why are you hiding away up here, and as drunk as a skunk?'

'Because if I go downstairs, Rex Kelly will send me to bed,' Daisy confided, and now the fizz seemed to go out of her and she slumped in her chair.

'Why?'

'He'll take one look and be convinced I'll tell everyone. But I won't.'

'Tell everyone what?' Bertie glanced at Lynette, whose eyes were wide.

Daisy blinked. 'Nothing. Forget it.'

'Oh no you don't.' Lynette sat forward. 'Come on, something's got you skulking away up here and drinking yourself silly!'

'I'm not supposed to say.'

'You can tell us,' Lynette urged. 'We won't tell anyone, and it looks as if you're not happy about keeping it to yourself. You'll feel better if you let it out.'

Daisy looked from one to the other, clearly wavering. 'You have to swear to me that you'll keep this just between us,' she said at last. Lynette took Daisy's hand. 'We promise.' She turned back to Bertie. 'Look at me, holding this famous hand!'

'Don't.' Daisy pulled away. 'I know you're kidding, but please, don't.'

'What's wrong?' Bertie said gently. 'Why don't you want to see Freddie or Rex?'

'This is going to be my sixth picture,' Daisy said, meditatively.

'It's my fourth with Freddie, my third with Rex ... And my last picture with anyone at all.'

A silence fell between them. In the grand scheme of things it wasn't a huge announcement, but it had been Daisy's entire life, and the decision seemed to be causing her some conflict.

'But you're only, what, twenty-four?' Lynette ventured.

'Twenty-five.'

'You're at the peak of your career!'

'That's what Rex says. And Freddie too. But it's alright for them, as men get older they get more popular. Us girls get picked apart before every role, and one of these days I'm not going to fit. So, much as I love it, I'm quitting before that happens. While I'm on top.' Daisy sat forward, and now she didn't seem drunk at all, just terribly earnest. 'I made my mind up ages ago, but this place has convinced me.'

'What?' The last thing Bertie wanted was for it to get out that Fox Bay had somehow deprived the public of more Daisy Conrad films. 'Don't blame us!'

'I'm not blaming you, I'm thanking you!'

'I'm sure Rex Kelly won't be,' Bertie muttered. 'Why doesn't he want it getting out?'

'Can you imagine? The moment he takes over as the producer of the Conrad–Wishart movies, one half of them quits? His reputation will take a hell of a beating. He might never recover from that, professionally.'

'Can I fetch you ladies a drink?'

They all turned in surprise, to see a young bar steward with a tray.

'Guy's taken our order already,' Bertie said. 'About five minutes ago.'

The young man looked confused. 'Mr Bannacott's not on duty tonight, his shift ended hours ago. Mr Bickle sent me up to do this room and the sitting room on first.'

'Oh, our mistake,' Lynette said brightly. 'Champagne please!'

'Lynette!' Bertie laughed. 'Don't listen to her, Simon, she's had quite enough!'

The steward gave an indulgent little shake of his head, and made a note on his pad before vanishing down the stairs.

Bertie turned back to Daisy, still finding it hard to believe she was sitting here talking to such a huge star as if they were friends. 'So this is it then. *Dangerous Ladies* is your final film.'

'And I'm going to go out with a fanfare,' Daisy said. 'Leah has taught me so much already, I'll miss her when she's gone, for sure.'

Bertie remembered the gentleness and persistence with which Leah had nursed and encouraged her, and, with a surge of guilt, the bitterness and bile with which she'd been repaid. 'I'll miss her too, but she'll be a wonderful nurse.'

'So how's the accent coming along?' Lynette asked Daisy, breaking through the faint air of melancholy.

Daisy sat up straight, wriggled her smoothly rounded shoulders, and shook back her hair. 'It's going very well, actually,' she said, in a surprisingly good accent and understated manner. 'I was born in a little village in Surrey, and I live in a cottage near a post office, a pub, and a library. There are farms too. The pavements are narrow, but the roads are well maintained.'

'That's amazing,' Bertie murmured. 'You'd never know.'

'It was hard enough to learn to drop these Rs,' Daisy went on in her usual voice, 'but Ts were my main problem so she taught me to say this, are you ready? Betty bought a bit of butter, but she found the butter bitter, so Betty bought a bit of better butter, to make the bitter butter better.'

'I can't even say that sober!' Lynette laughed.

'It took a while,' Daisy admitted. 'But it was worth the effort. This movie is going to be huge, and it's going to be fun to play a . . . a kind of, what's it called? A grifter.'

'Like a con artist?'

'Yes! She's a great character.'

'And Leah's teaching you this,' Bertie mused, enjoying the irony. 'Well you're certainly going to be leaving your public wanting more, but what do *you* want next?'

'Ah, just in time, I was beginning to sober up.' Lynette gestured Guy over. 'Thank you, Mr Bannacott. Have you seen Xander?'

'He and Miss Porter are dancing, miss.'

'Heaven protect everyone else then.' Lynette grinned. 'Or at least their feet. So, Daisy, you were saying?'

Daisy waited until Guy had withdrawn once more, then she looked at Bertie. 'You're marrying soon, aren't you?'

'I don't know about soon,' Bertie said, 'but I'm supposed to be getting engaged. Tonight, as it happens.'

'Yes, where *is* that boyfriend of yours?' Lynette muttered. 'Come on, Daisy, you were supposed to be telling us what you want to do now.'

'What's he like?' Daisy persisted.

Bertie thought for a moment. 'Good,' she said at length.

'That's it? Good?' Lynette took the champagne Guy had left, and splashed some into each of their glasses. 'He's the solid, dependable farmer type,' she said to Daisy, 'but that doesn't mean he's boring or plain.'

'Or here,' Bertie said drily.

Daisy laughed. 'No, but honestly? That would be enough for me. A good man. A farmer would be fine. So would a fisherman, or a blacksmith ... Or anyone that isn't part of that phoney world.'

'What about Freddie?' Bertie asked. 'The papers all say you two are the perfect couple.'

'And Rex cultivates that, because the public *wants* there to be something between us. But there isn't and never could be.'

'Why not?'

'Because he's ... Just because!' Daisy was clearly going to go no further, so Bertie didn't push although she sensed Lynette was all for it.

'Why don't we go down now and wait for Jowan?' she suggested. She was beginning to wonder if the Nancarrows would turn up at all, and it felt as if by being downstairs it might somehow speed up their arrival. 'And you girls can't really want to spend your New Year's Eve up here and away from all the fun.'

'Oh, believe me, it's bliss,' Daisy sighed, and lay back in her chair.

'One party's like any other,' Lynette agreed. 'Drink up, plenty more where this came from!'

'I can't have too much,' Bertie protested. 'I don't want Jo to get here and find me fast asleep!'

'Especially not tonight,' Daisy agreed. 'I'll take hers, Lynette.'

'And I don't want to be explaining you to Rex either,' Bertie added, aware she was sounding a little schoolmistressy. 'There's a lot of evening to get through yet.'

'Alright, Mother. So, tell me.' Lynette replaced the bottle in the bucket and turned to Daisy. 'Who are your best Hollywood friends? Have you met Greta Garbo, or Alfred Hitchcock? Or ... How about Clara Bow?'

Daisy spoke of her life at home, carefully stepping around the questions Lynette dropped in about Freddie, while Bertie's attention wandered more and more to the window, and to whether Jowan and his family were even now pulling up outside. It wasn't a night for walking, especially since they'd all be dressed up, and she strained for the distinctive sound of the farm's van over the music from downstairs, the wind from outside, and the chatter here in the lounge.

'Let's go down,' Lynette said, breaking into her concentration. 'I can tell you'd rather be hanging around that draughty lobby than up here in the warm with us.'

'You'd better not let Mum hear you call it draughty,' Bertie warned with a grin. 'Daisy, you can stay here if you want, we won't tell Rex where you are.'

'No, it's alright.' Daisy stood up and straightened her extraordinary dress. 'He'll come looking sooner or later. Just so you know though, he's not an ogre. He just doesn't want me to go telling people I'm quitting. Not yet.'

'No one'll hear it from us,' Lynette said. 'Now, let's go and play Hunt the Farmer.'

* * *

Fiona looked at the huge, silver-framed clock on the wall by the piano and saw it was already past eleven o'clock, and there was still no sign of the Nancarrows. Perhaps Jowan hadn't yet been able to raise the money to repay his loan, and reclaim the ring, and that's why he was staying away? What would it be, a manufactured farm emergency? Perfectly believable, of course. But even Bertie must admit it was rude not to have sent a message, even if it was a lie.

Amy was dancing up a storm tonight. As soon as Billy and his band had moved from quiet, introductory music to some of the more popular numbers, it was as if someone had flicked a switch inside Amy's head.

'I know these songs!'

'You don't have to pretend to *me* about your memory coming back,' Fiona reminded her, amused.

'No, I mean these are the songs I learned to dance to at home. Remember I told you about Belinda Pearce's lessons? Come on, I'll show you how!'

'No, thanks!' Fiona had pulled back, still smiling. 'And you need to be careful too,' she added, in a lower voice. 'We definitely don't want you slipping over.'

'I won't! Watch!' And she had disappeared into the throng, emerging a moment later with her hands in the air, dancing with as much confidence and skill as anyone in the room.

Fiona watched, just as she had at Bertie's birthday party, admiring the dancers without feeling the slightest inclination to join them. Now and again she broke away to speak to someone, or to help out as Ben waved her over to the bar and thrust a tray of drinks into her hands. She watched her mother too, not on duty tonight and dressed for a party, but with an odd air of melancholy about her. She recalled Bertie often telling her about the New Year's party ten years ago, describing all the finery, the clothes, the excitement. Fiona had been too young to really understand, all she remembered was that Ben had been in terrible trouble the next day. She guessed a big part of her mother was somewhere back there even now, in Bristol, but that she wasn't thinking about Ben's behaviour.

Now, with the time nearing midnight, the party was in full

swing and Amy was still cutting a rug, this time with Leah who kept stopping and making Amy repeat a move so she could copy it; there was something almost desperate about her determination to get it right, which was quite interesting to see and made Fiona wonder if she had something up her sleeve. Time would tell.

Guy Bannacott slipped from the room, and Fiona followed him out to the lobby, her heartbeat picking up as she realised this was going to be her best chance to catch him alone. Bertie and Lynette were out there, laughing over something, and were clearly both giddy with drink, but both of them kept looking at the door ... Fiona was fond of Jowan, but she could have kicked him for being so late, turning her fiercely strong sister into what amounted to a wallflower.

Guy had turned the first corner on the stairs and Fiona hurried after him, twisting her way through people drifting up and down, and hoping to catch him somewhere quiet. Most of the human traffic was moving between the first floor sitting room and the party downstairs, so Fiona was glad to see Guy already halfway up the second flight, though she made herself hang back.

'Fi, darling!' Granny came out of the sitting room. 'I wouldn't have thought the old fuddy-duddies room was for you!'

'Hardly fuddy-duddies!' Fiona laughed, trying not to follow Guy's progress too obviously. 'No, I'm just fetching something from my room.'

'Well, in case I don't see you when the moment comes,' Fleur said, drawing her close for a hug, 'Happy New Year to you. May it bring you everything you want.'

'Same to you,' Fiona murmured. She hugged her grandmother back, and hoped her impatience didn't show.

'Are you alright, sweetheart?' Fleur asked, holding her at arm's length. 'I suppose you'll miss your little friend when she goes home.'

'I will, yes.'

'Well I'm sure you'll both write. Where is she, anyway?'

'Dancing. She's very good, I'm going to change my shoes so she can teach me,' she added in a burst of inspiration. 'So I'd better hurry.'

'Gracious, yes.' Fleur dropped a kiss on her brow. 'Off you go, you don't want to miss your chance.'

Fiona thought she saw a flicker of sadness on Granny's face, and promised herself she'd go back again later to talk to her, but there was no time now. She took the next set of stairs at a fast trot, and stopped dead at the top. The open lounge area was nearly always shunned over the Christmas break, in favour of the more sociable areas downstairs, but Guy was talking to someone who sat in one of the chairs over by the picture window.

'I must have looked a sight,' he was saying. 'I didn't see you so I tried to give the impression I was only passing by, but I had to take their drinks orders, and I'm not even working tonight!' His laugh was short, and forced, and wasn't returned.

'It's better to meet here, rather than somewhere overtly secret.' It was Freddie's voice, and he sounded subdued. 'At least that way you can pretend to just be taking *my* drinks order, right?'

'Yes, I understand that.' Guy fell silent for a moment, and Fiona tried to melt into the wall, scared her heavy breathing would give her away. This would either confirm her suspicions, or put an end to her hopes of getting extra money for Amy.

'Look,' Freddie said, 'I don't know if this was such a great idea. Maybe we should just—'

'We need to talk.'

'Why? You haven't told anyone, have you?'

'No!' Guy lowered his voice. 'But don't you think you should at least tell your family?'

'That's easy for you to say!' Freddie's voice was louder and clearer now, as if he'd stood up. 'They'll be wrecked if it gets out. It's different for us in the public eye, the papers go crazy over this stuff!'

'Freddie! Listen.' Fiona imagined Guy taking hold of Freddie by the shoulders, but she couldn't lean around the corner to see. 'I know it's hard, but if you keep drinking tonight you're going to end up letting your emotions get the better of you. Then where will we be?'

'I won't! I'm not stupid.'

'Good. Look, it might be too soon to say this, but ... I love you. It'll be alright, I promise.'

Fiona backed away, her face burning, but a great relief stealing over her. As distasteful as it was to have this hold over Guy, it meant Amy would be alright for money, and Fiona's deeply regretted promise would at least be honoured. She went back downstairs, thinking hard. When should she approach him? Amy would have to leave by the morning of the third, at the latest, if Mr Glasson was right about the ship on Saturday. And they had to arrange passage—

'They're here!'

She had reached the bottom of the stairs, and saw Lynette jump up out of her seat.

Bertie spun her chair around to face the door, where Jowan stood, windblown and soaked and worried-looking. 'Why so late, and why haven't you got the van?' She looked beyond him.

'Where are the others?' She started towards him, but he met her halfway across the lobby.

'It's just me,' he said. 'Mum and Uncle Alfie have taken ... Bertie, can we talk somewhere?' He looked around for a quiet corner.

'The upstairs lounge is probably still empty,' Lynette suggested.

'No, it's not,' Fiona put in quickly. 'I've just come past it.'

'Here will do,' Bertie said. 'What is it? Have you changed your mind?'

'No! God, no.' Jowan took a deep breath. 'The thing is, the ring's been stolen.'

Fiona started, and she felt a stirring of real anger. It was a good thing Amy hadn't heard this.

'Stolen?' Bertie repeated in shock. 'From the jeweller's? Was there a robbery?'

'No.' He crouched beside her. 'Jory picked it up, since it was his day off and he was going in anyway. But we think someone must have been watching him.'

'Why?'

'On his way back through the town he took a short cut up through Pathfields, you know, the little alley that's narrower at the bottom end? He was on his way to the station, and that's where they got him. In the dark. They beat him up ...' Jowan took a short breath '... and stole the ring. Along with his wallet and the pocket watch Dad gave him the birthday before he died.'

Bertie put a hand to her mouth. 'Is he alright?'

'He will be.' Jowan's face was pale. 'But there's no chance of getting the ring back now.'

'Never mind the ring!'

He flinched, and Bertie lowered her voice. 'I mean, I know

257

it was your grandmother's, and I'm so sorry it's gone. But your brother's been *hurt*! They could as easily have killed him.'

'Do you think I don't know that?' Jowan stood up, agitated. 'If only I'd gone myself—'

'Oh no you don't! We went through this with my accident, and your father's. This wasn't your fault.'

They were silent for a minute, and then Jowan nodded. 'Jory says the same thing.'

'Do you want to go back home?'

Jowan looked torn. 'I do, and I don't. I want to be with you, but I want to be there when they fetch Jory back.'

'Back from where?' Fiona couldn't believe he was taking it so far.

'The doctor's. Alfie was worried about the bang on his head, said he might have concussion, and Tam Rowe would be able to tell. That's where the van is.'

'Then go,' Bertie said in a low voice. She leaned in and pressed her cheek to his, but from where she stood Fiona could see the bitter disappointment she was hiding from him. 'We can talk about the ring tomorrow. I still want to marry you, you don't get out of things that lightly.'

'Damn.' He turned slightly so his lips touched hers, and they stayed there for a moment, while Fiona's fingers clenched tight. Should she tell Bertie she was letting Jowan make a mockery of her trust?

Jowan touched Bertie's face and stepped back. 'I'm sorry, I truly am.'

He gave Fiona and Lynette a quick, uncertain smile, and pushed his way through the revolving door.

'Poor Jory,' Bertie murmured, 'and poor Jo too, thinking I'd be angry with him.'

That was enough for Fiona. She hurried after Jowan in time to see his figure in the crazily bobbing lights, disappearing around the side of the building.

'Jowan!' Her voice was whipped away as soon as it left her mouth, but she ran a few steps and shouted again, and he stopped.

'Fiona?'

'You're a liar!'

He splashed his way back to her, the rain streaming down his face making him look unfamiliar and a little frightening. 'Come here!' He grabbed her arm and pulled her against the side of the hotel, where the light from the windows spilled across him and made him look even wilder. 'What the hell are you doing following me? And what do you mean, *liar*?'

'Amy saw the ring in Templeton's.'

He blinked. 'Templeton's? What's ... Oh, I know it!' His expression cleared. 'Well whoever stole it must have pawned it. That's brilliant, Fi, we can get it back!'

'Oh stop it!' Fiona shook her wet hair out of her eyes. 'Amy was in Templeton's *hours* before it got dark! She came back to Trethkellis on the half past two train, and you said Jory was attacked in the dark.'

'But he's ...' Jowan looked genuinely baffled. 'He's all over cuts and bruises!'

'So you say.'

'It's the *truth*!'

'Mr Templeton told her who brought it in. He gave her *your* name, and he said they must have had identification.'

The wind surged, and almost knocked Fiona off her feet, even in the shelter of the wall. Jowan caught her arm and held her steady.

'Go back in.' His voice was tight now. 'Promise me you'll say nothing to Bertie. I'll try and sort this out.'

'It wasn't you?'

'Fi, I promise you, I knew nothing about this. Go on, you'll catch your death out here.'

She watched him stride away over the grass, and right up until he left the reach of the lights she could see how rigid his shoulders were beneath his coat. A gust of wind whipped her hair back into her eyes and she turned and made her way back indoors.

'What on earth possessed you to go outside?' Bertie exclaimed. 'You'll catch your death!'

Fiona hadn't even spared a thought for what excuse she'd use. She wiped rain from her face, glad she hadn't decided to try out any make-up tonight, after all. 'I . . . just thought we ought to pass on our good wishes for Jory's health, especially since it was your ring he was picking up.'

'There's no need to make it my fault!'

Fiona was about to respond with equal anger, until she saw her sister's white face. 'No, I'm sorry. Anyway, that's why I went out.'

'It's nearly midnight,' Lynette said brightly. 'Shall we go in to the party?'

As she spoke, the lounge door burst open and Amy came out. She stared at Fiona's bedraggled state in surprise, then gestured them all into the lounge. She was flushed and happy-looking, and Billy Lang himself was staring at her with unabashed admiration – Fiona felt the sting of envy, not for the first time, then shook her head; Amy might be the belle of the ball tonight, looking so much older than her years even in her comparatively plain dress, and catching the attention of the popular band leader, but in a few days she would be setting off on the first part of a lonely journey towards an unknown future. And she had an unborn child to protect. Fiona knew who was better off out of the two of them.

The countdown began, and when they reached midnight the room erupted in streamers, cheering, and singing. Fiona looked around at the guests – both resident and invited for the evening – and wondered how many of them were telling lies, right now, as they kissed and shook hands, and wished one another health and happiness in the coming decade.

She also remembered the dismay and betrayal she had seen on Jowan's face as he'd realised what his brother had done, and knew that, while she still meant to keep Guy to his promise to help out with Amy's passage to Ireland, she could never risk doing anything to make Bertie look at her like that. Any thoughts of gaining extra money by using what she knew about Guy and Freddie were firmly quashed; she would just have to think of something else.

CHAPTER SEVENTEEN

Trethkellis Village Square
1st January 1930

Leah watched from her seat by the well, as more and more villagers came to the centre of the village for the dedication of the war memorial. She herself had been looking at the shrouded stone monument, lost in the past as her mind took her back through the war years. As a nurse in four different field hospitals and clearing stations she had seen so much, done so much and yet now it felt as if she had done nothing of value at all. Her mind and her memories told her otherwise, but her heart did not believe it.

Daniel's name was on that stone, along with so many others, but his body was still somewhere out there beneath the unknowing feet of people who walked the fields. Nothing more now than bones, mingled with those of the men who'd died with him; his fellow sappers, some of them miners as Daniel had been, drafted to tunnel beneath no man's land, always aware that the enemy was doing the same and might be just feet away. Working in near silence lest they give away their position; dying in a noise too awful to bear thinking about.

Leah raised a hand to her forehead, trying to massage away the tension there, but it had settled in the form of a pounding headache that threatened to push her right eye from its socket. A hand on her arm brought her head around and she smiled to see Helen sitting down beside her on the bench.

'Fleur has been busy, lots of people I've never seen before.'

'Mrs Finch has been giving me evil looks since she got here,' Leah murmured. 'Look at her.'

The owner of the Sandy Cove guest house, who'd been utterly taken in by her play-acting, was standing with her friends and kept shooting disapproving looks her way.

'Well you can hardly blame her,' Helen pointed out. 'She thought you were some poor little Scotswoman called Susannah, weeping in the corner, and then running away from that nasty Mr Coleridge. *And* you promised her a travel bag she never got. The one with the butterflies on the handle, remember?'

'I'd completely forgotten about that!' Leah sighed. 'Well, when I leave she can have it.'

'She'll probably burn it.'

Leah looked at Helen in surprise, then had to smother an inappropriate laugh.

'Look sharp,' Helen said. 'Fleur's moving into action. Come on.' She stood and held out her hand, and Leah took it, a sharp pang of mingled regret and panic taking her by surprise. Was she really doing the right thing? She was lying to these people yet again, and leaving them to pursue a life of danger and uncertainty with a man she no longer loved ...

'Nice to see you, Mrs Marshall.' Father Trevelyan took her

hand and pressed it between his. 'We're all so grateful for the courage of men like your husband.'

'Thank you, it's a great comfort to see they're remembered.'

He wove his way through the gathering, taking a hand here, pressing a shoulder there, no doubt substituting *husband* for *father*, or *son*, where appropriate.

'Do you suppose they'll ever commemorate women in this way?' Helen mused. 'They ought to, with all you've told me.'

Leah was momentarily in the thick of it again; the screams, the weeping, the dead . . . She didn't want that to be remembered, but the sacrifices, and the women who'd died for their country, yes. It was only right for them and she hoped that one day they would have their names carved alongside the men they'd fought beside, and for.

Fleur was gesturing, and Helen let go of Leah's hand, leaving her to stand with those whose loved ones' names were being unveiled today. Fleur guided her to stand beside someone she recognised from her occasional wanders through the village, and she reflected how so many sorrows were private ones; she'd never stopped to think how many of the people she saw every day were suffering loss and grief as intense as her own.

She felt quite alone despite the shuffle and the conversations rising and falling around her, but at the same time a little prickling touched the back of her neck. She'd heard people say that they felt as if they were being watched, but she'd never actually felt it herself before, and had dismissed it as implausible nonsense. How could you feel the weight of a pair of eyes on you? But she did.

She turned, expecting to see Helen or Fleur trying to catch her attention, or maybe – she allowed herself the wild hope – Adam had come along after all, to lend her his support. But of course he hadn't, and Helen and Fleur were talking to Beth Nancarrow, who looked drawn and worried. She faced the front again, concentrating on memories of Daniel, both before and during the conflict that had claimed his life.

Father Trevelyan raised his hands until the hubbub fell silent, and when the shuffling had stopped he spoke in grave tones.

'Our thoughts today are, of course, with those who sacrificed all for the Allied Forces and the liberation of Europe during the Great War. Our thanks and prayers will be offered in their names shortly. But first, I would like us all to take the hands of our neighbours, and bow our heads in prayer for the souls of the poor children of Paisley, Scotland, who lost their lives in the terrible, terrible tragedy at the Glen Cinema.'

A low murmuring arose, and Leah heard the words *crushed*, and *fire*, from those who'd heard the news on the BBC that morning. She herself had not heard it, but the news chilled her to the bone. Between sixty and seventy children, they were saying. *Children* . . .

As the shocked mutters turned to a heavy, emotionally charged silence, that feeling of being watched intensified. She felt it beneath the collar of her coat, and the scarf, and the heavy fall of hair tied back at the base of her neck, and finally it was too much to bear, and she whipped her head around. But there were only bowed heads, with rain running off the brims of hats.

Her heart thumping uncomfortably, she faced the front again and felt a deep relief as George Trevelyan began his eulogy to the fallen, and his dedication of the memorial. The names inscribed on the stone were also listed on a sheet of paper, which had been copied and was now passed around to everyone. Leah found

Daniel's name at once: mid-list and stark, and the years since learning of his death fell away until it felt raw and agonising all over again. A glance around showed her that almost everyone was feeling the same, and it was a sombre group that moved away once the reading of the names was over.

Leah scanned the crowd again as she joined Helen and the others, but saw no one she might have expected to be watching her; not even Mrs Finch would have bothered, once she had made clear her initial betrayed feelings. There weren't usually many visitors at this time of year, and even the artists had dispersed back to their homes before Christmas, but some families had moved away since the war, and the crowd had been swelled by their return today. Perhaps someone thought they recognised her but couldn't quite place her. Someone who remembered her from her days as Daniel's 'wife', or had seen her as Susannah, or Millicent ... A guilty conscience was a powerful thing, and an unsettling one.

The news about the Glen Cinema tragedy cast a pall over the guests at the hotel too, particularly after such a successful party. The common thread to conversations was the guilt that they'd been laughing, dancing, and drinking the night away, while only that afternoon so many innocent lives had been stolen and their families changed forever.

Many of the guests had reached the end of their stay anyway, and since it would be another few days before the hotel opened again to regulars, the gradual emptying of the place had a rare melancholy to it. Even the Hollywood party kept to their first floor rooms, and had their meals delivered to them.

Leah began once more to pack her things ready for tomorrow's departure. At least she only needed to take enough for the next few days, she'd have the rest sent on as soon as she could find a suitable address; Helen would find it highly suspicious to be sending it all to a boarding house instead of a nurses' home. It was odd, and unsettling, to think that this would be the last time Leah would be staying here as one of the family. She'd come back someday, she was sure of that, but it would be different; she'd be an occasional guest again just like those old, bleak days before she'd met Helen.

A knock at her door stopped her as she was trying to pull the buckle tight enough to secure her case, and with a grunt of relief she let it go and went to open the door.

'Daisy?'

'Hi, Leah. I just wondered … You know, I heard you were leaving tomorrow, so would it be okay if we spent a little time together now? Get me doing all that Betty and her butter stuff again one last time?' She exaggerated the "t"s the way she knew rubbed Leah up the wrong way, but her grin was disarming; it was hard to be irritated with Daisy Conrad.

'Certainly,' Leah responded in kind. 'Would the lounge be acceptable? It should be quite empty at this time of day.'

'Perfect! Rex is very pleased with the way it's going,' Daisy went on as Leah followed her down the stairs. 'Right now he's cornered Mrs Fox, and they're talking about all the things little Jimmy Haverford is going to need when he gets here. He's going to love it!'

'What's he like?'

'I only met him once, but he seems sweet. Not at all spoiled. Not yet, at least! This is his first picture though, so who knows?'

They went into the lounge which was, as predicted, empty and a little sad-looking. The decorations would remain until twelfth night, but the train set had stopped sometime during the party last night – possibly thanks to a carelessly spilled drink. The excitement of the previous week or so seemed a distant memory now.

They sat near the window that looked out over the deserted tennis courts, and worked further on Daisy's tendency to over-pronounce her "t" sounds, and the time passed pleasantly enough for twenty minutes or so until Martin poked his head in and spotted her.

'Ah, Mrs Marshall. Do you know where Mrs Fox is?'

'Apparently she's talking to Mr Kelly. Do you want me to fetch her?'

'Perhaps you could just ask her something for me? I know we don't open officially until Saturday, but I have a guest trying to check in.'

'Without a booking?' This would have been unusual at peak times, but it sometimes happened over the sparser months and Helen generally welcomed it.

'I don't see why there'd be a problem. Ask them to wait in the lobby, I'll check with Helen.' She left Daisy practising, and went to find Helen in the Foxes' private sitting room, but she was only halfway across the lobby when she heard the familiar voice.

'Leah?'

Her heart stuttered, and she turned to see Glynn, half-risen from his seat. 'I *thought* that was you I saw in the village,' he said with a wide, patently false, smile.

That prickling feeling of being watched suddenly made perfect sense; Glynn had always been good at only being seen when he wanted to be. Acutely aware of the openly curious Martin, Leah managed to sound bright and friendly.

'My goodness, hello! Is it you asking for a room then?' She

crossed the floor and took the chair opposite Glynn, registering a bruise that shadowed his chin. A common enough sight; she couldn't have expected him to change that much.

'I told myself I was going mad,' Glynn said, his smile disappearing. 'What are you doing here?'

'I might ask you the same thing,' she said in a savage whisper. 'Did you *follow* me?'

'No,' he ground out, equally angry now. 'I was invited here by the WI.'

'To this hotel?'

'Of course not! Sandy Cove only had a room free for one night, and the closest bed and breakfast after that is halfway to Bude. When I realised I was going to need a second night Mrs Finch recommended this place.'

She turned her head, suddenly worried Adam was watching. 'Well you can't stay here.'

'*This* is where you made your home? In my old village? I thought you were just staying here.' A look of further realisation crept across his face. 'You were at the front of the memorial group, with the widows and parents.'

There was both betrayal and disgust in his voice, and Leah felt a sudden sense of relief that he was going to make it easy for her to change her mind. To stay.

'Yes,' she said calmly, 'I was.'

'Did you ... tell everyone you were married?' This time he sounded hesitant.

'Of course.' She silently urged him to blow up at her, to make a scene, to bring everything to a boiling, ugly head. 'We lived as man and wife, from the moment you were sent down until the moment he was killed.'

He flinched. 'I knew you were lovers, but I had no idea.'

'Well you have now.' *Tell me you can't forgive me that!*

'I should have realised before,' he muttered. 'My big brother and my wife.' He shook his head, his face cast down. 'All that time I was in prison I thought about you, and I thought about Daniel, but I never put the two of you together until I got out. I'd come to terms with it though.'

Leah looked around again, still nervous. 'Look, we can't talk about it here. Tell the receptionist you've changed your mind, I'll come out to your car and we can talk there.'

'Won't that look a bit odd, you sitting here chatting, and me suddenly changing my mind?'

'You've never once cared how something would look,' Leah said, trying not to snap. 'Alright then, tell him you're going to fetch something from the car while I talk to Helen.'

'Helen?'

'Mrs Fox.'

'You're friends with the owner?'

'The best of friends.' Leah's heart twisted. 'We have been for years, this place is like my home.'

'Did you tell her why you're leaving?'

'Of course not.'

Glynn did not respond with words, but she saw the expression on his face, and knew him well enough to read it. He was right, and hadn't she thought the very same thing only that morning? How could she call herself a true friend when all she did was lie?

'Look, I didn't think I'd be pulling you away from anything much,' Glynn said at length, in a low voice. 'I had no idea you'd built such a life for yourself.'

'You'd no idea about a lot of things. How did you get that bruise?'

He shrugged. 'Card game got out of hand. But I got enough out of it to start us off in style in Liverpool. That's if you still want to come with me?'

Leah wanted to take this chance and tell him *no*, but an image rose into her mind of Adam, the day he and Helen had between them saved Fox Bay. Fleur had suggested they drink to success, to *all* of them, and that Adam should propose it.

Adam's arm had been around Leah, and she had looked up at him, filled with pride and hope, and longing for him to smile down at her in return. But he'd been staring directly across the room, his voice soft and filled with meaning as he tilted his glass in salute. *Vulpes latebram suam defendit. To Helen.*

'Yes,' she said now, her voice suddenly thick. 'I do. Go and wait in the car. I won't just come and talk, I'll come away with you now.'

Upstairs, the last of her things thrust hurriedly into her case, just as they had been at Christmas, she belatedly realised she'd still not seen her pink beaded dress since Helen had taken it away to press. She smiled sadly, remembering the times she'd worn it and felt like a movie star. It would be useful for Liverpool, but she couldn't bring herself to see Helen now just to ask for it. She had to leave quickly, before she changed her mind. The dress would follow, along with the rest of her things.

She fetched her butterfly-handle travel bag from the top of the wardrobe, and wrote a quick note.

Dear Mrs Finch,
Please have this, with my fondest regards.

271

After a moment's hesitation over how to sign it, she scribbled, *Thank you for the kindness you showed to Susannah Paterson.*

She fastened the note to the side of the bag with a hat pin, and dragged her case to the lift, still secretly certain that something must happen to stop her. Bertie, Fiona, or Helen herself, even Adam – someone would come out of a nearby room, and ask her what she was doing and where she thought she was going. She wanted someone to tell her not to be so foolhardy and impulsive, that Glynn would ruin her, or get her killed. But no one did.

Martin gave her a mildly concerned look as she passed through reception. 'I could have asked a bell boy to do that for you. Would you like me to carry it to your taxi?'

'It's quite alright.' She smiled brightly. 'It's not as heavy as I'm making it look.'

'Going back to Wales for a while?'

'Yes.'

'Well I'm glad you could come for the holidays. Have a good trip, and see you soon!'

And that was that.

As the Lancia turned onto the road that would take her away from Fox Bay, Leah Marshall said her silent goodbyes to the austere-looking former monastery, and tried not to think of the beloved people who walked its lushly carpeted floors and sheltered from the bitter west wind behind its solid walls; those people were no longer hers to think about. Her life lay hundreds of miles away now, in Liverpool.

CHAPTER EIGHTEEN

Higher Valley Farm

From the other side of the fireplace Beth surreptitiously watched Alfie scowl at the window, as if he could bring the weather under control by the force of his disapproval. The wind had picked up again since teatime and was buffeting the farmhouse; the screech of loose slates was punctuated by the banging of the gate, the latch sure to be hanging loose, and probably even broken.

'We didn't get around to talking about how Keir's doing,' she said. 'How was the funeral?'

'Went well enough. Young Eddie's still in pieces. He and Keir have one another to lean on though, or I'd have stayed longer than two days.'

'How about the farm?' She was aware she was talking for talking's sake, but it was better than thinking about Jory and Jowan. 'Is it managing alright?'

'Keir's taken a lad on, to make up for what Ellen used to do. He's staying in the house until Keir can get the stable loft fixed up, so it's good for them to have someone else around.'

'Did you and Keir get the chance to talk?'

He nodded. 'He seemed like he needed distracting so I told him about how our family would soon be all mixed up with the Foxes.'

'Did that work?'

He gave her a brief grin. 'In between hearing about them taking strays off lifeboats, and hosting Hollywood picture stars, I'd say he was distracted for an hour or so. Told me no two families ever seemed less suited to being joined.'

'Much as I want Jowan and Bertie to be happy, I can't say I disagree!' Beth's smile faded as the raised voices from upstairs grew louder. Jowan's sympathy for his brother had vanished the moment Tam Rowe had dismissed any worries about concussion, but Beth couldn't understand why; even if Jory wasn't in any danger he was still to be pitied. As her sons' muffled voices rose and fell she could see even Alfie was finding it hard to ignore them, and was darting increasingly frequent glances at the ceiling.

'I'm going up,' she said at length, putting down her mending. 'They're going to start throwing things in a minute.'

'What are they arguing about?' Alfie rose and joined her, rather than persuading her to stay out of it as he usually did. She didn't know whether this was a worry or a comfort.

'Jowan's been off since we got back from Tam's last night,' she said, 'but I've not seen Jory all day. You've seen more of them than I have.'

'They were working apart. Jo was down at the river, Jory was with me so I could keep an eye out, make sure he wasn't overdoing things.'

They'd only reached midway up the stairs before Beth's prediction seemed to come true: a crash, followed by a yell, came from

Jory's room, and Alfie shouldered past Beth, leaving her staring after him in dismay.

'What the hell is going on here?'

Beth rounded the top of the stairs in time to see Alfie disappearing into Jory's room. From inside she could still hear shouting, but thankfully no more crashes, and when she stepped into the room her sons were at opposite ends, and Alfie stood in the middle to prevent them coming together again.

'Tell them,' Jowan managed, his hand raised to his mouth which, Beth was alarmed to note, was bleeding.

'Tell us what?' Alfie demanded, when nothing was forthcoming from Jory. The younger man's bruises had come out overnight, and one side of his face was a vivid cushion of swollen purple and black, but he said nothing, just stared at his brother with a look of desperate pleading.

'What?' Beth asked, more gently. 'Please, I hate to see the two of you at each other like this.'

'He's a liar,' Jowan said in disgust. '*He* stole Bertie's ring.'

Beth looked to Alfie for help, but he shook his head, bewildered. 'The bruises are real enough.'

'Of course they are!' Jory was massaging his own fist, Beth saw now, and looking at the reddened knuckles she realised, with a dull pain, that he'd struck Jowan with his own hand. Somehow it seemed worse than if he'd thrown something in temper.

'You'd better tell us what happened,' she said bleakly. 'Get cleaned up, the pair of you, and come downstairs.' Without waiting for a response she turned and stumbled her way down the stairs, only stopping when she felt Alfie's hand at her elbow.

'Steady, love.'

She turned on the stairs to see him looking down at her, his dark blue eyes so kind that she had to blink rapidly to clear the sudden blurring in her own. 'I hate it,' she muttered. 'They used to be so close.'

'I know.' He came down so he stood on the same stair, and folded her into his arms. 'But they're crowding thirty now, and they need space apart. Come on.' He took her hand and led her to the kitchen. 'Sit down, I'll make tea and we'll find out what Jo was talking about.'

A few minutes later Jowan came in, and slid into the seat next to Beth. 'I'm sorry. I know it hurts to see us fight.'

'Wait 'til your brother gets here,' Alfie said. 'Give him the chance to have his say.'

'He won't be getting here.' Even as Jowan spoke they heard the front door slam.

'He's never gone out!' Beth half-rose, but Jowan shook his head. 'Let him go. I'll talk to him tomorrow.'

'But it's late, and the rain—'

'He's got somewhere to go.'

'What, her in the village, that Sally Penneck? Her father won't have him in the house looking like that.'

'He will, he knows him. He's as bad.'

'As bad? What's he talking about?' Beth looked to Alfie again, but he said nothing though he didn't look surprised; it seemed he knew more than he'd been letting on. Certainly more than Beth did.

'It's her father that runs the card school,' Jowan told her. 'That's how Jory got involved in the first place.'

'But her father's on the lifeboat crew, he's a good man!'

'Jory's a good man too,' Alfie pointed out quietly. 'It doesn't stop him throwing all his money away.'

'But Jory's not *running* things! Bill Penneck should know better.'

'Hold on, was it Bill's boys that beat him up?' Alfie half-rose in his seat, and Beth, suddenly scared, put a hand on his arm. To her relief he lowered himself to his seat again, but she could still feel the tension beneath her fingers.

'Jo, why don't you stop dancing around and just tell us what happened?' she said, her own voice hardening. 'You're doing nobody any favours keeping it to yourself, least of all Jory. How can we help if we're kept in the dark?'

'Alright.' Jowan looked from her to Alfie. 'It's true, what I said. He was beaten up, but by then he'd already pawned the ring.'

Beth's heart stuttered. 'Pawned it?'

'Charlie Templeton's, in Bude.'

'The place on the Strand?' Alfie demanded.

Beth realised it was the same place where she'd bought his hip flask, and remembered how she'd felt seeing all the debts and difficulties the shop's contents represented. 'We don't have the money to get it back, Alfie' she said on a sigh.

'Just tell us everything,' Alfie said, ignoring her. 'Start from the beginning.'

'The ring was too small, you knew that, so when Bertie and I took it in to be re-sized they said to come back New Year's Eve and pick it up.'

'Must have cost a bit,' Alfie observed.

'It did.' Jowan looked ill, as if he'd only just thought about what he'd lost on that. 'Jory was on his day off yesterday, and he offered to pick it up for me since he was going in anyway. Only he never said the reason, which was that Penneck's card school had a mid-morning session. He lost almost every hand, and ended up owing.'

'Well Bill knows him, and he and his boys wouldn't have turned on him, surely?'

'There are other people in the game, Mum,' Jowan said gently. 'They hold the games in Bude, in the back room of a pub Bill knows. He might run the thing, but he can't control what the players do to get back what they're owed.'

Beth felt the blood drain from her face, and Jowan shot her an apologetic look for his bluntness, but went on, 'Jory had to ask for time to pay. Lucky for him, they gave it to him.'

'Well then—'

'About twenty minutes,' Jowan went on grimly. 'Long enough to pick up the ring, and then pawn it. His mistake was to try and make it back to the train station without handing over the money he got from it, so three of them caught up to him in Pathfields, took the money he owed them, and taught him a lesson at the same time. And they got the watch Dad gave him too.'

Beth flinched. Her poor boy. Foolish and weak, but not wicked. 'He must have been terrified, to do something stupid like that,' she said quietly.

'That's no excuse.' Alfie stood up and drained his cup. 'I'll have a few words for him tomorrow. Then he's coming with me to get it back.'

'How?' Jowan shook his head. 'He might have got nowhere near what it's worth, but you can bet Templeton won't be selling it cheap, especially once he knows the story behind it. Mum's right, we can't afford it.'

'I'll go,' Beth said. 'I can pretend it was stolen, and—'

'It was,' Alfie pointed out.

'I mean by someone outside the family.'

'Won't make any difference to Templeton,' Alfie said bluntly.

'Makes you wonder how many times Jory's done this before, and with what. I've got a good mind to ask.'

'You'll find he's never done it at all,' Jowan said.

'Except yesterday.'

'Not even then, according to Charlie Templeton.' Jowan gave them a bitter smile. 'He used my name this time, so the chances are, if he's done it before, he's given my name before.'

'I'll skin him alive if he has.'

'That won't achieve anything,' Jowan said. 'I just hope he's learned his lesson this time.'

'I hope so too.' Beth hated this sense of helplessness, particularly when it came to her boys.

Alfie seemed to read her mind. 'I'm going round to Penneck's tannery, I'll tell Bill to turn the lad away if he tries to join another game.'

'He'll just join another school instead,' Jowan said. 'Bude's full of them, and most even less lenient than Penneck's.' He softened his voice as he turned to Beth. 'This isn't nice to hear, but I know for a fact he's dealt out his share of bruises too.'

Beth snatched a sharp breath. 'Never!'

'He's out of his depth and you know it,' Alfie said grimly.

'He's not a child!' Jowan's anger matched his uncle's now, as they stood facing each other, eyes blazing. 'He's ruined my engagement to Bertie, he's lied, he's stolen – from *your mother*! And he's cheated us all. He's brought everything down on his own head.'

'He's your own brother! You'd have me stand aside and him beaten to a pulp, would you?'

'You can't fight his battles for him!'

'And what would Toby have done, then? Tell me that!'

279

Seeing their outward anger, and loving them both the way she did, Beth could also see what each of them could not; Jowan's secret fear for his brother, and Alfie's sense of helpless inadequacy, not knowing whether to give in to fury or to fear.

'You're not obliged to do anything, and nor would Toby have been,' she said, standing up to clear the cups. 'Jo's got no ring to give his girl now, and—'

'Which Jory said was only right and fair,' Jowan put in hotly, then he shook his head. 'And he's right in a way, since it was a family heirloom. The point is, he had as much right to pawn it as I had to give it to Bertie.'

'That is not the *point*!' Alfie's voice rose to a shout, and Beth and Jowan jumped as he slammed the edge of his fist on the table. 'The point is, it was given to you, Jo, and we've promised to do what we can for him too, when the time comes. The *point*, is that he's lied, ruined your good name and the name of this family. Toby's name!'

To Beth's dismay, Alfie's voice shook as he went on, 'I've done my best to help here since Toby died. To steer you pair in the direction I know he'd have wanted to take you in himself. And what have I done? Lost half his farm, and—'

'We both chose to sell part of it, love,' Beth reminded him, but he ignored her.

'Now I've sat by and watched his son go bad. And—' his voice turned heavy '—I can guess what happened to Toby's hip flask, and to mine too.'

Jowan looked baffled and frustrated, and as if he were about to question the importance of a couple of hip flasks, but Beth shot him a tight-lipped glare and he subsided.

'Dad had *two* sons,' he reminded Alfie, quietly now. 'You have two nephews.' The ghost of a smile hovered around his eyes. 'That's a fifty per cent success rate, at least.'

Beth looked at Alfie to gauge his response to this attempt at defusing the explosive atmosphere. Alfie's jaw, which had been quilted and jumping, relaxed and the tension in his posture likewise. The reluctant smile that flickered across his face was so like Toby's that a wholly unexpected pain shot through Beth's body. After all this time . . .

'Wait until tomorrow, at least,' Jowan was saying. 'I'll go over to Fox Bay on my lunch break and talk to Bertie, and then we can think about what's to be done.'

'Agreed.' Alfie looked over at Beth. 'I've got those slates to fix in the morning, I'm going to turn in.' Was she imagining it, or was there a question in his eyes? If there was, she chose to ignore it. Tonight was not the time for them to take that one step closer, not with Toby so heavy on both their hearts.

She climbed the stairs alone, and an unsettling thought was beginning to worm into her mind: with Toby all around them, in his sons, in the fabric of this old place, and especially in Alfie, would she ever be ready to take that step with him after all?

* * *

2nd January

Although it wasn't yet twelfth night, some of the bigger decorations were coming down; Piran Burch was even now helping Ben to dismantle the railway, and soon that would be packed away for another year, and where wreaths and garlands had graced the walls it now looked stark and bare. It wouldn't be long before it all began to feel normal again, but at the moment Fiona couldn't help feeling a little sad at the loss of it all; the twinkling lights, and the warm atmosphere created by the sense that things were just slightly out of the ordinary, and that anything might happen. She was also finding it hard to keep biting her tongue when her sister voiced her worries about Jory; if Jowan didn't tell her soon, Fiona would take matters into her own hands.

In the meantime she and Amy were stripping the bedrooms of every trace of their former inhabitants ready for a deep, New Year clean. Wherever possible, however, Fiona made Amy sit and watch while she did the heavy lifting.

'I'm not an invalid,' Amy grumbled. 'I can do *something*!'

'Polish, then.' Fiona tossed her the cloths and the tin of Mansion, and returned to bundling sheets into the basket. 'You can go and get some magazines from the little sitting room if you like, ready for tomorrow.'

'Tomorrow?'

Fiona gave her a disbelieving look. 'Your ship sails on Saturday,' she said with exaggerated patience. 'We have to leave tomorrow, to make sure we can book passage.'

'I'd forgotten what day it was,' Amy admitted. 'I can't believe it's time.' Her sudden melancholy transferred itself to Fiona; despite the girl's up and down moods, her occasionally selfish manner, and their frequent arguments – or even perhaps because of all that, Fiona knew she was going to miss her. She told herself it would mean she could spend more time down at the lifeboat station again, but she'd never known she was missing a companion her own age until Amy had burst so dramatically into her life, and things would feel a great deal flatter once she'd gone.

It was little wonder Amy's temper was short, with all the

uncertainty and fear that lay ahead of her. Fiona saw her reach automatically for the spoon pendant, as she always did when she was worried or restless, but she was forbidden from wearing it beneath her uniform blouse and her fingers closed on air. 'How will you get the money I need?' she fretted, squinting out of the window as if she planned on jumping out and running away in the next few minutes.

'Don't worry about that.' Fiona hadn't been able to bring herself to ask Guy, hoping that instead he would come to her, but it was becoming clear she would have to, after all.

She changed the subject. 'I hope little Jimmy Haverford appreciates all the fuss that's being made over his arrival.' She looked around the room. 'This has one of the best views in the hotel, but it's not much fun for a ten-year-old.'

'When's he getting here? I thought he was supposed to be here by now.'

'It keeps being moved, but I think he's due to arrive on Saturday. Which is good for you, as it'll distract everyone's attention.'

'Oh yes.' Amy's voice was part sarcasm, part bitterness. 'Who's going to care about a missing sixteen-year-old misfit, when there's a Hollywood child star to pander to?'

'You won't be "missing", everyone will just think you've gone home.'

'You assume anyone will *just think* of me at all.'

'They've – *we've* – all been very kind to you,' Fiona pointed out, her temper rising. 'I needn't have brought you here to live at all. Particularly as you've lied to me from the start.'

'I know.' Amy sighed. 'Look, it's not that I expect anyone to make a fuss over *me*, it's more that I don't understand why the fuss is made over film stars at all. They're just people, and there are a lot nicer ones out there who do better jobs and deserve the money.' She dug into the polish again and turned back to the dressing table. 'Let's get on with it, I don't want to spend *all* of my last day cleaning up for spoiled rich babies.'

They worked in silence for a while, and finally Fiona, reluctant to spoil her last normal day with her friend, decided to share the secret she'd been clutching to herself.

'I know something about those Hollywood stars you love so much,' she said.

'Oh?' Amy didn't look up, and her lips were still a thin line as she rubbed hard at a stubborn spot of face cream on the wood.

'Stop that a minute, and listen.' Fiona locked the door, and returned to sit on the stripped bed, smiling in anticipation of Amy's reaction. 'It's about Freddie Wishart.'

'Oh, you mean him and Daisy are getting married.'

'No. Quite the opposite.'

'Alright, they're *not* getting married then.'

Fiona sighed. This was going to be harder than she'd thought. 'But do you know *why* they're not?'

'Because they don't want to?'

'Amy! Put that down and come here!'

Amy gave a heavy sigh and slid the polish tin away from her, but she took a seat at the dressing table. 'What?'

'Freddie Wishart, sophisticated ladies' man, is no such thing after all. He's having an affair with a *man*,' she added, when Amy made no response. 'What do you think of that?'

'I think you're talking utter nonsense,' Amy said. 'I might not like the way you all fawn over these idiots, but it's plain to see he adores women.'

'They adore *him*,' Fiona corrected. 'But I've seen him with ... someone. And I've heard him saying how his father would react badly, and how he's to be allowed to break the news himself.'

'Who have you seen him with?'

'What does that matter?'

'Are you going to tell me?'

'No! I just thought you might enjoy knowing that Rex's worker bees, as Adam calls them, aren't all they're shined up to appear.'

'Daisy Conrad is still an absolute *angel* though. Of course.'

'And she'll be heartbroken when Freddie tells her he doesn't want her after all,' Fiona agreed.

'No she won't. She only has eyes for your brother.'

'That's Lynette, not Daisy.'

'Why can't it be both? He's a charmer.'

'Yuck.' Fiona pulled a face. 'Anyway, that's just a little piece of gossip for you, to cheer you up. Look,' she said more gently, 'I understand why you think it's unfair, when your mother and you both had such a hard start in life, but it's not their fault.'

Amy shrugged. 'I know, but when I think of the hard work, and ... Oh, it doesn't matter.' She picked up her duster again. 'Come on, if Jimmy's room isn't ready when the little darling arrives, he'll probably throw a Hollywood-style tantrum and have us all fired.'

'Don't be horrid,' Fiona said with mock severity. 'He might actually *be* a little darling.'

'Bet you anything he's not!' Amy threw her duster at Fiona, who plucked it off her shoulder and threw it back, and suddenly they were both smiling. Amy's humour was so easily lost lately; Fiona remembered the fun they'd had running around the garden at Pencarrack House and it seemed doubly cruel that all that laughter and delight had been crushed out of her by such a strict, even cruel, home life. Amy's fear that this Kitty woman would make her give up her own child, or worse, made it imperative that Fiona see Guy as soon as possible and get Amy away to safety.

They finished the room, and two others, and when they went downstairs to lunch there was a strangely heightened sense of expectation in the lobby. Only a few guests remained, among them the Hollywood set, of course, but for once it wasn't the likes of Daisy and Freddie who had caused a stir.

Adam, who'd been tight-lipped and grim ever since learning of Leah's abrupt departure yesterday, was doing his best to present a friendly and welcoming face to the two applicants for the position of Nicholas Gough's sous-chef. Having passed the first interview, they'd now come to the Fox Bay kitchen to prove themselves; one was a pleasant-mannered blond man of around forty, who'd apparently come from the Royal Oak Hotel in Penzance, and the other, Fiona recognised as the rather roughly put together chef from the Cliffside Fort in Caernoweth. Hadn't Bertie said his family actually owned the hotel? It seemed odd then that he'd want to take a lower-paid position in a hotel where he'd have very little influence.

Xander had left just after breakfast, to get settled in at the Caernoweth air base before he began his training on Monday, and Lynette, who'd also been on the verge of checking out, had evidently *just* decided to wait a little longer and catch a later train. Fiona couldn't help smiling as she remembered the way the young woman had barely been able to tear her eyes away from the Cliffside Fort's chef. It seemed she'd been wrong about where Lynette's fancy lay, after all. She and Amy joined Lynette and Bertie in the seating area of the lobby, and watched Adam introducing the two nervous chefs.

'What will you do if he gets the job?' Bertie asked Lynette with a laugh. 'Book in for the next six months?'

Lynette adopted an innocent look. 'I'm sure I don't know what you mean. I just wanted to get the later train so I'm not waiting for hours in Plymouth for the connection.'

Bertie nodded wisely. 'Of course.' She caught Fiona's eye, and they shared a grin.

Granny emerged from their private sitting room, and gestured for them to go in to lunch. 'Make your menu choices quickly, Chef will need time to instruct the candidates.'

Bertie turned to Guy as he seated them. 'Can you please ensure Mr Strommer prepares our meal?'

'I have no say in the matter, Miss Fox.' Guy handed out the heavy, gilt-edged menus. 'But I'll pass on your request to Mr Gough.'

Fleur looked baffled. 'Why would you want that, when you already know Mr Batten's food is so good?'

Bertie gave Lynette a sly look. 'I was just thinking we'll have to remember to mention how tough Mr's Strommer's meat was, and how the sauce could have done with more seasoning.'

'But you haven't even …' Fleur realised then, and raised her eyes to the ceiling. 'Playing with a man's career, eh? I do hope you were joking, Roberta.'

'Of course I was!'

'Well you have to admit,' Lynette retaliated, 'Bertie and jokes aren't normally associated with one another.'

Bertie Fox, twenty-one years old, sophisticate and soon-to-be pilot, poked her tongue out and earned herself a little sound of disbelief from her grandmother. Fiona recalled the flicking of water at the luncheon table at the Cliffside Fort, and reflected that no one brought out the fun side of Bertie like the Nicholls siblings, not even Jowan. It was a pity she was going to lose them just when she had most need of them.

Rex, Freddie and Daisy made their appearance just after Guy had taken the Foxes' orders, and sat close by in order to make conversation, and Fiona saw Amy looking at Freddie as if expecting him to have grown scales since she'd last seen him. She kicked her under the table. Amy turned a bland, innocent face back on her, then winked, and despite herself, Fiona smiled into her glass of water.

As they left the dining room after their meal Fiona looked around for Guy. She didn't see him, but Ben was coming down the stairs, his clothes neat but his hair wanting the attentions of a comb.

'You're up early,' she observed. 'It's only just two o'clock.'

'I have to help Guy and Jeremy with a stock evaluation. Who'd have believed so few people could put away so much gin and champagne?' He pulled a face. 'I've barely slept, to be honest, with that wind howling outside.' He stopped abruptly as the dining room door opened again and Rex and Daisy came out. Fiona would have sworn to anyone that her brother had forcibly stopped his own hands from smoothing down that mop of hair. Freddie went upstairs, ever the recluse, but Daisy and Rex came over to talk.

'So nice to see you at this time of day, Ben,' Daisy said, smiling.

'Likewise,' he muttered, then perked up. 'What were the meals like? Has Guy decided who to take on yet?'

'I think your mother said she and your grandmother are to

interview them both,' Rex said. 'I figured that's why you were up, actually, to sit in.'

'No, Adam's doing that.'

'Seems to me Coleridge has a finger in all the pies,' Rex said drily.

'Well as part-owner, and the bloke who selected the final two, I'd say he's invested in this, wouldn't you?'

Fiona and Bertie looked at one another and said nothing; Rex was clearly unaware of the closeness between Adam and the younger Foxes.

'Fiona,' Daisy said, into the faintly tense silence, 'since Leah's gone, would you be able to maybe spare me some time to help me with my accent? She's got me on the right track, but I could do with someone to listen and correct.'

Fiona was caught between Daisy's eager, lamplight smile and Amy's narrow-eyed *don't you dare* ... She was also keen to find Guy, but couldn't tell anyone that. Instead she shot Amy an apologetic look, and turned to Daisy.

'Of course! Just for a little while though, then perhaps Bertie or Lynette could take over. If Lynette hasn't left by then, of course.'

Lynette was peering over towards the office door behind reception, and was dragged back to the conversation with evident reluctance. 'Hmm? Oh, I'm not planning on going just yet.'

'I'm going upstairs then,' Amy said, pulling her necklace from her pocket and slipping it over her head. 'It's going to be a long day tomorrow.'

When no one asked her why, she gave Fiona another betrayed look and ran up the stairs.

'Don't mind her,' Fiona said to Daisy. 'She's just tired.'

'I wonder who got the job?' Lynette mused, still distracted.

Fiona followed her gaze towards the front of the lobby, and so was one of the first to see Jowan hesitating on the other side of the revolving door. She nudged Bertie, who beckoned him in, but Jowan pointed to his right, indicating he wanted to speak to her in the privacy of the cloisters.

Ben frowned after Bertie as she hurried off. 'What's going on there, Fi?'

She told him, in as few words as possible, what Jowan had said on New Year's Eve, and watched his face darken with each word. Before she'd finished, he'd set off in the direction of the cloisters too, and Lynette turned to Fiona.

'You'd better run along and teach Daisy how to say "alright, my bird?" and I'll go and make sure your brother doesn't kick young Mr Nancarrow into the middle of next week.'

'It's not Jo's fault!' Fiona protested.

'I doubt if that will matter to Ben. You know how protective he is of you girls.'

'Where's Freddie?' Fiona asked Daisy, as she led her towards their private sitting room.

'Oh, he just wanted a little chat with Guy about something.'

'So do I.' Fiona couldn't help wondering if Daisy knew what she did, and as they settled themselves in the sitting room she tried to think of a way to draw the girl out. It shouldn't be too hard, given Daisy's newly emerging enthusiasm for chatting.

After a few minutes she steered the subject in that direction. 'You're ever so good! Does Freddie do accents as naturally as you?'

'I guess if he wanted to, he could. He's not playing a Brit in this movie though.'

'In *English* English, please,' Fiona said, and her pompous tone made Daisy laugh.

'Very well. I imagine Mr Wishahht,' she exaggerated, 'would possess such an aptitude, should the situation require it, but this picture doesn't have need of it.'

'Better! What about his family? Girlfriend?'

'What's this, an excuse to talk about Freddie? You can ask him this stuff you know, he won't mind.'

'Just trying to widen our discussion,' Fiona said hurriedly. 'Why don't you give me a line from the film?'

'Oh, I was just kidding, don't mind me,' Daisy assured her. 'I know you're not some film fan who won't leave him alone. Your friend *definitely* isn't.'

'Yes, I'm sorry about Amy. She's never been to the pictures, you see.'

'No one ever said everyone has to be a fan of the movies. Maybe she'd like it if she went, maybe not, but there's no need to be rude.'

'I'll have a word with her. I expect his girlfriend must get very fed up with people always trying to talk to him.'

Daisy's eyes narrowed. 'That's the second time you've mentioned Freddie and a girlfriend.'

'Is it a secret?'

'Have you read about a girl in the papers?'

'No.'

'Then I guess it's a secret.' Daisy visibly painted on a smile, and because she was so good at it, Fiona would never have guessed it was false if she hadn't just heard the sharpness in Daisy's tone. Daisy lifted an eyebrow. 'Shall we go on?'

'If you still want me to,' Fiona said, embarrassment making her sound a little stiff.

'Of course I do. I have to get this right. And,' she added, putting a hand over Fiona's, 'I didn't mean to snap.'

'No, I'm sorry. It must get terribly tedious, people always asking about things like that.'

'It's just ... well, it's not my place to talk about Freddie, is it? Ask me anything you like about myself,' she offered, her eyes kinder again now. 'I suppose you'll know soon enough, but I'm planning on giving all this up after this movie.'

'No! But you're so young!'

'I'll explain another time. Meantime you know nothing about it, okay?' Daisy sat up straight. 'Give me a real stinker of a sentence, go on!'

Fiona wrestled with her curiosity, but was fast learning there was steel behind Daisy's pliable appearance, and that there was no earthly use in trying to bend it.

CHAPTER NINETEEN

Helen looked up at a knock on the office door, expecting to see Fleur. Instead, Adam gave her a quick on-off smile as he came around to draw a second chair up to the desk next to her.

'I told Fleur she needn't concern herself with the final interviews,' he explained. 'She looked fagged, so she's gone upstairs to rest.'

'Are you sure she didn't want to help?'

'Quite sure. She looked relieved, actually.'

Helen pursed her lips but didn't argue; Fleur had been working all the hours under the sun to complete the arrangements for the war memorial before New Year's Day, and she must be exhausted now.

'Who's first?' she asked instead.

'Mr Strommer from the Royal.' Adam sat back in his chair, his fingers laced across his stomach, his legs comfortably extended. 'Good luck, I'm just going to learn from the best.'

'You're not,' Helen warned. 'Sit up and behave.'

He grinned. 'I'm not a wayward child,' he protested. 'You can't talk to me like that.'

'I can if you behave like one. What happened to Leah?' Her voice caught, as she voiced the question that had been gnawing at her since last night when she'd realised her friend had gone without saying goodbye.

Adam's grin faded and he sat up straight. 'I don't know any more than you do,' he muttered.

'You don't seem disappointed.' She herself had been at first disbelieving, when Martin had told her he had seen her with her case, and then angry. It hadn't been until late that night, when the hotel had fallen silent and she had automatically looked around for Leah to talk to, that the anger had given way to a feeling almost like grief. Certainly guilt. Had Leah hoped someone would try to persuade her, at least? Had Helen failed as a friend, in her efforts not to stand in Leah's way?

'We knew she was going.' Adam shrugged, and she watched him carefully, noting the way his eyes slid away from hers. 'It was just one day sooner than we expected.'

'Yes, but why? What did you say to her when she told you she was going?'

'Nothing!' He raised his hands. 'Honestly, I told her I respected her decision, and wished her the best.'

'You didn't try to persuade her to stay?'

He turned on her, his eyes suddenly hard. 'Did you?'

Helen blinked, knowing he was right to throw it back at her. 'She has a new career ahead of her,' she stammered, 'it would have been selfish of me to try.'

'Well then.'

'But I had nothing new to offer her, Adam! If anyone could have kept her here, it would have been you. What aren't you telling me?' She glanced at the door. Still closed. The clock said the first interviewee wasn't due for another five minutes, and something about Adam was making her uneasy. 'Come on,' she said, her voice sharpening. '*Something* made her leave early, what happened between you two?'

'She said ...' Adam rubbed at his face. 'She said that this doesn't suit me, whatever that means.'

'What doesn't?'

'Being here. The hotel. She said I needed to be in the thick of things and that I didn't owe it to you to give up my lifestyle.'

'Owe me? Whoever said you did?'

'*I* said so,' Adam said, his voice softening. 'Because I do.'

'You don't—'

'Buying this place, gifting half of it to you and the kids, I thought that would make me feel I'd repaid you the debt I owed for Harry. But it hasn't.'

'Then nothing ever can, so you might as well stop trying.'

Adam looked hurt at that, but it was the harsh truth and Helen could think of nothing to say to mitigate it. But he hadn't finished. 'She said I was giving everything up for love, just like Harry did. She's right, I am.'

Helen fixed her gaze on the door, and her voice came out very small. 'No, you're not.'

'Helen—'

'No!' She rounded on him with a ferocity that took her as much by surprise as it did him. 'I'm not stupid, or blinkered. I know you feel *something*, what you think is romantic love, but it isn't.'

'How can you know what's in here?' He tapped his chest, then took her hand. 'Hels, we've known each other almost all our lives, and been close friends for a lot of it. But this is more. Can't you feel that?'

'I do love you, of course I do. But not in the way I loved Harry.'

'Of course not, but—'

'I love you in the way *you* loved him.' She saw a startled look cross his face, and nodded. 'You and Harry had a wonderful friendship, and since his death it's had nowhere to go, until we became close again. The fact that I'm a woman doesn't mean that same friendship has now become romantic. It hasn't changed, it's just been passed to me.' She laid her hand over his. 'What we have now isn't more than that, because it doesn't need to be.'

His face reflected so many realisations in that moment that Helen wanted to laugh, but it would have been cruel, and in any case there was something desperately sad about it.

The silence was broken by a rap at the door, and Helen released his hand as Martin announced Kurt Strommer's arrival. The nervous chef came into the room, but Helen allowed her eyes to remain on Adam's for a moment, until she saw the tiny smile crease the corners and he sat straighter, as if a burden had been lifted.

She directed her smile to the interviewee. 'Good afternoon, Mr Strommer.' She held out her hand. 'I hear your meal was quite delicious, and Mr Gough has passed on his notes to us. Now, can you tell me why you want to work at Fox Bay Hotel?'

Just before dinner Helen went upstairs to check Fleur, and to let her know which of the two chefs she and Adam had selected. It still struck her as odd, and a little worrying, that her mother-in-law had opted to sleep rather than be involved in something as important as this appointment. She hoped Fleur wasn't sickening for something; she had certainly been pushing herself for the past few months.

Walking past the little sitting room she heard a raised voice, and stopped, startled, as the door was flung open, and Guy came out looking uncharacteristically harried.

His gaze fell on the surprised Helen, and he closed the door and visibly pulled himself together. 'Who did you and Mrs Fox select in the end?'

'Mr Strommer.' Helen tried, and failed, to see past him to whoever else was in the sitting room. 'The younger chap was apparently very talented in the kitchen, but came across as a bit ... intense. To be honest I don't think having him and Nicholas Gough in the same kitchen would be good for anyone.'

Guy laughed, but it sounded a bit forced. 'Very wise.'

'It wasn't Fleur who interviewed with me,' Helen added, 'it was Adam.'

'Why ever didn't Mrs Fox do it? She said she was looking forward to it.'

'Adam said she was tired, so he suggested she have a little nap instead. I'm going to see her now.'

'I see. Well I hope she's not coming down with anything, she's been out walking a great deal in this awful weather.'

'Just what I was thinking.' Helen checked her watch. 'Well, I won't keep you, it'll soon be time to start readying the restaurant for this evening, and I believe it's your night off after that.'

'It is. I'm off to see the Alfred Hitchcock talkie.' Something passed across his face as he mentioned it, but Helen couldn't quite identify it. A sort of bitter amusement, perhaps?

'Have a lovely evening then,' she said, still faintly mystified.

She waited until he had descended to the lobby, then crossed to the sitting room. She half-expected to see Adam in there since he

297

was the one who seemed to be getting everyone up in arms lately, but there was only Amy, who was picking up a stack of magazines and shuffling them together into a neat pile.

'Hello, Mrs Fox. I think I've annoyed Mr Bannacott by making a bit of a mess.'

'He did seem a bit flustered.'

'It's my fault. I'd spread them around on the floor, and when he told me to pick them up I'm afraid I told him I wasn't his employee. Which was very rude of me.'

Privately Helen agreed, but then Guy could be a trifle sharp when he forgot who worked under him and who did not. 'He's had a very busy week,' she said, 'but I'll make sure he knows you didn't mean to be rude.'

Amy finished neatening the magazines, and placed them carefully in the walnut cabinet against the wall. As she sidled past Helen in the doorway she kept her face low, and Helen had a twinge of unease; she seemed secretive in a way she never had before, when she hadn't known who she was. Did that mean she'd remembered something unsavoury? Perhaps it was as well she was leaving tomorrow after all.

She continued up to the family rooms and knocked gently on Fleur's door, and was surprised to hear her mother-in-law answer right away.

'Come in.'

'I just thought I'd pop in and see if you're rested,' Helen said, 'and to let you know we selected Mr Strommer for the position. He'll start in a week.'

Fleur was propped against her pillows, a copy of Nash's *Pall Mall* magazine open on her lap. She looked washed-out and pale. 'Thank you,' she said. 'I tried to sleep but I'm just not tired.'

'You look it,' Helen said, concerned. 'Would you like me to call for a doctor?'

'No, no, no.' Fleur closed the magazine and swung her legs over the side of the bed. 'I'll come down now.'

'Are you well enough?' Helen plucked Fleur's cable knit cardigan off the back of the door and handed it to her. 'Adam said he thought you ought to get some rest.'

'Adam!' Fleur scowled. 'You know I've—'

'Always liked him, but . . .' Helen finished with a little smile. 'In this case I'd say he was right.' She sat on the bed. 'What's wrong, Fleur? You can tell me, surely?'

'Oh, I don't know.' Fleur slipped her arms into her cardigan and it was as if she had pulled on every one of her seventy-seven years along with the heavy woollen garment. Tears shimmered suddenly in her eyes; 'I just feel as if it's all . . . slipping away.'

'Slipping away how? Nothing's slipping anywhere.'

Fleur wrapped her arms across her body, and gave Helen a helpless look. 'That's just it, I know it's not, but I can't help *feeling* it is. Robert built this place from nothing, and our entire marriage was spent shaping it into what it became. When I lost him, it was . . .' She shook her head. 'Well, you know. And then poor Harry, who should have taken it over. How we take it all for granted, that it will go the way we imagine.'

Fleur gave a laugh that was more like a sob, and Helen put her arm around her. Her own tears were close to the surface, but Fleur didn't deserve the guilt of causing her to spill them, so she held them in, blinking hard and fiercely, willing them away.

'*We've* done it for Robert and Harry, haven't we? Kept it special, and unique. They'll be looking down on us with pride . . . even though they'll probably be complaining about those dull paintings in the first floor sitting room.' She felt Fleur's little huff of laughter against her neck, and hugged her tighter. 'Please don't upset yourself, Fleur.'

Fleur drew away, wiping her eyes. 'Running the hotel with you at my side was a joy I never thought I'd have,' she said. 'Even though it wasn't mine any more by then. But almost losing it last year, and then having it saved from the jaws of that awful little Pagett man . . . Since then I've felt almost like a stranger here.'

Helen didn't know what to say. Part of her wanted to protest: *we've involved you in everything!* But had they? Adam had almost certainly been acting from the best of intentions with every change he had suggested, and even today when he'd offered to take over in the interview, but how must it have appeared to Fleur to have had even that one small thing whisked away from her at the last moment?

'Why don't you help him select the artist for the new pictures he . . . *we* want?' she suggested. 'You have such a keen eye, and he doesn't know a thing about art anyway.'

'He'll be able to pick anyone of the usual crowd,' Fleur said dismissively. 'It doesn't matter which one. Look, don't mind me. I think it's just now that the memorial is done, the families contacted, the stone dedicated . . . ' She straightened her sleeves and gave Helen an apologetic smile. 'I have nothing else to occupy me now. You and Adam run the hotel, I'm just . . . here.'

Helen remembered her first thoughts when she'd brought the children here ten years ago, believing she owned half of it, but still feeling like a guest. 'I know what you mean,' she said gently, 'but you mustn't feel like that. I promise we'll do more to make sure you feel part of it all.'

'Ah, but that's just it, isn't it?' Fleur's smile was pensive. 'You shouldn't have to make me "feel part of it". Either I am or I'm not.'

'You are!'

'I was,' Fleur corrected, 'but no longer. That's why I've decided to leave.'

Helen looked at her, stunned. 'Leave? But … where will you go?'

'To my brother, in New Zealand. You remember the Christmas card he sent?'

'Of course, it was lovely.'

'Geoffrey and his wife are retired now of course. They've invited me many times over the years since Robert died, and they did again, in that card.' She took a deep breath. 'I think it's time to take them up on it.'

'But just to visit, surely?'

'Maybe.' Fleur touched Helen's arm. 'Don't fret, either way. If and when I come back it will be because I'll have missed you, the cubs, and this hotel, so you can be sure this is where I'll be staying. In the meantime, let's go down and spend some time with the youngsters. Tomorrow you can help me make my arrangements.' She looked around the room, and, like Adam, a new lightness seemed to possess her now she'd spoken her feelings aloud. 'You're never too old for a new start, Helen. Always remember that.'

* * *

Bertie lifted her glass to allow Ben to top it up. He would be starting work soon, so was drinking soda water with a twist of lime, but the gin was mellowing nicely in Bertie's blood, calming some of the tremors that had set in when Jowan had told her about his brother. On top of the shock of Leah's sudden and secret departure, it had been about as much as she could bear to learn what Jory had done.

Ben's arrival in the cloisters had fired things up as he'd caught up with what had happened, and he had taken a great deal of persuading that it wasn't Jowan's fault after all. Lynette's presence had eased things somewhat, and Bertie was glad she'd come out to join them, though equally glad to be alone now with her brother.

'Does Mum know anything about this?' Ben asked. 'I can't see her sitting still for it.'

'No. She doesn't even know he's given me a ring. I told her he planned to propose, but nothing else.'

'Good thing too. What was the ring like, anyway?'

She described it, feeling a little wistful at the loss, for the first time. 'Until now I'd just felt angry, and a bit cheated,' she said. 'But it's such a delicate, pretty little thing, and it meant so much to Jowan.'

'It's rotten,' Ben agreed, frowning as he settled himself in the chair opposite. 'I only have a few minutes, but I don't want you to be left alone. Where's Lynette gone? She did a good job of calming things down out there earlier.'

'She's packing. You can go, though, don't worry about me.'

'But I *do* worry, you know that. Especially now.'

'It's Jory you should be concerned about.' Bertie took a sip of her drink.

'I'm not in the least bit bothered about that idiot,' Ben said with a dismissive shake of his head. 'There's absolutely no reason at all he should have got himself into that kind of trouble. He

302

could have stopped his betting at any time, and the worst that would have happened would have been a few jeers. A punctured ego.'

Bertie looked at him through narrowed eyes. 'You sound as if you know a lot about it,' she observed. 'Don't tell me you're part of that card school too?'

'I'm not.'

'But?' He'd definitely hesitated.

'I'm not!' Ben chewed the inside of his lip for a moment, then shrugged. 'Not that one, anyway.'

'Ben!'

'It's not some dirty little den like the Pennecks' place,' he protested. 'It's in a suite at the Summerleaze. A lot of very notable people play, including several town councillors.'

'The Summerleaze?' Bertie stared, aghast. 'For crying out loud, don't let Lily know about it, she could lose her job!'

Ben smiled and twirled the lime in his glass. 'Lily runs it.'

'*Lily* does?'

'I know, not very ladylike, is it? I rather like that about her though.'

'It's nothing to do with it not being ladylike,' Bertie countered hotly. 'Is that how you got involved, or did it happen the other way about?'

'She's run it for years. She invited me in one night back in October, and it turns out the room gets booked to a Mr King. I presume his first name is *Jack*, and they're members of a special *ace club*.' He gave an exaggerated wink, and Bertie rolled her eyes.

'And do you lose much?'

'Hardly anything.' Ben finished off his drink. 'That's because

I know when to stop. It's down to Jory to do the same, but now look what he's done. And using his brother's name? Despicable.'

'Goodness knows what else he's pawned over the years,' Bertie said, staring into her own glass. 'Jowan says he's pretty sure things have gone missing from around their home, including his father's and Alfie's hip flasks that they'd had since they were eighteen.'

'Like I said, despicable.' Ben looked closely at her. 'How are you doing? I mean, since Leah left.'

'A bit ...' Bertie lifted a hand helplessly. 'I mean, we'd not long begun to make things right between us. It seems doubly awful now, that she's gone again. And so suddenly. I'll miss her, I hope she writes.'

'Of course she will,' he said gently, then stood up and stretched. 'Right, I'm going to start work now. I saw Guy earlier, he looked as if he'd got a wasp stuck in his trousers. Thank goodness he's off duty now, I wouldn't like to be on his bad side today.'

'Are you good at it?' Bertie asked, as Ben opened the door.

'Being on Guy's bad side?'

'Gambling.'

Ben considered, then a small smile crept across his face. 'Actually, yes. How do you suppose I managed to afford a Bugatti? But don't you dare tell Mum.'

'You sound like you did when you were ten!' Bertie smiled back. 'But you haven't just been scrumping apples now,' she added, more soberly. 'This is serious.'

'Only if you end up like Jory Nancarrow. But I don't care about how he got into debt, it's what he's done to you and to Jowan that makes me want to pin him against a wall.'

'You'll do no such thing,' Bertie said hurriedly. 'Let his family sort him out.'

'They're welcome to him.'

When he'd left, and closed the door again behind him, Bertie's thoughts turned back to Jowan, and how his relationship with Jory must have changed. They'd always been close, though very different, but what would this do to them?

The door opened and Lynette poked her head around. 'On your own?'

'Come in.'

'No fear, I don't want to hide away in here for my last night.' Lynette jerked her head towards the lounge. 'The Hollywoods are in there, let's join them. I might end up being whisked away for a starring role in Mr Kelly's next picture, especially if the divine Miss Conrad is leaving him in the lurch.'

'Hush!' Bertie gestured at the open door. 'You never know who's listening!'

'I told you, they're in the lounge. Come on, we might be missing something exciting!'

'I doubt it—' Bertie grinned '—going by all the non-excitement we've had so far.' She wheeled herself over to the door. 'It's a pity Mr Batten didn't get the chef's job,' she said. 'You'd have enjoyed your visits here even more.'

Lynette pulled the sitting room door shut after they'd passed through it, but before she moved to take the handles of Bertie's chair Bertie saw a little smile lifting the corners of her mouth. 'Well now, I might have another reason for wanting to go into the lounge,' she murmured, just loud enough to hear.

'He's in there?'

'He might be.'

'But why?'

'They're both staying overnight.' Lynette began pushing. 'Or so I'm reliably informed by your brother.'

She steered Bertie close to where Mr Batten sat talking to the man who'd secured the sous-chef position. Mr Batten looked up casually, and Bertie saw recognition flicker on his face, but it was an unfocused kind; he knew he'd seen her before but evidently couldn't remember where. He smiled briefly, and was about to return to his conversation when Lynette held her hand out to his companion.

'Congratulations on getting the job! Bertie here is a dear friend of mine, and I visit often.' She turned to Mr Batten. 'Hello again. We met at your parents' hotel a little over a week ago.'

'Ah, yes of course.' A memory visibly clicked into place, and his lips twitched. 'One of your party was . . . very keen on recommending Fox Bay over Cliffside, I remember.'

Lynette grimaced. 'Sorry about him.'

'Your husband?'

'My brother. I'm Lynette Nicholls.'

'Henry Batten. Harry to my friends.'

Bertie flinched, but couldn't suppress a smile as her friend held out her hand to the chef and dropped her voice to a soft murmur.

'Lovely to see you again. Harry.'

By the time Bertie was ready to turn in, Lynette had decided she really *must* visit Caernoweth again while she was in the area, to see how Xander was settling in at the air base.

'I'll leave tomorrow on the same train as Harry, just for the sake of convenience. Then we can share a cab from the station to the hotel.'

Bertie had laughed outright. 'Convenience, is it? Alright, I'll keep your room for you until Sunday, shall I?'

'Please. Then I can tell you all about it on Sunday night, and travel home to Brighton on Monday. I'm sure you'll want to know how Xander's getting on.'

'He won't have done anything yet,' Bertie began, then held up her hand. 'But yes. Of course I will.'

She rolled slowly along the corridor to her room, and now that she was away from the distraction of Lynette's chatter, and the company of "The Hollywoods", as her friend had called them, her mind turned once more to Jowan, and to Jory and the ring. As she pulled herself from the chair onto her bed she wondered if it were possible to be happy in the bosom of a family filled with so much mistrust, and where her brother-in-law was a known thief. The answer came swiftly; no matter how deeply she cared for Jowan, as soon as she was competent on her new prosthetic leg, she would apply to the air base and move away from Fox Bay. She could only hope Jo would decide she was worth following.

* * *

The lobby was deserted except for Ian Skinner at reception, who was idly flicking through the visitors book. Fiona's eyes drifted shut time and time again, only to fly open as her head jerked painfully on her neck. She mustn't sleep now, Guy could walk right by and she'd miss her chance. Amy had gone back upstairs after dinner, and Fiona had tried several times to catch Guy since he hadn't appeared in the dining room, but when she went looking in the lounge he wasn't there either.

'He's not on duty, so he went out to the pictures,' Jeremy Bickle said, hooking a wine glass onto the overhead rack. 'He wasn't looking in the best of tempers, so I hope he's better tomorrow. Mind, since we're light on guests now I don't suppose it matters too much.'

But it mattered to Fiona. Tonight was the absolute last chance she would have to ask Guy to make good on his promise; they would have to leave tomorrow lunchtime at the very latest, to get the connecting train from Bude to Plymouth.

Amy was already tucked up in bed, asleep, and Fiona knew she'd need to be well rested ahead of her long journey tomorrow, so chose not to disturb her and tell her what she was doing. Instead she'd fetched the Agatha Christie book she'd bought in Caernoweth, and settled into a chair facing the door. For a while the entertaining dialogue between Hastings and Poirot kept her attention, but as the evening drew on she found her eyes beginning to burn and the print blurred.

Several times she had to turn back a page, because what she was reading made no sense and she realised she'd skipped passages. Ian Skinner chatted a little now and again, but she didn't know him the way she knew Martin, they had little to talk about, and he soon fell silent. Fiona asked him to tell her when Guy returned, and then allowed herself to doze a little in the chair, but when she woke to find Ian had nipped into the office, she knew she only had herself to rely on.

So she faced the door squarely, willing Guy to return and desperately hoping he wasn't going to be staying out all night as he sometimes did. Her patience was eventually rewarded as she saw car headlights illuminating the drive, before plunging the night back into darkness as they died along with the distinctive-sounding engine. Suddenly wide awake, Fiona sat upright in her chair and rehearsed the way she planned to ask, and even the tone she would use.

Guy came in looking relaxed enough, and even greeted Ian cheerfully. Ian looked over at Fiona, but as Guy followed his gaze his expression closed down. He didn't acknowledge her, nor did he call in to the bar as she'd expected, but made his way directly to the stairs.

'Guy!' Fiona hurried across to him. 'Wait, please!'

He stopped, with one hand on the stair rail, and turned politely. But when she drew close enough to hear him he pre-empted her plea with a low, angry message of his own.

'I hope you're not going to ask me for money for that vile companion of yours.'

Fiona stopped dead, her heart thumping hard in shock. 'What?' she managed.

'I would no more help that girl than I would help a thief mug your grandmother,' he clarified, his voice cold. 'Now if you'll excuse me, Miss Fox, I've had a long day and I'm very tired.'

'Wait!' Fiona grabbed his sleeve, and although he didn't pull away, he remained very still, looking at her fingers caught in the material, until she let go.

'I'm sorry,' he said, more gently now, but no less firmly. 'It has nothing to do with my respect and affection for you, but I simply cannot, in all good conscience, provide anything that's going to help that . . .' He let his words fall away, and Fiona stared at him in dismay.

'I don't understand,' she said at last. She looked over her shoulder at Ian, who was paying them no attention. 'Come into the sitting room, and tell me what's happened.'

He shook his head. 'I'm sorry, I don't want to talk about it. You'll have to find someone else to lend you the money.'

'But I can't! Guy, please, we need you. If you hadn't said all along that you'd be happy to help, we might have found another way, but it's too late now. And you *promised*!'

'I did no such thing.'

'Well *I* did!'

'Then you're a ... then you shouldn't have,' he amended, apparently realising he was about to overstep his mark, even as a family friend. 'I told you, if any of this got out I'd be liable to lose my job.'

'It won't! Look, I don't know what's got you rattled, but neither of us will say anything. You have our word.'

'*Your* word, I would believe.' Guy sounded sad now. 'I wouldn't question it in a month of Sundays. But hers?' He shook his head. 'I'm sorry, but the answer is no. If she must wait for the next boat, then that's what she'll have to do. Or she could go home.'

'She can't do that.' Fiona caught herself about to explain Amy's predicament, but bit down on the words. 'I don't know when the next boat will be.' She refused to entertain the nagging thought that kept rearing its head: that she had something she could use to force him if she had to. It would make her the worst kind of bully, it would destroy every shred of respect and affection between Guy and the Fox family, and it would probably drive him to leave altogether.

'Alright, I'll tell her she'll have to wait,' she said dully. 'Won't you at least tell me what's happened to change your mind?'

Guy looked over at the sitting room. 'Has everyone gone to bed?' She nodded. 'Alright then, come in here.' He led the way and shut the door firmly behind him. Fiona couldn't sit down, despite her tiredness, and Guy remained standing too, his long, finely boned face tight.

310

'I had a little chat with your friend late this afternoon,' he began, and Fiona instantly tightened up. His eyes narrowed slightly. 'Do you know why?'

'How could I? I was with Daisy, working on her accent.'

'And where do you think your friend was while you were doing that?'

Fiona bristled. 'I'm not her keeper!' She shrugged. 'She went off in a bit of a sulk if you must know.'

'I know exactly where she went. She went to see Freddie Wishart.'

Fiona felt a chill crawling over her, but feigned bafflement. 'What?'

'She went to see him, because she thought she knew something about him that would force him to give her money. I'm talking about blackmail, Miss Fox. Oddly enough, the title of the film I've just been to see. Horribly ironic, wouldn't you say? Such a cowardly weapon.'

She flinched, her own abandoned intentions still fresh in her mind. 'What on earth could she possibly have to blackmail Freddie with? We never see him.'

'I do find it interesting that your reaction isn't to instantly refute this. To defend her.'

'She's desperate!' Fiona lowered her voice, worried they might bring Ian Skinner to the door. 'So what did she claim to know?'

'She told him she knew he was … drawn to men rather than women. That he had been seen with another man. Something like that would utterly destroy his family, and his career, yet she said she would go to the press if he didn't pay her.'

'And presumably he refused.'

'He told her he needed time, but that he'd pay her, just to send her away happy. Then he came to see me. Of course, he'll do no such thing, and I told her as much.'

Fiona's heart sank. 'No, of course not. And what did she say?'

'She threw a pile of magazines at me.'

'What?'

'She was taking them for the trip. Your idea, I gather.'

'Yes, but—'

'Now she knows I've been aware of her plan all along. And that Freddie isn't going to be paying her anything.' Guy sank into a chair at last. 'The poor boy was distraught.'

'What's he going to do?' Fiona asked. If only she hadn't been so desperate to cheer Amy up, this would never have happened. She could have ripped her tongue out. 'He can't call the police if it's true, can he?'

'It's not true!' Guy scowled. 'Not in the least.'

Fiona raised an eyebrow. 'You sound very sure of that.'

'Of course I'm sure.' Guy shifted in his seat, then sighed. 'The truth of the matter is, he has a fiancée waiting at home. But she's something of a secret so I don't want that getting out. And neither does he.'

He was a very good liar, Fiona realised, and the thought was unsettling. 'Who is she?'

'It doesn't matter who she is. The point is, your vagabond friend has jumped to entirely the wrong conclusion, and has made a very grave mistake in trying to profit from it.' He stood up, cold once again. 'In case she hasn't quite grasped it, you can tell her she's made an enemy of us both, and I do not give my hard-earned money to my enemies. Nor,' he added regretfully, before Fiona could speak, 'to friends who consort with them. I'm sorry I've had to let you down, but you can place the blame squarely on the shoulders of that little cuckoo you've brought into our nest.'

Fiona pushed past him, not daring to say anything at all in case the wrong words came out. She didn't know whether she was angrier at him, at Amy, or herself, but she'd had as much as she could stand of it all now. All she'd done was try to help, and now she was caught up in an ever-tightening web of deceit. Including Guy's.

She lay in bed, once again wide awake, listening to Amy's light snores. She had no idea now how to get enough money to keep her promise, and she was sorely tempted to go back on it, to cut Amy loose and send her home. Except that there was a baby to think about too, and from what Amy had said it would be no life to return to, and perhaps even worse. The girl was right, her mother would be the only one who would understand; Ruth must have been devastated all those years ago, when Amy had been snatched from her. Fiona tried to imagine what it must have been like to return from work to find your child gone, and she drifted into an uneasy sleep at last, to dream of an empty room and a distraught mother with no child to hold.

CHAPTER TWENTY

Bertie was only halfway down the drive and her arms were already tired, when her sister ran up, panting, and told her off in tones very like their mother's.

'Where do you think you're going?'

'To see Jowan, thank you very much.' Bertie couldn't help laughing, despite her nervousness; today she would have to talk about the decision to which her endless sleepless hours had led her, and what it meant for their future. If indeed they had one.

'Why on earth didn't you ask Guy or Ben to drive you?'

'Ben's asleep, and Guy has his own job to do. They're not just here to drive me around when I need to go somewhere! I'll go by the road, don't worry. It'll take longer, but—'

'Longer? It'll take hours! Come on, we'll go by the field path, and I'll push.' Fiona turned and Bertie saw that Amy had been trailing her down the path. 'Amy! We're going to the farm. She's a bit miserable,' she confided in a lower voice, 'she'd hoped to be leaving today.'

'Why isn't she then?'

Fiona shrugged. 'I think her mother has asked her to stay a

bit longer.' As Amy joined them she gave her a bright smile. 'We were going mad cooped up indoors, weren't we, Amy?'

Amy seemed less convinced, but she didn't argue, and by the time they turned from the muddy farmyard onto the smooth path through the front garden, Bertie was glad she had come along; she mightn't like the girl much, but she'd been a help whenever the wheelchair had become stuck in a few waterlogged ruts along the field path, although Fiona was reluctant to let her.

Fiona rolled the chair to the front door of the farmhouse and stepped forward to knock. It was a few minutes before they heard scuffles and murmurs from inside, during which time Bertie almost turned the chair around and went home, but eventually the door opened. At Bertie's knee-height, the Nancarrows' dog's head appeared, panting, and Bertie fought the instinct to draw back; Reynard might have saved her life by bringing Helen to her at the bridge, but he had also caused the accident to begin with. No matter how often she saw him, it was hard to forget.

Beth put a knee out to prevent the dog from squeezing past, and blinked in surprise to see the delegation at her door. 'Hello, Miss Fox ... Reynard! Back!' She gave them an apologetic smile and reached down to seize Reynard's collar. 'Don't mind him, we're keeping him indoors for a few days while his leg heals. Come in.'

They filed into the warm hallway, and Beth closed the door, letting out a sigh of relief as Reynard shot away towards the kitchen at a fast limp. 'He's been driving us to distraction these past few days.'

'What's he done?' Bertie saw Jowan's oilskin hanging up and felt the same mixture of relief and nerves she'd felt on Christmas Eve; no escaping it this time though.

315

'Just caught it on some wire, he'll be alright.' Beth gestured for them all to follow her into the little sitting room. She looked ill at ease to suddenly have so many guests, and immediately set to plumping cushions and straightening antimacassars. Bertie wished she could tell her to relax, but it would only sound patronising.

'I'll shout Jo for you,' Beth said at length. 'He's not long come in, and just having a wash. Can I fetch you some tea?'

They accepted, and Beth left the room. Bertie looked around at the other two. 'Would you mind just doing the same as Reynard, when Jo comes down?'

'Running around with a limp?' Fiona deadpanned.

'Going into the kitchen!'

Fiona grinned. 'Of course we don't mind, I know you'll want to be alone.'

Bertie nodded. This was going to be hard, her throat was already thickening at this tiny show of understanding from her sister. 'Thanks.' She looked up as the door opened and Jowan came in. He seemed surprised to see the two younger girls, and even more so when they abruptly realised Beth needed help with the drinks.

'What's got into them?'

'They know why I came,' Bertie said, and he looked at her more closely.

'I'm not sure I like the sound of this.'

'We do need to talk, Jo, you know that. Fi offered to push me over here, to get some fresh air after being stuck indoors.'

'Pushed? I thought someone must have driven you!' Jowan lowered himself into his chair. 'Well I'll drive you all back.'

For a moment they only looked at one another, then he sat forward. 'You've decided, haven't you? You're going.'

'You knew I was.'

316

'But ... you're not just going to train, are you? You're leaving Fox Bay.'

She nodded. 'As soon as Doctor Russell says I can.' She couldn't look at him, but she could feel his eyes on her. 'What I need to know is, will you come with me?'

They were both momentarily distracted by shouts outside the window, and Bertie looked up to see Fiona and Amy, with Reynard on a lead, marching across the farmyard.

'He still needs his exercise,' Jowan said, in a distant voice, 'but we can't let him run loose.'

'Never mind the dog! Do you have any notion of how much sleep I've lost over the thought of asking you this?'

'And do you have any notion of the hours I've spent wondering how I'll react when you do?'

For a moment they glared at one another, then Bertie subsided. 'You guessed, then.'

'That learning to fly wouldn't be enough? That when you left it would be for good? It took a while, but I finally realised, yes.'

'You said you hoped, by the time my leg was fixed, that you'd have had time to come to terms with it.'

'We're not there yet.'

'But you gave me the *scarf*, Jo!'

Jowan shifted in his seat, his eyes cast down. 'I suppose all I was thinking about was how you'd cope with the flying ... and how I would cope with the worry. I gave you the scarf to show you I'm behind you whatever you choose. But I never really thought about what it would mean for us as a married couple. Where we'd go, how we'd live.'

Bertie knew there would be no better time. 'There's something else, and I don't want you to fly off the handle when I tell you.'

'Xander Nicholls is going to be training in Cornwall, not Brighton?'

'How did you know?' It was a relief, despite the surprise, that she didn't have to say it herself.

'Just a guess. I was hoping you'd say I was wrong though.'

'Jo, you have to—'

'Look, this isn't about Xander,' he said. 'You've probably been tying yourself in knots over how to tell me, but I do realise you and he are only friends. This is about you and me.'

A timid knock at the door brought the conversation to a halt, and Beth came in with a tray filled with clinking china. It looked as if it must be her best, and once again Bertie wanted to tell her she shouldn't worry.

'The young 'uns are taking Reynard out.' Beth placed the tray on the sideboard with nervous care. 'Just as far as the barn. Tea'll keep hot 'til they get back.' She placed a knitted cosy over the teapot, looked from one strained face to the other, and cleared her throat. 'Well, I'll be leaving you to it then,' she said, with forced brightness. 'Alfie'll be in d'rectly.'

Bertie smiled, and waited until the door closed behind her, then continued as if the interruption hadn't happened. 'What if I changed my mind? Decided not to do it after all. Would we live here with your family?'

'No,' he said, 'I couldn't ask you to do that.'

'Why not?'

'Well, because ... Because it's so far from what you're used to, I suppose.'

'So you'd move into the hotel?'

'No!' Under other circumstances she might have laughed at his vehement response, but it all felt too much as if their plans were

318

built on sand. 'We'd find our own place,' he said firmly. 'Start our own family, like anyone else.'

'And how would that be any different to living here?'

'My family wouldn't be there for a start,' he muttered, and she realised with relief that he wasn't happy here any more, either. That was another hurdle cleared.

'But our home would be no better than this, would it?' she persisted. 'We certainly couldn't afford to live in the same luxury as I'm "used to", as you put it.'

'Why are you pushing this?' he asked, his voice tightening. 'Are you trying to remind me that your station in life and mine are completely different?'

'No,' she said more gently. She took his hand onto her knee. 'Because they're not. I'm trying to remind you that whether it's here or in Caernoweth, we'd still be starting a new life together, and you knew that, when you asked me to marry you. So,' she went on, 'in all those hours of wondering what your reaction would be, did you reach a conclusion?'

'No. I realised I wouldn't, no matter how many times I played it out in my head. Not until you actually told me.'

'And now?'

He looked at her, exasperated. 'I still don't know how it would work.'

'I see.' She let go of his hand, but he caught her fingers before she moved away.

'Which doesn't mean I'm not keen to find out! Bertie, I still want us to marry.'

Bertie took a deep breath and let it out slowly. 'You'd move away from your family?'

'I told you, *you'd* be my family. You and our children.' He looked

319

at her earnestly. 'Look, Uncle Alfie's friend has a farm just down the road a bit from the air base. I might be able to start off with a job there, while you're training. Just to see if it's really what you want to do.'

'And after that?' It was Bertie's turn to gradually realise that this might happen after all.

'Let's just take it one step at a time, shall we? I don't even know if I'd have a job yet.'

'It'll be a while before I'm ready too,' Bertie reminded him, 'so there's no rush to work it all out. I just ... I had to know if it's something you were prepared to do.'

'Leave here?' Jowan looked around him with a strange mixture of fondness and impatience. 'I'm nearly thirty, if I don't move on soon I'll take root.'

'And your family? The farm?'

'Uncle Alfie knows I'd be looking to move away once I'm wed, he'll find another pair of working hands. Mum ...' He shrugged. 'Mum'll probably shed a tear in private, and cling on to poor old Jory a bit too tight for a while, but she likes you, and she's glad we're starting out together.'

'We have time,' Bertie repeated quietly. 'As long as we need.'

Jowan leaned in and touched his lips to hers. 'Then let's make the best of it. We'll save every penny, and find the perfect home for us and our children.'

For a while Bertie allowed herself the simple pleasure of his hands in her hair and his forehead on hers. When he eased back, she remembered the other reason she'd wanted to speak to him. 'Do you know if there's a way yet, to get your grandmother's ring back?'

'There's only one way I can think of,' Jowan said, and now he looked nervous again.

Bertie's heart sank as her suspicions were confirmed. 'You're going to sell the bike, aren't you?'

'It's the only way.'

'No, it's not. I'm sure we can help. The hotel, I mean. Let me talk to Adam.'

'Not your mother?'

'Adam understands better why I wouldn't want you to sell the Squirrel. I think Mum would just be glad to see it gone forever.'

The back door slammed, and a moment later Fiona and Amy came into the sitting room, and Fiona shot Bertie a questioning look. She nodded, and Fiona found the tray of tea and began pouring, while Amy went to the window and stared out across the yard.

'Did Reynard behave himself?' Jowan asked.

'Got quite lively out by the barn,' Fiona said. She handed him his tea and looked over at Amy. 'And so did she.'

Amy turned. 'What?'

'When Reynard pulled the lead out of your hand.'

'Oh, that. Haven't run *that* fast in a long time!' Amy smiled, she looked oddly alight today, there by the window with the feeble sun struggling through the thickened glass. Also a tiny bit tense, Bertie thought, as she accepted a cup from her sister.

'Good thing you got to him before he made it through the gate,' Jowan said. 'He'd have been up over the hill to the golf resort, and then you'd have had a job getting him back.'

'Why?'

'Where they've dug out the deeper foundations, for the storage area, they've disturbed an old warren. He spends hours sniffing around there, it's where he cut his leg on the wire fence.'

They heard Beth's voice greeting Alfie as he came in, and then it lowered, presumably while she warned him they had a sitting room full of guests. A moment later he came in, hair in disarray and still in his grubby work clothes, and went straight over to where Bertie sat.

'About what Jory did,' he said, without preamble. 'There's no forgiving it, but I want you to know how sorry we all are.'

'The ring wasn't mine,' Bertie said quietly, feeling sorry for the discomfort she could see on his face. 'It was your mother's, and we're going to try and help get it back.'

'We'll talk about it later,' Jowan put in, as Alfie frowned and opened his mouth to speak again. 'I'm going to drive them home, so I'll need the van.'

'I'll walk,' Amy said. 'That little bit of exercise has made me realise how little I've had. Besides work,' she added, as Fiona raised an eyebrow. 'Fresh air, I mean.'

'I'll walk with you.'

'There's no need.' Amy turned back to the window, but in its reflection Bertie saw a faint frown crease the girl's brow. 'Besides, Bertie will need you at the other end.'

'I'm quite able to manage,' Bertie insisted. 'Thanks for helping me to get here, but I'll be alright with Jo to help.'

'I could do it if you like,' Alfie said quickly. 'I need a word with … with Adam, anyway.'

'He's not there today, he's in Truro. What do you want to see him for?'

'Oh.' Alfie shrugged. 'Nothing important, it's just … We've done well with the eggs again, since Reynard's not been out barking at the hens, thought you might like to increase your order.'

'Well we've got fewer guests now,' Bertie said, picking up her gloves, 'but I gather our new chef starts in a few days, and he's supposed to be a whizz with a whisk. Meringues to die for apparently. I'll tell Adam you'll be down tomorrow then.'

Jowan settled Bertie into the van, and tucked her blanket around her knees. 'Can't have you catching a chill.'

'It's five minutes at most,' she protested, laughing, and he grinned back.

'You're going to have to learn not to argue when someone does something nice for you, and just get used to it.' He dropped a kiss on her cheek as he backed out of the van, and went around to his own side, still smiling. Relieved, no doubt, that they had begun to lay their plans for their new life together.

But Bertie couldn't help thinking back over their conversation, and wondering suddenly if they wanted the same things after all.

* * *

Helen traditionally used this pre-season Sunday to go over the Christmas books and ensure all the figures were up to date. As today was also twelfth night, the remaining decorations were being taken down, and the serious cleaning begun; she retired even more gratefully than usual to her office, glad to escape the scurrying and shouting, and the general air of restlessness as Fox Bay was returned to its usual pristine self.

She sipped a cup of strong coffee as she worked, but her thoughts soon turned away from profit and loss, to Bertie and Jowan; Bertie had returned from her visit to the farm yesterday in a more settled, though thoughtful, mood. She'd been so disappointed by Jowan's absence from the party, but he must have had a good reason after all since Bertie would never have forgiven a feeble one. Helen found her lips curving in an appreciative smile for her daughter's strength of character.

Her own disappointment for that night, she pushed to the back of her mind. Alfie Nancarrow didn't belong in her thoughts at all, and since he had only that day returned from the funeral of his friend's wife he'd likely been in no mood for a party anyway. The fact that she'd worn a new dress, and taken special care over her appearance, meant nothing; it was expected of her.

She bent to her ledger again, but all the numbers began to look the same, and eventually she picked up her cup, and turned to look out of the window instead. She gazed out at the empty cloisters, the driving rain, and the madly blowing trees beyond, and for a moment wondered if her thoughts had confused her eyes; Adam was walking the length of the cloisters, deep in conversation with Alfie Nancarrow.

Helen was wholly unprepared for the jolt she felt at the familiar sight – it wasn't as if Alfie had changed physically, or suddenly done something courageous and selfless, nor had he shown any kindness she didn't already know him to possess ... She'd told Leah it was flattery, but she finally had to admit this new pulling sensation deep inside her was more than that. And it was too late to do anything about it.

As the two men passed the window Alfie's gaze swivelled towards it, and a brief smile lit his face and was gone in an instant. Adam waved, and then they had gone, passed round the building to the kitchens where they would no doubt conclude whatever business Alfie had come to discuss. Helen turned back to her desk and opened the ledger again, determined to concentrate this time.

It must have been perhaps ten minutes later when Martin knocked at the door. 'Mr Nancarrow to see you, Mrs Fox.'

Helen's heart turned over. 'Thank you. Show him in.'

He seemed huge, suddenly, standing in the doorway in his work clothes, where he had stood a hundred times before, and this time there was no smile to soften his hard features.

'Alfie. Sit down, won't you?' She waited until he was seated, giving her time to collect herself. 'How can I help?'

'I came to see Adam, about . . . No.' He waved that away. 'That was just an excuse, I wanted to let you know how sorry I am.'

'For what?' She wanted him to repeat what he had said to her in the churchyard, perhaps as a way of reminding herself he had said it at all, and she was already framing her reply. But he surprised her.

'For what Jory did. It was unforgiveable'

She stared at him blankly for a moment, trying to reconcile what she had heard with what she had expected to hear. Then she shook her head. 'I'm sorry, what are you talking about?'

'Jory,' he repeated. 'The ring.'

Helen gave a helpless half-shrug. 'What ring?'

'The engagement . . . You didn't know?'

'Clearly not.' What would his engagement ring have to do with her?

Alfie's eyes narrowed beneath the straight dark eyebrows. 'Jowan was getting my mother's ring re-sized. For your Bertie,' he added, unnecessarily.

'That was nice of him, and nice of you to give it to him.' Helen paused, waiting for a further explanation, but when it came she wished it hadn't. As he told her everything her heart sank, and she sighed. Poor Bertie . . . That fool Jory! And to use his brother's name, too.

'No wonder she was so upset on New Year's Eve,' she said when he'd finished. 'What are you going to do about it?'

Alfie shook his head. 'Jo's planning on selling his motorbike. Bertie's bike,' he amended, 'since it's still in her name.'

'She'll hate that,' Helen murmured. 'Is there no other way?'

'We certainly can't afford to pay for a ring like that, not in the time before it's sold anyway.'

'But we could,' Helen said slowly. 'Is that why you're here?'

'No, it isn't.' Alfie's voice hardened. 'I came here to apologise for my nephew's actions, and to explain why *your* daughter's finger won't be graced with *my* mother's engagement ring. I had no idea you didn't know about it, and even less notion of asking for your money.'

'Well you must admit,' she said, her own voice tight, 'when you come here saying the only alternative is for Bertie's beloved Squirrel to be sold, then add that you can't afford to prevent it, it does rather point to that, don't you agree? Whether emotional blackmail was your intention or not. You *know* how heartbroken she'd be! What else am I to think?'

'I don't know. I don't even know why I bothered, to be honest.' He rose to leave, his eyes flashing with an anger Helen had never seen in him before. Remorse for the sudden animosity made her feel a little ill, but she could have done without his attitude. He seemed as if he wanted to say more, but snatched up his hat and strode to the door.

'I don't want your money, Mrs Fox. I just ...' He shook his head and yanked the door open. 'I'm sorry I came.'

Helen stood up too, but before she could think of anything to say he had gone, and the door stood open so she could see him crossing the lobby. She watched as he shoved his way through the revolving door as if it were his personal enemy, and she was disturbed to find her own irritation did not make her feel

326

better at having angered him. Yes, he had responded predictably, pridefully in fact, but he hadn't given her any chance to explain that she was quite happy to get the ring back. But for Bertie, not because she wished to appear the Lady Bountiful to the poor farmer up the road.

Helen closed the door, harder than necessary and not caring that it would cause raised eyebrows on the other side of it. She had no idea how much retrieving the ring would cost, since she'd never even seen it, let alone guess how much the Bude pawnbroker would charge, but she would ensure the money was available. For Bertie.

CHAPTER TWENTY-ONE

Lynette had been full of the joys of her brief stay in Caernoweth since her return last night. Bertie listened to her chatter all the way to the railway station, noting that most of the talk, unsurprisingly, centred on a certain young chef.

'Now, when you and Xander are both in Caernoweth, I won't have to make a decision about where I stay when I visit. I can see all of ... *both* of you at the same time.'

'You don't have to pretend to me,' Bertie pointed out with a smile, and added gently, 'Harry seems a very nice young man.'

'He is.' Lynette gave a contented sigh. 'I can't wait until I can come back down. I'll miss your sister, too, though she seems to have been a bit frosty lately. What's wrong?'

'I think her friend is proving something of a bad influence,' Bertie said. A tiny sound came from Guy, whose eyes were on avoiding the huge puddles left by yesterday's torrential downpours, though he said nothing during the short trip. Bertie reflected that it had been days since she'd seen his usual indulgent smile; Granny's announcement that she was leaving was bound to have hit him hard.

Bertie slipped her arms through the leather bands of her crutches and followed Lynette to the platform to await her train eastwards. The westbound from Plymouth was idling as its few Trethkellis passengers climbed down and slammed doors behind them. Among them, a woman in her early thirties was wrestling two bags while struggling to hold a small baby, and her face was white and worried beneath the mass of red curls that was escaping her hat.

'Guy, look.' Bertie lifted one crutch and waved it. 'Help her, won't you?'

'Hmm?' Guy followed the direction Bertie was pointing in. 'Oh! Of course.' But before he reached her, a porter stepped in and the woman looked ready to burst into tears with gratitude, as he lifted her two bags and gestured with his head. She adjusted the baby's hat and pulled its blanket higher to cut out the slicing cold wind, and followed the porter gratefully to the office.

'Must be all but impossible to travel like that,' Lynette mused, staring after her with sympathy. 'Where's her nanny, do you suppose?'

'She probably doesn't have one,' Bertie pointed out patiently. Really, Lynette was lovely, but she did inhabit another world sometimes.

The train pulled away in a rush of steam and belching black smoke, and Bertie accompanied Lynette to the waiting room. Guy followed, with Lynette's bags, and through the murky window they watched as a taxi arrived and the porter helped the struggling woman climb into it with her baby.

'She looks awfully worried about something,' Lynette mused. 'I hope the baby's alright.' She nudged Bertie's arm. 'That'll be you one day soon, once you and Jowan start producing.'

'Oh, for goodness' sake! That's a bit previous! Besides, he knows I want a career.'

'Every man wants an heir,' Lynette said, only half-smiling. 'He'll let you learn to fly, because he knows he has no choice, and he's a lovely chap. But mark my words, it won't be long before he starts making noises about starting a family.'

Lynette's words raised the niggling concern that Bertie had tried to deny since her talk with Jowan. He'd mentioned children more than once, as if it were beyond question, and the thought of giving birth was terrifying in itself, but to then have all that responsibility, all that anxiety, and the fear that she was making awful mistakes that would affect another human's entire life? How anyone did it she would never know. She remembered how she'd blamed her own mother, who'd had to make the heart-breaking decision to let the doctors take Bertie's leg to save her life; she'd been absolutely vile, and Helen had absorbed it, some-how, and not turned away once. Bertie doubted if she herself would have been so forgiving.

And now, that poor woman fighting her way off the train with her precious bundle, ready to weep at the simplest act of kindness, and *she* appeared to have all her limbs intact. What if a tiny life depended entirely on Bertie's prosthetic not giving way or coming loose? Bertie gave an involuntary, inward shudder as she pictured herself falling, clutching helplessly and ineffectually at unravelled swaddling, watching as it plummeted beyond her reach ...

No. Motherhood was not for her, and she knew now she would have to tell Jowan that too, before he made irrevocable plans to come with her when she left Fox Bay. She felt more than a little sick at the thought that the gap between them was widening again – they kept closing it, but each time it got harder and harder. How many more differences would force them apart before it finally became too wide to keep them within touching distance?

Back at the hotel, and already missing Lynette's company, she found Fiona cleaning the lounge on the second floor. 'Where's your friend?'

'She went to the village for Granny, but she should be back soon.'

'How long is she staying, anyway?'

'A few days. Something to do with a – a flood, at the farm where she lives.'

Bertie wasn't convinced, and she could see Fiona knew it, from the flush that stained her sister's cheeks.

'Has there been any luck yet, getting the ring back from the pawnbroker?' Fiona asked, before Bertie could say anything more about Amy.

Bertie shook her head. 'Alfie went in, but Charlie Templeton says he bought it in good faith, and he wasn't giving it up until we either pay him, or the police turn up.'

'Why not tell the police, then?' Fiona dug her cloth into the can of Mansion. 'Jory doesn't deserve to get away with what he's done.'

'Jory gave Jo's name, and we can't prove it wasn't him. In which case it's perfectly legal.' She sighed. 'Jo wants to sell the Squirrel to buy it back.'

'Oh no, that would be too bad.'

'I've told him I'll speak to Adam about borrowing some money from the hotel.'

Footsteps on the stairs announced Amy's arrival, and the end of the conversation. She seemed brighter than she had when they'd left the farm on Saturday, and she smiled at Bertie but turned to Fiona. 'Are you coming down for lunch?'

Fiona tilted her head. 'Did you hear that? It sounded like a baby.'

'You sound surprised,' Amy observed. 'Don't you get babies here?'

'Not generally, no. Sometimes in the summer, but then we don't normally have new guests during this week anyway.'

'I wonder if it's the same woman Lynette and I saw at the station,' Bertie mused. 'She was having a bit of trouble with her baby and her bags, but they found her a taxi. Didn't expect her to be coming here, though, Mum didn't say we had anyone booked.'

Fiona gave the low table one last wipe over. 'Maybe her husband is coming later.'

'Perhaps. But she didn't look very . . .' Bertie stopped, hearing Lynette's innocent prejudices in her own words. 'Never mind. Might not be her anyway.'

'Well?' Amy prodded Fiona. 'Are you coming?'

'What's the rush? You've only just got back from the village, and you said you'd help me here.'

'Alright then, I'll go on my own.'

'But—'

'I'll see you in the dining room.'

When she'd left Bertie gently took the duster out of her sister's hand. 'What's going on?' she asked.

Fiona shrugged. 'She's bored, I think, and would rather go home now.'

'That must be disappointing for you.'

'I'll miss her,' Fiona conceded, 'she's brightened things up here for me, and can be wonderful company. But you can see the way she's been behaving lately. One minute so tense I catch myself thinking twice before I speak, and the next minute she's as happy as you like. It's a bit exhausting, to tell the truth.'

Bertie nodded. 'I thought the same on Saturday at the farm. Look, I really came to find you because I wanted to ask you about Guy.'

Fiona stilled. 'What about him?'

'Well, I found him doing something odd recently, and ever since then he's been a bit … off. The past few days though, he's been worse than ever. Do you know what's going on?'

'No.'

But Fiona's abrupt answer only fuelled Bertie's conviction. 'Come on, Fi! He found something in a bin outside Mrs Burch's shop but he wouldn't tell me what it was. Now he really has a bee in his bonnet about your friend.' She waited, and when Fiona didn't answer she sighed. 'Alright, if you won't tell me either, I'll find out some other way.'

She wheeled away crossly and returned to the ground floor. There she saw Amy going into the dining room, and as she was about to follow her she heard the lift ding behind her. Expecting to see Fiona, she turned with an apology on her lips, but the cage rolled back to reveal the woman from the station. She must have left her child in their room, and her face was far more composed, her hair neatly brushed, and she had swapped her travelling coat for a woollen suit, smart, but with visible mends here and there. She stepped out into the lobby, staring around her in fascination before crossing to the reception desk and shyly asking Martin something Bertie couldn't make out.

Bertie went into the dining room, determined to find out the truth about the bin, certain now that it had something to do with Amy. Without being invited she settled at Amy's table.

'Hope you don't mind if I join you,' she said brightly. 'Fiona will be down in a minute.'

'No, of course not.' Amy's smile looked genuine enough, and, encouraged, Bertie pushed on.

'Do you know anything about why Mr Bannacott is acting strangely lately?'

Amy gave her a guarded look. 'Is he?'

'He seems awfully grumpy.'

'It must be a strange time, with everyone leaving and the new guests not here yet. Does he have any hobbies?'

'Hobbies?'

'Well, like Fiona was telling me about one of her lifeboat station lads, who has his own outboard motor.'

Bertie blinked. 'Oh, you mean Constable Quick's son.'

'Yes. She said he was going to teach her how to drive it. Does he keep it moored by the slipway? I imagine it must be fun to take it out on the open sea.'

'I have no idea,' Bertie said, bemused by the swift change in subject. 'I think he keeps it there, yes. Anyway, about Guy—'

'He seems very kind.'

'Exactly! Yet while we were at the station today he had to be prompted to help a lady in difficulty, which is most unlike him.'

'The lady with the baby you talked about?'

'Yes. It turns out she *is* the one we heard earlier.'

'I hope she's coping better now,' Amy said politely, helping herself to a bread roll.

'She does seem to be. I saw her in the lobby just now and

she looks a lot fresher. Lots of lovely red hair, all set in curls a bit like Fiona's. The child must be sleeping now, giving her some peace.'

'That's lovely, it must be dreadfully hard to travel alone with a young child.' Amy put down her roll. 'I'm just going to see if Fiona needs any more help. Maybe speed things up a bit so we can eat at the same time.'

Bertie looked after her as she left the dining room, frustrated but reluctantly impressed; the girl had deftly managed to engineer the conversation away from Guy, twice, and with only the slimmest of opportunities. She made up her mind to keep her questions more direct when Amy returned, but the minutes ticked away and there was no sign of her. Fiona came in and looked around as she shook out her heavy cotton napkin.

'Where's Amy?'

'I was about to ask you that. She came to help you, didn't she?'

Fiona shook her head. 'The last time I saw her was when we were all in the sitting room upstairs.' She paused, then replaced her napkin. 'I'll just go and see if I can find her.'

'Why? She'll be down in a minute. Let's just eat.' Bertie raised a hand to call the waiter.

'Order for me,' Fiona said. 'I'll just have soup.'

Left alone once again, Bertie sighed and gave their order. Those two girls were definitely up to something.

* * *

'Ah! There she is. Fiona?'

Her mother beckoned her over to where she and a nervous-looking woman were just coming out of the office, and Fiona cast a quick, frustrated glance at the stairs, then went over. The woman gave her a hesitant smile.

'This is Mrs Buchanan,' Helen said. 'Mrs Buchanan, Fiona will be able to take you to your daughter.'

'Please,' the woman said, 'call me Kitty.'

Fiona's mouth dried up. From Amy's descriptions, Fiona had built a picture in her head of a tall, angular woman, stern and cold-eyed. Kitty Buchanan might have been Daisy Conrad's older sister; short, and sweet-faced, her hair only a slightly more muted red, and very curly.

'Do you know where Amy is?' Kitty asked anxiously. 'I've been so worried.'

A hundred responses dashed through Fiona's head, from denying Amy had ever come to stay, to saying she had caught the train home only that morning; anything to buy a little time to get Amy safely away. But she uttered none of them.

'Evidently there has been some ... misunderstanding,' Helen said, her eyes boring into Fiona's. 'Kitty *hasn't* asked Amy to stay away due to flooding, in fact she's neither seen nor heard from her since the middle of December.'

'But Amy sent ...' Fiona's protest faded, because she'd never actually seen Amy post the letter in Caernoweth. In fact hadn't Amy directed her attention elsewhere? She hissed annoyance at herself for being so naïve. 'I think she's upstairs,' she said instead. 'I'll go and find her for you.'

'Do take a seat in the lounge, Kitty,' Helen said, indicating the way. 'It's wonderful to meet you at last.' She flashed Fiona a dangerous look, that told her this was by no means the end of it.

'I can't thank you enough for caring for her,' Kitty said,

gratitude trembling in her voice. She turned to Fiona. 'And of course yourself, Miss Fox.'

Fiona smiled mechanically and hurried up the stairs. Perhaps it would be better after all, for Amy to return to her home. Kitty seemed so far from the way she'd been described, too, and it was hard to imagine her being cruel, or even particularly strict. But, she reminded herself, you could never tell just from the way someone looked; you only had to see the way Leah fooled people to be reminded of that.

The bedroom was empty and when Fiona looked at the back of the door, where Amy's new coat usually hung, she saw the coat was gone. Her stomach shrank, but she told herself that if Amy *had* seen Kitty when she passed through the lobby, Kitty must surely also have seen her. It was more likely she had simply gone out for some fresh air, but there was only one way to be sure. Fiona pulled open the drawer given over to Amy's few belongings, and her heart sank. Empty. If the spoon had gone, Amy had gone with it.

Her gaze fell on a note, hurriedly scribbled on the back of one of Fiona's Christmas cards.

Thank you for everything. I'll write when I can. I have money, don't worry.

Fiona groaned softly as she realised Freddie must have paid up after all, and she wondered if Guy knew. She took up the note and went downstairs to break the news. Kitty was standing by the window, her arms crossed, continually looking towards the ceiling as if that might help her hear better if her baby were crying. When Fiona came in she started towards her in anticipation, but stopped when she saw she was alone.

'I think we're too late,' Fiona said dully, handing her the note.

337

Kitty read it, and folded it, taking great care over making the edges neat. It was only when Fiona saw how her fingers trembled that she realised the woman was doing her best to hold herself together.

Kitty absently handed her back the tightly folded Christmas card. 'How long is it since anyone's seen her?'

'Close to an hour now. She'll probably be on the train to Plymouth already. She has money,' Fiona added hopefully, 'she said so. That will help her stay safe.'

'Money, yes.' Kitty raised her eyes to look around her. 'I didn't understand how she could afford somewhere like this, but your mother told me how she came to be here. That you'd been on the beach when she was brought in. Thank you for taking her under your wing.'

'She was very welcome here.'

Kitty's eyes glittered with tears. 'It's too dangerous for her to travel alone,' she said, in little more than a whisper. 'She's so young.'

'There's more,' Fiona said, in a voice just as quiet. 'There's a . . . a baby. I'm so sorry,' she rushed on, as Kitty's face turned white, 'she was desperate you shouldn't find out.'

'But why?' Kitty sank into a chair, and her fingers knotted around themselves; hard-working hands, reddened and calloused. Fiona remembered how she'd imagined those hands raised in anger against the defenceless Amy.

'She knew you'd be absolutely furious,' she said, 'and try to make her . . . do something about it.'

'She said *that*?'

'She said the only person who'd understand would have been her true mother, because she'd been in that predicament too.'

'Oh yes.' Kitty sounded bitter now, but the tears that had stood in her eyes began to roll down her cheeks. 'Ruth Wilkins would certainly know about that.'

'She's going to Ireland to find her.'

'Ruth's not in Ireland.' Kitty pulled a cotton handkerchief from her bag. 'As far as I know she's still in London.'

Fiona looked at her, baffled. 'But she said her father had had letters from a village there.'

'Frank? He's not heard from Ruth in years.'

'Then why . . . ' Fiona's legs suddenly wouldn't hold her up, and she fumbled her way to a chair. 'She's been lying to me too, then?'

'It seems so.' Kitty wiped her eyes, but kept the handkerchief balled in her fist as if she knew she'd be needing it again. 'I wonder what story she'd have come up with if you hadn't realised she was pregnant.'

'She *what*?'

They both turned as Bertie came towards them, looking from one to the other. 'Did you know?' she demanded of Fiona, who nodded miserably.

'And you helped her to run away?'

'No! I've only just seen that she's gone.'

'But you'd planned to help her anyway.'

'I *promised*!' Fiona's own eyes brimmed with tears now. 'I only found out a few days ago, when she was trying on Leah's beaded dress. You know how small that one is.'

'So she's showing?' Kitty dabbed at her eyes again. 'Do you know how far along she is?'

'She thinks she's due in June, she says. When we brought her ashore there wasn't the faintest sign. There's only a tiny bump now, but she's so small, and it's such a distinctive shape, not like she's put on weight.'

'Did she say who the . . . Who she . . .'

'I'm sorry, I don't think it's my place to say.'

'My poor little girl.' Kitty sounded distraught, far from the cruel harridan Amy had painted her, and Fiona felt a growing anger towards her friend.

'The only reason I agreed to help her was because she made you out to be some kind of monster.'

'I still can't believe she said that,' Kitty said. 'We've had our ups and downs lately, who hasn't? But we've always been so close. She's always trusted me and her Mr Arch.'

Fiona and Bertie exchanged a questioning look, and Kitty gave them a faint smile. 'It's what she's always called my husband, Archie. They're devoted.'

'She said you had both changed since you came back from the war,' Fiona ventured. 'And that since you'd had your baby together you had no time for her.'

'That's rubbish.' Kitty was clearly attempting to sound brisk, but the tears were clear in her voice. She looked around, as if for an escape. 'Speaking of the baby, I'm going to check him. I don't like him being so far away and not being able to hear him.'

She brushed past them and out of the lounge, and Fiona looked helplessly at Bertie.

'What's been going on, Fi?' Bertie asked, more gently now.

Fiona told her, and as the relief of unburdening herself grew, she saw certain things click into place for Bertie too, particularly when she came to the part about Guy finding the discarded posters in the bin. The only thing she omitted was any question of blackmail, it wouldn't be fair to Guy.

'Does Mum know?' Bertie asked, looking over at the door as if she expected their mother to be there listening.

Fiona shook her head. 'Not all of it. She doesn't know about the baby, or the posters.'

'Do you know when the next boat to Ireland is?'

'No, but now I know she wasn't going there to find her mother.' Fiona told her what Kitty had said about Ruth.

'Then perhaps she wasn't running to Ireland at all,' Bertie said. 'We only have her word for it that the RMS *Drake* itself was going there.'

Fiona put her head in her hands. She hadn't even considered that. 'It would be easy enough to find out, Mr Glasson would know.'

Kitty re-entered the room, this time with her baby in her arms. She sat down carefully, and Fiona saw fatigue written in every line of her face.

'This is Lawrence,' she said. 'He's named for a very dear friend of mine.'

'He's beautiful,' Fiona murmured, mostly out of politeness though when she looked more closely she was rewarded by a sunny smile, and a gurgle that made her smile in return. She brushed the child's soft, rounded cheek with one finger.

'He's the image of his father,' Kitty said. 'We waited such a long time for our own child, but Amy has no reason to think we no longer have time for her.'

'I'm sure she doesn't really think that, any more than she believes herself that you're cruel parents. She just wanted my sympathy, and my help. If what you say is true about her relationship with Mr Buchanan, she's probably convinced this news would ruin her in his eyes.'

Kitty nodded wearily. 'It wouldn't, but I hope you're right.' For a moment she stared down at Lawrence without speaking, then she sighed. 'So now we have to ask ourselves whether Ireland was the lie, or whether finding Ruth was.'

'What if they were both lies?' Fiona said, her forehead tightening as an awful thought occurred. 'What if she just wanted the money for ... for an abortion?'

Kitty drew a sharp breath. 'She wouldn't!'

'Wouldn't she? Not even knowing how you'd have felt?'

'No, let's think about this,' Bertie said. 'If she were truly looking for Ruth she would be going to London. So why was she on a ship heading for Ireland? Assuming that *was* the truth.'

They fell silent; they would probably never know now.

'Why don't you tell us more about her?' Fiona said at length. 'She never really said much, apart from the fact that she liked dancing.'

'Oh, she does love that.' Kitty's faint smile seemed to lift years off her as her memories temporarily banished the worry. 'Ever since her very first harvest festival, when she couldn't take her eyes off the dancing. When she was old enough she begged me to let her go to Bel's dancing lessons in the village, and luckily Bel's a dear friend and let her join for free.'

'She said she had to sneak ...' Fiona shook her head. Of course she hadn't had to sneak out, any more than she'd been threatened with "Mr Arch's" leather belt. 'What was the spoon for?'

'I'm glad she still has that with her, at least.' Kitty looked ready to cry all over again. 'She had that when Frank, her father, found her in that hovel in London. Her mother was ... selling herself.'

She stumbled over the explanation, but it didn't seem that she found it distasteful, more that she was deeply upset by it. 'Ruth was working as a kitchen maid, but fell pregnant and was let go.' She waved her free hand dismissively. 'The details aren't important. She went to London but had no real family there either, and fell into prostitution the way so many do.'

Kitty was really struggling now, and Fiona glanced at Bertie, troubled. 'Don't, Kitty, if it's too hard,' she said gently, but Kitty shook her head.

'I want you to understand. Frank was worried about Amy, what that life would do to her, and so he stole her away. The only possession she had was that spoon, and if you tried to take it from her she'd scream the place down.' She shrugged. 'Because of the life she'd led she was a little … backward, for a four-year-old, and it took a while for her to learn to trust us, but she came to live with us at Dark River Farm and we became her family. She's been very happy.'

'Then why was she so worried about telling you, when you're so loving towards her?'

'Perhaps because she was worried we'd think she took after her mother.' Kitty dropped her gaze, not quite masking a flush by fussing with Lawrence's shawl. 'Perhaps it was my fault. I might have reinforced too strongly how she must be careful around boys, especially living on a farm, but I had my own reasons for that.'

Fiona was about to ask, but Bertie put a hand on her arm and shook her head briefly. It didn't matter. 'So what will you do now?' she asked.

'Go home, I suppose. Telephone Frank, and if he *is* in touch with Ruth—'

'You do have a telephone then?'

'Of course we do. That's another reason I was surprised she didn't at least call, to let me know she was safe if nothing else.'

'How *did* you find out?' Bertie asked. 'If she didn't put up the posters, or contact you, how else would you know she was in Trethkellis at all, let alone here?'

'A friend of mine saw her in Caernoweth.'

'Oh, was it a Miss Parker?'

Kitty nodded. 'We've been friends since I left the ambulance corps. Both bookworms, you see. Emily's known the Penhaligon family since she was a child, and often goes down to the bookshop to help out.'

'But Amy didn't come into the shop.' Fiona again remembered the girl pulling her hat down lower over her distinctive hair.

'Exactly. Emily couldn't be certain who it was, only seeing her from a distance. But she was helping out at the new recruits' party in the civic offices in Caernoweth on Saturday, and got talking to a young friend of yours, a Mr Nicholls.'

'Might have known Xander would be involved,' Bertie murmured.

'Just making conversation, you know,' Kitty said, 'but he mentioned he was staying here over Christmas, and that you, Fiona, had a friend staying too. She made the connection then, but didn't think too much of it because she didn't know Amy was missing. But she came home yesterday, and stopped in to pass on her greetings for the New Year. Of course I told her then.'

'And where's your husband?'

'He's in Breckenhall searching for Amy, and not due back until tomorrow.' Kitty held her child closer, and the infant squirmed uncomfortably but she didn't seem to notice. 'Where did she get the money from to leave, if not from you?'

Fiona felt the heat stealing up her face, there was nothing for it now but to tell the truth. 'I think she was blackmailing Freddie Wishart,' she said in a small voice.

'Freddie Wishart, the film star?' Kitty's eyes were huge.

Bertie just stared at Fiona. '*Blackmailing* him?'

Fiona told them all she knew, concluding with what Guy had told her when she'd waited up for him. 'I was going to confront him with it myself,' she confessed, 'it was the only way. But I couldn't, when it came to it.'

'So now she probably has a great deal more money than you could ever have secured for her,' Bertie said, 'and poor Freddie's life has been turned inside out.'

'She won't tell anyone,' Fiona protested. 'She's got what she wants now.'

'Until she needs her funds refreshed.'

'But by then he'll have gone back to America, she won't have any way of contacting him to demand more. She wouldn't tell just for the sake of it, she's not like that.'

'And how do you know what she's like?' Bertie's voice rose. 'What do you really know about her?'

'*I* know her,' Kitty said quietly. 'And she wouldn't have done something like this unless she was desperate.'

'I still don't understand why she is though,' Fiona said. 'There must be more to it than just not wanting your opinion of her to suffer.'

Kitty just shook her head helplessly. 'If there is, I don't know what it could possibly be.'

CHAPTER TWENTY-TWO

Higher Valley Farm

Beth hung her oilskin by the front door and gingerly removed her leaky boots before padding down the hall in stretched, sodden socks. It had been a long trek out to the bottom field, especially in weather like this, but at least the men needn't break their day coming inside for lunch, and now it was her turn; there was half a beef pudding in the range, which had been warming since before she went out, and she could smell the rich gravy from here. Some leftover mashed potato, with a bit of farm butter to soften it, would finish the meal nicely.

She heard the back porch door slam, and was cross with herself for leaving it open in this high wind, after all the tellings off she gave the twins. She was only glad they weren't home to tease her about it, they could be merciless at times. She allowed herself a little smile. Maybe so, but she'd certainly miss it when they were gone.

With a small sigh of pleasant anticipation she went into the kitchen and her attention immediately went to the range, where the iron door hung open, slightly crooked on its worn hinge. The pudding was still there, but the bowl of mashed potato she'd left covered on the side was gone, and the door to the cold larder also stood wide open. She hadn't left the porch door unlatched at all.

Dismayed, Beth crossed the kitchen and passed through the porch in time to see a boy stumbling away from the house. He was clutching something to his body . . . Beth's potatoes no doubt. Little thief! A flash of fury drove her out into the stony yard in her socks, though there was no hope of catching the intruder now, but a sharp pain in the bottom of her foot stopped her, and left her hopping and hissing curses she'd have given either of her own boys a thick ear for uttering. But now she had stopped her headlong rush she was able to pay more attention to the fleeing figure, and she realised it was in fact a girl. And not just any girl; that white-blonde hair was as distinctive as the face it framed.

Beth limped back into the kitchen and closed the range door, then went to close the larder as well, noting the absence of her Dewar flask of cold milk. That decided her. Still muttering some of Jory's favourite curse words, she pulled her boots on again and shrugged back into her oilskin. In a few minutes she was striding down across the field towards the path that led to the back of Fox Bay Hotel.

Until now she'd thought quite a lot of quiet, polite little Fiona Fox, but she needed to accept responsibility for her house guests, and so did her mother. This wasn't the same as scrumping apples, or picking fruit that had fallen and lay rotting – all of which the local children were fond of doing – this was theft.

Her anger had not abated by the time she had arrived at the back of the hotel, and Beth barely waited for the door to open fully in answer to her knock, before pushing her way into the short

347

hall. She was overheated from walking so fast, but wet from the persistent rain, and it made her even crosser to know she looked a sight compared to the ever-cool and composed Miss Tremar.

'I'd like a word with Mrs Fox, please.'

'Mrs Fox is busy just now, Mrs Nancarrow.' Miss Tremar frowned in concern. 'Is anything wrong? Can I help, perhaps?'

'No thank you. I'll wait, if I may.'

'Certainly.' Miss Tremar plucked a towel from a pile on a tray. 'Give your hair a rub down, love.'

Beth hadn't been expecting such a kind response, and it took a moment for her to take the towel Miss Tremar proffered. 'Thank you,' she said at length. 'I'm sorry to barge in.'

'Not at all. Come into the kitchen, I'll fetch you a hot drink.'

'Do you know how long she's likely to be?' The surge of angry energy was fading now, and Beth was beginning to wonder exactly what she planned to say to Helen Fox when she saw her. After all, she'd only had a distant glimpse of white hair that had looked a little like Amy's . . . She recognised that her resolve was weakening, and gave herself a mental shake. If she left now she'd only berate herself all the way home, so she would wait. But, she reminded herself as she replaced her teacup in its saucer, she was not hotel staff; no matter how scruffy she looked she would wait out in the lobby like any other visitor.

* * *

Mum had insisted Kitty stay overnight, and after some protest an exhausted Kitty had at last agreed, and accepted the use of the telephone so she could try to contact Amy's father. Fiona helped her settle baby Lawrence in a makeshift cradle in the

348

family sitting room, then went in search of Guy to tell him what had happened.

Passing through the lobby she was surprised to see Beth Nancarrow, her head bent over a magazine, seated near the reception desk. She almost went over to say hello, but glimpsed Guy through the swinging dining room doors, and instead hurried in before he vanished again. If she had been surprised to see Beth, she was doubly so to find Guy deep in conversation with Rex Kelly, in the otherwise deserted room.

She hesitated in the doorway, but Guy looked up and saw her, and his expression darkened. He said something in a low voice to Rex, who also frowned.

'We'll continue this later, Bannacott.'

Guy inclined his head, the old, formal, suave gesture, but his face was tight as Mr Kelly brushed past Fiona with only the faintest nod of acknowledgement.

'What's going on?' Fiona asked, troubled. She hadn't even known they knew each other well enough to argue, but that's clearly what they'd been doing. 'Was the service off this lunchtime?'

Guy's tone was disappointingly formal. 'If it was, I'm sure your mother will be the one to remonstrate with me. What can I do for you, Miss Fox?'

'I've come to tell you, you don't have to worry about Amy any more. She's gone.'

'Gone?'

Fiona nodded, then took the bull by the horns. 'I'm afraid to say you were wrong about Freddie though, he did pay her after all.'

Guy looked as though he'd been slapped. 'I don't believe you,' he said in a low voice. 'He wouldn't.'

'She left a note. See?' Fiona showed him. 'Where else would she have got enough money to leave? Oh!' She looked at him with sudden hope, but he shook his head.

'Certainly not from me.'

'Then it *must* have been Freddie.'

'She has nothing to blackmail him with!' Guy insisted. 'She's mistaken. He's not . . . fond of men.'

'How do you know?'

'I told you, he has a fiancée at home!'

'*I* saw you together!' Fiona wanted to bite the words back, but it was too late now. She had to push on. 'And I heard you.'

Guy's eyes were flint-hard as he looked at her. 'So you had to run off and tell your little friend, did you?'

'It wasn't like that! She was upset, and we'd rowed, and—'

'I don't care about your arguments! This is a private matter and nothing to do with either of you.' He calmed himself with what seemed like a great effort. 'What did you see and hear, if I might ask?'

She told him what she'd heard when she'd returned for a plaster for Daisy, and what she'd seen through the keyhole. Then she added what she'd heard on New Year's Eve, in the second floor lounge. 'You told him you loved him, and he said it back,' she finished, feeling like the worst kind of spy.

Guy took a deep breath and sat down at the nearest table. When Fiona didn't immediately join him he looked up at her and gestured to the seat opposite. Playing with the corner of a freshly placed napkin he avoided her gaze and remained silent for a moment, until it became unbearable.

'Guy?'

'He's my son.'

Fiona's words failed her utterly. She waited for him to speak again.

'Alright. From the beginning then,' he said. 'You might have heard that your father and Adam had been told of the growing motion picture trade, from an old friend of mine who'd moved out there.'

'I'd heard something of that. Who was he?'

'She. Gabrielle Fleming, a nice young lady from a modest background. We were engaged to be married, and while we were never love's young dream it suited both of us quite well. She enjoyed the life I could give her, and for me she was a . . . disguise. You understand?'

Fiona nodded, still stunned, but now fascinated as well. He'd had a rich life, it seemed, albeit a shadowy one. 'She found out, though?'

'She did. She felt humiliated, and left immediately, with her brother who was keen to start a new life in America. By then she was already pregnant, and so she married someone she met on the ship. A businessman named John Wishart.'

'Didn't her new husband guess? I mean, I heard Freddie say that it would kill him to find out.'

'He knew. What would kill him was not that he would discover he wasn't Freddie's father, but that he and I were growing close. Until now I've been far enough away to be no . . . threat, if you like.'

'So that's why you collected all those American magazines,' Fiona said. 'How on earth must you have felt when you knew he was coming here?'

'It took a while to sink in,' he admitted, 'but I knew I would have to tell him the truth when he got here. He's not usually half so reclusive, but the poor boy's been in shock since I told him.'

'He's covered it very well,' Fiona murmured. 'So you told him not to give in to Amy, then.'

'He absolutely wouldn't.'

'Then where did she get the money?'

Guy shrugged. 'I have no idea, but I'd be inclined to check the petty cash in your mother's office.'

'No!' Fiona shook her head. 'Whatever else she is, she's not a—' She stopped, remembering the day she'd picked Amy up from the police house. 'She wouldn't steal from us,' she amended. 'So it's true that Freddie has a fiancée?'

'That's what Mr Kelly was so angry about,' Guy said. 'He doesn't like scandals leaking out where his "kids" are concerned.'

'How is it a scandal?'

'Freddie's intended is the niece of someone ... well, let's just say *unsavoury.*'

'In whose opinion?' Fiona couldn't hide her indignation. 'What's it to do with him who Freddie marries?'

'I don't mean someone of a questionable social standing,' Guy said, lowering his voice even further, 'I mean someone dangerous. What they'd call a gang boss.'

Fiona had thought today couldn't possibly throw any more surprises at her, but now she just stared at Guy in stunned silence.

'Look,' he said, 'that doesn't matter, Freddie's not part of that world, but Rex is determined it shouldn't come out.'

'Does he know you're Freddie's father?'

'He'd never have brought him over if he did.' Guy changed the subject, clearly uncomfortable. 'What will you do about Amy?'

Fiona shook her head. 'There's nothing I can do. She'll be long gone by now.'

'Are you *sure* she has money? That she didn't just say that to stop you coming after her?' Guy patted her hand. 'Check the cash box, and be happy if she's proved me right. And now, I must go and speak to Mr Gough about dinner. Try not to worry. And don't tell a soul what's passed between us today, do you promise?'

'I won't,' Fiona muttered, making up her mind that she would never promise anything aloud, ever again. She went out into the lobby where she found Daisy pushing Bertie out of the lift and towards the lounge.

'Is Kitty alright?' Bertie asked.

Fiona nodded. 'But I'm not sure that Amy has money after all,' she said. 'Which means she could have actually run away, not just left. She could be anywhere. I'm going to check the petty cash box just in case.'

'Miss Fox?' Beth hurried towards them. 'Are you saying you don't know where your friend is?'

'Why, have you seen her?'

'I have, not an hour since. She'd been stealing food from my kitchen. That's why I'm here, I came to speak to your mother.'

'What happened?'

Beth told them, and all the while Fiona's worry was growing; if Amy had money she certainly wouldn't need to be stealing from a farmhouse kitchen.

'I don't understand where she can have gone, unless she's hoping to beg her way back to Plymouth?'

'Oh!' Bertie looked startled. 'She was asking about the lad's boat!'

'Danny's? When?'

'At lunch.' Bertie frowned. 'I was trying to get her to talk about what was upsetting Guy, but she kept going off at what I thought was a random tangent. But maybe it was more deliberate than I thought. She was asking if he keeps it moored at the slipway, and I said I thought he did.'

'He does,' Fiona confirmed. 'She didn't seem at all interested the other day, but I did tell her how to get it going . . .' She felt queasy. 'She can't be thinking of taking it, surely? Not on her own, and in her condition?'

'Telephone Mr Glasson,' Bertie said grimly. 'And then the coastguard, what's his name?'

'Pasco Penberthy,' Fiona said. 'Can you do it? I need to find Ben to drive me to the station.'

'He's sleeping,' Bertie reminded her. 'What about Guy?'

'He's with Mr Gough. Adam?'

'In Bude with Granny, getting her travel papers in order.'

Daisy spoke up. 'I can do it. If you don't think Ben would mind me taking his new car?'

'Can you drive?'

'Of course. You have to back home, if you don't want to be stuck in one place, everywhere's such a long way.'

'Right,' Bertie said. 'Go! I'll telephone ahead and see if someone can be there to meet you.'

Daisy turned out to be an admirably fearless driver. Fiona clung to the door handle of Ben's treasured Bugatti as they rocketed through the lanes towards the village, while Daisy peppered her with questions.

'Did you mean to say back there, that your friend is pregnant?'

Fiona filled in as many of the gaps as she could, and before long they were sweeping down the steep lane towards the lifeboat station at the top of Trethkellis beach. Before Daisy had fully pulled the car to a stop, Fiona was scrambling out onto the path and noting immediately that there was no one around. Danny's little boat was pulled high onto the beach and turned upside down. He must have taken the outboard motor off it and stored it in the shed. Fiona drew a huge breath and let it out on a sigh of relief. She shoved her hands into her pockets to warm them, and found the Cornish penny in the corner. She couldn't help a little smile; it seemed a token worked just as well as a real lucky penny after all.

Daisy joined her on the beach and looked both ways, towards the rocks at one end and the jutting headland at the other. 'Nobody?'

'No.'

'I guess that's good though.' Daisy pulled her coat sleeves down over her fingers and shivered. 'Want to go back, or can you think of someplace else to look?'

'She won't be able to get at the motor, even if she turns up. I suppose we could check the railway?'

'Sure. You'll have to remind me of the way, though.'

Fiona turned back towards the car, only to see the familiar stocky shape of Mr Glasson appearing over the lip of the hill. She waved and ran to meet him.

'Thank you for coming down but it's alright. We were worried Amy might be trying to take Danny's boat, and get into difficulties out there.'

'He's took the motor off,' Glasson pointed out, unnecessarily.

'Yes. Thank you again, but you can go home now.'

'Hmph.' He looked past her, saw Daisy, and did a double-take. 'Is that—'

'It is,' Fiona said, amused despite her rising impatience to get away. 'She's helping me look for Amy.'

'Well, you know, I could help you too,' he ventured. He held out his hand to Daisy, who shook it, but spoke quickly.

'Great to meet you, Mr Glasson. Fiona's told me a lot about what you guys do here. So brave. Anyway, we have to—'

'Kind of you to say, Miss Conrad.' Glasson flushed with shy pleasure. 'Perhaps you might like to come down one day when we're training. See it all in action.'

'I'd like that very much.' Daisy gently disengaged her hand from his, as a relieved Fiona climbed into the passenger seat. 'Meantime we really ought to make our way into the village.'

Fiona twisted in her seat to see Glasson's disbelieving eyes on the car as it turned carefully and made its way back up the hill. She watched him turn back towards home and was about to face the front again, ready to direct Daisy towards the village, when another figure caught her attention.

'Stop!' The car jerked to a halt. 'Down there, look. Who's that?'

Daisy peered through the drizzle, but shook her head. 'Someone you know?'

'I don't know, they're wearing a hat and I can't see a face. But whoever it is seems really keen to get to the beach. Go back.'

'You think it could be Amy?'

'Maybe. Similar build, but it's hard to tell from here.'

As Daisy turned the car again and nosed her way down the hill, Fiona kept her eyes on the running figure. She gave an exclamation and sat forward, as the hat blew off, but saw with disappointment that it wasn't Amy at all, it was a slightly built young man with dark blond hair.

He was making directly for Danny's boat, only to realise before he reached it that he was wasting his time, and that the motor had been detached. He twisted left and right as if in faint hope of finding some other means of escape, and as his gaze fell on Fiona and Daisy he made a small sound of alarm and began to run again. Fiona's legs, strengthened by fighting countless tides and used to running on sand, easily matched his stride. She reached out to seize his flapping coat, dragging him to a stumbling halt. He fell to his knees just as Daisy joined them, and Fiona was startled and dismayed to see he was sobbing.

'I'm sorry! Let me go!'

'Who are you?' Fiona demanded, kneeling on the wet sand beside him. 'Why were you trying to steal that boat?'

But the boy only wept harder. He was clearly more than upset, he was in shock, white-faced and shaking, his eyes flitting from Fiona, to Daisy, to the sea, to the rocks.

'What's happened?' Fiona asked, more gently. 'You're not in trouble for the boat, don't worry.'

'There weren't nothing I could do,' he managed at last. 'Oh, God, I shouldn't have left her—'

'Left who?'

'And where?' Daisy added, more harshly. 'Does someone need help?'

The boy's face swivelled to her again. 'Amy. She only went for food.'

Fiona's blood chilled, and her grip on his coat slackened. 'What's happened to her?'

'It was the ladder,' he muttered. 'The hole collapsed. I think she's dead.'

Fiona could neither move nor speak, she just stared at him in mute horror.

'Where?' Daisy demanded again, grabbing his collar.

'The hole in the ground. Up by the farm.'

357

Daisy turned to Fiona. 'Where's he talking about?

For a moment there was only a rushing sound in Fiona's ears, stopping her from thinking. Then she snapped her head up. 'The golf resort!' She somehow found her feet, and tried to drag him too, but he remained on his knees, his head bowed. 'Come on!' She pulled again, and Daisy tried to help, but he was like a dead weight between them. Fiona lost her temper and shook him, but rather than bring him back to his senses it only made him curl up and bury his head in his hands.

She dropped him. 'We haven't got time for this. Come on.'

Most of the strength had run out of her legs now, but somehow she made it back to the car, her heart thundering with fear, and looked back to see the boy hunched over on the sand. As the car roared up the lane again Fiona could barely speak to tell Daisy which direction to take, but within a few minutes they were on the road that would take them to the top of Higher Valley Farm.

'We should have called in to someone on the way,' Fiona realised, as they left the village behind.

'Too late now, and no time to go back.' Daisy eased the car around a corner and speeded up again. 'Who is he, anyway?'

'At a guess I'd say he's the father of her baby. I don't know how, but he must have come ashore at Porthstennack after all.' She saw Daisy's puzzled frown. 'It doesn't matter, I'll tell you later. Go right, just up there.' She pointed, and Daisy nosed the car into a gap in the wall, which had been widened to allow building materials and larger vans to pass through it.

The wheels spun in the muddy ground for a heart-stopping moment, then found traction, and the car jumped forward and crossed the grass before sliding to a halt near a wire fence with a hole torn in the bottom of it. On the other side of the hole was the area of land set aside for the clubhouse, or at least what would be the storage area of the basement; an area that measured no bigger than half a tennis court, and covered by a huge, flapping tarpaulin. Fiona ducked through the hole in the fence, feeling a tug as her collar snagged on the broken wire, but she pulled free and just managed to stop herself from stumbling forward onto her knees.

The tarpaulin snapped and writhed in the wind where it had come loose at the far end – that must be where the ladder was that the workmen had been using, and Fiona's feet squelched in the churned mud where countless feet had trekked back and forth from the excavation. She kicked something hard as she went, and looked down to see a Dewar flask half-submerged and lying in a puddle of diluted milk.

She didn't need to glance upwards to know the river water was cascading down the hillside and gathering in the flat land above the planned clubhouse; the overspill was churned and brown, the ground had a sickeningly bowed look, and as the tarpaulin lifted again in a gust of wind Fiona saw that the side of the foundations had given way under the sudden deluge from undrained flood land, just as the boy had said.

She was aware of Daisy sloshing through the mud behind her, and began to run again, shouting Amy's name. There was no reply, and it was as much as she could do to remain on her feet, her stomach roiling as she imagined how it must have happened; a small-boned, slim girl climbing down, one hand on the ladder, one clutching whatever food she had been able to steal, only to be sent crashing down into the mud as the wall collapsed. The basement wasn't deep, certainly no higher than eight feet or so to allow a full-grown man easy access and allow for a floor to be laid, but there was no way of knowing what the ground was like in there.

Fiona seized the edge of the heavy, waterlogged tarpaulin, and felt Daisy add her own efforts, and between them they flung it aside to uncover the small, triangular gap near the corner. The unshored wall beneath had come away in a wide semi circle, the earth washed down into the excavation in a stony trail of mud, and the ground on the other side of the mudslide was one huge pool of dark brown water. There was no telling how deep the pool was; they must have dug the ground out deeper there and it might be inches, or several feet.

Fiona peered down, her heart slithering against her ribs; if Amy had gone into that water when the ladder had broken ... Was that what the boy had witnessed? She felt sick at the thought, and turned to Daisy. 'I'm going down.'

'No!' Daisy grabbed her arm just as she began to step onto the mudslide. 'You can't see how soft that is, it could suck you right down!'

'Alright, I'll go over along there.' Fiona ran to the middle section of the hole and began pulling at the wooden peg that had been keeping the tarpaulin in place. Daisy lent a hand, and together they were able to pull it free, flinging it away as they had with the corner section. Fiona shrugged out of her coat and threw it on the ground, and was about to lie on it when Daisy stopped her again.

'If you lie on that, you'll slip right in, coat and all. Here.' She picked it up and began to tie one sleeve around Fiona's wrist. 'Okay,' she said, when she was satisfied. 'Now you do me.'

Though frustrated at the time it took, Fiona realised the sense of it, and nodded. Her fingers were shaking almost too much to complete the job, but soon they each had a sleeve secured around one arm, the coat hanging between them like an exhausted child.

'Now we'll find out how good this stitching is,' Fiona muttered, and lay down with her feet dangling over the foundation. She slithered backwards until her hips touched the edge and allowed her to bend at the waist, and the sleeve tightened around her wrist as the ground beneath her crumbled away a little more.

'Are you okay?' Daisy asked anxiously. 'I'm keeping hold of this end, don't worry.'

'It's not that deep.' Fiona stretched her toes, and felt the sucking of the mud at her boots. 'I'm alright,' she called back, 'but it's slimy underfoot in here.' She turned to squint into the darkness, fear stealing over her again. 'Amy? Can you hear me? Can you make a noise?'

At first there was nothing, and then a faint, incredulous voice came from somewhere just ahead. 'Fi?'

Fiona's heart skipped. 'She's alive! I'm going to untie the coat now.'

'Don't! I'll stretch out further instead.'

'It's not enough.' Fiona ripped at the sleeve, cursing the way the knot had tightened. 'It's alright, Amy, I'm coming!'

At last the sodden, mud-coated sleeve fell away and Fiona pulled one boot free from the mud. 'Speak to me, where are you?' She leaned forward, and stared, wide-eyed into the darkness, which receded a little as her eyesight adjusted, until she was able to make out the full outline of the basement.

She dropped her gaze lower, and found the white face of her friend, streaked with either mud or blood, it was impossible to tell which. She was half lying, half sitting next to the mudslide, her lap filled with broken stones and mud.

Fiona took a short, relieved breath. 'Are you hurt?'

'I, I don't think so. I've been waiting for help.'

'You'd have been waiting a long time,' Fiona said grimly, taking an unsteady step away from the relative safety of the wall.

'What do you mean? Is Micky alright?'

'He's fine.' Fiona would have preferred all her concentration to go on keeping her balance, with that pool looming, dark and possibly lethal, just a few steps away, but talking would be good for Amy. 'Why does he think you're dead?' Her foot slid away from her, sending her heart into her throat, and her arms pinwheeling, but she regained her balance and steadied her voice. 'He seems to think it's his fault. Is it?'

'No! He wasn't even down here. He was up there, waiting for me when I came back with the food. I gave him the flask and the bowl and started to climb down, but there was this awful rushing noise, and then the mud started to . . . *bend* inwards, from underground. It looked as if the whole wall was coming away. I don't know what happened but I fell backwards.'

'The ladder's old, must have been standing here in the rain for months, and just rotted through.'

Amy nodded. 'I landed awful hard, on my back. Micky shouted to me, but I couldn't get my breath to answer. He didn't come down, so he must have gone for help.'

She sounded so desperately bewildered that Fiona didn't like to tell her the truth. 'Can you stand?' she asked instead.

'I think so, but there was no point trying to climb that—' Amy pointed to the river of mud '—so I thought I should wait for Micky to get back.'

'Don't try to move yet. I'm going to see if I can salvage part of the ladder.'

362

'Should I go get help?' Daisy called down.

'No, she's fine, and we need you!'

Above them the wind tugged at the loose side of the tarpaulin, and Fiona could see further glimpses of daylight at points along its edge, as the wooden pegs had worked loose. She tested the solidity of the ground with her boot; it was still slick, shifting and unstable, and although neither she nor Amy was particularly heavy, it was too dangerous to attempt to climb it with that pool so close.

Her teeth were already chattering as she leaned forward again and felt carefully, and with rapidly numbing fingers, along the wall below the level of the water. The splintered bottom half of the ladder was there, but when she tried to pull it, it held fast. Either there *was* a much deeper shaft here, or the ladder was sunk deep into the ground. The top half was the better option but it was likely buried under several tons of mud now.

'I'm going to have to lift you,' she said to Amy. 'Are you sure you didn't hurt your back when you fell?'

'No, it just knocked me breathless.'

Fiona helped her to brush away the heavy debris from her lap and legs, and pulled her unsteadily to her feet. Together they crossed the soft, sucking ground to the wall, where she made a stirrup with her icy fingers, hoping they weren't too numb to hold firm while Amy climbed. The tarpaulin snapped and strained at the pegs in the ground, and then another one tore loose and skidded into the hole. Fiona eyed it, the beginnings of an idea tickling her tired mind.

Daisy dangled the empty sleeve of Fiona's coat, and Amy caught hold of it and put her foot into Fiona's linked hands.

'One, two, three ... hup!' Fiona boosted as Amy stepped,

and a moment later the girl was up, and out of the dank, earthy excavation, leaving Fiona feeling oddly alone.

'Your turn,' Daisy called, throwing the coat down again, but Fiona had no friendly boost down here for herself, and although her arms were strong they were very, very tired now. She looked down and saw the wooden peg that had fallen near her, and the tentative idea flared into life. She bent and picked it up.

'Get me that peg we pulled out earlier!'

Grasping the peg tightly with both hands, she shoved it as hard as she could into the wall at around knee-height. It took several blows, and drilling twists, and her arms were shaking with fatigue, but eventually she was able to drive it deeply enough so that it might bear her weight for just long enough. If she was quick.

Daisy had, in the meantime, found the first peg they had pulled out and now she tossed it to Fiona, realising what it was for. 'My word, you're one smart girl!'

'We'll see!' But Fiona couldn't help grinning, despite her blistering fingers, as she leaned against the wall and removed her boot. Daisy's admiration spurred her on, and she used the boot to hammer at the sharpened peg until it too was sunk into the wall to around half its length. Never had she been so glad for the years of hauling on waterlogged ropes down at the lifeboat station.

The tarpaulin was billowing wildly in the stiffening wind now, and the glimpse of the sky was intoxicating. Fiona pulled her boot on again, then took a deep breath and took hold of the dangling coat sleeve.

'Are you ready?'

'Let's go!' Daisy was laughing now, and Amy yelled encouragement as Fiona wrapped the sleeve around her wrist and placed one foot tentatively over the first peg. Two quick steps, a mighty heave, and she was over the ledge. Her free hand grabbed at the grass, and she felt hands at her collar, pulling her onto the flat ground to lie, panting and smiling up at the sky.

'We did it!'

She twisted to see Amy, standing near her head. 'No thanks to you, you rotten little thief!' But she was still smiling as she climbed to her feet. 'Come on, let's get you back to the hotel and cleaned up.'

'I can't,' Amy muttered, pulling back from Fiona's reaching hand. 'I told you, I have to—'

'Kitty knows everything, don't worry.'

'Everything?' Amy put a hand to her stomach.

'She's desperately worried about you, Amy. She just wants you home.'

Amy hesitated, then took a deep breath, looking resigned and relieved at the same time. 'Alright.'

They started to walk towards the car, and Daisy shuddered as she looked back at the muddy hole. 'I'll be glad to get away from there— Oh! There's the farmer-lady's bowl. She'll want it back, right?' She went back to pick it up, and laughed. 'What do you know, it's even still got the mashed potatoes in it!'

A snapping sound, almost like a crack of thunder, came from overhead and they all looked up, startled, as the huge, flapping tarpaulin billowed upwards. The corner they had flung back unfolded, and rose straight up in the air before the tarpaulin slammed back down.

In the time it took to blink away the shock, Daisy had vanished.

CHAPTER TWENTY-THREE

'It was good of you to drop me back,' Beth said, as the car pulled in to the farmyard. 'Jory should be back d'rectly, he's always first home. Won't you come in for some tea while you wait?'

'No, it's quite alright, thank you,' Helen said, 'I'll wait in the car with Guy.' How could she possibly tell Beth that the thought of speaking to Alfie, knowing he was so angry with her, was making her quake inside? It was ridiculous; they had disagreed on many things over the last few years since he had come to live here, mostly to do with business, but this was different. His opinion of her as a person mattered more to her than she'd ever liked to admit, and now it had plummeted.

'You'll freeze,' Beth pointed out. 'Both of you should come in, it might be a while yet.'

Helen and Guy looked at one another, and when Guy pointedly blew on his fingertips, Helen relented; it wasn't fair to make him wait in the cold, just because she was nervous of speaking to Alfie.

'Thank you,' she said. 'That's very kind of you.'

'It's the least we can do. And Jory will tell you everything you need to know, don't you worry about that.'

They managed to stop the dog from nosing his way past them at the door, and followed Beth into the kitchen. Guy dropped the key to his ignition lock on the table with a clatter, so he could hold his hands before the range to warm them. Helen eyed the chair where Leah had tended to Toby after the accident that had taken his life; did Alfie sit there now, reading his paper and warming himself after a day out in the cold and rain? As if to reinforce the notion a gust of wind rattled the slates, and Beth looked at the ceiling and sighed.

'Need to get them fixed before they blow off. Alfie's all set to do it but it's dangerous up there just now.'

Helen just stopped herself from asking why they didn't employ a builder to come and make the repairs, and instead accepted a cup of hot tea and looked around.

'This isn't comfy but it's the warmest room at present,' Beth said. 'The fire's laid in the sitting room, but won't be lit yet.'

'This is lovely,' Helen said truthfully. She imagined the family seated around this big table, with Alfie at its head, talking about their day, or probably knowing each other so well they could eat comfortably in silence. She shook the image away, appalled at the jealousy that uncurled in her heart.

'Do you suppose your Fiona will have caught up to Amy yet?' Beth asked.

'I hope so. I'm so sorry about that wretched girl stealing your food.' It would no doubt have put Alfie in an even fouler mood to discover that, she acknowledged miserably. 'If we'd known anything about her we certainly wouldn't have allowed her to stay.'

'Well, no matter what she's done since, she was still in need then,' Beth pointed out, quite generously, Helen thought.

'Well that's true, but—'

'Though after Fiona put life and limb in danger to rescue her, I'd have thought she'd have been more grateful.'

'Well, she wasn't in any danger on the beach, but I see your point.'

'Oh. Yes, the beach.' Beth turned away. 'That's what I meant. Is that Jory coming back?' She wiped at the condensation on the window. 'No, just the gate banging.' She wouldn't look at Helen for a minute, but when she turned back Helen saw the remnants of a blush high on her cheeks and felt a flicker of suspicion.

'Are you saying there was more to Fiona saving Amy than helping to pull the boat in?'

'Look, t'isn't for me to say.' Beth busied herself in the cold pantry for a minute, and Helen made a mental note to get the full story out of Fiona later.

Jory's arrival put an end to the faintly awkward minutes that passed, and when he came into the kitchen Helen was appalled to see the yellowed bruises on his face, and the puffiness around his eye. She'd known he'd been beaten of course, but it must have been bad to still be so swollen.

'Jory,' Beth said, before he'd had a chance to express his surprise at seeing them, 'Mrs Fox wants to ask you about Mr Templeton, and the ring.'

'I just want to know how much he's asking for it,' Helen said. 'I don't want Jo to sell Bertie's bike, and put himself further in debt.'

'*You'll* buy it back?' Jory said doubtfully.

'And you'll repay Mrs Fox,' Beth put in. 'As much as you can afford, and when you can afford it. Isn't that generous?'

'It wasn't *her* ring,' Jory pointed out. 'Why should I pay her back if it's her choice to buy it?'

'Then you'll pay me,' Beth said, her voice like iron. 'Either way.'

Before anyone could speak again, a shrill voice cut across the farmyard. 'Help! Someone! *Help!*'

'Fiona?' Helen whispered, her blood going cold. 'What ...?'

Jory raced for the back door, beating Helen by a hair's breadth, and dragged it open. Fiona almost fell through it, her face like milk; she was dragging shallow breaths and trying to speak through tears of terror.

'Fallen ... stuck ... oh, God, please ...' Her gaze fell on her mother but she was too distraught to register surprise at seeing her there. 'The resort. Come quickly.'

Jory snatched up the key to Guy's ignition lock and followed. Helen tore after them both, but they had scrambled into Guy's car before she got there, and she could only watch in breathless dismay as the car spun away from the yard and up the hill.

'Come back inside, Mrs Fox,' Beth urged. 'You'll catch your death out here. I'll run and fetch Alfie ... Wait, he's here.'

'Stay with Mrs Nancarrow,' Helen said to Guy, seizing her coat, 'I'm going up to find Fiona.' She ignored Beth's protests and ran outside, shouting at Alfie not to turn off the engine. 'Golf resort!' she gasped, as she yanked open Jowan's door and gestured for him to shuffle across. 'Now!'

For the second time in a few short months, she found herself in Alfie's van, with nothing but a daughter on her mind, but at least this time she knew the girl in question was safe. The desperate matter now was if they were going to be too late to help Amy.

As they went she was able to tell Alfie all she knew, which was precious little, and by the time they arrived she had run out of words, and sat silently clutching her coat in her lap, as the van slithered to a halt next to Guy's car.

'Isn't that Ben's?' Jowan asked, pointing to a third vehicle. 'Is he here too?'

'Oh God,' Helen moaned.

'Wait here,' Alfie said, and held up a hand as she started to protest. 'Please!'

Helen acquiesced, and sat obediently in the van as Alfie and Jowan scrambled through the broken fence and onto the site. She waited until they had begun to make their way across to the excavation, then climbed out. The wind up here was fierce but at least it was no longer raining, though the sun was low in the sky now and it would be dark soon.

She ducked through the fence and followed Alfie and Jowan, peering ahead to see that Alfie had dropped flat onto his stomach, before turning and wriggling backwards until he disappeared into the hole in the ground. Helen fought a growing dismay, and told herself that Alfie knew what he was doing. She might not be able to see how deep it was, but he could. It must be safe.

Her eyes moved away from the hole to see Fiona sitting hunched nearby, and she gave a startled, relieved cry and ran to her. 'Fi! What's happening? Is Ben alright?'

'Ben?' Fiona looked at her dazedly, then shook her head. 'No, it's Daisy! She borrowed his car. She's the one down there. Jory went in to help, but I . . .' She raised her muddied hands to cover her face and gave a sob. 'I think it's too late.'

'Oh, darling.' Helen dropped to her knees and put her arms around her daughter, holding her close to share her warmth. She knew she should be relieved Ben wasn't in danger, but everything seemed to be happening at a blurry distance. 'What happened?'

'We got Amy out quite easily, but then the cover blew back and Daisy was knocked back in. There's a pool in there . . .' Fiona's voice trailed away, and Helen hugged her tighter, frightened by the violence of the girl's shivers.

'Are you hurt?'

She felt Fiona shaking her head. 'Amy took my coat and went back in, and she dragged Daisy out of the water while I came to the farm. But when Jory and I got back here, they'd both slipped in again, and Amy had to struggle to find her in the dark. She . . .' Fiona's breath hitched. 'She said she couldn't wake her up—'

'Steady, Jor!' Jowan's shout dragged their attention away, and a moment later a muddied, white-blonde head appeared over the lip of the pit. Fiona gave a cry and scrambled to her feet, and Helen followed her to the excavation. Inside she could see Jory and Alfie between them lifting Daisy's limp form clear of the water, and her heart shrank to see their grim faces.

'Jory found her,' Jowan muttered beside her. 'Whatever happens now, at least he got her out . . .' But his own face was just as bleak.

'Is she alive?' Fiona was asking Amy anxiously. 'Amy! *Is* she?'

'It's all my fault,' Amy said dully. Helen wanted to scream, *Yes, it is!* But she was too numb and terrified to speak.

'Amy!' Fiona repeated, shaking her. 'Was she alive when you found her?'

'I couldn't tell if she was breathing or not. I just wrapped your coat around her and held onto her.'

Fiona stopped asking, and hugged her instead, before holding her away. 'Are *you* alright?'

Helen did not miss the way her daughter dropped her glance to Amy's midriff, and her breath stuck for a moment. How much more had been going on with her children, while she had been focused entirely on the hotel?

371

The three of them stood silent while Alfie and Jory slipped and slid their way across the basement, with their precious burden held between them. Helen crouched beside Jowan at the side of the hole, and between the four of them they soon had Daisy laid out flat on the grass. She was unrecognisable from the twinkling star of the Hollywood screen; some flashes of the famously white skin showed, where either Amy or Jory had wiped mud from her eyes, nose and mouth, but for the most part she was a lumpen brown mess, with clumps of thick mud clinging to her cheeks and jaw, and filling the open parts of her coat. She lay still as death.

Jowan was about to roll her onto her side but Jory, boosted out of the hole by his uncle, stopped him. He tilted her head back and ran a finger inside her slack mouth before fastening his lips to hers. He blew, then began to press rhythmically on her chest. Jowan instead gave his hand to help Alfie, who knelt, exhausted, beside Helen.

'Does he know what he's doing?' Helen asked him quietly.

Alfie nodded. 'Our dad taught us, and Toby'll have taught the boys. It works, I've done it myself, down at Porthstennack. As long as she's alive, this will—'

'Come *on*!' Jory shouted, between breaths. He sounded at once furious and frustrated. He bent once more, and this time when he blew he was rewarded with a mouthful of dirty water, as Daisy retched and then took a huge, strangled-sounding breath.

Now he rolled her onto her side, and sat with his head bowed and his hair hanging in his face, as she convulsed and vomited up a seemingly impossible amount.

Through the relief, Helen felt a large, rough hand covering hers where it lay on the wet grass, and looked up to see Alfie, his eyes closed, and evidently oblivious to what he was doing.

She turned to look at Daisy, and as Jory held her hair back

from her face she could see a livid welt on the girl's cheek, and a reddening area across her jaw that would likely blossom into a deep bruise soon. Blood crept, sly and barely noticed, from a cut at her hairline, the darkness of her wet hair disguising it until it reached a clear patch of skin near her eyebrow.

'Let's get her back to the farmhouse,' Jory said, when Daisy's uncontrollable heaving had tapered off into gulps.

'No,' Helen said quickly, 'look at her head. We should take her to Doctor Rowe.' She slid her hand from beneath Alfie's, and stood up. 'You did a wonderful thing, Jory. Thank you.'

The young man nodded briefly, but did not seem able to speak. She saw his hands clenched at his sides, and he made no attempt to wipe the dirt from his own face, but slipped his hands beneath Daisy's shoulders and knees ready to lift her.

'Let me help,' Jowan said, and Jory looked at him warily for a moment, as if he expected his brother to suddenly remember the wrong he'd done him and draw back. Helen was certain he would refuse the offer, but Jowan reached out and clasped his brother's shoulder. 'Come on. For her.'

Jory nodded, and between them they lifted the limp form onto the back seat of Ben's car, and Jory climbed behind the wheel.

'Wait!' Helen called. 'You should go with her, Amy,' Helen said. 'You need to be looked over, too, after what you've been through.'

'I'm fine,' Amy said quickly. The two younger girls' eyes met, and Helen was relieved to see Fiona silently urging Amy to change her mind. After they'd glared at one another for a moment, Amy subsided and climbed into the front of the car.

Jowan offered to drive Helen and Fiona back to the hotel in Guy's car, picking Guy up on the way. They accepted, and when

Alfie paused with his hand on the door of the farm's van Helen willed him to look at her. She didn't know what she would do if he did, but from that moment of closeness had come an even deeper yearning to communicate. Even if it were only silently. If he looked at her now it would mean he felt it too, and that might be enough.

He didn't.

CHAPTER TWENTY-FOUR

Fiona woke while it was still dark, with a distant, unfocused troubled feeling. Gradually the events of the previous day filtered through the tiredness, and she glanced towards the other bed, not needing her bedside light to remind her it was empty. Amy and Daisy had been taken to hospital last night, both suffering from exposure, and Daisy had the worrying addition of severe bruising, from the impact of the weighty tarpaulin that had knocked her unconscious.

Doctor Rowe had said nothing about Amy's "condition", so Fiona hadn't asked. It wasn't her place, and the nurses would realise anyway, as soon as they stripped her of her muddied clothing.

She slipped from her bed, had a token wash at the sink, and dressed in her oldest clothes before leaving a note for her mother, and going out through the back of the kitchen to avoid Ian Skinner's inevitable questions. There was still a steady, fierce wind coming off the sea, and the air was dry now but bitterly cold. Fiona pulled her good coat tighter as she walked the familiar road to Trethkellis, and thought of her favourite one, still lying in the mud up at the excavation pit. Probably buried forever now, along with the lucky penny in the pocket. That token had certainly done its job yesterday, and she felt a twinge of disappointment at its loss now, but it had little to do with superstition, it simply reminded her of the fun she'd had running around at Pencarrack with an altogether different Amy; quite likely the same Amy that Kitty and Mr Buchanan knew.

The lifeboat station was deserted at this hour, although she knew Mr Glasson, Michael Sherborne and the others would be sleeping with one ear tuned for the sound of the siren. She walked down onto the beach, now enjoying the snap of the wind so much that she took her hat off. She could practically hear her mother begging her to replace it, and smiled as she stuffed it into her pocket. Her curly hair whipped first forward and then back, and she could feel the roots tugging as if they'd pull loose at any moment. The tide was out, but making its hissing and rolling way back in, and Fiona saw Danny's boat and wandered towards it, for no particular reason other than it provided a focus.

'Oi!'

She jumped, and turned to see Danny himself striding down the beach towards her. 'Trying to nick it yourself this time, eh?'

'What?'

'Instead of sending one of your friends to do it. I told you, I'll take you out on it when I'm good and ready.'

'I never sent anyone to—'

'Get on, 'course you did! Ratty little tacker, he was.'

Now he was closer Fiona could see he was grinning, and she relaxed. 'How did you know about him, anyway?'

'Me and Andrew were on our way down here yesterday, saw you and that film star hurtling off up the road in your brother's posh car, and your little friend curled up in a ball over there.' He pointed to a spot beside the rocks.

'Really? What happened?'

'Nothing.' Danny dropped the bag he was carrying. 'Give us a hand, then, make yourself useful.' He indicated the boat, and although Fiona knew he was perfectly capable of turning it the right way up by himself, she just rolled her eyes, gave the heavy sigh she knew he expected, and bent to help him.

'Where is he now?' she asked, as they set the small boat firmly on the sand. 'He's not from around here, so he'd have nowhere to go.'

'Dad took him in. For his own safety, I'm not bothered about him trying to nick the boat.' Danny looked at her closely. 'Are you alright, Fi?'

It was so far from his usual teasing tone, that Fiona felt her throat closing up, and swallowed hurriedly. 'I'm fine. What are you doing today?'

He kept looking at her a moment longer, then apparently realised she wasn't going to confide in him, and indicated his bag. 'Now the rain's finally stopped I've got some repairs to make and a bit of painting to do. Want to help?'

'I'd love to,' Fiona said truthfully, 'but I'll be expected home for breakfast.'

'You must have started out before first light,' he observed, 'sun's only just up now.'

She nodded. 'I like it down here when it's quiet.'

'You like it down here when it's noisy, too,' he pointed out. He sat down, and patted the space beside him, knowing she wouldn't flinch at sitting on the wet sand. 'Are you sure you're alright?' he asked, nudging her with his shoulder.

'I'm a bit worried about Amy and Daisy, but yes.' In fact she was better than alright; sitting next to Danny, with the wind in her face and the taste of salt on her lips, was about as close to perfect as she could think of.

'When your friend goes home will you come back to the *Dafna*?' he asked.

'Why, do you miss me?'

He snorted. 'Like I miss chicken pox.'

Fiona laughed, and was about to respond when she heard a voice drifting down the beach.

'Fiona!'

They both turned, and Danny's face lost its expression. 'Looks like you don't have to worry about her, at least.'

Amy came closer, and Danny stood up. He offered his hand and pulled Fiona to her feet too. 'I'd better get on.'

Fiona felt a flash of resentment at the interruption, but she was relieved to see Amy looking healthy. She said goodbye to Danny and walked up to meet her.

'That looked cosy,' Amy said. She tried to link her arm through Fiona's, but Fiona turned away and started back up towards the lane. 'How did you get here?'

'Mr Kelly sent a taxi for Daisy, and they brought me too. I had a feeling I'd find you here, so I asked them to drop me off at the top of the hill.'

'How *is* Daisy?'

'Much better, they wanted her to stay in for the day but she wanted to go back to the hotel. I can't say I blame her.'

'Why didn't you go there too, then?'

'Because I wanted to talk to you. Away from everyone.' Amy slowed her pace. 'I wanted to apologise.'

'For the lying, or for risking people's lives to save you?' Fiona realised she sounded harsh, but the betrayal of the past weeks had risen again with the memory of how close Daisy had come to death.

'For all of it.'

378

Fiona kept walking at the same speed, forcing Amy to run to catch up with her. When the girl gasped for breath she relented a little, and slowed down. 'Go on then. Apologise. No, first explain.' She stopped abruptly, and Amy cannoned into her. 'I'm waiting.'

'Can we sit somewhere?' Amy looked around helplessly.

'Only the grass.' Fiona found a patch that would accommodate them both, and sat down cross-legged. She waited for Amy to sit opposite, then fixed her with a hard look. 'Why did you lie about Kitty? Was *anything* you told me true?'

'Yes!' Amy took a deep breath, and seemed to be searching for the right place to start. Her hands went to her necklace and she clutched the spoon, frowning.

'Tell me about Micky first,' Fiona prompted.

Amy nodded. 'We were going to Ireland, that part was true. The thing is, he's in trouble back home, and he needed to get away even more than I did.'

'What sort of trouble would make you risk that?'

'I don't want to tell you,' Amy muttered.

'Goodbye, then.' Fiona braced herself to stand up, but Amy grabbed her trouser cuff.

'Wait. Alright. Look, it wasn't just him, he and a friend were seen selling something that wasn't theirs, in Tavistock market.'

'Selling what?'

'Horses. He didn't steal them,' she hurried on, but after a look at Fiona's face she subsided. 'Two very good ones, belonging to a manor house out near Callington. Micky dyed their coats after his friend stole them, but someone recognised them anyway. Micky would go to prison if they caught him.'

'Looks as if he's taught you well,' Fiona said grimly. 'You make a good couple.'

Amy accepted the rebuke without argument. 'We planned to stay with Micky's brother in Cork. We wanted to start a new life together, to pretend to be married, so the baby had a proper home.'

'But you're sixteen!'

'I can look older, you know that. Why do you suppose I was so glad to find a dress that would do that?'

'And you said you were glad for my sake,' Fiona said, cross all over again.

'I was!' Amy threw a glance back towards the beach, where Danny was now working. Her mouth lifted in a faint smile. 'What were you saying about spots and a big nose?'

'Never mind that, what happened?'

'We became separated when the *Drake* got into bother, and Brian, the cook, didn't have time to go back and find Micky. I'd hoped Micky had come ashore at Porthstennack, you know that. Well it turns out he did, after all.'

'When did you find that out?'

'Not until Saturday just gone, when we went up to the farm with Bertie. Remember when we took Reynard out for his exercise and he got all excited out by the barn?'

Fiona nodded. 'When you had to catch him before he got out of the yard.'

'He'd seen Micky. It was the barn itself he was excited about, not getting away to find rabbits.'

'So he was at the farm? Under their noses?'

'He'd got there just that morning.'

'I don't understand how he knew where to find you though, or how he got ashore without anyone knowing about it.'

'Porthstennack sent two tugboats out to the *Drake* with supplies, and to reposition her so they could work on her. Micky jumped overboard, swam to one of them, and hid. When he came ashore he found work at the first farm he came to after he left the beach. The same farm where Alfie Nancarrow used to live.'

'Lucky for him.'

Amy shrugged. 'Anyway, Micky was living-in there when Alfie went down for that funeral. He heard Alfie and his friend talking, and they mentioned me. Or at least,' she amended with a wry little smile, 'they discussed how exciting life was up here, with film stars and stowaways at every turn.'

'So he knew where to find you.'

'Sort of. He knew where Alfie lived, so came to hide out in the hopes of hearing something about me.'

'For someone who ultimately ran away at the first sign of trouble, he seems to have been very keen,' Fiona observed. She felt a twinge of guilt as Amy flinched, but didn't take it back; after all that's exactly what he had done. 'Go on,' she said, getting restless now. 'I have to be getting home.'

'Well, when I saw him there I wanted to stay behind and talk, but you insisted on walking with me—' she ignored Fiona's stony expression '— so I had to go up later. When I told you I was going into the village for your grandmother, remember? I told him what I'd heard about the broken fence up by the golf resort, and that the foundations had been dug out, so he went up there instead. Beth doesn't lock up when she goes out, so he was able to take the odd bit of food. I told him Kitty had turned up, and that we had to leave.' She had the grace to look embarrassed. 'I also said we might be able to get our hands on a boat that would get us at least around the next headland.'

'You told him to steal Danny's boat.'

'He'd have got it back!' Amy rubbed her face tiredly. 'Well, I took the milk and the potatoes from the kitchen yesterday, I was going to take the meat pudding too, but it was too hot and Beth came back before I could find a cloth to carry it in. You know the rest.'

'Yes,' Fiona said roughly. 'When you needed him the most, he ran away.'

'He thought I was dead! It wasn't his fault, there was nothing he could do.'

'We thought you were dead too,' Fiona pointed out, 'but it didn't stop us from helping.'

'I know.' Amy lowered her head, and Fiona saw the slender shoulders shaking.

'I'm so sorry,' Amy managed through her tears. 'I don't know how it's all gone so wrong.'

'You could at least have posted the letter to Kitty. Why didn't you do that?'

'Because I saw Emily Parker, and you said you'd told her where you were from! I really meant to, I promise.'

'Promises don't mean anything,' Fiona said shortly.

'Not even Cornish ones?'

Fiona met the half-hopeful smile with a glare. 'Stop it. What will you do now, go back to your first plan?'

'How could I? He's gone.'

'If you could though, would you?'

Amy slowly drew herself upright from her defeated slouch. 'No,' she said. 'I don't think I would.'

'Because he ran away?'

'Because I couldn't do it to Kitty.'

Fiona shook her head and stood up. 'You'll forgive me if I don't believe you, you didn't care two hoots about that before, after all.'

'I was being stupid. And ungrateful. And I really thought she would be angry with me when she found out I'd got pregnant, but she's come all this way so I know she loves me, at least.' She started to walk towards the main road again. 'Is she? Upset with me, I mean, now she knows I'm safe?'

'She's shocked,' Fiona allowed, 'and she says she has her own reasons for being worried, but she's not going to do any of those things you said she'd do.'

Amy nodded. 'Then no, I wouldn't run off with Micky, even if I could.'

'Easy to say.'

'I swear it's true.'

'Prove it.'

Amy stopped. 'What?'

'I said prove it. Micky is at the police house with Constable Quick. He's not in trouble, no one knows who he is, or what he's done. He could leave anytime.'

For a moment Amy just looked at her. Then she glanced towards the village, but when she turned back she had a look on her face that convinced Fiona she was telling the truth. It wasn't resolve; she might not have believed that. It wasn't defiance either. It was regret, and longing, and a slowly fading hope.

'Let's go back to the hotel,' she said quietly. 'I have some apologies to make.'

When they arrived at Fox Bay the daytime lights were burning brightly against the cold grey day outside, and there was a fresh, clean atmosphere now that the last of the decorations and the trees were gone.

'Do you suppose she's still here?' Amy asked anxiously, looking around. 'What if she left, thinking I'd gone too?'

'She's still here. Mum moved her to one of the first floor rooms so she can—'

'She won't be able to afford that!'

'Do you think we're *charging* her?' Fiona shook her head. 'For goodness' sake, Amy!'

'No, I wasn't thinking. Sorry.'

'If you want to go up, it's room six, nearest the stairs.'

Amy had just put her foot on the lower stair when Kitty appeared at the top. She and Amy looked at one another in silence for a moment, then Amy flew up the stairs to meet her halfway down. They embraced wordlessly, and Fiona turned away to give them their private moment.

Ben came out of the office, presumably from where he and Helen had been doing their daily handover. He looked at the stairs, and started at the sight of Amy. 'Where's Daisy?'

'I don't know, she's back, though, I know that.'

'She's having a bath,' Helen said, following him out of the office. 'I saw Rex ordering her to bed, but she doesn't want to go.'

'He can't order her anywhere,' Ben snapped.

'I didn't mean literally, just that he was trying to persuade her to rest.' She gave him a teasing little smile. 'Really, Benjamin, that was quite a reaction.'

'Well, I don't like that bloke,' Ben muttered, flushing. 'He comes across all very friendly, and gentlemanly, but I know he's—'

'Well I'm sure she'll feel better after a bath,' Helen broke in, and smiled brightly. 'Good morning, Rex, I trust you slept well?'

Ben's expression closed down into a professional blandness, and he offered Rex a polite nod by way of greeting.

'Nope, not at all,' Rex said, 'but that's nothing against your beautiful rooms, I promise. I'm feeling a lot better now Daisy's back.' He looked around the empty lobby. 'Anyone seen Freddie this morning?'

'He went out earlier,' Ben offered.

'Where?'

'Guy has given him a lift into Bude, I think,' Helen said, as surprised as the others at the abrupt question. 'He said something about visiting the bank.'

'Oh. Okay. Look, can we talk for a few minutes before Daisy comes down? I don't want to embarrass her.'

'Of course.' She gestured to the sitting room, and Rex turned to Fiona.

'This concerns you too, Miss Fox.'

Fiona's heart sank. Now she was going to be torn off a strip for putting Daisy in danger, on top of everything else.

'She offered,' she said as she followed him into the sitting room, hoping to pre-empt the scolding. 'We didn't ask her to—'

'I know.' Rex returned to the door, and Fiona glimpsed a deeply suspicious-looking Ben before it closed, and then it was just the three of them.

'Okay,' Rex said, 'so I heard about what happened, but I want the details from you. All of them. Miss nothing out, you hear?'

Fiona gave him a cool look, surprising herself. 'I'll do no such thing, Mr Kelly, I'm sorry. I'll tell you what Daisy did, and how she helped save Amy's life, but that's all.'

'Fiona!'

'No, Helen, she has a point.' To Fiona's surprise Rex was smiling. 'I'm too used to being in on the ground floor, knowing everything about everything. Her friend's situation has nothing to do with me.'

Fiona risked a glance at her mother, who was looking both

baffled and even, she thought with relief, a bit proud. She turned back to Rex, and told him what Daisy had done, and how, at the last moment she had returned to recover Beth Nancarrow's bowl and nearly died as a result.

'Amy just dragged her out of the water, but both of them were in danger of sinking into the mud,' she finished, trembling as she recalled the cold, sickening terror. 'She just screamed at me to run for help, it's all we could do.'

'And how about the farmer's boy? What exactly did he do?'

'He got them both out, and then brought Daisy back when we thought ... thought we'd lost her.' Fiona's voice was shaking now too, and she felt the smooth warmth of her mother's hand sliding into hers. She clutched at it tightly.

'I gather the kid has some trouble, financially. That right?'

The abrupt change of direction made Fiona and Helen look at each other blankly.

Rex shrugged. 'I guess you'd say again, that has nothing to do with me. But I want to reward him. He's ...' This time it was Rex's turn to break off and clear his throat. His face worked as he tried to swallow a surge of emotion and regain his usual brisk tone, but in the end he just sank into the nearest chair and put his hands over his face.

Helen poured a large brandy from the crystal decanter on the side table, and waited until Rex had gathered himself a little before pressing it into his hand. 'I know it's early, but you've had a big shock.'

'I don't know why it's hit me all of a sudden,' Rex said, pulling a large silk square from his pocket. 'Thank you.' He gulped at the drink, and Fiona and Helen took seats of their own.

'Anyway,' Rex said at length, 'I'd like to clear young

Nancarrow's debts for him, and give him a little extra to, you know, get on his feet.'

'I'm sure he'll be glad of that,' Helen said, 'though if it were his brother he'd probably refuse it out of gallantry. Jory wouldn't.'

'Hey, I won't hear a word said against the kid who saved Daisy's life.' Rex blew his nose and tucked the pocket square away. 'Whatever his situation, or his character, he did an amazing thing.'

'What do you know about Jory's character?' Fiona asked, curious. 'And how did you know he was in debt?'

'I hear things.' His eyes met hers, and she couldn't suppress a shudder at the suddenly bland expression. 'Will you ask him to come here, or should I go to the farm?'

'I don't think it's right to just summon him, like some kind of servant,' Fiona said. Ben had begun to say something earlier, before their mother had cut him off at Kelly's approach, and she had to wonder exactly how Rex *heard things* that had no connection with his film stars, or their film.

'Why don't we invite them all for a meal instead?' Helen suggested. 'The Nancarrows, I mean. Just our two families and Adam, plus Amy and Kitty, and—'

'If they're still here,' Fiona said. 'I'm certain they'll be going back home today.'

'Oh. Of course. And then there's Rex, Daisy and Freddie.'

'Great idea,' Rex said, and now he was back to his former beaming self. 'Give these two girls the day to get over it all, and then get everyone together for a great celebration!'

'It can be a farewell for Fleur too,' Helen said.

'What about Guy?' Fiona asked.

Rex's expression faltered. 'Well, he'll be working, won't he?'

'Oh, we can spare Guy for the night,' Helen said. 'He's practically family.' She smiled at Fiona. 'Can I leave you to do the inviting, darling? I'll go and talk to Mr Gough about the menu.'

'Can I invite the Nancarrows by telegram?' Fiona was ready to wilt. 'I can't face going all the way over to the farm again.'

Her mother looked suddenly stricken with remorse. 'Oh, Fi . . .' She drew Fiona close, and kissed the top of her head. 'Go and rest, I'll ask Bertie to invite the Nancarrows, I'm sure she said Jowan was popping down at lunchtime to talk about the bike.'

'So . . . you've forgiven me then?' Fiona mumbled. 'For keeping Amy's secret?'

'*Secrets*,' Helen said, but Fiona could hear a little smile in her voice. 'You've more than made up for those.'

'I did Cornish-promise.'

'And that's binding,' Helen agreed. She held Fiona at arm's length and studied her closely. 'You're exhausted, I imagine you didn't sleep too well last night, and you've done as much as anyone to sort all this out. Come down bright and breezy for dinner tonight, and we'll toast your courage along with Amy's and Jory's.' She shook her head. 'Imagine, the two most troublesome people I've ever met, and my adventurous baby girl . . . between them responsible for saving the life of one of the world's biggest moving picture stars.'

'Also responsible for endangering it, don't forget,' Rex put in, but the teasing laugh that accompanied his words did not fool Fiona for an instant.

Late in the afternoon, groggy from sleep, Fiona opened her eyes to see Amy putting the last of her few things into the bag Helen had provided for her. She was dressed in the same clothes in which she'd been pulled from the sea, but she looked fresh now. Calm. Happy, even, though there was a new, adult look about her.

'You're leaving then?' Fiona hauled herself upright, and Amy nodded.

'I wouldn't have just gone without saying goodbye, but Kitty asked me to pack my things ready. We won't be going for a while yet.'

'Will Micky come back too, do you think?'

Amy shrugged. 'I doubt it, not with the threat of prison hanging over him.'

'What will you do if he does though? Would you marry him?'

'No. Not even to give the little one a name.' She sat on Fiona's bed. 'I don't know how I can thank you for what you've done for me.'

'I'd have done a lot more if I could.'

'I know.'

Fiona shoved her hair out of her eyes. 'You should have told me the truth, Amy.'

Amy nodded, and was silent for a while. 'Will you let me write to you?' she asked at length.

'You'd better. Do you still feel the same about Hollywood film stars?'

'Not all of them. I think I might ask Arch to take me to Cinema.'

'Where?'

'It's the picture house in Tavistock. Belinda Pearce goes there all the time and can't say enough about it.'

'She's your dance teacher?'

Amy nodded. 'I suppose that's over for a while, too.'

'But just think, if that one's a girl—' Fiona nodded at Amy's waist '—you can teach her all those nifty steps you showed Leah and me on New Year's Eve.'

'What if it's a boy?'

'Oh, well then I'm not at all interested. I mean, boys are dreadful, just look at Ben.' She smiled, then asked quietly, 'Are you frightened?'

Amy swallowed hard and looked away. 'Terrified,' she admitted.

Fiona leaned over and hugged her. 'Kitty will be there to help you. And the little one will have her Aunt Fiona to spoil her rotten. You must come and stay anytime.' She climbed out of bed. 'Let me wash and dress, and I'll meet you downstairs.'

'I'll wait. No rush.'

But when Fiona went down to the lobby it was empty, and the key to room six was back on the hook behind the reception desk. For a moment she stared at it, sure she must have misread the number, but there were no bags waiting, and no sign of either Kitty or Amy.

She felt the swell of betrayal, and the sting of disappointed tears, but after a moment a cool calm dropped over her. It wasn't Amy's fault, in fact Fiona owed her a debt of thanks for teaching her that friends were ultimately unreliable. She should have realised before; Mum had been devastated when Leah had moved out, Guy was losing Fleur to a life in New Zealand, Bertie's only real friends lived miles away, and now Amy had gone back to Plymouth without even waiting long enough to say goodbye. It might take her a while, but Fiona had always learned her lessons eventually.

CHAPTER TWENTY-FIVE

The guests gathered in the lounge before dinner, and Billy Lang, solo this time, played soft piano tunes to try and break down the barriers between farmers and film stars. It was a hopeless task, but he kept at it, smiling and nodding at the guests now and again, but Fiona saw him rolling his eyes more than once, and sent him a sympathetic smile.

Jowan was, of course, glued to Bertie's side, but their conversation seemed to flow mostly from Jowan, absorbed by Bertie but hardly returned. She still had that soft look in her eyes when she looked at him, but Fiona couldn't help noting that it was tempered by uncertainty, a silent question seemed suspended above her, not quite falling, as if she deliberately held it at bay.

Jory kept his distance from the Hollywood set, but was clearly transfixed by Daisy; his eyes slid away from her, only to be drawn helplessly back time and time again. With the help of her assistant, Miss Porter, Daisy had carefully applied make-up to cover as much of her bruised face as she could manage, and had used plenty of dramatic eyeliner to draw attention away from the injuries. But the wet tarpaulin might as well have been a block of wood, for the severity of the impact, and her cheek was swollen, making it difficult to speak and painful to smile. A large plaster covered much of her forehead, and she'd brushed her hair forward over it, but it showed stark against the rich red of her hair.

Beth Nancarrow had sent her apologies, claiming a migraine, but the three men were here, and had clearly made a special effort with their appearance. Jowan and Jory in their Sunday best, and even Alfie himself wore a slightly old-fashioned, slim-fitting light wool suit, the jacket open to show a neat waistcoat with frayed cloth buttons. He was clearly uncomfortable in it, which was quite endearing, but Fiona was intrigued to note how her mother studiously kept her eyes averted.

She thought back to when they had knelt, side by side with Daisy at the excavation, and how Alfie had laid a hand over her mother's, drawing no reaction at all. You had to be a very special friend to do that . . . But now Alfie was engaged to Beth, so where did that leave their friendship? Another loss.

Fiona was about to bring up the subject of Alfie and Beth, but thought better of it as Adam pushed through the doors and came straight over to them, only pausing to lift a drink from the waiter's tray.

'I'm going to bring her back,' he said, before either of them could greet him.

Helen and Fiona looked at one another, then turned questioning eyes on him, and he shrugged. 'Leah, of course. I'm going to find her, I'm going to break into that nurses' home, and I'm bloody well going to bring her back.'

'Are you sure you want to?' Helen asked. 'You were happy enough to let her go.'

'I was not!' Adam drank half his drink. 'Well, perhaps I was a bit relieved, but that was before I realised. God, it's killing me,' he groaned theatrically. 'What am I going to do if she won't have me, Hels?'

Helen laughed. 'She will! She's bananas about you. But you'll have to prove yourself, you know how she is.'

'I do,' he agreed mournfully. 'She's a perishing nightmare.'

'You're made for each other then.' She grinned, and plucked the glass from his hand. 'Come on, you two, make yourselves useful and help me round everyone up for dinner.'

With the dining room to themselves it had the potential to feel a little empty, but Guy and Ben had placed the other tables so that they felt more like a highly decorated border than the sign of an empty hotel. Fiona sat next to her mother, with Jowan on her other side, and tried not to think about how much more fun it would have been with Amy there, helping her feel less like the youngest child at the party.

The awkwardness had faded somewhat, with the serving of food, and when the time came to toast Granny's farewell, Helen's carefully prepared speech deserted her and instead she let all her years of gratitude and affection pour out. By the time she had finished, Fiona's eyes were burning, Helen and Fleur were sobbing and laughing in equal measure, and Adam pointedly re-filled both their glasses, to general amusement and another toast.

Rex rose to his feet and tapped his glass with his knife. The group fell quiet again, and he passed a glance over them all, his lips moving silently as he counted.

'Thirteen of us,' he said, 'let's hope it's not an ill omen, huh?'

'Amy was rescued on a Friday the thirteenth,' Fiona supplied with a smile.

'And look what happened there,' Rex said, causing an embarrassed silence to fall across the table. Fiona felt heat creeping across her face, but it was born of annoyance.

'I'm joking!' Rex chuckled. 'No, the reason I'm glad you're all here tonight is because I want to pay tribute to a fine young man, who selflessly, and without hesitation, risked his life to save our shining star Daisy Conrad.' He raised his glass. 'To Mr Jory Nancarrow.'

The guests began to repeat the toast, but Helen pushed her chair back and stood up, halting them.

'And to the absent Amy Markham,' she said firmly. 'She might have been the reason Daisy was up at the building site, but she was also the one who jumped into the hole and kept Daisy's head above water for almost an hour. And, of course—' her voice softened as she turned to Fiona '—to my courageous and generous-hearted daughter, who helped bring Amy ashore. Yes,' she added, as Fiona's flush deepened, this time with guilt, 'I know you were out on the *Lady Dafna*. I also know that you will never do it again. Don't I?'

She said this last with a mock glare and a very pointed tone, and Fiona nodded, then shook her head, then nodded again more fervently, and laughter rippled through the group.

'Absolutely,' Rex said. 'To Jory, Amy, and Fiona.' The toast was echoed, and he went on, 'This brings me on to what I'd like to say. Jory, son, I'd like to reward you for what you did. When we're done with this delicious dinner I'd like to meet with you, and discuss how I might be able to ... make your life a little easier. Financially.'

The awkward pause that followed this statement drew out, until Adam grinned. 'Give him a part in one of your films, that'd do it!'

'Better still, make a film out of what's happened here!' Bertie said. 'It's got everything! And Daisy and Jory can even play themselves!'

Fiona looked at Jory, who looked both appalled and fascinated by the notion. Ben's face was less entranced, she noted with an inward smile.

'Yes, a beautiful romance,' Fleur put in. 'But we'd need a conflict. I know, Freddie could play the young man Daisy had been going to marry before she fell in love with her rescuer! What do you think, Daisy?'

Daisy gave her a twisted half-smile, half-wince. 'That sounds like a wonderful idea,' she managed carefully, eliciting clucks and frowns of sympathy around the table.

'But it'll never happen.'

All eyes swivelled to Freddie, who'd said even less during dinner than his screen partner. His eyes were glittering, his face expressionless ... Fiona recognised the signs of someone who'd been getting quietly and completely drunk for the past hour.

'Freddie,' Rex warned, 'leave it, son, okay?'

'It'll never happen, because she's giving it all up. Aren't you, Daisy?'

'Please, Freddie,' Daisy said in a low voice, 'you've had a little too much—'

'And now I've discovered that, because *she's* giving it all up, my career is over too.'

Fiona's uneasiness grew the more nervy she saw this was making Rex, and it seemed her mother felt the same.

'Would you like to go and sit in the lounge for a bit, Freddie? Jeremy Bickle will see you're comfortable.'

'No, I don't want to *sit in the lounge*, Mrs Fox. I want *him* to explain to me how we're going to get out of all this?' Freddie gestured to Rex with his glass, slopping red wine over his starched shirt cuff.

'Get out of what?'

Guy reached across and took the tilting glass out of his hand. 'Mr Wishart, let me help you—'

'Mr Wishart!' Freddie laughed, but his eyes were haunted as he turned to Guy. 'Rex calls me son, *you* call me Mr Wishart! Is that irony, or what?'

Fiona started. Rex was staring at Guy as if he were ready to take the knife he had used to tap his glass, and do something awful with it. But there was no surprise on his face; it seemed he did know everything, after all.

Freddie lit a cigarette, and squinted at his studio head through the smoke. 'I'm done with all these lies, Rex. I think it's time you told everyone what's really going on, don't you?'

Adam leaned back, his arms folded, and a look of amused interest on his face. 'Let's hear it, Kelly.'

'Come on, now.' Rex gestured at the Nancarrows with his glass. 'These good people don't need to hear any of this.' The heartiness was clearly forced, and it dropped into a low, warning tone as he went on, 'It's just industry stuff. Nothing that concerns them, and not worth spoiling a good meal over. Why don't we just enjoy our coffee, we can talk later.'

Fiona watched as Alfie's gaze swept the table and fixed on Helen's white, mortified face, and she silently willed him to stay seated. But she couldn't blame him when he stood up.

'We've been honoured to accept your hospitality, Mrs Fox. Please give my thanks to your chef, but we'll be going now.'

'You don't have to,' Helen said, and Fiona's heart contracted as she saw her mother's fingers twist into the tablecloth.

'I don't like to ... to leave Beth for too long, you know.'

Helen's voice was stiffly polite, though her hands clenched harder. 'Of course. Do give her my kind regards, and tell her she was missed.'

'I will, thank you. Jowan, Jory, it's time we left.'

'I guess your uncle's right, boys,' Rex said, 'you don't want to leave your mom if she's sick. And you'll just be bored here when we start talking business.' He looked over at Jory and felt in the inside pocket of his jacket. 'Here, kid.' He withdrew a packet and passed it across the table. 'We won't forget what you did, none of us.'

Jory was about to open it, but Alfie gently closed his hand over his nephew's. 'It's very good of you, Mr Kelly. Come on, lads. Say your goodbyes.'

Jory's gaze lingered on Daisy as he pushed his chair back, and her smile seemed to be the only thing likely to distract him from the money in his hand. Fiona felt a flicker of misgiving as she noted that Jowan's face was alight with a quiet joy as he squeezed Bertie's hand, but that Bertie's answering smile faded too fast, once he'd moved away from her to say goodbye to his hostess. So much being said in that one silent moment.

Helen only half-rose, accepting a polite kiss on the cheek from her future son-in-law, but she didn't look at Alfie again until his back was already turned; Fiona saw behind that perfect-hostess smile to the intense disappointment, and her certainty grew that there was something new and complex happening in her mother's heart.

With Ben taking over where Jory had left off, his eyes stealing towards Daisy every second breath, and Bertie still in some kind of quandary, it seemed only Fiona herself had her emotions under control tonight. Thanks to the nature of Amy's departure, so much like Leah's, she was entirely settled in her view that the only person on whom she could rely was herself.

Rex took his time pouring himself a fresh drink, and Fiona could see his hand was shaking as he replaced the glass stopper in the decanter.

'Well?' Adam said calmly, when the door had closed behind the Nancarrows.

Rex didn't look at him. 'Well what?'

'Aren't you going to tell us what young Freddie's talking about?'

'*Young Freddie*,' Rex said in a hard voice, glaring at his star, 'is drunk. He doesn't know what he's saying.'

'Oh, I've never been more certain,' Freddie said, and looking at him Fiona saw only truth in the famously bright eyes. 'You know, pretty much all you've ever seen me do is speak lines that aren't mine. Well this is one time I won't be told what to say. You owe it to this family to tell them the truth.'

'I don't owe anyone a damned thing!'

'Now you know *that's* not true.'

'I swear to God, Freddie—'

'Tell them!' Freddie's fist came down on the table, and everyone jumped as glasses and cutlery rattled. 'If you don't, I will, so it might as well come from you. Come on, you've ruined everything, so why not salvage a little dignity before it's too late?'

'Alright!' Rex snapped. 'But you have to know that if I do, your own secret will come out with it.'

Fiona looked at Guy again, and although his face was impassive, his jaw was tight as he looked at Freddie. She held her breath.

'I don't care,' Freddie said tiredly. 'It's not like it matters any more. In fact,' he turned to Helen. 'Your friend Guy here is my father.'

The silence that fell across the table was soon swallowed up by a barrage of questions, which subsided as Guy reluctantly took up the narrative. As he unravelled his past, he looked half sick, half relieved, as if it had been choking him until now.

'I'd never intended to tell Freddie,' he finished, 'but it'd been too long. Seeing him standing there in the lobby just ...' He shrugged. 'I had to.'

'Sweet little scandal, which I just found out yesterday,' Rex said bitterly, 'and only adding to the biggest blow to my professional career.' He sent Daisy a look of deep betrayal, and her eyes flashed – the first sign of anger Fiona had seen from her.

'You can't hold me hostage, to save *your* career.' She lifted a hand to her bruised face. 'Even before this happened I knew I was done making pictures, and the things people have said to me since have just confirmed it's the right choice.'

'What things?' Ben asked, frowning. 'Who?'

'Some of those nurses, and even the doctors. I guess they meant well, but they were all telling me not to worry, that I'd be able to film again soon. When the image is more important to people than the pain, it's time to let go.'

Ben's hand curled on the table, and Fiona saw it was an effort for him not to reach out to her. He caught her eye and gave her a rueful smile, which she returned with a sympathetic one.

'The thing is,' Rex said, and now he sounded defeated, 'Freddie's fiancée's family have been bankrolling Good Boy Productions, and as soon as they learn Daisy's out, they'll pull the plug.'

'Why would they do that? Freddie's still hot property.'

'Hot?' Rex gave a hollow laugh. 'Come on, even Freddie knows he doesn't still have that kid appeal that got him started. He's nothing without Daisy.'

'Thank you,' Freddie said distantly, and reached for Alfie's abandoned drink.

'I'm sorry, kid, but you know it's the truth. Maria's the only reason the Falciones are involved. Once they're out, we fold.'

Adam shook his head. 'But surely they're not the only investors in town, you'd still be able to get funding. Unless . . .' His eyes narrowed and he leaned forward. 'What are you up to, Kelly? What have you done with that company?'

Rex ignored him, and turned pleading eyes on Daisy. 'Please, honey, reconsider? There's still time.'

'Leave her alone,' Bertie snapped. 'It's her career, her choice.'

'You have no idea what—'

'Which came first,' Helen wanted to know, 'the fiancée or the funds?'

'What are you talking about?'

'I mean,' Helen said, her voice hard, 'did Freddie meet this girl through people you put him in contact with, or did he bring her, and her wealthy family, to you?'

'Freddie met her through Good Boy.' He caught their frowns as they tried to puzzle it through, and elaborated. 'Okay, way back when we were all starting out, the Falciones decided they wanted a foothold in the movie industry, so they bought out Good Boy.'

'And then Good Boy took over Horizon,' Adam put in. 'Which was why mine and Harry's investments never got off the ground.'

'Why did they need to take over Horizon as well though, if they had their foothold already?' Fiona wanted to know.

Rex looked blank for a moment, then shrugged. 'I guess

maybe my studio head at Horizon was keen to sell. Anyway, hey presto, the Falciones have their investment in a reputable, successful company, and I get to stay on, as studio head. I always wanted to produce though, not just executive produce, so when Cliff Brennan left, I got my chance with Daisy and Freddie. An all-round win.'

'Wait,' Fiona said, sitting forward as she remembered. 'Guy, you said that this girl's family were dangerous. Mobsters, or something?'

'Bannacott!' Rex tore his napkin loose and twisted it between his hands; perhaps he wished it were Guy's shirt collar. 'You told this kid that?'

'It's only the truth,' Guy snapped back. 'Everyone knows the Falciones, but I didn't know they were financing your company!'

'So not such an all-round win then,' Helen said, her voice quiet. 'I think we can assume the boss at Horizon was ... *persuaded* to sell, rather than keen to.'

Fiona fell a chill fingering the base of her spine, and saw looks of shock on her brother's and sister's faces. 'And Mr Brennan?'

'I'm assuming he found out what was going on,' Adam said, 'and either took himself out of the picture, or was put in the same position as the Horizon studio head. Am I close?'

Rex looked as if he were about to deny it, but in the end he just nodded. 'You see my problem then. Freddie told Maria that Daisy was quitting too, and it didn't go down well. They're getting the sense that it's all falling apart, and their reputation's being put on the line just as they're starting to see some real profit.'

'Did you know about Maria's family, Freddie?' Fiona asked.

He nodded slowly. 'To a point. I knew they ran rackets; extortion, protection, fencing, that kind of thing. Not that they had anything to do with the company though, I didn't find that out until after I told Rex about Daisy.' He gave a bitter little laugh. 'Seems like I'm finding out all kinds of interesting stuff lately.'

'So,' Kelly went on, frowning at him, 'when Freddie heard I was coming over to check the place out, he thought it was a good idea for them both to come with me, make themselves scarce for a while.'

'Why?' Ben spoke quietly, but with a hard edge to his voice and it was clear there was only one thing he cared about. 'Is Daisy in danger over this?'

Rex dashed off his drink in one gulp. He looked ill now, and there was sweat on his upper lip. 'I'll make sure she isn't.'

'That's not good enough!' Ben rose from his seat. Helen put a hand on his arm and drew him back down, but his eyes were spitting fire as he glared at the producer. 'If I have any reason to think you've put her in danger, Kelly, I'll be onto the police before you can blink!'

'Oh, I don't think you will, son.' Kelly's face was bland, and his voice soft, but the chill spread up Fiona's spine like icy water. 'You have no idea what you'd be stirring up.'

Daisy was even paler than usual. 'Rex, why did you never tell us who was paying for these films?'

'You paid for them,' he insisted. 'You were bringing in big bucks, you two.'

'But this gangland mob, whoever they are, put up the money,' Adam argued. 'You placed these young lives in danger for the sake of taking over Horizon pictures. You saw Clifford Brennan kicked out as their producer, and you used your own contacts to build up this new company out of the wreckage ...' His words tailed away, and he sat back, his eyes almost disappearing beneath

402

a sudden heavy frown. 'Are you laundering money through this company, Kelly?'

Fiona looked at him, puzzled. 'Is he what?'

'He knows.' Adam glared at Rex. 'Well? Are you pushing mob funds through your not-so Good Boy Productions?'

Rex eyed him with sour amusement. 'Takes a rogue to recognise one, eh?'

'Takes one to work out why you needed to stage a legal takeover to begin with, I'd say. Speaking of recognition, I'm assuming *you* only got to stay on because they spotted corruption and greed they could use.' Adam gave a soft, derisive laugh. 'And to think you gave me such a hard time about trying to get my girlfriend a part in one of your rotten little films.'

'That has nothing to do with it!' Rex poured yet another drink. 'You're still a snake, Coleridge, nothing will ever change that.'

'What happens now?' Helen wanted to know. 'Are Daisy and Freddie supposed to go back and carry on with this farce, just because you made them sign to it?'

'Sign?' Daisy looked at Freddie. 'Did you sign anything yet, Freddie?'

He shook his head, a half-smile suddenly playing across his lips. 'Nope. Not a thing. Contract's still in my suitcase.'

'Me neither.'

Rex looked from one to the other, in disbelief. 'Come on, kids! This movie is going to be amazing, no matter where the money came from. Don't throw your careers down the pan.'

'I'm not doing it,' Freddie said tightly, 'and I don't blame Daisy for getting out either.'

'If I hadn't already planned on quitting,' Daisy added, 'this would sure as hell do it.'

Rex wiped the back of his hand across his lips and took a deep breath. 'Look, it's not just about you two. Think how your director's going to feel. And young Jimmy. Not to mention the guy who wrote the screenplay.'

'The guy who wrote the screenplay,' Daisy mused. 'Andy Discaro, right?'

'Right! This is a hell of a script, and you know that.'

'Did *he* sign yet?'

Rex looked as if he were about to say yes, then he shook his head. 'We were keeping him on the back foot while we ironed out the final budget.'

'So,' she mused, 'once he knows what he'd be getting into bed with at Good Boy, he can back out, maybe take it to Stone Valley, or even MGM. He'd do well at either of those, and so would Freddie and I. Especially if we told them this was my last picture.'

'They'd be keen as hell to get us, for that reason alone,' Freddie added. 'Even as untalented and too-old as I am, I've been approached several times by Stone Valley to come back. I've always turned them down out of loyalty to Cliff Brennan.'

'And my dad still runs that company,' Daisy reminded Kelly with a little smile. 'Just because he didn't want to be seen to be giving me my start, doesn't mean he won't help me out now I'm bowing out of it all.'

'Well,' Ben said, turning back to Rex. 'I'm no lawyer, Mr Kelly, but it seems they're under no obligation to continue with Good Boy Productions after all, and neither is your Mr Discaro.'

Fiona thought about the name, and the way Daisy had said it, and as a light went off in her head she looked across at the actress, mentally checking off the letters. Daisy met her eyes, and her lips twitched before she looked away, and Fiona felt like laughing for the first time since Amy had left.

'You can't do this to me!' Rex was pale now. 'You've just pulled this movie out from under me, you think the Falciones are going to take this lying down?'

'You still have Jimmy Haverford,' Freddie said coldly. 'He's got, what did you call it? Kid appeal. I'm sure you'll find a vehicle for him that they'll bankroll, after all, they still need someplace to launder their money.'

'Listen to me!' Rex shouted over him. 'They wanted the studio that produced Conrad–Wishart movies, because *those* are the ones that are making the most money. They wouldn't have been interested in you when you did *The Boy at the Window*, and they won't be interested in Jimmy Haverford now. They'll take their money someplace else and that'll be it for Good Boy. And that's if I'm lucky.'

'You must have realised that the partnership would break up one day,' Daisy said quietly.

'But not yet! This movie would have bought me some time, at least. I'm going to have to do some real fast talking if I'm going to stand any chance of keeping my livelihood.'

'You can't blame me for your failure to plan ahead.'

'What will happen when you go back?' Fiona asked her. 'Will you be alright?'

'Don't worry,' Freddie said. 'I'll see that she's left alone. Maria loves her, which is a good thing.' He gave Rex a thin smile. 'She doesn't think a lot of you, Mr Kelly, but she does listen to me. I hope you understand me.'

Rex wiped his forehead with his napkin, and laid it down again carefully, then he pushed back his chair and stood up, and although he still looked ill, he sounded oddly stiff and formal. Tightly controlled.

'Thank you for a delicious dinner, Mrs Fox, and my compliments to the chef. I'll be in the lounge if anyone wants to cross-examine me further.'

For a moment after the doors swung shut it seemed as if no one would accept the invitation, then Adam and Ben looked at one another and rose as one; Ben threw his napkin down, Adam swigged the last of his drink, and they followed the producer into the lounge.

Helen smiled tiredly around at the others. She looked as close to tears as Fiona had seen her since Bertie's accident. 'I'm going to get some fresh air.'

Fiona found her a few minutes later, leaning against a pillar in the cloisters and staring out across the dark tennis courts towards the invisible sea. She turned as the door clicked shut, but shifted her gaze back again. 'Is everyone alright?' she asked, her voice almost stolen by the gusting wind.

'Stop worrying about everyone else for a minute,' Fiona said gently. 'This must be awful for you, too.'

'Worse for Daisy and Freddie. Not to mention poor Guy.'

'At least Guy can be open about Freddie now, with us at least. Freddie himself . . . well, he's clearly used to being at the centre of a lot of conflict, he needn't have forced Rex to tell us everything. Though I'm relieved he did.'

Helen turned properly now, and Fiona could see she had indeed been crying. She wished she were more like Leah, who would have jollied her mother out of her sadness with a single quip or wry observation, but all she could do was put her arms around her.

After a moment, she ventured, 'What will happen to the hotel over this? Will Rex still pay what he owes?'

Helen drew back and wiped her eyes. 'The hotel will be fine. Uncle Adam and Ben will put all that straight, I'm sure. Rex paid a deposit when he arrived, and they won't let him get away without paying the balance. I'm sad for poor Daisy. Those bruises!'

'I'm so sorry about Amy, running off like she did,' Fiona said in a low voice. 'If it weren't for her, Daisy wouldn't have—'

'Let's not dwell on that side of it.' Helen touched Fiona's cheek. 'It's a shame for you that she's had to go home now, but she'll be back, and next time there'll be no need for subterfuge. In the meantime you can write to one another.'

'If she wanted to write she'd have left a note, and her address. Or at least waited long enough to tell me so. More to the point,' she added, 'why would I want her back?'

'Because . . . Because she brought you to life,' Helen said softly. 'And you were a good friend to her despite her behaviour. She might have used you at the start, but anyone could see she thought the world of you, and you of her.'

'I did not!' Fiona wanted to forget all about Amy Markham. For tonight, at least, and Helen evidently sensed it.

'Alright, have it your way.' She smiled. 'This has been quite an eventful evening.'

'An eventful few days,' Fiona agreed, then took her courage in both hands. 'Can I ask you something personal? About Alfie?'

There was a long pause, then Helen looked away. 'Not yet,' she said quietly, staring out at the night as if all the answers lay in the darkness beyond the hotel. Fiona heard the weight behind those two words, and wished she could weave some magic spell to ease it. It was her turn to change the subject.

'If Daisy stays a while there could be a battle for her favours,' she said, giving the words an exaggeratedly romantic emphasis. 'Did you realise she's the one who wrote the screenplay for *Dangerous Ladies*?'

'No, that was a man name Discaro—' Helen stopped. 'Oh, good grief!'

Fiona grinned. 'I told you she was clever. Ben's doomed.'

Helen started, then smiled, but there seemed to be an ache behind it. 'Doomed?'

'Utterly.' Fiona shivered as a gust of wind whistled down the passageway. 'I'm going in, are you coming?'

'Well, you know you could have put on a coat,' Helen said, slipping back into a more familiar role as they went indoors. 'Where's that ratty old thing you insist on wearing?'

'Buried in mud, you'll be glad to hear.'

'Oh, no!'

Fiona turned, her suspicions confirmed as she saw the look of mock dismay on her mother's face. 'The sewing actually turned out to be quite good, you know!'

As they passed through the lobby Ian Skinner stopped them. 'Miss Fox, Martin left a package under the desk here for you after his shift. And a note. Sorry, I've only just seen it.'

'Martin did?' Fiona exchanged a puzzled look with her mother, then took the small box and the note.

Dearest Fi

I am so sorry for slipping away like this, I've learned a lot about myself these past weeks, but one thing I always knew was that I am hopeless at saying goodbye.

You are the dearest and most generous friend I could have

*wished for – from the moment I woke on that beach and saw you
so worried for me, a complete stranger, I knew you would be.*

*I also know you don't believe I'll be back, but I Cornish-
promise I will. Look in the box.*

Love, Amy.

*ps, you're quite right, Danny Quick is the ugliest young man I
have ever seen!*

Fiona opened the box, and blinked quickly to clear a sudden,
unexpected mist of emotion.

Inside was a leather case, with an image stamped on it that
indicated it held a pocket compass; a joint birthday and thank-you
gift, she'd said. And now a farewell one too.

Nestled in tissue paper beside the compass case was a tarnished
silver spoon pendant.

ACKNOWLEDGEMENTS

My gratitude once again to **The RNLI**, not only for their dedication and courage, but also for being so generous with their time and their information, and for helping me to put young Fiona through her paces in this book.

Huge 'thank you' also to my online community of writers. The most supportive and lovely bunch, helping each other through what can be a fairly lonely job, particularly this strange and difficult year. **Savvies**, **Connectors**, and all the rest – you're the sugar in my coffee, the ice in my Baileys, and the Marmite on my toast!

Special shout-out to the **TSAG** and the **Author Support Network**, especially **Glynis Peters**, **Christie Barlow** and **Deborah Carr** ... by the time this comes out, we'll have made some more memories in person – let's hope we haven't also been arrested!

As always, my thanks to **Eleanor Russell**, my brilliant editor at Piatkus, and to the whole creative and editorial team who have put their time and talent into producing this second volume in The Fox Bay Saga.

To my loyal and very kind **readers**: thank you for your continued support. Now brace yourselves for book three!

A Cornish Homecoming

Liverpool
February 1930

Soaring frescos painted on the multi-levelled ceilings, glittering glass chandeliers and highly-polished silver, so many mirrors it must take an army of cleaners to work on them alone, and a wide staircase with a deep blue carpet dotted with silver stars . . . The lobby of The Empire Park Hotel was like the set of a Conrad–Wishart movie; Leah half expected Daisy herself to appear at the top of those stairs, swathed in winter-white fur.

The music that came from the piano in the corner was soft but not slow, giving the atmosphere a lightly charged feeling, a sense that one must keep moving, talking, circulating, or be left behind. Unlike Fox Bay, the Empire Park was not a residents-only hotel, and the numbers were clearly swelled tonight; beautifully dressed, loudly chattering guests regularly spilled out of the main ballroom and spread to the three different bars. The party was clearly in full swing, but where was the host?

Leah stood straighter and reminded herself that she was dressed appropriately, but she still felt a little like a cabaret artist in her headband and beads, and her figure-hugging halter-neck gown. Her gloves itched, and she peeled them off now that she was in the dense warmth of the hotel, feeling the heaviness of the ring on her wedding finger like a lead weight. She forced herself not to look at it. Why would she? She was used to it, it was nothing new and certainly nothing to twist around her finger as her nerves reached snapping point. She gave her coat to the attendant and moved through the lobby, keeping her head up, and with a sense of purpose in her manner that she didn't feel. It wouldn't do to seem aimless, not here. Not tonight. She avoided the myriad mirrors with an effort, except to ensure her pageboy was perfectly in place after her short walk from the taxi to the front door, and to hastily adjust the silk rose at her shoulder, crushed flat by her coat.

'Mrs Scripps!'

She turned towards the voice, hiding her relief behind a mask of pleased surprise. 'Mr Freeman.'

The bearded, bespectacled man beamed and gestured her over. 'I'm so glad you could make it after all.' His Cockney accent was more subdued than she'd become used to but was still distinct amidst the more Northern voices all around her.

She went over to the little group. 'Thank you so much for inviting me, I do hope your host won't mind?'

A man of medium height and bland, forgettable features inclined his head towards her, and she guessed him to be the man in question. Mr Freeman drew her closer, one hand at her bare back in a too-familiar gesture. She would have strong words for him later on.

'Here, let me introduce you,' Freeman said. 'Mr Neville, this is the lady I was telling you about, Mrs Millicent Scripps. I was fortunate enough to receive the point of her umbrella in the small of my back, at Ma Egerton's earlier today.'

'I'm so sorry about that,' Leah began, but he brushed it away.

'We'd never have got talking otherwise, would we? Mrs Scripps, this is Mr Leonard Neville, well known philanthropist, and the generous host of this magnificent party.'

He went on to name the others in the group, but Mr Neville was the only one of interest, though Leah kept her greeting brief then stood silent while Mr Freeman held forth at great length about his latest investment.

'America is where the clever money's going,' he said. 'RKO, Good Boy, Paramount, you name it. Since the depression hit they're desperate for overseas investors, they'll snatch our hands off.'

'Of course,' one woman broke in, 'with you being American, Mrs Scripps, you'd know a lot about the movie industry, wouldn't you?'

'Oh!' Leah laughed lightly. 'I'm not from California. I live ... *lived*,' she broke off, and now she allowed herself to twist the huge engagement ring, just once, 'in New York with my husband.'

'Oh ...' the woman looked uncomfortable. 'And now?'

'I moved away after he died late last year.'

'I'm so sorry,' the woman murmured, and when Leah only smiled sadly at her she turned back to her companion and allowed Mr Freeman to continue his story.

Eventually the others drifted away and left only Leah, Mr Freeman and Mr Neville.

'Do please call me Leonard,' Neville invited, deftly lifting a drink from the tray of a passing waiter and handing it to her.

'Thank you. It's very gracious of you to allow me to come along tonight. I'm afraid I'm quite adrift here. Or I was, until Mr Freeman kindly took me under his wing.'

'It's my pleasure.' Mr Freeman's hand was on her back again, this time lower, and she stepped smoothly away under the pretence of examining one of the glossy-leaved ferns in a pot nearby.

'I do hope you enjoy the party,' Mr Neville said. 'Perhaps, if you're still at a loose end tomorrow you might join me for lunch? Both of you, of course,' he added.

'Oh! That'd be so nice, thank you.'

'Well, I understand from Mr Freeman here that you have a little ... difficulty you'd like help with?'

Leah shot a look at Mr Freeman, who recoiled slightly. 'I spoke to you in confidence, during a difficult moment. I don't appreciate you discussing what I told you with a perfect stranger.' She turned back to Neville. 'I'm so sorry, Mr ... Leonard, I wouldn't dream of imposing on your good will and your time.'

'It's no imposition, I assure you. I'd talk tonight, but as you can see,' he gestured with his cigar and no small amount of satisfaction, 'I have rather a lot of circulating to do.'

'Nevertheless, I'm afraid Mr Freeman here spoke out of turn, and—'

'Please, Mrs Scripps.' Neville took her hand, his eyes grazing the ring before returning to meet hers. 'I'd be delighted to help if I can. Shall we say here, at twelve-thirty? If you choose not to confide in me, then we'll simply call it lunch, and an introduction to Liverpool.'

Leah hesitated, then nodded and smiled shyly. 'In that case, thank you, and I'd be delighted.'

'Ask for me at reception. Now,' Neville was already getting a faraway look on his face, 'I must mingle. Do enjoy the rest of the party, won't you?'

'I'm sure I shall.'

But ten minutes later, Leah was shivering on the steps as she waited for the car to pull around. What a waste of a wonderful dress and two hours with a curling iron. Although perhaps not a waste exactly, given the lunch invitation, just a shame to have to cut the evening so short. She wondered idly if Mr Neville would be looking for her as the number of guests dwindled, and decided that even if he did he would assume she was too annoyed with 'Mr Freeman' to want to stay.

The car she was waiting for eventually pulled up, and the driver waved away the commissionaire who stepped forward to greet him. Leah pulled her coat closer and hurried down to slip into the passenger seat.

'Where were you? I'm freezing.'

'I couldn't just leave at the same time as you,' he pointed out reasonably, the East End now back in his voice in full strength. 'Home, then?'

'If you can call it that.' Leah shrank down into the seat, crossing her arms over her chest to keep warm. 'What's Glynn been doing while we've been wangling lunch invitations from dodgy philanthropists?'

'Sorting it from his end.' The man Neville knew as Freeman, but who Glynn had introduced to her as Wilf Stanley, negotiated the late evening traffic towards the ferry terminal. Leah neither liked nor trusted him, but Glynn had assured her he was perfect for the job. Besides, the whole thing had been his idea, conceived when the two men had shared a cell in Cardiff Prison, so she couldn't exactly refuse to work with him. But he made her skin crawl when his hand brushed it, as it did far too often, and she knew it wouldn't be too long before she gave him short shrift for doing so. In the meantime, it was best to keep his temper sweet.

The trip back across the Mersey to Birkenhead passed in silence, and Wilf dropped her off outside the West Bank boarding house before ten o'clock. It might be hours yet before Glynn returned, and Wilf looked at her with a hopeful expression as she climbed out of the car, clearly expecting an invitation for a night cap.

She smiled brightly, pretending not to notice. 'See you at the hotel tomorrow then. Twelve-thirty.'

He didn't reply at first, and Leah steeled herself for a more firm farewell, but eventually he nodded.

'Twelve-thirty then, darlin'. Dress smart.'

The cheek of him. Leah raised a hand and smiled, waiting for him to drive off before pushing open the door to the dingy little boarding house and climbing the three storeys to the room she and Glynn shared. It was such a far cry from the place she'd just left, yet so close as the crow flies, that she felt as if she'd been plucked out of a fairytale and dropped straight into a Dickens novel.

She hung the dress carefully on one of the few rickety hangers in the wardrobe, and, shivering in the cold, she quickly pulled her robe over her rayon slip before going through the belongings that had come over from Fox Bay. They'd been delivered to the nurses' home at Pembroke Place, and once she'd safely intercepted them Leah had written to Helen to give West Bank as her new address, thankful her friend would never see this hovel for herself. She'd be appalled.

She carefully selected tomorrow's outfit. Lunch at the Empire Park, particularly in the company of Leonard Neville, would place her at the heart of much scrutiny and analysis, and she wanted to appear bright and personable, but not overly so, in light of her recent widowhood. It was a tricky balance, but she eventually selected a handkerchief-hemmed dress in royal blue, and laid aside the matching hat and light scarf to tone down the open neckline. She had just found the perfect watermelon tourmaline brooch to pin to her shoulder when she heard the downstairs door open, and a man's voice murmuring to the landlady. There weren't many guests at this time of year, so Leah was reasonably certain it would be Glynn, but she still tensed when she heard a heavy tread on the creaky boards outside their door; the last thing she wanted was a late-night visit from Wilf Stanley. She relaxed as the door opened and Glynn came in, looking dapper in a well-cut suit, his hat dark with rain.

'Everything go alright?' he asked, dropping his coat onto the bed.

Leah tutted and picked it up before the damp could transfer onto the sheets. 'Perfectly. Wilf's done his background well, Neville seems to have accepted him as Freeman.'

'Excellent. And?'

'And we're having lunch tomorrow, at the hotel.'

'Good.' He caught her from behind as she moved to the dressing table and began brushing out the smooth waves she'd spent so long creating. 'You looked beautiful tonight, it's no wonder he's so keen to help.'

'We don't know that he will be, yet,' she pointed out. 'Just because he wants to hear what I have to say doesn't mean he'll fall for any of it. He's no fool, I'm sure of that.'

'He doesn't need to be a fool. Just needs to be greedy, and we know he's that at least.'

'Why him, anyway?' Leah put down her brush and turned to face him, effectively breaking his embrace. 'I half-expected some

417

monster. What's Wilf got against him that he cooked this whole thing up even before he got out of jail?'

'No idea.' Glynn moved away to begin undressing. 'Didn't ask, doesn't matter. We'll get enough out of it to start our new life.'

'You're still keen to go to America then?'

'Aren't you? Just think how well we'd do out there. I could get a job anywhere, and you could teach actors how to speak with different accents, just like that Kelly bloke said you might.'

'I told you what Helen said about him and his film studio,' Leah said. '*Dangerous Ladies* isn't going to be made after all, so my name won't be on any credit roll.'

'Still, there's work there if you want it, I'm sure of it.' Glynn pulled on his pyjamas and picked up his washbag. 'I won't be long.' His gaze drifted across her robed body, and she could tell what he was thinking, but deep down she knew it still wasn't time. They had been back together only a little over a month, and she couldn't surrender to his touch without feeling a surge of longing for that idiot Adam Coleridge.

Leah sighed, and as soon as Glynn had gone down the hall to the bathroom, she used the bowl and ewer in their room to complete her own ablutions and climb into the lumpy bed before he returned. When he came in she didn't bother to feign sleep, but managed to convey by her posture that tonight wasn't the night. To her relief he didn't try to persuade her, and they lay talking quietly over Leah's role for tomorrow, until they both drifted off to the comforting sound of the rain on the window.

The following morning Glynn left early, and Leah took her time dressing and, after another disappointing breakfast, readying herself for her lunch appointment. Then she slipped her smart shoes into her bag and walked to the ferry, once again wishing they could have stayed somewhere both brighter and closer to the Empire Park.

But the cash Glynn had won from his final card game in Bude was fast disappearing and maintaining the impression of wealth was eating into it alarmingly fast. As always, Leah's mood lowered as she thought of that game, and how he had brushed off her questions about the bruise on his face with how it had simply 'got out of hand'. She was as certain as she could be, now, that he had been one of those who had attacked Jory Nancarrow in the lane and taken the money he'd been paid for pawning Bertie's engagement ring. The thought that she was even now living off those ill-acquired gains had almost made her turn tail more than once. But what would have been the use? She couldn't return to Fox Bay, not after having lied to everyone, and continued to add to those lies with every letter she sent. A new life in America was all that was left to her now.

The ferry docked at Pier Head, and Leah turned up her coat collar against the biting cold and waved down a taxi. During the short ride to the hotel she slipped off her comfortable Mary Janes, and into a pair of high-heeled satin pumps, and went over her story yet again – this wasn't like those days at Fox Bay, when Millicent had merely been a diversion from the emptiness and the sorrow; Glynn had made it perfectly clear that, despite his outward charm, Leonard Neville was not a man to be crossed. If he discovered what they were doing, things could get very sticky indeed.

The hotel was much quieter today, even for a Saturday lunch-time, and Leah, now fully immersed in her Mrs Scripps persona, marched confidently across the gold and brown carpet and gave the reception bell a single, imperious tap.

'I'm here to see Mr Leonard Neville. Tell him it's Mrs Scripps.'

'I'll call up to his room for you now, madam.'

Wilf appeared from nowhere, his hand outstretched. 'Good afternoon, Mrs Scripps. So good to see you again. Might I buy you a drink?'

'No, thank you, Mr Freeman, I'll wait for lunch.'

They didn't have to wait long. Leonard Neville came out of the lift within a few minutes, pulling at his shirt cuffs to expose square cut silver cufflinks with an inset that might have been either ebony or onyx. Despite the obvious wealth that draped him like a cloak, he still seemed as forgettable as yesterday's rice pudding, and Leah tried to put a finger on how that could be. He was distinguished-looking, with grey wings brushed back from the temple, and the smile he gave her was perfectly pleasant as he extended his hand, but his eyes were a rather ordinary mid-brown, his eyebrows neither bushy nor thin, his moustache neat but plain ... she might have passed him four times in a day and not recognised him.

They exchanged pleasantries, and he showed them into the dining room. After Fox Bay, Leah had thought she knew what to expect, but the Empire Park had taken Fox Bay's quiet elegance and covered it in glitter and gold, so much so that it actually made her wince and long for the fresh, clean decor she knew and loved. The food, however, was delicious, and since Mr Neville did not bring up the reason for inviting them she took the time to enjoy every mouthful. After West Bank's limp bacon and watery scrambled eggs it was hard not to wolf everything down and exclaim at every bite.

But she made herself stop eating long before she had finished her main course, and pushed her plate away. 'I'm so sorry,' she said in a low, embarrassed voice. 'This is so kind of you, but my appetite ...' She let the words trail off and took a sip of water. 'I hope I haven't put you to any inconvenience.'

'Not at all. Mr Freeman here said you were looking for some advice. Is that the case?'

She looked at Wilf, frowning slightly. 'I really don't want to put you to any trouble.'

'It's no trouble. Tell me what you need.'

Leah looked over her shoulder, then at the waiter, hovering nearby, and lowered her voice. 'I have a substantial sum of money to invest, and I'm looking for somewhere ... safe.'

'Safe?'

'I can't run the risk of losing it. It's too ... the cost was too high.'

'All investment is a risk, Mrs Scripps,' Neville pointed out gently. 'What do you mean, the cost was too high?'

'My husband, my *late* husband,' she amended with a little hitch in her voice, 'left all his money tied up in Blue Chip stocks. He was told to get the money out, by a, a friend, who warned him the market was unstable, especially after the London crash, but he paid no attention. When Wall Street went down he thought he'd lost everything, and he ... I'm sorry!' She stifled a sob in her napkin, and felt a warm hand on her shoulder.

'Please, Mrs Scripps, don't upset yourself. Would you prefer to take this conversation somewhere quieter?'

She gave Neville a grateful look. 'Perhaps, if it's not too much trouble.'

'Not at all. The lounge has booths that offer more privacy.'

Once settled, Neville ordered drinks and prompted Leah to begin her tale again. 'You said your husband *thought* he'd lost everything,' he said. 'Can I take this to mean you were in fact able to cash in his stocks without him realising? How was that possible?'

Leah didn't answer right away. She picked up her drink and took a generous slug, glad she'd at least eaten something; there was a great deal more gin in it than she'd expected. 'The friend who tried to convince him, was his stockbroker.'

Neville sat forward, his expression sharpening. 'Are you talking about insider dealing?'

'I couldn't say.' But Leah made sure her lowered eyes said it for her, and heard Neville mutter a little oath under his breath.

'This is extremely serious,' he said aloud. 'Mrs Scripps, this man could go to prison.'

For a moment Leah wondered if they had misjudged him, but she ploughed on regardless. 'George's entire savings, our house, everything was tied up, and he tried to save it! In the end, between us we ...' Leah broke off again and rose. 'I'm sorry, I should never have come to you—'

'Please sit down, Mrs Scripps. Mr Freeman, did you know about this?'

'Certainly not! When Mrs Scripps and I met in Ma Egertons she told me she had a sum of money to invest. I'd mentioned I was an investor, you see.'

'But you didn't tell her your specialism is the film industry.'

'It was just conversation; I didn't see the need.'

'I misunderstood,' Leah confessed. 'It's all so confusing.'

'An easy mistake, my dear,' Wilf said, taking the opportunity to pat her on the knee. She was just able to stop herself pulling her leg out of the way.

'And why aren't you interested in putting your money into that industry?' Neville wanted to know. 'It's a flourishing business, I'm given to understand. You heard what Mr Freeman was saying last night.'

Leah lowered her face, plucking at a button on her dress. 'I would prefer to take my money out of America just now, I'm sure you understand that.'

Neville gave a short laugh. 'I do, especially given what you've just told me.'

'Mr Freeman was kind enough to suggest that you yourself might have some advice for me.'

'Why are you here? As opposed to London.'

'Because the *Samaria* runs here from New York,' she said, sounding puzzled at the sharp question, but sending silent thanks to Glynn for his thorough research. 'I'll be moving on soon.'

Neville pursed his lips. 'How soon?'

'I don't know. I hadn't planned to stay long though, I have family back home who don't really understand why I've come away so soon after ... you know. Obviously I couldn't tell them the truth.' Leah gave him a hopeful look. 'Do you? Have any advice, I mean.'

'About your money? Perhaps. How much is it?'

Leah took a deep breath. 'A little under fifty thousand dollars. Minus the cost of travelling here, and my hotel.'

'A not inconsiderable sum,' Neville conceded. He cast a slow glance around as much of the room as they could see from their booth. 'Leave it with me, I'll talk it through with some colleagues. In the meantime, I'd very much like to meet the man who gave your husband such good advice.'

Leah's heart leapt. '*Meet* him? I, I don't think that would be possible.'

'I take it he's still in America then?'

She nodded quickly. 'Yes, he is.'

'How soon could he travel here?'

Leah lifted her hands helplessly. 'He's so busy. It would take a real long time to organise, and then there's the voyage—'

'I agree with Mrs Scripps,' Wilf put in. 'A very bad notion, Mr Neville, if you don't mind my saying so. You'd be putting your own reputation at some risk, were it to come out later what ... what this man has done.'

A tense silence fell over the little group, while he nursed his drink and Leah's fingers went white twisting around each other.

'When did he get your husband's money out?' Neville asked mildly, after a few minutes had passed. 'The exact date, I mean.'

'October twenty-third.' It didn't seem enough, and she went on, 'When it was just coming up to close of trading, we finally accepted that George wasn't going to take his advice, and things were already starting to slip badly ... as you'll know,' she added, 'being an investor yourself. I gave the word to go ahead and just sell everything, right there and then.' She wondered if she'd committed the liar's sin of explaining too much; he'd only asked for the date, after all.

Neville shifted on his banquette, then leaned forward and closed his hand on Leah's. She gasped as his fingers tightened, grinding her knuckles against the band of the ring she wore. His eyes dropped to it, and his smile was thin as he released her.

'I don't believe you, Mrs Scripps.'

'I don't understand,' she whimpered, her eyes filling with tears that weren't altogether deliberate; that had hurt, and the sudden change in his demeanour was chilling. She rubbed at her hand, resisting the urge to look around to see if anyone else had seen what he'd done. But he was subtle; it would have looked like nothing more than a friendly gesture even if they had. 'You don't believe what?'

'That, after risking everything for you, this man is only your husband's stockbroker. Admit it, Mrs Scripps, you and he are having an affair, aren't you?' He smiled again, though it was anything but friendly. 'And it wouldn't surprise me either, to learn that you'd realised poor old George would be unable to live with losing everything, especially after being warned. After all, *you* neglected to tell him his money was safe. It was deliberate, wasn't it?'

'No!' Leah breathed. 'My husband never came home that night, I didn't have time to tell him before the markets opened—'

'But your broker *is* here in England.'

It wasn't a question, and there was no sense arguing further. 'Alright, yes. He was worried, with me bringing such a large sum in cash, so he escorted me here. He's not in town,' she hurried on, 'I decided to break my journey for a few days. but he travelled ahead to London, to investigate various other options.'

'Then, as I said, I'd like to meet him.'

'But—'

'Mrs Scripps.' Neville leaned forward again his nondescript features suddenly iron-hard, and Leah instinctively jerked her hand out of his reach. 'You have freely admitted, to both myself and my friend Mr Freeman, that you have come by your wealth through nefarious means. You have broken the law, and your husband's stockbroker mightn't be the only one going to jail when, *if,* it becomes known how you've benefited from this.'

Wilf spoke up, sounding horribly nervous too. 'Surely, Leonard old thing, we don't want to get—'

'She's played you for a fool too,' Neville reminded him, 'I would lay good money that the meeting you thought was accidental was anything but. She has her uses, at least. Arrange things, Mrs Scripps.' He sat back, and now his face had relaxed into its former easy smile. 'I'm sure you'd prefer to share your lover's expertise than your own wealth.'

Leah forced herself to meet those mid-brown eyes for a moment longer than was comfortable, and nodded. 'I'll try.'

'And I'll do some asking around in the meantime.'

'A ... asking around?' Her voice trembled.

'To see what's up and coming, in the line of legitimate businesses looking for cash injections, of course.'

'Oh. Of course. When should we meet you?'

'Not you. If and when your broker friend proves himself genuine, and useful to me, I'll be back in touch. If he doesn't, or if he doesn't agree to meet me, you'd better watch your back. Before you go,' he added, as she rose, 'you'd better give me his name.'

For a heart-stopping moment her mind went blank, then she dragged a name from the shadows. 'Jacob Bitterson.'

'Have you heard of him?' Neville asked Wilf.

'No, but I can ask around for you.'

'Good.' Neville turned back to Leah. 'Tell him to call the hotel as soon as he arrives in town, we'll arrange a meeting.'

'Is this really necessary?' she pleaded.

'Absolutely. If you wish to avoid a nasty court case, that is. Wait behind if you would, Mr Freeman, I'd like to talk to you.'

Wilf paused, half-standing, then sat back down again without looking at Leah. 'Of course.'

She left, hugely relieved to be away from him, though part of her wished she could have stayed to listen to the ensuing conversation, but there was a car waiting around the corner and she hurried to climb in.

Glynn started the Lancia and nosed out into the traffic, and when she said nothing, he glanced at her, his eyebrow raised. 'Well?'

She blew out her pent-up breath and let her head fall back against the head rest. 'Well, I hope you've been busy, because the game is afoot.' She gave him a slow, triumphant smile. 'He wants to meet you, Mr Bitterson.'

Look out for *A Cornish Homecoming*, coming soon from

PIATKUS